Passion's Promise

"There is so much you have to learn, Christina MacTavish, and it looks like I must be the one to teach you," said Damien Drayton.

When his lips closed over hers, she was lost in the delights of this mad sensation. Her eyes flew wide open with surprise as his tongue possessed her mouth.

Her arms went about Damien's neck of their own accord. Her body ached to be closer to his, to be entwined against his long length, and he obliged by moving carefully over her.

Then his voice whispered near her ear, "I intend to make you mine, whether you will or no."

And the last shreds of Christina's resistance vanished in the savage sweetness of surrender. . . .

LOVE BETRAYED

by

Patricia Rice

AN ONYX BOOK

NEW AMERICAN LIBRARY

NAL BOOKS ARE AVAILABLE AT QUANTITY DISCOUNTS
WHEN USED TO PROMOTE PRODUCTS OR SERVICES.
FOR INFORMATION PLEASE WRITE TO PREMIUM MARKETING DIVISION,
NEW AMERICAN LIBRARY, 1633 BROADWAY,
NEW YORK, NEW YORK 10019.

Onyx is a trademark of New American Library.

SIGNET, SIGNET CLASSIC, MENTOR, ONYX, PLUME, MERIDIAN and NAL BOOKS are published by New American Library, 1633 Broadway, New York, New York 10019

First Onyx Printing, February, 1987

1 2 3 4 5 6 7 8 9

PRINTED IN THE UNITED STATES OF AMERICA

Part One

1

Long woolen skirts wrapped roughly about her legs in the strong wind, but Christina paid them little heed. Sheltering her eyes from the late-winter sun with one hand and hanging on to her bonnet with the other, she stared out over the choppy gray sea.

Like all the other idlers on the cliff, she fastened her eyes on the majestic billowing of white sails on the horizon, but her imagination did not carry her in the same direction as those of the minds around her. While she dreamed of feeling the heaving decks beneath her feet, the wind whipping wildly through her hair as she sailed to the freedom of foreign ports, the others turned their tongues to more pragmatic matters.

"Lookee there!" A young boy in tattered trousers pranced in excitement before his slower elders. "Her's a Yankee ship! See them colors?"

Muffled ejaculations and curses followed this news as others strained their eyes to see what the boy's had, but Christina's sharp gaze fastened immediately on the streaming ribbons of red, white, and blue.

The ship flaunted its glory with triumphant pride, making no haste as it sailed within sight of enemy shores. British ships on American waters were not an unusual sight, but it took a daring recklessness for a Yankee ship to hover off the shore of England in this year 1781.

"Must be that damned Paul Jones fella." A squirt of tobacco juice shot past Christina's whipping skirts, splattering against the rocks. One of the older men jostled closer to the edge, following the full white sails as they turned toward the horizon. "Nobody else that much of a fool."

"Fool, nothing. I heerd he got the courage o' the devil hisself. Stand up to any man and do him better. Didn't he beat the best the British Navy had to offer? Them Yankees are a dangerous breed."

Christina glanced gratefully at the young man appearing at her side. She had been taught to hold her tongue before her elders, but Thomas had uttered her thoughts.

"Mebbe it ain't that Paul Jones. Mebbe it's that *Sea Lion* we heerd of, the Yankee they say's been chasin' the British Navy all over the sea, bringin' in prizes to France faster'n we can send 'em out. Mebbe they comin' here at the invitation of our new earl. Hee hee," an elderly merchant cackled knowingly.

Voices erupted in sudden heated discussion of this fascinating new topic, some swearing they had seen the "Yankee Earl" delivered some months back in the dead of night in a ship as mighty as the one disappearing over the horizon, others claiming he had arrived by coach roaring drunk, just as his uncle the late earl had done. Christina ignored the debate, watching with a sliver of sadness as the majestic ship slipped over the horizon and out of sight. No excuse remained for further dalliance.

"There be 'bout as much chance of that besotten lord bein' captain of the *Sea Lion* as there be of his bein' the highwayman. He's got all he needs up there in that castle o' his'n and all to lose by bein' down here with the likes o' us and the highwayman. Mebbe the highwayman will catch him out some night!" Thomas spoke with not a little relish at the possibility.

"Hee hee! Did ye hear of Lord Aiglin's comeuppance t'other night?" The scrawny merchant tugged at his aged vest, searching for a snuffbox that no longer existed. "They say the highwayman sliced off all them fancy gold buttons he's so proud of, just whooshed them away"—he made a swift slicing motion with his hand— "with his sword. Then pricked his noble lordship in the arse and made 'im pick 'em all up out of the dust and hand them over, and his lordship with his breeches down about his feet!"

The fishermen behind them roared at this tale and someone else inquired as to how an "old goat like 'e" would know of goings-on between Lord Aiglin and the highwayman, but this tale was followed swiftly by others, rapidly bordering on the bawdy, and Christina turned away.

Tugging what had once been a fine woven shawl about her shoulders, Christina secured the drab brown bonnet more firmly over her tawny curls, and lifting her woolen skirt from the mud of the road, stepped gracefully back toward town. The notorious highwayman had been a heated topic for some weeks, but one well beyond the realm of her present concerns.

"Christie, wait!" Thomas hurried up beside her, tugging at his dark forelock, his husky farmer's frame sheltering her from the wind. "Let me walk with you. You ought'n to be out here alone."

"And who else would be with me?" With a wry emphasis that completely escaped her escort, Christina's voice drawled her words softly, in strange contrast to the harsh, uneducated tones of her companions.

"You should be home with your ma. You got no call to be out here standin' on the cliffs." Thomas did not dare touch her golden fineness, but satisfied his protective urges by speaking with firmness.

Christina continued walking in the opposite direction from her home. The cliffs had only been a diversion, a momentary escape from the dreariness of reality, and now she was running late.

"That's all well and very good for you to say, Thomas, but there is no one but me to buy the medicine my mother needs, and by the cliffs I must go to get it."

She made no further explanation, hastening down to the town's main street in an obvious effort to shake her companion. Why should she have to explain where she went or why? It was nobody's business that the late mayor's daughter now had to work for her living, and that if she were any tardier, she would most likely lose her new position. Word would spread soon enough, it always did, but she was not the one to spread it.

Thomas made as if to protest, but a hail from a nearby tavern caught his attention, and while he stopped to offer a pleasantry, Christina pointedly hurried on.

Thomas was a well-meaning lad, probably the best the town had to offer, but Christina could not imagine him as the man of her dreams. Although these past two years of hardship had forced her to accept practicality, they had also given Christina no other escape but her fantasies. Straight from the country, she had been quiet and shy among the more boisterous, sophisticated girls at school, and had learned the advantages of imagination at an early age. She needed little encouragement to indulge in that pastime now.

These past months, Christina had pleasantly entertained the prospect of the gallant highwayman sweeping her off her feet, playing Lord Robin to her Lady Marian, and rescuing her from the desperation of her plight. But the ever-present shadow of the gallows tree eventually dimmed the glory of that fantasy and Christina had found an even better one in the arrival of the new Lord of Westshipham. The lonely Yankee would discover her quick wit and intelligence and fall head over heels in love with her sympathetic nature. . . . A grand dream until the rumors of the new lord's gambling and drunkenness soured this too with reality.

But now the captain of this mighty ship, a dashing privateer with courage beyond all others—surely there was a man to dream about! He would be handsome and brave, and unfailingly polite and kind. He would be a gentleman, but capable of wild adventures and rash actions when the circumstances warranted them. . . .

Creating this lovely list carried her well down the path out of town. Christina had resigned herself to the fate of spinsterhood two years ago when she had been forced to leave Mrs. Grenoble's Academy for Young Ladies and return to her village home without the benefit of a coming-out ball in London. At the time, there had been too many other emotions to experience regret. Now, at eighteen, Christina had too many other worries and responsibilities to do more than make pleasant daydreams out of lost possibilities.

Her father's death when she was just sixteen had been the most traumatic experience of her young life. Argus MacTavish had been a giant of a man, a towering, brawny, stalwart gentleman of amazing tenderness and exuberant spirits. He had been the center of her world and her mother's. Nothing could dim the MacTavish spirit or health. He had thrived on the conflicts as well as the rewards. He had fared well at his shipping business, and later as an import merchant. Loved by all, envied by many, his small family had flourished in the protection of his generous care. Until one night they had found him facedown in the rocks on the shore, a knife in his back.

Determinedly stifling a sob and brushing away a sudden tear at the still vivid memory, Christina increased her pace. The shock of her father's death had done more than destroy her social life, it had nearly paralyzed her always delicate mother. The love of Argus MacTavish had held his wife aloft through all manner of misfortune and adversity, and without it Eleanor MacTavish was reduced to helplessness. Christina understood that, had always understood it, knowing the story behind it well.

But romantic stories did not put food on the table, and the last few shillings of her mother's small hoard were nearly gone. If the old Earl of Westshipham had known of that small hoard, he would probably have taken that too, as he had the shop and everything else but the roof over their heads and the clothes on their backs. But once he had his gold from the sale of all their worldly possessions, he had forgotten the existence of the MacTavish women.

Christina did not believe her money-wise father had been foolish enough to sign all those notes the earl had produced, but her opinion counted little in the court of men. Anger was not an emotion she entertained frequently, but the thought of her delicate, ladylike mother being reduced to penury by the falsehoods and greed of that debauched old man—even now Christina shook with fury at the memory.

At one time, many had compared Christina to her spirited and handsome father, but the hardships of these past two years had taken their toll on a child's exuberant spirits. With the entire fabric of her existence rendered into shreds, Christina had held the threads together with her father's pride and stubbornness and the hard, ladylike carapace she had learned at finishing school. Her only gaiety now existed in her mind, in an imagination that ran rampant when she held a quill between her fingers and a blank piece of paper under her hands. But as the demands of harsh reality grew stronger, those moments grew fewer and farther between. Until the silt of poverty threatened to bury them, as it had her childhood.

Footsteps dragging as she approached her destination and her fate, Christina gazed dispiritedly at the crumbling walls now lining the lane she walked. Westshipham Hall rose up before her in all its decrepit extravagance. The towering brick walls cried out for repairs, the lawns and gardens had not been tended in many a year, and the carriage lane wandered through a wilderness of weed and briar. From the tales Christina had heard, she knew the interior to be not much better, but she had only glimpsed the outdated kitchen on her last visit.

Thinking back to that day she had been reduced to the desperation of pleading for work, Christina fully realized the butler of this decrepit household had agreed to hire her too readily. The lascivious glint in the eyes of the skeletal old man had not escaped her notice. She had no experience, no references, nothing to recommend her but the MacTavish name, and she doubted if the old lecher recognized it. No, common sense told her the butler belonged to the old regime of the late earl, when drunken debauchery reveled through the old halls and no self-respecting female dared enter the grounds.

But Christina had heard from excellent sources that the new lord, the "Yankee Earl," did not molest his maidservants. Indeed, he did not venture from his study at all, but drank and cursed and swore violently throughout the day—at the fates, his ancestors, the moldering walls, at anyone daring to intrude upon his tirade. Yet he had ordered servants hired and meals cooked, and Christina had no objection to working for a madman as long as he paid in hard cash.

The cold wind beneath the overhanging trees sent a shiver coursing through her thin frame. She had long since lost the need to wear anything to keep her tiny waist within the fashionable confines of her gowns, though she had not owned a new bodice in two years. True, her bodices had to be laced much more loosely over her bosom than was seemly now that she had developed more of a woman's roundness, but with skillful use of lacy chemises and kerchiefs, she had succeeded in keeping her modesty. Still, Christina knew herself a stone lighter than before, and none the stronger for it. With the last of their larder disappearing, she must find work or starve for a certainty.

Her mother had been elated at hearing her daughter had found employment in the new earl's household. In her mind's eye, Eleanor had seen the hall as it had been in the old days, well scrubbed and livened with youthful excitement. Perhaps she even imagined this new earl as the young viscount and his brother she remembered. Whatever, Christina had played upon her mother's memories and skimmed over the true description of her duties. "Housekeeper" had a genteel ring not too demeaning for an educated lady without funds. "Scrub maid" would be a more fitting description.

2

Christina held her hand to her side and gasped for air. The pain knit tighter with the first ragged breath but relaxed slightly with the next. She had not known a flight of stairs or length of hall could be so long, but she had escaped him, for now.

She cursed mentally as she cowered behind the drapery of the second-floor window. Since that first day, the lecherous butler had made his intentions toward her clear, but Christina had outwitted his ploys with one stratagem or another. It had become a degrading game she dreaded, but desperation and sheer perverse obstinacy kept her struggling for self-respect. This job was all that stood between her mother and starvation, she must keep it at all cost, but at times like these, death had almost become an attractive alternative.

Christina rested weakly against the hard panel partially hidden by the drapery. She had not eaten a decent meal in months, and the strenuous activity required of the hall's servants had depleted what remained of her little strength. Her inability to sleep worrying over the best means of evading the goatish butler had brought her nerves to a state of tension bordering on the hysterical. Nothing else could explain her insane flight to this forbidden second floor.

She did not know who had given the orders preventing access to this floor—whether it was the master's order or some ruse to keep her within the butler's reach—but Christina cared no longer. At the first sound of the decrepit old man's footsteps approaching the room in which she worked alone, Christina had fled through the nearest exit and up the stairs. It seemed the safest place to be while the butler searched the rooms below for her. She heard no ranting or raving in these upper-story halls. Perhaps the mad lord slept or had fallen into a drunken stupor. In either case, he would not notice her trespass.

A slow tread upon the staircase sent Christina's nerves into careening panic. She would kill before she allowed that foul creature to lay another hand upon her. Hanging seemed preferable to the mauling she had endured thus far. In sheer terror at her thoughts, Christina whirled and tried the door behind her. It slid open smoothly. Quickly she slipped through and carefully eased the heavy panel back into place. Exhausted, she slid to her knees and rested her head prayerfully against the wood.

"*What in hell*?"

This resonant curse and a heavy footstep behind her sent Christina's heart plunging to her stomach. In shock she turned to find her gaze confronted with an immaculately polished, finely cut pair of black leather boots. Trembling with fatigue and fear, she inched slowly from the floor, following the path of the boots upward to long, sturdily masculine thighs encased in tight buckskin breeches. Their owner's virility was thinly disguised by the tailored cut, and Christina hurried to push herself upward, her gaze quickly sliding past slim hips and flat belly until she stood full height, her nose nearly pressed against the thick mat of tight dark curls covering the bronzed torso of a half-dressed male. Shakily her gaze continued its journey upward, past the casually unbuttoned white silk shirt over well-muscled shoulders to the flashing dark fires of the furious gaze boring into her.

"Damned fools cannot obey the simplest orders! I told you . . ."

But the words seemed to slither to a halt in the cascading silence as dark fires encountered the slender grace of the sight before them. A number of tawny golden curls had escaped their pins and now tumbled in soft confusion about an oval face of ivory perfection, framing huge wells of velvet sadness flecked with gold. Long lashes swept upward in sensuous appeal above cheeks tinged with rose, and no word escaped the half-parted lips of dusky red.

The clash of their eyes sent a shock wave rippling through both of them, and Christina made no sound of protest as the large hand behind her moved from the door lock to protect the slender curve of her waist. She could feel the heat of the man's fingers through the thin material of her bodice, but she gave it no thought as her mind raced rapidly over the series of events to find her place in it. Who was this man and what was he doing here?

But Christina's mind remained as paralyzed as her eyes by the dark play of lightning in those flashing black eyes above her. The stranger's rigid face seemed carved in stone, yet the loose dark hair tied back in a rough queue gave his harsh cheekbones a shadow of hunger and not sternness.

Even as he muttered, "You are the best idea anyone has had in months," and bent his head toward hers, Christina did not budge. In a sudden imaginative flight of fancy, she knew how his lips would taste on hers, and she welcomed them without thought.

The first shock of the heated contact of his mouth burned all else from her mind. The stranger's lips twisted across hers with terrifying demands of which Christina knew nothing. Her own cried out a protest of pain, but did not lessen their clinging.

Large hands enclosed her waist and slid knowingly up the slender column of her spine, forcing her closer into his embrace, forcing her to raise her hands to his chest in self-defense, only to find her fingers wrapping achingly in the mat of fur she found there.

With a whimper of bewilderment, Christina parted her lips beneath the onslaught of his, and gasped at the exquisite torment vibrating through her center at this new contact. Balanced within the circle of this man's strength, possessed by the electrifying magnetism of his lips upon hers, his tongue claiming the honeyed interiors of her mouth, Christina found an excitement and a security she had not known existed, and she bent her lips willingly to this new lesson. Her body quivered at the suddenness of the exploding sensations within her as he crushed her eagerly against his hard male length.

Not until the hand protecting her waist slid lower to cup her buttocks suggestively and then to sweep her from the floor did Christina crash back to reality. As the dark stranger swung her up in his arms, she screamed and struggled to gain her feet again.

"I am a starving man, me lass. Do not hold my haste against me," he responded in answer to her vigorous protests, crossing the room in easy strides as he spoke. "There is time enough to do it properly later."

With that outrageous remark, he dropped her on the broad length of a divan and unceremoniously stripped his shirt from his breeches in preparation for his conquest.

The wind momentarily knocked from her lungs, Christina squealed weakly as the tall madman's hand moved to the fastenings covering his loins. Her squeal turned to piercing shrieks as she struggled to rise, and he moved swiftly to kneel over her, catching her arms over her head and pinning her easily between his knees.

"For God's sake, woman! Do you wish to give the whole household warning of what we do? Or is that the game my uncle preferred to play?"

Dark eyes watched her with curiosity and a trace of disgust, but his fingers did not slow their quick work. The linen handkerchief disappeared from the low neckline of her bodice, revealing the swelling flesh beneath the lace edging of her chemise.

Christina gasped and writhed frantically to elude his questing fingers as they loosed her laces, but a strange lethargy gave her movements little veracity.

"Don't, my lord, please! It is a mistake, stop . . ." she cried hysterically as his hand slid beneath her chemise and circled the warm flesh beneath, yet the sensation was not unpleasant.

A groan escaped her as his fingers gently manipulated a tender peak to tautness, but her body's growing desire to allow these liberties caused an equal and opposite reaction in her mind. Christina's struggles grew frantically.

The man's heavy weight held her casually, his powerful thighs pinioning hers while his hand easily prevented her from striking out.

As Christina attempted to bring up one knee, he cursed mildly and adjusted his position, giving her a look of disdain. "There is no need to act the damsel in distress for me. I will pay you better for your willingness."

Before another scream could escape her lips at this outrage, the stranger's mouth persuasively crushed hers once more, and Christina felt his tongue between her teeth, gagging all further outcry. She strained against him, hoping to find some release from the pressure of the hard body covering hers, but every move placed her more firmly within his hands. As she gradually realized the futility of the situation in which her foolishness had placed her, a small tear trickled from the corner of her eye, but the man above her paid it no heed.

If he would only be satisfied with kisses, Christina could find enjoyment in the warm hunger of his mouth upon hers. The sensations of his strong hand possessively manipulating her bare breast sent shocking thrills of pleasure to the very center of her being. She wished time to learn more of these sensations, but his hand did not linger in one place long. With shocking rapidity it found the hemline of her skirt and eased it upward, and Christina knew she had only moments left.

Shaking her head violently, tearing her mouth from his, she screamed with terror. She had no experience with half-naked men, but this baring of herself sent terrifying explosions careening down her spine. With a violent jerk nearly fracturing her wrist, she freed one hand from his hold and beat soundly against the madman's shoulders.

"Let go of me, you beast! Let go of me!"

The last became a wail of horror as his masculine hand succeeded in tugging her skirts upward about her waist and proceeded to caress the bare flesh above her garter with intoxicating skill.

"Scream as you will," he murmured softly against her ear. "These fools have been trained well by my uncle and will not come without my order. Relax and enjoy it. It will not harm your price any, I assure you."

Gazing upward into the blazing dark fires of his eyes, Christina shuddered violently as the callused palm of his hand slid unhindered over the bare curve of her buttock, and his gaze watched her knowingly. Unable to bear the sensation of that mocking scrutiny, she closed her own eyes, only to discover this heightened the intimacy he forced upon her. With a whimper of fear she felt the hard strength of his masculine hand move to gently caress the sensitive junction between her thighs, and she knew all was lost.

Her tongue would not function and her struggles ceased as she surrendered helplessly to the brute force claiming her. This could not be happening to her, Christina MacTavish, daughter of the mayor of Westshipham and granddaughter of the Baron of Adderly. It must be happening to some poor maid she did not know, and she must endure it, must become whatever it was this madman made of her, for this was her life now.

She felt his powerful legs part hers easily, felt the smooth cloth of his tailored breeches slide caressingly along her opened thighs, and waited for what must inevitably follow. Never had she felt so naked and vulnerable as she did now, knowing she had lost all control of her own fate, or even of her own body. For the ache between her legs told her much she had not known. She clenched her eyes closed, refusing to acknowledge what was happening, praying her rapist would disappear if she could not see him.

She knew nothing of what happened between men and women except from the furtive whispers of the older girls at school, and these she had mostly ignored. Now she wished she had listened closer, for a hard lance seemed to be pressing against her stomach as his hand released her wrists and he reached below her to bring her hips closer to his.

She shivered as hard fingers bit into soft flesh and he raised his weight slightly from her. But even as his mouth closed coaxingly over the quivering peak of one breast, Christina felt that strange hardness probing between her thighs, and her muffled groan became a scream of horrified anguish as she was pierced to the very quick by a pain of untold dimension.

His swift movement halted at meeting this unexpected resistance, and he swore a violent oath, but then without further hesitation returned to his plundering.

Christina's screams died in her throat as she felt his body invade hers with a weapon of a force she could not imagine. The first tearing pain still ached at her insides, but the remainder of his thrusts tore along already opened passages and did no more than reduce her to the final depths of humiliation.

With a sudden swift movement the madman jerked away and collapsed on top of her, grasping her tightly as he shuddered with a violent passion. Christina felt a sticky moistness cross her uncovered belly, but turned her head away and kept her eyes clenched tightly closed, wanting to know nothing of what happened.

In a moment her rapist had recovered himself and with cool aplomb adjusted his breeches and produced a cloth with which to clean her.

"Where in hell did a damned virgin come from in this brothel?" he muttered rhetorically, for Christina's averted face showed no inclination for answering.

Judging he had done the best he could under the circumstances, he carefully drew down her skirts to cover lovely ivory limbs, and then abruptly he rose from the couch.

At his departure, Christina swiftly opened her eyes

in hope, only to swallow her disappointment as she located her assailant pouring a glass of wine at the desk. He turned and caught her look.

No expression crossed his face as he returned her gaze. He seemed to be studying her, and Christina cast him a glare of her own. She judged him to be of above average height, well-built, with rugged shoulders beneath the rippling silk of his loose shirt. That broad torso that had so frightened her at first narrowed to a lithe waistline and flat stomach beneath skintight fawn breeches, but she dared not look lower, knowing now the meaning of the virile bulge men kept hidden beneath those deceptive buttons.

Blushing furiously, Christina lost the battle and turned away first, fumbling at her laces before daring to sit up. The sight of her breasts bared before this strange man caused further embarrassment, but she bit her tongue and with shaking fingers clumsily rearranged the lace in some semblance of modesty. She did not dare look about for the linen cloth that had covered the cleft between her breasts; she feared where she might find it.

The subject of her scrutiny watched this performance with mingled alarm and interest. That he had just tumbled an innocent and not the whore he imagined caused a certain amount of consternation, but the predicament was no worse than the one he had already enmeshed himself in. The wench herself, however, held his attention. At the moment, she appeared some fragile flower harshly treated, bruised and crumpled, but aside from her earlier screams, she seemed to be recovering from the ill treatment with amazing rapidity. He had a strong feeling that this flower would quickly regain her earlier grace and beauty to tempt many another plucking. And he contemplated that possibility with an audible sigh.

A deep golden cascade of curls tumbled about Christina's shoulders as she set about righting herself, preventing her from noticing the stranger's movement until he was almost upon her.

"Drink this. It will help."

Startled, Christina swung away from the sound of his voice. Still clutching her lacing, she sat up and stared back at the madman.

With deceptive normality he held out the fragile goblet, and not knowing what else to do, Christina accepted it. Her training as a lady acted for her. A lady did not refuse a gentleman's assistance, and whatever else he might be, this toweringly awesome stranger could be no other than the new Earl of Westshipham.

Once in her hand, there seemed to be no other choice but to sip the wine, and Christina did so without thinking. Her hands shook as she watched the earl's restless pacing.

She almost jumped as he swung around unexpectedly and confronted her.

"I suppose you must be some whore he bought and did not have time to lay before he died. Or did he keep you as you were to satisfy some stranger urgings? It makes no matter. I should be grateful you are not riddled with the pox he died from." He turned away with a disgust that seemed to be aimed at himself more than her.

But Christina heard only his crude words. Her screech of fury reached a crescendo as he calmly reached for his wineglass, but he did not turn back again until her goblet sailed dangerously near his head and crashed against the opposite wall. Christina raced to the door and had nearly negotiated the lock before the earl caught her. He calmly secured the door and pocketed the key before releasing her again.

Christina's heart beat rapidly against her ribs as she faced the tall stranger in this close proximity, the fury of long pent-up frustration hammering for some release. He had made no apology, no explanation, but treated her as a whore, even knowing what she had been! He had ruined her for life, probably filled her with his bastard, and he stood calmly contemplating her as if she were some interesting specimen to be added to his collection! Words were useless under the circumstances.

"You do speak English, do you not?" he inquired mildly when she did nothing but glare furiously at him.

Realizing how foolish she must look, Christina gathered her strength and stepped away from him.

"Better than you, I venture," she replied calmly in an accent that was the envy of even the most upper-crust of Mrs. Grenoble's girls. The Yankee's abominable drawl could not compare.

A measure of wry amusement lit dark eyes to almost human warmth, but the moment quickly passed.

"Is there a name to go with that pretty face, then?" He guarded the door carefully with his large frame, forcing her to retreat from the only means of escape.

"Christina MacTavish, sir, daughter of the late mayor of Westshipham. If he were alive, he would have you flayed for what you have done today."

A momentary frown of consternation etched the bridge above his patrician nose, but it did not linger long.

"Sit down, Christina MacTavish, and let me give you another glass of sherry. You are in no state to be hurrying from here, and we have much to discuss. Although, I must admit, your hysterics have vanished admirably."

"I have no desire to sit or drink in your presence, and the time for discussion is long past. Please allow me to pass." She held her ground firmly, lifting her chin in as grand a manner as she could summon.

"I will not. You came in here against my express orders, responded in a way that left no doubt as to your reasons for being here, and then screamed the news to the world when I reacted as I assumed was expected. You will sit down there and tell me what the mayor's daughter is doing here and then we will discuss what is to be done about it."

The Yankee earl led her firmly to the couch and saw her seated before returning to the bottle of sherry.

"The *late* mayor, and I was but seeking to hide from

the lecherous billy goat you call a butler," Christina sighed wearily. She ached in places she had never dreamed existed, and her disheveled attire left her feeling even more humiliated. How could she convince him he had just dishonored a lady when she looked the part of filthy slut he thought her? There was no fairness in this battle; she had lost without even knowing the rules. Fighting the urge to weep, Christina forced her chin up and regarded her molester with defiance.

With his back turned toward her, the earl could not see the girl's brave charade, but he could hear the tears and defiance in her voice. With a thoughtful frown he gazed upon the vial of powder on the desk, and then with a careless shrug he sprinkled a few grains in the goblet.

Christina searched the Yankee's sun-darkened face as he approached. The lightning had left his eyes, and their nearly black iridescence seemed to have withdrawn behind a cold curtain. Thick russet hair framed the rugged lines of his face, and though a certain sternness marred the handsomeness of his features, the marks of good breeding betrayed themselves in the line of his aristocratic nose and the firm curve of thin lips. Yankee or not, this earl bore the certain signs of English aristocracy, and arrogance played no small part in the portrait.

"So you chose my study in which to hide? How long have you worked here?"

He handed her the goblet and, as before, Christina accepted.

Christina could not take her eyes from his, though she shivered at his frightening proximity. This was the man who had held her and raped her, robbed her of her one possession, yet she accepted his wine as if he had just asked her to tea. She moved to set the glass aside, but his hand came up to stop her, tilting the glass slightly toward her mouth.

"You are shivering. The sherry will warm you and calm your nerves. You have not answered my question."

"I have been here a week," she whispered, praying if

she obeyed him in this, he would allow her to go soon. When he did not move away, she sipped the sherry.

Nodding approval, the earl turned and poured a glass for himself. "Your father is dead, then?"

No emotion betrayed his words, yet Christina sensed he asked nothing that did not hold his full interest.

"Murdered, two years ago. My mother has not been well since. I had heard, with the old earl gone, that this place was safe to work in . . ." She stumbled over the words, knowing she was not placing them well. She had never been good at artful speeches, and lack of practice these last few years had not helped her cause.

The earl inelegantly straddled a chair, not caring that his open shirt exposed an unseemly amount of his broad furred chest. He looked the part of dissipated pirate, or worse, as he faced her, watching her carefully. "That rumor will be quickly dispelled after today. Your screams have safely ruined both our reputations. Mine does not matter, for I will not be here long. I suppose I must find some means of making amends for yours."

Christina sent him a murderous glare and made no reply.

The dark stranger laughed shortly at the message he read quite successfully in her eyes. "Not a chance, my lady. Not only am I not inclined to marry, it would gain you nothing to be my wife. You would inherit a moldering estate, a mountain of debts, and a reputation that would bar you from every decent home in the country."

"You can be assured, after today, I have no inclination whatsoever to marry, either, and if I did, it would not be to a vile beast such as yourself. Do not concern yourself with my reputation, my lord. Simply let me out of this place." She sent an entreating glance toward the door.

"There is no hurry. The damage has already been done and cannot be worsened by lingering awhile longer. You may just be the answer to my needs, and I would know more of you. Have you no relatives to whom you may go? I daresay the rumors of this encounter will be in no hurry to follow if you leave quickly enough."

Christina shivered and sipped the sherry for warmth. He regarded her with a strange expression as she drank, and she grew increasingly uneasy. She could not fathom how she had come to this state. Other girls kissed and were not raped for their actions. How was it that the momentary pleasure of a kiss had led her to this bruised and bedraggled state, with her attacker so calmly interrogating her? And what was wrong with her that she had actually enjoyed the brute's kisses and did not faint or have hysterics when he had his way with her? Did normal women act this way? Shouldn't she hysterically be insisting on marriage now? She must be as mad as he.

"My father's family was starved out and hunted down like animals in the Jacobite rebellion of '45; he alone survived. My mother has not heard from hers since she married, and I know nothing of them. I will survive. Simply let me go." Christina did not plead, but stated her case calmly.

The earl nodded and swirled his sherry in the glass before sipping it again. He watched approvingly as she did the same. The afternoon sun sneaked through a high window and glittered across tawny curls, reflecting golden highlights in an angelic halo about the girl's porcelain face. The strain of keeping her emotions safely hidden away seemed in danger of cracking that smooth facade, but he admired her stately control. He knew few other women capable of it.

"I take it, then, that you are the sole support of your ill mother, and your father's estate was not exactly ample to provide for both of you?"

Christina shrugged and continued to look longingly at the door. A strange lethargy again seemed to haunt her limbs. She could not remember the source of the sudden anger that had sailed a full glass of wine at this man's head. She simply wished to be left alone to sort out the day's disaster.

The earl studied her glazed expression for a moment before speaking.

"I am leaving for London shortly. I can take you and your mother with me, out of gossip's reach, where your mother can obtain medical care. There would be only one condition attached."

Christina stared at her adversary without curiosity. His prominent cheekbones were displayed handsomely by the frame of thick russet hair pulled back from his face, and she wondered idly how he would look in a periwig. Perhaps Yankee lords did not wear periwigs. Disturbed by the intense penetration of those dark eyes, she looked away again. His look made her aware of how his strong fingers felt against her breast, and she did not want to remember. The final act had been too degrading to accept.

"Christina, are you listening?"

His words brought her back to the present, and she nodded absently, aware he had been speaking and not caring what was said.

"I find celibacy is not to my taste. These last months at sea and in this sorry household have convinced me to seek companionship, but I cannot afford casual acquaintances. It is too dangerous."

Realizing he had finally caught the girl's attention, the earl held her gaze as he continued slowly, seeking the proper words, though he did not know what madness inspired them. "I need a mistress who knows how to be loyal, discreet, and quiet. A well-bred girl such as you would suit my purposes nicely. I would pay well, and when I am gone, you would be free to start your life again anywhere that you wish." The proposal seemed justified through the murky light of wine and circumstances, and the earl concealed his satisfaction at this perfectly credible answer to both their problems.

Christina's eyes widened with horror as she realized what he asked, but a certain fascination kept her from screaming with fury at this outrageous insult. With genuine curiosity at the depravity of this monster, she asked, "And what would happen to any bastard we breed together, my lord?"

He shrugged unconcernedly. "There are many means of taking care of these things. I will see you provided for in whatever way you choose."

She wanted to scream and fling the glass at his smug face, but could not. She despised him with every fiber of her being, but she was helpless before him. Shaking her head emphatically, she finally managed to speak.

"No. Never. Never, never *never!* I never want to be touched again. I detest you and your entire abominable family! Seek elsewhere for your companionship. Just let me go home."

A trace of hysteria and tears again tinged her voice, and the earl quickly rose from his chair. Lifting the hand still holding her glass, he tilted it soothingly to her lips.

"You have not drunk it all," he admonished gently. At Christina's resistance, he settled down on the couch beside her and was rewarded with her hasty gulp of the remainder of the liquid. "That is better. Now I need to undo the damage I have done by taking you so crudely earlier. You must not leave here thinking lovemaking is such a cruel process."

Christina shrank away in horror as his shirt-sleeved arm slid behind her and strong brown fingers gently removed the goblet from her hand.

"No, please don't!" she whimpered, this time with all the pleading she had kept from her voice earlier. She could not bear the torment of being touched in such a way again, and she recoiled from the touch of his manly arm about her waist. His musky male scent quivered in her nostrils and she became overly aware of the hard lean body beneath the gentlemanly clothes. She wished to shove him away, but did not dare touch her hand to the black curls of his chest again.

"Do not fight me, Christina. You have nothing more to lose and everything to gain by letting me have my way in this."

The earl's deep voice rumbled soothingly against her

ear from the depths of his chest as his arm curved around her. To Christina's amazement, her shivering slowed, and when his hand returned to the curve of her partially covered breast, she did not flinch, but considered it wonderingly.

Strong fingers stroked the curve of her bodice, then worked their way up to the warm flesh swelling above the tight lacing. With amazing gentleness for one so large, he traced a path along the low neckline to her throat, stroking the underside of her chin before tilting her head back with the tip of his finger.

Some secret amusement tinged his voice as the Yankee gazed down into bewildered depths of amber. "My uncle's depraved knowledge has its uses, it seems. It is scarcely sporting to drug innocent maidens, but in this case, I believe the ends justify the means."

At his words, Christina cast a frantic glance to the empty glass on the table. At his low chuckle, her heart shrank away from her ribs. In panic she struggled to free herself from his embrace, but her movements were sluggish and without effect. As his devil's hand lowered to unlace her bodice, a shiver of mixed anticipation and fear shot through her, but she felt no urge to stop him. Her blood raced with a strange excitement as her bodice fell open and she felt the full heat of his gaze upon her. The black coals of his eyes burned with an admiration that made her giddy.

"That is much better, my dear." Lowering his head to her level, the earl plied her lips gently with wine-scented kisses while his fingers lovingly explored the unhampered pleasures of her young, firm breasts. The rosy crests puckered hard and pointed against his palm, and he forced back a surge of impatience. This time he would be gentle.

A surge of ecstasy pierced Christina's lethargy as strong fingers plied her reverently, and his lips promised more. She felt herself responding to his kiss more fervently than before. She wanted his mouth on hers, the pressure of his hard body holding her tightly while his lips nipped and caressed and invaded hers. Sheer madness possessed her as her fingers came to rest on his hard chest, and her lips parted invitingly beneath his insistence.

With a groan of delight the Yankee lord swept her up in his arms. With the muscular ease of an athlete, he lifted her from the divan and carried her toward a tapestry-covered door in the far wall.

Suspended in his strong arms, Christina dizzily registered this change in location, but not until he laid her across the rumpled sheets of his unmade bed did she understand the significance. Instead of fleeing for her life, she lay nervelessly watching as his silk shirt floated to the floor like the dust motes in the fading sunlight, exposing his sun-bronzed torso to her gaze once more. Everything seemed to move in slow motion, as if swimming languidly through a thick salt sea.

Beads of sweat formed upon Christina's brow as the remainder of the Yankee's clothes joined his shirt upon the floor, and she could not turn her head or avoid the sight. Weighed down by some oppressive effect of the drug, Christina could not even express her terror of the naked man swimming through the dim haze of her mind.

The Yankee watched as the girl's golden head rolled from side to side in wordless denial, her young, fair form seemingly frozen where he had placed her. Sympathy blackened his eyes deeper, but determination ruled the set of his jaw. With calm deliberation he set about the task of stripping her clothing away, reducing her to her natural state, unhindered by civilization's proprieties.

Even in fear, the slight body beneath him responded vibrantly to his touch, and Damien Drayton could scarcely control his eagerness. No woman had driven him to such madness before. Not even a hunger of many months' duration could explain his response to this golden woman. Perhaps his uncle's dark spirit inhabited this place and had invaded his soul. No matter. Her beauty and innocence illuminated the black world he had endured these past months, and he would grasp this light while he could.

The bodice slid easily from Christina's shoulders and the gown and petticoats were quickly divested, but the chemise proved an awkward bit of business. After contemplating it thoughtfully, Drayton left it alone. Blond curls tumbled in lovely disarray about shoulders untouched by sun, and he satisfied himself with simply unlacing the ties binding the glorious globes of flesh he had but glimpsed before.

Christina whimpered as his hard masculine body stretched out beside her, heavy legs like tree trunks lying familiarly across her bare slender ones. She turned her head away as he bent over her, but strong fingers forced her to face him.

"There is much you have to learn, Christina MacTavish, and it looks as if I must be the one to teach you."

When his lips closed over hers, she was lost again in the delights of this mad sensation. Her eyes flew wide with surprise as his tongue possessed her mouth at the same time his hand released her breast from its confinement. Fully circling the soft flesh with his fingers, he raised the rosy peaks to quivering hardness. His mocking gaze stared back at her for a moment, before he moved and took the tight peak into the heat of his mouth.

Christina cried out with the joy of this new possession, helpless to fight the inundating sensations he aroused in her. With methodical deliberation he showed her the wild pleasures of her body, churning a frenzy of desire within her that she had never before experienced.

Her arms flew about the Yankee's neck of their own accord, her fingers newly sensitive to the hard bulge of cord and muscle beneath their touch. Her body ached to be closer to his, to be entwined against his long length, and he obliged by moving over her, carefully keeping his weight from crushing her into fear again.

The brush of his hair-roughened skin against hers, the awareness of an emptiness between her legs that he seemed admirably able to satiate, engendered all manner of confusion within Christina's drugged mind. Some awareness still existed that she must fight him before he possessed her entirely, but the aching need for that same possession remained paramount. She hugged him closer, and his lips whispered near her ear.

"I intend to make you mine, Christina MacTavish, whether you will or no."

She felt him fumbling between them where their hips touched dangerously near, but before she could rouse to any protest, the earl's fingers slid along the cleft of her womanhood, lingering with certain knowledge at the aching entrance. She cried out as he plied her with caresses, and her hips surged upward.

He was ready for her. With one swift movement he plunged home, and her cry of surprise became a muffled groan of pleasure as he pulled her against him, riding gently where she wanted him most.

No pain marred this joining and Christina surrendered to the urgency of his thrusts. She had no knowledge of how to respond, but felt her body opening fully to him, welcoming his hard maleness. The sudden thrashing plunge as he gained his pleasure brought an odd contentment.

With the heat of his body burning against hers, Christina closed her eyes and slept.

3

She woke alone, the covers pulled about her and the room shrouded in darkness. The fogs of sleep protected her for a moment, but the places rubbed raw by a beard and the chafing soreness between her thighs reminded Christina all too soon of her humiliation.

As memory returned, her cheeks burned crimson with shame. To be mistaken for a whore was shameful enough, but to behave as one. . . ! The memory of her complete capitulation burned clearly in Christina's mind, as clearly as the memory of the Yankee's hands upon her skin, and worse. The scent of him still clung to her if she still had any doubts as to the reality of this nightmare.

Panic crept through her veins. What had she done? What had she become? The demented earl had left her here, used and torn, as he would some play toy with which he had grown bored. He would come back when he grew hungry again and use her some more as it pleased him. He must be certain that he had made her his mistress, that she could not resist the pleasures and temptations he offered, for him to leave her so unguarded.

This thought brought Christina abruptly to her senses. She must escape. My Lord, what time was it? How long had she slept? Her mother would be panic-stricken. She must get home.

The thought of home brought tears to her eyes. How she wished for the strength of her father's powerful arms, the concern and affection he had showered upon her, the wisdom that would guide her from this morass she found herself in. She needed him desperately at this moment, but was grateful he was not here to see her humiliation. He could do nothing against an earl, a lord of the realm. She must act on her own.

With silent caution Christina slipped from beneath the covers, trying to ignore the aches of her newly opened body. Her trembling fingers sought and found the clothing discarded—when? Yesterday?

She glanced at the gray sky outside the uncurtained window—dawn, then. It must have been yesterday. She had been gone all night. How would she ever explain that to her mother?

Hastily she jerked on her clothing. She could not afford to think now, she must act. Somehow, some way, she must get out of here before the Yankee returned. Her fingers fumbled and jerked every lace and fastening, and her heart beat frantically within her chest in fear that any moment he would return. The fate that awaited her should he do so did not bear long consideration.

At last her clothing sat upon her in some manner or form, and Christina nervously grasped the door clasp. If it did not move, she would be reduced to shredding sheets and lowering herself from the window, but leave here she would.

With relief, she felt the clasp give way beneath her fingers, and in moments she was hurrying down empty corridors and dark stairs. She did not dare risk the huge portals at the front of the house; they would be locked at this time of day, she felt certain. She must risk the kitchens.

Hair streaming in a disheveled cascade down her back, garments in wild disarray, she raced through the cavernous kitchens like one possessed, startling the few morning occupants into thinking they had roused a ghostly apparition. Speaking no word, Christina flew by them and out the open kitchen door, through the gardens, and into the stableyard. Stealing a horse would only give him further reason to seek her out, and she resisted the temptation. Perhaps "out of sight, out of mind" applied to madmen and Yankees, and once she was gone, he would not seek her.

Dew-drenched fields soaked her shoes and gown, but they were safer than the road. Christina hurried through the morning mists of open pastures and into the shadowed grayness of the hedgerows. The sun had crossed the horizon, but its first faint rays scarcely tinged the ocean fogs settled against the far hills. She must be far gone before it rose higher and he discovered her escape.

She gasped with relief as she reached the mysterious darkness of the ragged evergreens. The paths were plain to one familiar with them, but the Yankee would know nothing of their direction. Wet slippers carried her through the bone-chilling cold of early morning darkness.

Lungs panting for breath, Christina collapsed to rest against the hairy bark of a sea-warped trunk. Gasping, she stared out over the high cliffs to the sea beyond. Had it been only yesterday that she had looked out over that same bay and longed for the freedom of those crashing breakers?

The memory drew her from the shelter of her wooded haven and closer to the rocky slope. Fog lay across the waters now, but some trick of the rising sun formed a ghostly ship among the vapors, strangely near the rocky shore. Christina glanced downward at the perilous drop beneath her feet, so near—yet so far. A stumble would put an end to her miseries, a ship would give her freedom. If only she dared either one . . .

Her breath caught in her throat before she could contemplate the thought longer. A dark shape climbed agilely up the treacherous path of boulders directly below her feet!

Fascinated by the impossible feat, wondering what strange trick her tired mind played, Christina could not bring herself to tear away immediately. Twists of fog twined about the shadowy shape, but as he rose closer, she realized the climber wore a cloak and hood. And far below, where the waves pounded against the shore, rocked a small shell of a boat.

Odd, but not unusual on these rugged shores. Smugglers inhabited many of these secluded coves. Thieves used the caves for storing their plunder. Neither would appreciate her observation.

Without waiting to see more, Christina darted toward the protection of the woods. It would not do to escape a madman only to be captured by a pirate.

Branches crackled underfoot, easily betraying her existence. Christina hesitated, uncertain of the better course—hiding, or running. Surely the smuggler would not expect to be observed at this hour. If she hid, he would pass on by. To run would give her away, and she did not have the strength or fleetness to outrun a pursuer. She hid.

The decision was a futile one. From her hiding place Christina watched as the black-cloaked figure pulled himself over the edge. As he rose agilely to his full height, Christina swallowed a cry of dismay. This creature of the night stood well over six feet in height and moved with the assurance and power of an untamed panther. His gaze focused immediately on the only possible place of concealment. As it became evident his steps would turn her way, Christina dashed from the underbrush and down the forest path.

To no avail. In a few long strides that agile figure had crossed the clearing and cut her off. With a cry of terror Christina found herself trapped in the long heavy folds of a damp cloak.

She struggled, but her wild flailing only succeeded in twisting it tighter. An amused chuckle brought her to a startled halt.

Cautiously she raised her eyes to the stranger's face—and saw nothing. A hood with eyeholes concealed his features, but the creature undoubtedly had a mouth, for he used it now.

"I have poached these woods before, but never have I snared such a handsome bird. How comes it that the worm catches the early bird?"

Christina stared at this apparition in astonishment. Living all her life in Cornwall, she had come to know a fair number of suspected smugglers, but none had spoken with the well-educated tones of Oxford or made clever witticisms. It would seem the highwayman would be of the same crude character, but she could think of no other who would be out at this hour, garbed in cloak and mask.

As if following the path of her bewildering thoughts, the hooded stranger did not wait for her to speak. "A pretty pickle we have here, is it not? You have chosen an odd time to visit the cliffs. Did someone send you?" His voice lacked any trace of the suspicion his words indicated, but Christina responded vehemently.

"No! Never! If you will just let me go, I will say nothing to anyone. I have no wish to betray my own presence here, either."

This close, the highwayman seemed even more a giant than at a distance, his firm grip betraying a terrifying strength. In her fear Christina decided this highwayman held an advantage even over the forbidding earl, and she knew the danger of the Yankee's strength. She was at his complete mercy unless she could talk faster than he thought. She had some doubt as to her ability to accomplish this feat, and his next words did nothing to alleviate her fears.

"And you expect me to believe that? Half the countryside seeks my hide. I cannot risk your revealing my presence." Feeling the girl's shivers beneath his fingers, the highwayman kept his cloak pulled about her shoulders, but set her back enough to study the distress in her pale face. "Though I do believe you would prefer it not to be known that I found you in this godforsaken place at dawn."

His voice took on a certain harshness as he inquired, "What *are* you doing at the cliff's edge at this hour?"

Christina heard the unspoken accusation and attempted to jerk from beneath his forceful grip. "It is none of your concern. I have told you I will not reveal you. My mother is ill and will be over worried if I do not appear with her morning tea. Please, let me go."

She could not hide the tears in her voice. In these last hours, she had been abused in more ways than she had thought possible, and this stranger's threats had pushed her beyond the border of control.

Catching the sob in her words, the highwayman relaxed his grip a degree. With a quick look up the hill to the wooded mansion grounds, he regarded her with a different interest, as evidenced by his next words.

"The new lord is as much a bastard as the old, then?" he asked with knowing tone.

Christina shook herself free and glared back at him. "H-how w-would I know?" she stuttered bravely, refusing to acknowledge what all the world would know shortly.

The hooded stranger's interest seemed to mount. "You expect me to believe you are out wandering the cliffs to watch the sun rise? Give me credit for more sense than that. How am I to believe you will keep quiet about me if you lie about other things?"

Christina's glare verged on the murderous. "You would have me reveal the trust of another to prove your trust in me? Fie on you, sir! Why don't you slit my throat and put an end to this mockery? It is obvious you have no intention of freeing me."

Again the black-garbed apparition chuckled with some amusement as he watched fiery sparks of amber light previously doleful eyes. "On the contrary, my lady, slitting your lovely throat is the least of my intentions. I only seek to preserve my own safety. Perhaps I should phrase my question differently. Answer me only yea or nay. Did his mighty lordship leave you untouched?"

"Y-yes!" Realizing he forced her to lie, Christina became confused and tried again. "No! That is an unfair question! If you do not mean to slit my throat, then I shall take this opportunity to bid you adieu, sir."

Furious at her confusion beneath the stranger's mocking eyes, Christina turned to flee down the forest path. He sought only to protect his back at the expense of her own embarrassment. She would give him no further amusement.

Twigs crackled underfoot as she raced down the hillside and back toward town. She hated to traverse that path revealing her to observant eyes, but it was safer than lingering in the woods with a highwayman.

A shrill whistle pierced the murky gloom of the damp woods, followed by the unmistakable beat of a horse's hooves not far behind her. In amazement more than terror, Christina dodged from the path and hid in the shadow of a stunted pine as a galloping black stallion careened madly down the path after her.

And reared to a halt in front of her hiding place.

The cloaked figure leaned down from the massive steed and held out his gloved hand. "Do you think I'd let you walk back to town? Who knows what evildoers might lurk in these trees?"

Christina heard the mocking taunt in his deep drawl, but sensed it aimed at himself as much as at her. Hesitantly she stepped forward and glanced askance at his mysterious steed.

"I did not see this beast climb the cliff."

He grabbed her hand and loosed his foot from the stirrup so she might use it. As he hauled her unceremoniously before him, he replied, "I summon beasts at my call. Would you come were you to hear me whistle?"

He held her distractingly close to the warm length of his hard body, and his voice whispered insinuatingly softly against her ear, leaving Christina momentarily confused. Another man had held her thus not so long ago, and the consequences had been horrendous. How was it that she now felt secure in the embrace of this dangerous thief? Perhaps the drug affected her senses, but she made herself comfortable beneath his protective cloak and answered almost saucily.

" 'Tis man who is said to be the beast. In the future, I shall learn to whistle when I wish to be amused."

He laughed shortly and set the horse in motion. "I doubt not you will be successful, my dear, but be certain the beast is fully tamed before you summon him."

And with those words of warning he turned the horse toward town.

At Christina's direction, they skirted the edge, keeping well hidden in hedgerows and fields, out of sight of snooping eyes.

At the entrance to the back gardens of her home, the highwayman brought his stallion to a halt and his arm tightened suggestively about Christina's waist.

"If his Yankee lordship does not suit you, perhaps you would care to dally awhile and sample the delights an Englishman has to offer," he murmured wickedly against her ear.

Despite his words, Christina sensed no seriousness of purpose in this mysterious stranger, and she replied in kind.

"N-no m-man h-has h-had me, sir, and none shall, for there is n-none g-good enough."

The answer did not come out quite as lightly as she wished; too much pain rang in the tattered remains of the truth. One man had had her. No other would.

She heard the disbelief in his reply.

"Do you always stammer when you lie, my dear?" he asked quizzically.

Instead of replying, Christina slid from her seat and hurried toward the garden gate, out of his embarrassing presence. She should have known better than to dally with a highwayman.

The stallion whinnied and reared in the forest behind her, but she did not linger to watch him go.

The highwayman watched her flee and cursed himself roundly. Months of hard work and he had just laid it all within the reach of a Tory temptress. Drastic measures would have to be taken at once, but the methods and means left much to be desired. He swore again and swung the stallion around. War and desperation went hand in hand and left no time for the niceties. He must act quickly.

4

The back door to the cottage was unlocked as usual, and Christina gasped with relief as she reached its welcoming warmth. Their servants had long since found employment elsewhere, but Mrs. Frymire, their neighbor, often came by to keep the fire hot and look after Mrs. MacTavish when Christina was out. The fire threw out a flickering warmth now, and Christina hastened to test the water over it.

Warm. Thank the Lord. With swift deliberation she hauled out the old wooden tub and emptied the contents of the kettle into it. She filled another at the pump and returned it to the fire, then added a pail of cool water to the simmering tub to fill it further. Then, with haste, she stripped off her soaked clothing and sank into the comfort of liquid warmth. She would not go to her mother reeking of that animal's scent.

Though she scrubbed vigorously, the lapping waters and lavender soap could not wash away the reminders of the Yankee's possession. Hungry dark eyes ravished her as she rubbed the cloth across her breasts, and with wonder Christina gazed down upon their puckering crests. He had found some strange fascination in rousing them that way, indeed, in just gazing upon them and the slender curve of waist and hips below. She had not thought of her body as attractive to men before. Now she could not stop thinking of how he had touched it, and what pleasures that touch had wrought. She must be as mad as he. Coupled with her memories of the highwayman's warm embrace, her thoughts did not encourage sanity.

Christina dried herself hastily and wrapped herself in a robe. Practicality must prevail over nightmares. She must see to her mother at once. She would be frantic with worry.

When the chamber door slipped open, Eleanor MacTavish turned her gaze from the sun-filled windows to her daughter's golden head and smiled serenely.

"Christie, my love! I did not expect you back so soon. His lordship's message made it sound as if you were sorely needed at the hall."

Christina nearly fell headfirst into the room at these words. Steadying herself, she tried to answer calmly. "His lordship? I thought him too busy to notice and feared you would be worried."

Mrs. MacTavish smiled and struggled to pull herself upright. Her once fair hair had grown thin and graying these past few years and slipped wispily from the plaits tied about her head. Her delicately boned face drew into a small frown of pain as she tried to adjust her position.

Christina hastened to help, tucking the pillows more comfortably behind her mother's slight frame before sitting down on the bed beside her.

Eleanor smiled and tried to pat away Christina's worried frown. "You bother yourself overmuch, my love. You are young and should be looking to the future. Of course your Yankee earl, as you call him, notified me of your delay. It would be extremely inconsiderate of him not to do so. You must tell me all about him. He must be much like his father. Anson Drayton was always a thoughtful, considerate man. I would have loved him dearly had I not loved another more."

Her mother always spoke thus, the words coming in the cheerful gay spurts of a bubbling fountain. She was a hopeless romantic, and Christina had to hide her smile at the images scattered like sparkling droplets before her. Her mother and the Honorable Anson Drayton? It was possible. Her mother had once been a great beauty, daughter to the Baron of Adderly. Why shouldn't an earl's younger son look her way? Only,

Christina prayed, the father had no resemblance to the son. Two of such a kind in the world would be catastrophic. She fancied the Yankee took more after his uncle than his father, if her mother's words were to be believed.

"I know nothing of this earl or his father, *ma mère*, but his household is a scandal. It would take an army of housekeepers to clean it."

"Oh, but then you must hurry back to help. He will learn to appreciate your help, and who knows? Mayhap he will not be able to live without you. You are becoming an extremely beautiful young lady. It would not be the first time such beauty turned the head of a young man. Tell me of him. Is he handsome? Does he speak well? Tell me all."

Christina groaned inwardly. Her mother had already conjured up impossible fantasies. It passed the time and kept her happy. How could she possibly say the man was a demented monster who had raped and drugged her? Again she longed for her father's silent wisdom and strong character. She needed someone to turn to for advice, but her mother was not that someone. She must be protected from all shock and unpleasantness.

"There is nothing much to say, *ma mère*. He is a busy man and soon leaves for London. He needs someone who will be able to accompany him and keep his house there. I am not that someone, Mother. Let me fetch you your breakfast."

If disappointment crossed her mother's face, Christina pointedly ignored it. She did not have a glib way with words to lie well and she skirted the truth as neatly as she could. Before she could be questioned further, she returned to the kitchen and breakfast.

With her mother safely napping, Christina sat down at the tall mahogany secretary and began to compose her thoughts. She could always think more clearly with pen and paper at hand. Insane fantasies of riding off with gallant highwaymen provided no solution to her immediate problems, though she stared at the window wondering what would happen should she whistle loud enough.

She must write her uncle. There was no other alternative. Once the rumors of her night at Westshipham began to spread, she would not only have to give up all hope of marrying well but of finding any work whatsoever. They would soon starve if she could do neither. Highwaymen hung for their criminal deeds, but not earls. And few had pity on their victims.

Surely her uncle could forgive what was long in the past. Her mother was his only sister, and with her father out of the way . . . Christina dashed away a tear and began to write. Now that he held the title of Baron of Adderly, perhaps he would be more generous and forgiving than when he was only an arrogant and somewhat insecure young man. A son must follow the father's orders, but he was a man grown now. Surely he could not be so unreasonable as to reject his penniless, ill sister and her daughter?

Begging did not come easily. In fact, it did not come at all. Instead Christina merely stated the facts of her father's death and her mother's illness and requested guidance from the head of her family. What man could resist the chance to flaunt his opinions or power? Grimly Christina completed the letter carrying her fate. If her uncle did not respond, she might as well fling herself from the cliffs. Or whistle for the highwayman.

By the time she had copied the letter in a fair hand and without the smudge of teardrops, it was too late to meet that day's post. It saved her the humiliation of venturing outside the safety of her own walls for one more day, but Christina chafed at the delay.

Emotionally drained and physically exhausted, she sought the escape of sleep while her mother napped. There was no question of returning to the hall, even for her wages. They must eke out some existence until her uncle replied. Christina could no longer bear the burden alone.

Garbed in a black cloak with his dark tricorne pulled

down over his face almost to the edge of his mask, the horseman selected a secluded nook among the bushes in the trees and waited.

The game should be almost over by now. He would not have long to wait. The fog settled like a cold rain about his neck and shoulders, and he moved restlessly within the confines of the warm material. This would be the last time he risked his damned neck on such foolishness. He had come here with a much higher goal in mind. To be forced to waste precious time on this nonsense for lack of funds irked him, but the revenge extracted in the process had served to soothe some of his ire.

He chuckled in memory of the fear in their greedy eyes and the elaborate precautions they had recited as their protection against the ill-famed highwayman. He had outwitted them all, but they were scarcely the kind of adversaries he preferred. He enjoyed a challenge, but he found little enough of that in these fat lords.

He had one last score to even before the highwayman disappeared forever. The sheriff's pockets should be plump this night after his winning hand. He found it hard to believe the old lord had been so dinged in the noggin that he could not spy the sheriff's cheating ways in the first round. Well, he'd gain it all back and then some this night, and then be done with it.

His gaze strayed to the cottage beyond the trees. A candle flickered briefly in an upper-story window and he wondered what she did up at this hour. Remembering the terror in those wide amber eyes as she gazed upon him, he grimaced beneath his mask. He had made a serious blunder there and regretted every minute of it. Almost every minute of it, he amended. He could still feel her slight weight in his arms and remembered well the flashing challenge of those golden-brown eyes. Now, there was one worth fighting for, had circumstances been different. But as it was, the best he could hope to do was give her a hand out of the mire he had thrust her in, and quickly, if he had heard rightly.

He did not linger long on such thoughts. His mount stirred uneasily beneath him, and within seconds he heard what the animal had sensed. Hoofbeats, and from more than one direction!

Damn! They would have him surrounded. How could that fool of a sheriff have guessed. . . ?

Remembering the churl he had thrown out on his witless head this afternoon, the horseman cursed again. If he survived this little encounter, he would make short work of the cowardly talebearer who had put him here.

Spying the sheriff's plump figure astride a horse cantering down the main trail, the highwayman smiled beneath his mask. He would not only escape from this mess, he would have the purse he sought also.

The stallion reared with a mighty scream as its rider jerked the reins. The highwayman's intended victim froze in the saddle, his head nervously turning from side to side as he sought the source of the ghostly cry. No amount of foresight could have prepared him for the terrifying specter flying out of the darkness and into his path. Paralyzed with fear of the winged creature bearing down upon him, the sheriff could do no more than shout a meager protest as the pouched belt at his waist fell away with a single flashing sword stroke.

Pounding hooves coming from all directions at once gave reason for hope, but the shattering blast of a gunshot whizzing past his ear sent him diving for cover. The highwayman waved his prize tauntingly at his attackers and stood his ground.

Out of the darkness a sword flashed, and the highwayman's silver blade instantly swung to meet it. The fog swirled about the furious clash of mounted swordsmen, and horses whickered fearfully through the haze. Steel clanged against steel, but through the mists only the occasional flicker of silver could be seen.

A cry of pain rang out, and the sound of muffled hooves echoed against the sudden stillness of the moisture-drenched night.

When she woke, the windows were dark. Hastily Christina jumped from the bed and crossed to her mother's room. The remains of a supper tray rested on the bedside table. Blessing Mrs. Frymire, Christina removed the tray from beside her sleeping mother and tiptoed from the room.

In the kitchen she lit a candle and placed the dirty dishes in a bowl of water to soak. Foraging through their depleted larder for some crumb to stave off the pangs of hunger, Christina scarcely heard the shouts of confusion and fury in the woods beyond. But the sudden wild commotion of gunshots and galloping hooves outside the window startled her into dripping hot wax on the floor.

Setting the candle on the sink, she approached the darkness of the window, her heart beating erratically. She had never felt fear in her own home. The villagers looked out for their own, and the mayor's widow and her daughter held their respect. But these past days had taught Christina something of the other shadows beyond her small world, and she had learned to be wary.

But not wary enough. The back door burst open and a cloaked figure dashed through. Grabbing Christina by the waist and covering her mouth with his gloved hand, the highwayman shoved the door closed and quickly blew out the room's only light. Panting for breath, he leaned against the wall, easily stifling his captive's struggles by wrapping his arm firmly about her. Holding her tightly against his masculine frame, he held his breath and listened to the sounds outside. The rapier in his hand remained taut, brushing against her skirts as they breathed.

Anger quickly replaced fear as Christina sensed he meant her no harm. His hold on her was firm but gentle, and eased as the sounds of horses disappeared into the night, leaving behind only the quiet ticking of the mantel clock in the darkened parlor. As the taut muscles of the man behind her relaxed, Christina recognized the direction his attention now took, and she shook her head free from his smothering grip.

"Let go of me! Have you gone mad, coming here like this?"

He did not immediately release her, but held her lightly against his chest, his breath ruffling her hair as he indulged his enjoyment of her lavender scent and the slightness of her gentle curves beneath his hands. Then, feeling her grow tight with fear, he relaxed his grip and watched ruefully as she darted to the opposite side of the room.

"I have to be half-mad to continue this treacherous profession, but not mad enough to endanger you. I just needed a moment's diversion." He shoved his rapier back in its belt, lest he frighten her further. "Would you have a cup of tea? It would warm the chill from my bones before I venture out again."

Christina stared at the dark cloaked figure outlined against the chimney. The darkness and his cultured tones hid his danger, but as he swept the tricorne hat from his head, her heart leapt in fear again.

"The fire for the water has died. There is some brandy in the cabinet behind you." She heard her voice speak, but could not believe she had said the words.

He said nothing, but with the ease of a cat located the bottle and a glass in the darkness. Politely he held up the bottle so it winked in the moonlight streaming through the kitchen window. "Will you join me?"

Christina shook her head, then, realizing he could not see her, whispered, "No, thank you." The enormity of entertaining a notorious highwayman as if he were an invited guest took away her breath, but she was quickly regaining her self-possession. As he offered a seat at the table, she remained standing. "I do not even know your name," she found herself protesting, incredibly.

A flashing smile lit the gloom. "And for your own good, you will not. Call me Captain, if you must. It will serve."

He waited patiently for her to sit, and Christina could no longer think of an excuse to avoid it. He evidently meant to stay safely hidden until his victims were far gone, and she scarcely had the strength to throw him out. Reluctantly she joined him at the table.

"Why are you here?" she asked nervously, watching as long gloved fingers wrapped about the bottle and poured a generous portion. She had felt the strength in those fingers when he held her. It would not do to anger such a man.

"The sheriff came too close tonight. I fear I have been betrayed by more than my own carelessness. The culprit will fear the prick of my ire before this night is o'er."

His voice floated through the darkness to her, the low tones seemingly reserved for himself more than his companion. Christina shivered at the ominous warning, but could not keep from questioning further.

"You have accomplices, then?"

His grin broke the gloom once more and Christina strained to see more of his face than the engaging charm of his smile—in vain, for his eyes were wells of darkness behind his mask.

"You ask too many questions, but so do I. Unfortunately, I do not always listen to the answers. Did you know his noble lordship has thrown out that diseased butler his uncle left to him? Devious old codger, with a vengeful streak—the butler, I mean. Getting sacked wasn't sufficient, I believe. The man needs a notch or two taken out of his hide."

Carried away on a stream of emotions, Christina did not immediately reply. Grateful the disgusting old man had received his just deserts, puzzled that the earl had even bothered to see justice done, and bewildered that the highwayman should know anything of him, she formed her words carefully.

"You are familiar with his lordship's household?"

The scent of brandy surrounded them with its familiar warmth. Her father had used to sit at the table like this, sipping his brandy and listening to his daughter's wild tales. This man across from her now carried with him an aura of danger and adventure, not her father's reassuring security, yet she felt comfortable in his presence. Christina listened expectantly for explanations.

"A man of my profession must be familiar with all the comings and goings of his territory. The rumor of your night at Westshipham Hall has already reached the village. Jarvis carried it first, but one of the maids has confirmed it. You knew it couldn't be kept secret forever, didn't you?"

She could not find the emotion behind his muffled words. They spoke quietly, to prevent waking her mother. Much could be hidden in whispers.

"I know and I do not care," she stated bravely.

"Then you are a fool." He took another swift drink from the glass. "There is a young farmer down in the tavern now, drinking himself under the table. His threats against the earl were quickly reduced by persuasive tongues to boasts of the conquest he intends to make of you. You have become fair game to every rutting male in the territory. The 'Yankee's whore' will not be safe in her own home much longer. Have you nowhere to go? I will gladly carry you wherever you wish."

The abrupt sentences said more than his hushed tones. Christina heard his anger and his concern and though she could not imagine its source, she was grateful to have someone to whom she could talk. She would not have been able to discuss such a topic with her father, but with this stranger the words came easily.

"I have written to my uncle. Drinking talk comes to nothing, and Thomas will do nothing but suffer a sore head in the morning. My concern is keeping the tale from my mother. She could not bear the shock."

"It does not matter to you that the poor swine suffers a broken heart? Is there no man here to step forward and protect you?" The grin had gone, replaced by a hidden frown scarcely concealed by his whispers.

Christina retaliated with anger. "Thomas suffers only hurt pride. He means nothing to me, nor does any man here. If they had wished to earn my affections, they would have hunted down my father's murderer and driven off the greedy earl with his false claims! But no, they choose to shake their heads and mutter curses and do nothing! Men are worthless!"

The highwayman chortled lightly and finished his drink, satisfied by her reaction. She was a survivor. He would not have to worry overmuch about delicate sensibilities; she would see reason. Out loud he admitted, "Your father's spirit lives on in you, it seems. 'Tis a pity you are female. Still, there are certain advantages to that also."

Christina could almost see the leer behind his words, but his humor kept her from being offended. She needed someone to lift the heavy oppression of her thoughts, and the gallant highwayman seemed too much like a storybook hero to be taken seriously.

He rose quickly, throwing back his cloak to produce a small sack that clinked lightly as he set it upon the table. "You need this more than I. Use it to take yourself to your uncle. I will claim your wages from the earl for you."

Christina rose to protest, but he silenced her words with an abrupt kiss in the vicinity of her forehead.

"Your mother's health is more important than pride. Remember that. I thank you for your hospitality, but I have work to do. Good night, fair Christina."

He touched her briefly upon the cheek and was gone before she could utter a word of farewell.

The morning light revealed the dark stain of blood on her skirts where his rapier had rested.

Not daring to contemplate the crime behind this evidence, Christina scrubbed the stain until all traces had disappeared. It would be best to pretend last night had never happened.

As she approached the village, letter to her uncle in hand, Christina could feel eyes of malice follow her, but when she would turn to meet them, all gazes quickly averted. The highwayman had spoken the truth. Rumor had already spread. She had become a fallen woman, a Yankee's whore, in the eyes of all who knew her. Christina shivered as a cold wind caught her mantle, and she hurried on. The highwayman's devious route to her doorstep had fooled no one. She was a branded woman for so long as she remained here.

Posting the letter, Christina quickly retraced her steps, pondering the news she had inadvertently heard in the town. Jarvis, the hall's butler, had been found stripped of all clothes and dangling by his thumbs from a tree just outside of town. Surely the earl had not committed this atrocity. But for what reason would the highwayman have done it? Remembering his threats against his betrayer, Christina shook her head and hurried faster toward home. Had the highwayman placed informants even in the earl's household? Or what connection dangled between the two men?

The gracious two-story cottage she called home was hidden from her sight by the parcel of woods in the bend of the road. She supposed they would have to sell the house now, but her heart fought against this last departure from all she knew and loved. They must leave it behind, but to burn all bridges behind her seemed a drastic measure.

Not until her footsteps carried her around the curve did Christina realize the bridges were already gone.

The earl's coach waited outside the cottage gate. It was unmistakable. No other in Cornwall possessed such a grand vehicle, even if the heraldry on the door had not acted as signature.

Christina was torn between the desire to run in two different directions. Escape seemed imperative. She did not know how he had found her or why, but she could not face that madman again! The very thought sent paroxysms of fear down her spine. She could not bear the thought of his hands on her again, and if he attempted more. . . . She gagged at the thought, her hand rising to her throat to hold back the bile.

Yet what would the cruel Yankee do to her mother if she did not return? What could he possibly be telling her now? If he spoke of her disgrace, her mother would die of the shock. That thought turned Christina's feet racing down the path. Surely even that monster would not rape her under her mother's roof, and she would dearly like this opportunity to give the beast a piece of her mind.

Throwing open the oaken door, she found the downstairs rooms unoccupied. A bustle of activity came from the bedrooms upstairs, and Christina hastened to find its source.

Passing her own room, she spied one of the maids from the hall packing a trunk with her last few precious gowns. She wanted to scream for a halt, but she must find her mother first. Screaming would not help her mother's health.

A low murmur of voices came from the room at the end of the corridor. Christina hurried toward it, rage exceeding caution. She threw back the partially open door and positioned herself boldly in the opening.

"*You!* What business have you here? I demand some explanation, and if your maid does not return my clothes at once, I will call the sheriff!"

The tall, lithe figure in the room's center turned slowly. Russet hair had been powdered and tied in a bagwig in respectable style. His fashionable plum-colored coat was cut away at the waist to reveal a buff waistcoat and impeccably styled buff knee breeches. He presented a figure of unimpeachable authority as he regarded her impertinence with a cold stare, yet Christina refused to quail before him.

Instead, her mother replied with horror, "Christina! How could you talk to his lordship so? And after he has been so kind as to make such a magnanimous offer! Apologize at once!"

Before Christina could open her mouth to protest, the earl suavely interceded.

"Miss MacTavish and I have had a small misunderstanding that must be resolved. If you would excuse us for a moment, my lady, I will send my maid in here to assist you while your daughter and I talk."

The words and intonations were deliberately designed to return stars to her mother's eyes, and Christina glared at the Yankee with contempt as he took her elbow and pushed her from the room without waiting for reply.

As soon as the bedroom door closed, she attempted

to shake herself free from his grip, but brown fingers only fastened themselves more strongly as he steered her toward the stairs.

"How dare you!" Christina demanded in harsh whispers. "Let go of me! This is my house. You have no authority here. How could you come here like this?"

The Yankee earl shoved her into the small downstairs parlor and slammed the door. No fire lit this little-used room and March winds kept it chilled. Yet the heat of rage coursed through Christina's veins as she turned on this despicable monster who had destroyed her life.

He gave her no opportunity to speak. Beneath powdered hair his face seemed darker and more lined than before, a weathered face of stern lineaments. The coldness of his tone did not lighten his appearance.

"I have invited your mother to accompany me to London. She cannot receive effective care in this backwater. In London she will be seen by the best physicians, and there will be someone to tend to her at all times so she will not be left alone while you are out dallying with the locals!"

His accusatory tone set her back, but it did not take long for Christina's brain to register the import of his words. He could no longer fool her with his pretense at gentlemanliness. She understood that beneath that fashionable facade lay an uncouth Yankee, a heart of stone, and a madman capable of anything, including blackmail. She retaliated with as much vehemence as he.

"You cannot just pack my mother up and take her away like this! Her health is delicate and cannot tolerate such a journey. Besides, I do not trust your words. We do not need your charity," she spat out angrily.

"It is not charity. You will accompany us, ostensibly as my guest, but you will act as hostess and housekeeper and whatever other duties a woman in the house fills. I am tired of looking after such things myself. I am also damned tired of sleeping alone, but since you insist on playing the recalcitrant miss, I will give you a fortnight to make that choice. Your mother will receive the best of care and you will have the opportunity to see what you are missing by hiding in this superstitious backhole. At the end of that time, you must choose to continue living in London as my mistress, or you and your mother will return here."

He spoke the words tonelessly, without warmth or ardor, reflecting the same lack of expression as his features. Christina stared at him, waves of cold horror breaking across her body as she realized the trap he had set for her. She must choose between her mother and herself! How could anyone be such a dastardly bastard? Yet she could not refuse him outright. Her mother's life might depend upon it.

"I have written my uncle of our plight. He travels much, but when he returns, he will surely come for us. We do not need to go with you," Christina stated proudly, the golden-brown lights of her eyes flashing in the room's twilight.

The earl's tight jaw relaxed a notch. She had taken the hook and needed only to be reeled in cautiously. He sensed his own streak of practicality had met its match in hers. She would not be able to refuse.

"Your mother's health cannot wait for your uncle's dubious return. You may write him from London with your new address. He will have a fortnight to make his appearance."

"You will kill her in the process! Leave us alone, I beg of you! There are whores enough in London. Find one there."

Point and counterpoint, but both sides sensed the outcome.

The earl watched as the girl pulled back the heavy, dusty curtains, unwittingly outlining her slender figure against the early morning light. Even without the hoops and bustles and panniers and other feminine fripperies, her proud stance held a ladylike grace that would shame half London. He knew little of feminine fashion, but those tawny curls piled high had a natural beauty of their own, and needed no additional adornment. He could speak such flattery to any other lady with impunity, but this one would fly in the opposite direction if he dared mention so personal a subject. Besides, it would not suit his purpose for her to hear praises from his lips. He preferred she continue to think of him as a monster. It would be easier for everyone when he proved her right.

Drayton grimaced and kept the conversation to the point. "How long has she been like this?" he demanded.

Christina swung around and stared at him. "She has ever been delicate. The shock of my father's sudden death sent her into a rapid decline. How can I answer such a question, and what matters it to you?"

"It means she is not likely to improve, but continue to waste away if she remains here. We must get her to London before she lacks the strength to do so. She is a brave woman and will find the strength somewhere. Do not underestimate her."

He had been shocked himself at the widow's frail transparency and realized the urgency of immediate action. Should the widow die now, the girl would be in even more dire straits than she imagined. Even if it had not met with his plans, he would have had to act in memory of his father's friend. But he had no intention of explaining himself to this obstinate little Tory. It would not right the wrongs done.

"How do you know this?" Christina asked incredulously. How would this Yankee stranger know anything of her mother?

"Does that matter? Go tend to your packing. I am in a hurry. We must reach the inn by nightfall. There is nothing further to be argued. You are going and that is the end of it."

The earl strode impatiently toward the door, tapping a riding crop against his leg. When she did not immediately follow, he turned on her in irritation. "Well?"

Amber eyes glared back at him with undisguised venom. "What reason have I to trust your word? I would prefer to stay here, a safe distance from the likes of you."

Black eyes regarded her coldly. "Madam, I assure you

that what happened the other day will not be repeated. I made a serious misjudgment of character, one you must concur I was led to believe by your own behavior. I attempted to rectify my error in the only manner available and thought you had enjoyed it as much as I. Again, I was obviously in error. I will not repeat the same mistakes. Next time you will come willingly or not at all. Now, move yourself upstairs and assure your mother all is well."

There simply seemed to be no other choice. If he kept his word, her mother would receive a fortnight of the best medical treatment available. Maybe that would be sufficient to perform a cure. If not, they would be returned here to live much as before. Her reputation had already been irretrievably ruined; what mattered another question against her name?

As she swept past his tall figure, Christina felt his calm regard upon her, and could not resist swinging around to score one further point.

"My mother lives in a fantasy world of her own making. She envisions romance in every encounter. You encourage her with such words as you have used today. That is cruel and can lead only to harm."

"It is not cruel if she does not know the truth, and if you do not tell her, I certainly will not. I can see no harm in happiness, and every advantage in encouraging her. Give me credit for some sense."

That was exactly what she could not do, but she did not dare betray her thoughts. She could never become this arrogant man's mistress, if simply for the fact that it would destroy her mother more surely than lack of proper medicines. But she would not tell him that now. Let him pay for his crime awhile, first.

Why did she have such an urge to whistle and summon the gallant highwayman?

5

Christina stared out the window of the jolting carriage at the desolation of the barren fields. All trees had been stripped from the windswept land to provide wood for the various ramshackle structures dotting the countryside. Outside the miners' shacks, filthy children on rickety legs played in tattered clothing, seemingly unaware of the icy wind blowing across the open land.

Christina shuddered but did not pull the curtain. The scene matched her mood. In a few years she could easily be one of those work-worn mothers with their bastard children. She could be carrying a bastard even now. Her fingers gripped convulsively within the confines of her old fur muff. Poverty left little choice in many things, she had gradually come to realize.

She glanced over at her mother's dozing figure. Heartbreak, not poverty, had put those gray hairs on her mother's head, lined her face with woe, and broken her gentle spirit. Eleanor MacTavish was essentially a weak woman. Loving too much was a symptom of that weakness. Another lesson Christina was learning the hard way.

Sighing, she returned a blank gaze to the window. At least the earl had spared her the agony of his company on this journey. She had learned of the Yankee's intention of riding on ahead with some shock, quickly followed by relief. His presence in the close confinement of this coach would have totally unnerved her. As it was, her mind worked at a feverish pitch and her hands twitched with an unaccustomed nervousness. What was she doing here?

She could not tolerate being in the same room with the man. He made her want to do irrational things. She wanted to smack the self-satisfied look from his arrogant face, to kick and scream and throw any available object at the tempting target of his towering frame. She had never had a violent thought in her life, never been stirred to the violent passions his very presence engendered, and had no wish to succumb to them again. How would she ever survive living in the same house with him for two weeks?

Simple. She would not. She would kill him first. He would drive her to it.

She dozed off, the silence of the rocking carriage too unsettling to cope with in any other way.

When she woke, it had grown dark. Christina studied her mother's slumped form anxiously, but her even breathing indicated she slept. She sighed with relief. She had feared the rough road would cause her mother more pain than was bearable, but either the apothecary's new posset was working or the earl had found some way to drug her mother too. Or both.

The possibility that the posset the druggist had given her came from the earl's evil larder had not occurred to Christina before, and she dared not consider it now. The man was wicked to a degree she could not fathom, but she must pray the Lord above watched over her mother.

Christina stretched her cramped legs and aching back and hoped the inn was near. She had always loved the excitement of traveling and seeing new places and could not entirely quench that feeling now, though dread overshadowed everything else.

Did she imagine it, or was the carriage slowing? Eagerly she gazed out the dark windows, hoping for some sign of the inn. Perhaps it was on the other side of the road, for she saw no lights ahead.

A horse neighed close by, a disturbingly wild cry echoed by the whinnies of the earl's matched bays. For some reason the cry raised gooseflesh along her arms, and Christina searched the night beyond more frantically. Did that sound not seem disturbingly familiar?

A thump overhead, and the carriage jolted more precariously than ever. Christina's hand flew to her mouth as she caught the soft murmur of voices. The carriage had a driver in front and a footman in back, but they had no means of conversing. Who was out there with them?

The answer came much too suddenly. The carriage door flew wide and a dark figure tumbled in, righting himself swiftly as he grabbed the door and slammed it shut. In a single movement he threw himself down at Christina's side, and a flashing white grin lit the evening gloom.

"We meet again, Miss MacTavish."

Leaning forward to observe her mother's sleeping figure, the highwayman nodded with satisfaction. "She sleeps. That is good. I would hate to terrify her with my presence."

"And what of me?!" Christina demanded acerbically. "Did you not think you would frighten me half out of my wits with such a wild appearance? What are you doing here?" A sudden thought crossed her mind, a memory of his threats the night before, and amber eyes grew wide with horror. "Surely you do not mean to rob the earl? There is nothing of his here. Why haven't his men stopped the carriage?"

Adjusting his cockaded tricorne to enshroud his masked face in deeper darkness, the highwayman took his time answering. His broad shoulders beneath the encompassing cloak filled the small space of the carriage, and Christina nervously shrank farther into her corner. He brought the scent of horses and leather and night air with him, a frighteningly masculine combination to which she could not quite adjust.

Laconically shrugging off her question, the highwayman studied her with admiring interest. "You do not strike me as the type of young lady who faints at the drop of a hat, though admittedly I am relieved you did not resort to your usual tactic of screaming. Why not? Did you fear you would wake your mother, or have you learned not to fear me?"

"Both," Christina replied with irritation. His persistent stare when she could not return the favor frustrated her. She wished she could see the man behind the mask. Was he handsome or common? Perhaps scarred beyond recognition? Fantasies took charge of her mind when she thought of him, but her practical nature wondered what would happen should she suddenly strike the lamps to find out. She bit back a grim smile at this thought. She would reserve that action as a desperate measure. "Why did the coachmen not stop you?" she persisted.

But he had found her first answer more amusing. Stretching his long legs so they crossed near hers, the highwayman grinned his appreciation.

"You do not fear me? Every high official and wealthy landowner in the south of England fears me. You ride in the coach of one of the area's most exalted personages. I should think you have every right to fear me, especially since you have so obviously rejected my offer in favor of the earl's."

Christina waxed indignant. "You have no more right to tell me what to do or not to do than that arrogant, mule-headed, insufferable Yankee madman. I have told you I will belong to no man. Now, will you tell me what you are doing here or shall I scream to the driver for help?"

The darkness kept all but his grin enshrouded. "A man in my business must have friends. The driver knows me and little of you. I doubt your screams will excite more than your mother. And if you think you will beat the Yankee at his own game, you are as mad as he."

"That may be so, but it does not answer my question. What are you doing here?"

He shrugged in a self-deprecating manner. "I heard of your abduction at the hands of the Yankee earl and thought to offer an alternative. The sheriff is close on my heels and it is time I seek greener pastures. Go with me, and the earl will never see you again."

A chill of suppressed fright and excitement careened

down Christina's spine at these words. Perhaps not the gallant white knight of her fancies, the highwayman still offered storybook escape. He had not harmed her earlier, as he could have easily. She trusted him as she did not trust the Yankee. His suggestion actually tempted, and if she were alone . . .

Christina shook her head at the imaginative trail her thoughts had taken. "Your offer is too kind, sir," she answered with a tinge of sarcasm. "What makes you think I would prefer the role of highwayman's mistress to earl's mistress?"

His flashing grin illumined the darkness. "I thought I detected some small amount of distaste in your manner toward his noble lordship, and since you did not openly reject my assistance—"

Christina interrupted irately. "You gave me little choice!"

The highwayman waved aside this objection. "I am not poor. I can keep you well, and if we suit, I can offer marriage, which the earl assuredly will not. You have caught my fancy, and I would not see you unhappy if it is within my power to prevent it."

Though he slouched leisurely in the corner, his long legs stretched across the carriage, and spoke with carelessness, Christina sensed some crumb of seriousness in his offer. Amazing how a criminal could offer more morality than the nobly born! In his own way, of course, she amended hastily.

Still, he asked the impossible. He thought her a whore, but she had no intention of ever submitting to a man's disgusting hungers again. His charm attracted, but his intent revolted her. Christina had no means of explaining this to him, but vented her distaste in sarcasm.

"You are indeed magnanimous. You would set me up comfortably in some inn while you went about your nefarious trade, and I would spend my time waiting for your return until one night, you did not. And I would be left to wonder if another woman's arms had captured you, or the hangman's noose."

The highwayman shrugged unconcernedly. "There

is that, I suppose, but I will warn you now, his lordship's fate is none more certain than my own."

Christina could understand that. Had she the courage, she would carve his lordship's heart from his chest with a saber. Many another with more courage would likely do the same. That did not affect her decision.

"His lordship may go to hell for aught I care. I seek only my mother's welfare," she whispered with urgency. "You must depart before she wakes and finds you here."

A gloved hand wrapped warmly around hers, holding it against the seat between them. "I should be safely past the sheriff's vigilantes shortly. Tell me this: If it were not for your mother, would you have gone with me?"

Strangely enough, tears pricked at Christina's eyelids as his deep drawl flowed sensuously around her in the darkness. She wished there had been time to know this man. Not since her father died had any other offered comfort or support as this man did. He spoke as a gentleman. Surely he had a story to tell, but she would never know it.

"I would have been tempted. Let us leave it at that," she answered softly, so softly he had to lean forward to hear it.

"There is hope yet, then," he murmured. Lifting her hand to his lips, he kissed the tips of each finger with caressing gentleness. Almost as an afterthought, he turned her hand over and kissed the palm.

Hot prickles of excitement danced through her veins, and with reluctance Christina removed her hand from this temptation. She would never see this man again, would not recognize him if she did, yet something had grown between them that she did not quite understand, nor ever would.

"It is farewell again, is it not?" she asked timidly.

The timbre of his voice was low and caressing, a sensuous touch against her ears. "Nay, mademoiselle, have more faith in me."

Before she could reply, he had lowered the window,

and whistling shrilly, brought the carriage to a slower pace, with the sound of racing hooves thundering from a distance.

In amazement Christina watched as the towering black steed broke into easy strides beside the carriage. Within moments the black-garbed highwayman had jumped from the carriage and mounted his stallion, rearing the horse in gallant farewell before darkness enclosed him.

Silence descended once more. Not trusting herself to speak, Christina stared out the window at the blank landscape, and for the first time since leaving home, tears welled in her eyes.

The lone horseman stood on a ridge above the highway, watching as the carriage proceeded on toward London, carrying away the sad-eyed daughter of a once noble Scotsman. For a moment he let his thoughts dwell on the angry flash of amber eyes and the defiant tilt of a proud but delicate chin. But only for a moment.

There were more important things in his life right now than lovely maidens in distress. He must use every tool given him to accomplish his goals before he could contemplate his very uncertain future. These past years had taught him ruthlessness. If the girl were to survive, she must learn some of the same. Weakness was a commodity only the rich could afford.

Still, he lingered, watching as the carriage rolled from sight. He had learned much and little from that last conversation. She had the hunted look of a wounded doe, but she sought no revenge nor betrayed her attacker. She knew the value of silence. Valuable knowledge to one in his position.

Yet he wondered about the look in her eyes when he had offered to take her away with him. He would have done it, too, had she accepted—hidden her away until she had had the time to heal from fresh wounds—but he had guessed she would not. Yet he knew she had wanted to. He had seen that desperate plea for freedom in her eyes, a plea that kept him standing there watching and wondering.

* * *

A blaze of candlelight greeted the carriage some time later as it jolted to a halt in front of the two-story inn. Wearily Christina unfolded herself from the back-stabbing springs of cushioned seats and lowered herself out the door without waiting for aid from the footman engrossed in noisy argument with the stable hand. She feared the exertion from the trip had been too much for her mother, and she hastened to seek assistance.

With grudging help from the berated footman and driver, the two women were escorted into the wide front hallway. The floors gleamed of recent scrubbing, and their hostess, a pleasant, plump woman of indeterminate age, hurried to greet them.

" 'Is lordship said ye'd be arrivin' soon. Let me 'ave my boys carry yer things for ye . . ."

As she bustled about, directing the placement of luggage, ordering up candles and hot water, a tall shadow detached itself from the noisy darkness of the tavern beyond.

Christina cast the earl's lounging figure a disdainful glare. Attired in the height of fashion, his elegant emerald cutaway revealing immaculate fawn breeches, the earl managed to look both splendidly decadent and thoroughly bored. Christina swept by him without a word.

"Mayva, set up a dinner for two in the parlor and send one upstairs for Mrs. MacTavish. I'm famished." With an authoritative voice accustomed to giving orders and having them obeyed, the earl directed his wishes at their hostess.

One foot already on the stair in the wake of her mother, Christina swung around with outrage at this presumptuous command from behind her.

"Sir, you must needs be famished to order up two meals for yourself. My mother will be too ill to dine on more than tea and toast, and the same will suit me well, so you might have the third meal sent in also, if you desire."

Her biting sarcasm seemed to bring the room to a

standstill as she glared at the lordly figure with flashing black eyes and he glared back, but in truth, all had gone about their tasks and only these two remained in the gleaming hall.

"I have waited here without my supper for the past hour or more so I might have the pleasure of your company while I dined. Will you deny me *that* too?"

The Yankee's emphasis on the last words and the knowing look he flicked over her slender figure brought color to Christina's cheeks. She could almost feel that dark gaze stripping her down to her shift and beyond, and with more knowledge than any other man. Her fingers clenched the stair rail with embarrassment and fury.

"I would deny you *everything*, my lord."

Their gazes clashed with as much furor as a clangor of steel in a declaration of war.

With a sudden about-face the earl shifted from his lofty position and crossed the space separating them in a single stride, taking her elbow with excessive care.

"You must be tired. Let me take you to your room. It was quite inconsiderate of me to expect you to entertain after such a tedious journey. You never told me—did you find your way home the other night without incident?"

Why did she suddenly have the feeling he tested her with his mockery? Christina's heart constricted in her chest as her thoughts flew back to that dawn when she had first met the highwayman. With a casualness she did not feel, she responded, "Qu-quite s-successfully, thank you."

Before she could dismiss him again, Drayton came to a halt on the landing, forcing her to look up questioningly at the angular lines of his chiseled face.

"I never noticed your stutter before, Miss MacTavish. How very charming. Then you had no need of my excellent swordsmanship to save your virtue from thieves and rogues?" he asked suggestively, the glint in his eyes slightly mocking.

He played with her, Christina realized, but to what

purpose? She refused to believe the conclusion to which her mind nimbly jumped. The Yankee earl's abominable American twang condemned him unmistakably no matter what charade he played. He could not possibly be the educated highwayman. Perhaps he was a smuggler or spy in some connection with the highwayman. . . .

That thought rounded her eyes with a new horror. Despite what had gone between them, this man at her side was a stranger, and a dangerous one. What evil trap did he lay for her now? She dared not let him guess her thoughts before she had worked them out, and hastily she tugged loose of his hold and proceeded up the stairs.

"Thanks to you, I have no virtue left, milord. I will thank you not to remind me of it," she threw over her shoulder.

Drayton stubbornly kept to her side as Christina located the open doorway through which she could spy her bags and their hostess. Instead of letting her escape to this haven of safety, he bowed grandly and ushered her in as if she were a countess and no words of acrimony had ever passed between them.

From the bed where she lay half-propped against the pillows, Eleanor MacTavish extended a pale, thin hand in greeting to the latecomers.

"Ahh, Christina, there you are. My lord, welcome. I fear I do not make good company. I hope my daughter has expressed her gratitude for what you are doing for us."

Bending over her fingers, the earl replied graciously, "Your daughter is kindness itself, madam, and you must call me Damien. A friend of my father's should not be forced to formalities. I did not think. I should have provided a maid to travel with you. You must excuse my ignorance. It will take me awhile to grow accustomed to traveling with ladies."

He turned to the innkeeper. "Miss MacTavish will dine with her mother, so we will not require your parlor, after all."

Eleanor protested. "That is nonsense! I am quite

capable of eating on my own. Christina, you need not fear the proprieties with Damien. Do not make him dine alone."

To Christina's shock, the Yankee shook his head decisively. "Your daughter can be an extremely sensible young woman when she chooses. She is correct in refusing to leave your side after such a journey. I have dined alone often enough since coming to this country, and I will suffer another night without any great hardship."

So saying, he dismissed the innkeeper to fetch supper, and after a brief exchange of polite farewells, he departed, leaving Christina to stare openmouthed at the closed door. She had enjoyed an unfeminine interest in natural history, but she had never heard of a case of a gila monster becoming a chameleon before. The man was uncanny.

Her mother intruded upon her thoughts. "I am happy to see Anson brought his son up to be a gentleman. I have heard such dreadful tales of Yankees . . ." Eleanor's voice dwindled off as Christina turned around and she read the look of stunned bewilderment upon her daughter's face. "Is there something wrong, my dear?" she asked mildly.

Although frail, Eleanor MacTavish was not foolish. The death of her husband had shattered her life, but she had prayed to live long enough to see her beautiful daughter well married. Poverty had a severe dampening effect on her hopes, but Christina's quiet obstinance and complete inability to notice the opposite sex had been Eleanor's biggest hurdle. She had despaired of the girl's ever falling in love with a man outside of her books, but now a certain amount of satisfaction crept into her smile as she observed her daughter's dazed reaction to a real man.

"Wrong? No, Mama. Let me help you with your gown. You will be much more comfortable in your nightrail."

Presenting her back for unfastening, Eleanor innocently chattered on. "It is a tragedy that boy had to grow up denied of his rightful heritage."

"I would hardly call him a boy, Mama," Christina replied dryly, lifting off her mother's heavily brocaded gown.

Eleanor ignored the interruption. "I cannot speak of his uncle without revulsion. It is dreadful to speak ill of the dead, but Bartholomew was a filthy degenerate when I was a girl and he did not improve with age. I suppose it was wise of Anson not to allow his son back here to live in such immoral company, but the boy has no knowledge of Westshipham to guide him now. I suppose we should all be relieved Bartholomew had no other legal heir."

She sighed gratefully as Christina removed the boned bodice and petticoats.

Thoroughly confused by the parade of long-dead names her mother produced, Christina paid little heed to her chatter. In her mind this earl was as evil as the old one had been rumored to be. Whatever came between had no concern to her. Yet all through the meal that followed, her mother's reminiscences kept the earl and his family on her mind when she could wish otherwise.

"Sophia and I were the best of friends, though the baron thought the vicar's daughter beneath me. Can you imagine?" Eleanor chuckled to herself, dabbing daintily at the corner of her lips with a napkin. "Love takes strange paths. It would have been so much better for all concerned if Anson and I could have loved each other, although I'm certain that would have horrified the old earl enough, but he would have come around eventually, and of course it was what the baron had always dreamed of."

Christina picked at her meat pie and let her mind wander. Her mother had repeated enough horror stories of the curmudgeon Baron of Adderley to make her glad she had never met her grandfather. Had his son become so crotchety and snobbish that he would no longer recognize his only sister? She knew they had stopped corresponding after her mother's marriage, but she seemed to remember it had more to do with the baron interfering and her uncle going off to war. Perhaps he had died and no one had told them? An icy wave of fear clenched at Christina's insides. If that were the case, they were in dire straits indeed. If they could not turn to her mother's brother, they would have great difficulty in unraveling themselves from the clutches of the malevolent Yankee.

"Still, there never would have been a duel if that devil Bartholomew had not forced the issue. To this day I cannot believe Anson would deliberately kill that poor man. Pistols were such an unfortunate choice, not a gentleman's weapon at all, I suppose, but that is no excuse. Anson could have aimed above his head . . ."

Eleanor shook her head, as much in annoyance at her daughter's lack of interest as in remembrance of things past. How would she make the chit learn to understand if she would not listen?

The story about the duel was a new one, and to avoid her own unpleasant thoughts, Christina feigned interest. "What did they duel over, Mama?"

Eleanor gave an impatient sigh, but encouraged by this small sign of interest continued on. "It is a long time ago and of little significance. What mattered was that Anson had killed a man. The old earl wanted to ship him off to the Continent until the furor died down, but Anson had other ideas. He refused to go anywhere without Sophia, and of course the old earl would not hear of that. A younger son must marry well—in this case, not only because of a need for wealth but also because it grew most obvious Bartholomew would never provide a legitimate heir of any kind. Bastards he had aplenty, some almost as old as Anson himself, but no decent woman would marry a degenerate rake, and he would have no decent woman. So there it stood. Anson's heirs must be suitable earls, and the vicar's bloodlines would not suit."

Despite herself, Christina grew fascinated with this story so closely paralleling her mother's own. No wonder her mother felt attached to a family she had neither seen nor heard from in a score of years! The romance of it captured her imagination. Two favored children of wealth and breeding falling in love with the vicar's daughter and the village mayor instead of each other! And the tragedy that must have separated them forever. Christina began to listen more closely.

"Well, the Draytons were ever a headstrong lot, and Anson none too different. I cannot condemn him for what he did—it gave me courage to do the same—but Westshipham has not been the same since he left. I still cannot believe a man of such immense vitality as he can be gone."

Christina almost cried out her disappointment at such an ending. "What happened? Did he marry Sophia? Did he run off to France? Do not leave me hanging, Mother!"

Smiling inwardly, Eleanor played with her tea. She had but this one chance to see her daughter happy; she must play it wisely.

"Why, I thought you knew, Christina. What have I been saying all along? Damien is his father all over again. Not quite as dashing and good-natured as I remember Anson to be, but I imagine it has not been an easy life over there. Isn't there a war or something going on in the colonies?"

Christina threw her hands up in a gesture of surrender. "It has been going on for well over five years, Mother. Are you telling me his high-and-mighty lordship is the son of your Anson and the vicar's daughter?" A tone of disbelief tinged her voice.

"Of course. Who else would he be? Those black eyes of his come from his mother. There are some who say there is a gypsy in her background, but they were jealous tabbies. Anson practically had to kidnap Sophia before she could be convinced he would rather hang here than go without her. I heard they married on the ship that took them to America."

Tired now, Eleanor sank back against the cushions and closed her eyes. She had done what she could to open her daughter's eyes; the rest remained to fate. She wondered what had occurred between these two that had already set walls of tension and flashes of lightning between them, but she had a feeling she did not wish to know. Anson's son had too much of his mother's wild nature in him and too little of his father's gentleness. Bred in a rugged land of no temperateness, he would be a dangerous force to tamper with, but Eleanor felt confident he had enough sense to judge true worth when he saw it. Wouldn't it be lovely if what was not meant for the parents could be given to the offspring?

Seeing her mother's exhaustion, Christina did not ply for more, but removed the dishes and completed her own undressing.

Clad only in her thin chemise, she stood within the moon's light from the narrow window, searching the darkness for answers. Why had this Yankee stranger stepped out of the past to wreak havoc with her life?

Without conscious thought, her hand covered the flat hollow between her hipbones. Could she even now be breeding his bastard? What had he meant when he said these "things" could be arranged? Would he give away his own child? She had heard of such, and worse, but recoiled at the thought. Even if he be the Earl of Westshipham, he was but the grandson of a lowly vicar. How dare he take her as he had, and refuse marriage?

At the thought of marriage to such a monster and all that it entailed, Christina blanched. She could almost feel his hard body upon her now, pressing her into the bedclothes, nearly suffocating her with his demands, and she nearly screamed out her terror.

Never! Never again! Not even the charming highwayman could tempt her to his bed with dreams of freedom. She would bear a bastard before she gave any man the power to do that to her again.

6

Wrapped in his stylish redingote against the chill of a March wind, Damien Drayton, Earl of Westshipham, sat proudly upright in his corner of the carriage, maintaining a proper distance between himself and his traveling companions.

Unlike his nemesis the highwayman, Christina thought waspishly, doing her best to ignore his aristocratic profile by staring out at the rolling countryside. It did little good. Though he maintained a respectful distance, she remained constantly aware of his threatening presence at her side. How different his cold hauteur from the highwayman's warm concern!

Without preamble the Yankee lord intruded upon her thoughts.

"I heard it said this morning that the highwayman was captured last night. They intend to hang him tomorrow at dawn, if all goes well."

Christina could not contain her gasp of horror and the icy sinking sensation in her stomach as she turned to gaze upon this fiend who spoke so calmly of death.

"Surely you jest, my lord?" she asked weakly. She had been confident there was some connection between these two disparate men who had entered her life, but he now seemed to be denying all responsibility.

Lord Westshipham turned his cold gaze upon her. "Men choose their own fates when they choose their means of living, Miss MacTavish, and he chose his. Do you find that so surprising?"

Tears burned the corners of her eyes and her fingers

clenched helplessly in angry balls as she fought back a great yawning chasm opening within her.

"Surely what he did does not justify death? Could they not transport him?"

A grim smile curled one corner of the lord's thin lips. "He took what was not his to take and knew his chances. They no longer transport thieves to the colonies, you know. I understand the outposts the British have found to dump their unwanted now are most unpleasant indeed. I think your highwayman might prefer a clean death to the slow torture of transportation."

His dark eyes seemed to pierce her thoughts, and Christina turned away, wordlessly wiping the moisture in her eyes. She did not even know the highwayman's name, but he had been kind to her in his own way. She could not believe a man of such immense vitality could be facing death.

Christina sat bolt upright in her seat. Her mother had used almost those identical words to describe the earl's father! A man of "immense vitality"! Wildly she glanced at her mother as if to see if the same thought had occurred to her, but Eleanor MacTavish slept, as she had most of the journey. Heart thumping irregularly, Christina sought to slow gyrating questions and answers and only succeeded in inducing a headache. It must be coincidence, her mother's words coming back at an opportune time. There could be nothing there. It made no sense.

She felt that dark gaze fasten on her, but did not dare face it. Her fingers clenched and unclenched nervously, and without thought her lips began to move in silent prayer.

"You would do better to pray for yourself. Thieves have been known to escape, but you will not."

Christina swung around and stared at him. "What are you saying?"

"It is better that the highwayman be thought dead and buried. You, however, must go on living. It is always hardest on those left behind."

He did not seem to be speaking in specifics, but

thinking out loud. Christina could not fathom how he knew of her relationship with the highwayman, but she understood nothing about this man at all. She searched his face for some clue to his meaning, but though momentarily she found no coldness in his chiseled features, she could discern no other emotion, either.

"My lord, you talk in riddles," she remonstrated uncertainly.

Turning a quizzical glance on her, he replied, "Do I?" and said no more.

Finding some hope in the earl's strange phrases, Christina looked away again. Now that she thought of it, the highwayman spoke in a cultured voice that had reassured her of his inherent gentlemanliness, despite his occupation. On the other hand, she had assumed the earl to be a gentleman because of his title, yet the hard line of his angular jaw and his rough Yankee accent spoke otherwise. What if. . . ?

But even Christina's active imagination could not fathom a reason for an earl to exchange places with a Yankee, and she gave up the attempt. If the man at her side was an impostor who had turned against the real earl and meant to have him hanged . . .

Her head jerked upward and, biting back the hysteria forcing its way into her thoughts, Christina spoke calmly to the window.

"Will he escape?"

The question assumed an understanding between them that was not there, just as his comment on her stutter had done the day before. Still, she must risk it. If he truly meant to kidnap her and murder the real earl, surely she could hear it in his voice, sense the lie in his words?

The answer was a long time in coming.

"To all practical effects, he will be dead to the world. Do not attempt to resurrect him. He will be safer that way."

Christina nodded dumbly. A sense of danger permeated the carriage with his words, but the danger had been there all along. The highwayman had brought it with him, and the Yankee carried it on his back. She did not know what the pair intended, but she knew now that they worked together.

They arrived in London in midafternoon of the next day. Christina gazed wearily at the teeming streets, houses built one on top of the other, the shop stalls and beggars, horses and carriages, and decided she preferred the angry sea to this bustling anthill. But here lay the talents and medicines that might restore her mother to life, so here they must stay, for at least a fortnight.

The towering town house to which the carriage led them seemed almost as gloomy as Westshipham Hall. Christina entered its dirty portals with reluctance and met the waiting staff with surprise. Aware of the drabness of her woolen traveling dress and of the grandeur of the wide paneled hall, she could only meet the staring sea of faces with trepidation. These would be her judges. She sensed it at once.

The earl's voice boomed out behind her, giving brisk orders and commands, sending footmen to gather baggage, maids to start fires, and both to assist Mrs. MacTavish to her room. Only one massive woman remained waiting patiently in the hall, her dark gown indicating her station but her lack of apron or uniform declaring it to be above the other servants. She stared at Christina with inquisitive eyes of the clearest blue, but said no word until spoken to.

Lord Westshipham came to stand behind Christina, his large hand resting protectively at her slender back as he greeted the woman.

"Miss MacTavish, this is Lorna Douglass, my housekeeper. Lorna, Miss MacTavish and her mother will be my guests for a while. Miss MacTavish will have a better understanding of English hospitality and entertainment than I, so you will do well to listen to her suggestions once she has settled in. In the meantime, I trust them to your care."

A glance of some sort was exchanged over her head,

but Christina was too tired to care. It was obvious the earl had little need of an additional housekeeper, and she could not imagine in what way she might aid such a formidable woman, but for the moment it appeared she need do nothing.

With relief she followed the massive housekeeper up the stairs.

In the hours that followed, Christina learned the Yankee possessed one redeeming quality—he kept his promises.

The physician arrived before they had scarcely unpacked, and none too soon in Christina's opinion. Her mother had visibly weakened during the journey, to a point where she could scarce lend a hand to a spoon and felt no need of it.

When the physician at last came out, he met her in the small sitting room separating the two bedrooms.

"How is she? What can I do to make her better?" Christina asked eagerly, rising to greet the dapper older man.

Not physically imposing, the doctor still carried an air of gravity and intelligence that commanded respect. He gave Christina's golden fairness a cursory look, rubbed his fingers over the bridge of his nose where his spectacles rested, and took his time in formulating a reply.

"Your mother has a weak heart, a congenital frailty, I fear, aggravated by strenuous circumstances. With rest and good nourishment, she may outlast us all."

Christina gulped a large breath of relief and sank back into the dusty velvet chair she had occupied earlier. Rest and food could not be impossible to obtain. Surely she could find some means of supplying that.

"However," the physician continued slowly, gauging this young woman carefully and deciding she appeared capable enough to bear the brunt of his observations, "any sudden surge of excitement or exertion could carry her away within seconds. There is no predicting this condition. Recent aggravations apparently have worsened it to a point where I can prescribe little that will be of use. I can give her laudanum to keep her calm and help her rest. You must see that she eats well, and between us we may see that she returns to her feet. That is the best I can do."

The doctor watched as sorrow and helplessness chased each other across the girl's delicate features, amber eyes growing dark as velvet, but the look of fear and determination that immediately followed startled him somewhat.

"I will do all you say, sir. Have you spoken with his lordship yet?"

"He was not below earlier, but I suppose I must, since it is at his insistence that I have come. I am certain he will have no objections to the regimen I am imposing, since it bears little hardship on anyone but the cook." The doctor continued watching her with curiosity, unable to determine why the girl seemed more concerned with his lordship than with what he had said of her mother. Tears he had expected, but the fear he had seen was another matter entirely.

"His lordship has much on his mind these days. He has done a great kindness by bringing us here to see you. I would not wish to impose further worries on him."

Though visibly shaken by his warnings, the girl continued holding herself proudly upright, those great dark eyes of hers speaking a plea the doctor did not hear in her words. Yet he understood what she asked and nodded agreeably.

"There is no need to burden his lordship with possibilities. As I said, there is every chance Mrs. MacTavish will live a long and rewarding life. Now, if you will excuse me . . ."

He bowed briefly and was gone. Gathering her strength, Christina returned to her mother's side, reassured that the Yankee would never know on what thin thread she hung. Without her mother she would be at the earl's mercy.

It was there Lorna found her some hours later. Seeing

Mrs. MacTavish slept, she gestured quietly to Christina, who rose and followed her into the sitting room.

"Yes, Mrs. Douglass?" Drained of all emotion, Christina gazed at the housekeeper dispassionately. The woman was nearly as large as the earl himself, though not built with the same lean, athletic grace. She carried her size well, though, and there seemed a kindness to those blue eyes that belied her stern expression.

"His lordship is expecting you to dine with him tonight. I have sent one of the maids to lay out a suitable gown. Would you be wanting me to dress your hair?"

A trace of a Scots accent remained in the broadening of her A's and the softening of her R's, but in the main part, she sounded much like the Yankee, and Christina winced imperceptibly. She needed no further reminder of that madman this night. Her mind rushed inexplicably to the gallant highwayman with the Oxford drawl, but she pushed aside the incongruity.

"I have no suitable gowns, Mrs. Douglass. If it is not too much trouble, I would prefer to dine with my mother. Give his lordship my regrets, if you would."

Dismay skittered across the housekeeper's features, dismay and a small amount of outrage at this impertinent chit of a girl standing before her. One of those high-and-mighty English ladies, she dared say. Well, she knew how to handle spoiled young ladies.

"I am certain that in that trunk full of gowns there is one that will suit. His lordship is not particular about the latest fashions. He has been more than considerate in bringing you here when he is ill-prepared to entertain. The least you can do is oblige his one wish!"

Christina stared at the quivering mountain of flesh before her. Never in her life had a servant spoken thus to her! What on earth had that wretched Yankee said to make this woman speak to her in such a way? Surely the beastly man had not already indicated the position he intended for her! Horror at such a possibility burned her cheeks to crimson, but stifling her fury until she could vent it more profitably, she acquiesced.

She followed the unsympathetic housekeeper to the

bedroom. Across the bed lay an amber silk gown of sophisticated simplicity, a gown she had worn once before her father had died. Tears welled dangerously near the surface as Christina remembered the occasion when her father had bestowed it upon her, but tears were of no avail now. Remembering Argus MacTavish's pride in her that day, her sixteenth birthday, Christina smiled grimly and began removing her heavy garments.

Observing the girl's grim smile with some trepidation, the housekeeper began helping her young charge to undress. From beneath the loose, heavy folds of the cheap gown, the girl's ripe young figure emerged, and Mrs. Douglass bit her lip in sudden doubt. The silk had seemed suitable for a young girl, and so Christina had seemed earlier, her quiet slenderness overshadowed by the earl's imposing figure and her charming but gravely ill mother. But behind those overlarge eyes and frail features waited a young woman of unknown depths.

Amber eyes watched expectantly as Mrs. Douglass raised the lovely gown and brought it forward. Refusing to back down, the older woman determinedly brought the silk down over the golden disarray of curls, smoothed it over milk-white shoulders, and straightened it over the frilly circle of petticoats. Taking a deep breath, she began lacing the bodice.

It became quickly obvious that where the lacing fit quite snugly and stylishly about Christina's slender waist, it gaped most distressingly as it rose higher. Amusement began to dance in the gold flecks of Christina's velvet eyes as she watched the massive housekeeper struggle to pull the lacing into some semblance of respectability over her bosom. Anger was not an emotion Christina knew well, and before this farce it began to pale.

The lace of her chemise spilled shamefully above the too-low décolletage, and the loose lacing left too much of the valley between her breasts exposed to view. Christina felt fairly naked beneath the light silk after these past years of wearing mourning, but she began to enjoy the possibilities. The Yankee obviously had a low threshold of resistance, yet he apparently prided himself on being a man of his word. If she could provide the irresistible force, what would happen to the immovable object?

Nothing worse than she had already suffered, she surmised bitterly as Mrs. Douglass threw up her hands in despair.

"It wil'na do, it wil'na do," she moaned. "Do they all be so?"

At Christina's amused nod, Mrs. Douglass made as if to attack the lacing again, but Christina waved her away and prepared to meet her fate.

The new lord waited impatiently in the hallway below as Christina began her descent. Eyes dancing with shameless mirth, she descended gracefully in Mrs. Grenoble's best manner, her slippered foot just barely peeking out beneath the frills of lace, her hips swaying gently, though she sported no wide panniers to enhance the movement. Not until she had reached midstair did the full impact hit the man below.

With true Yankee independence, Damien had dispensed with the nonsense of powdered hair, wearing his own dark russet locks pulled back in a severe queue and knotted in a bow. The effect emphasized high, wide cheekbones and hawklike nose, but most noticeably the flashing dark pools of his eyes. Sheets of lightning lit their interiors now.

Christina's humor faltered beneath that steady gaze, but she had gone too far to retreat. Bravely she traversed the distance between them, until she stood upon the bottom stair, her eyes nearly meeting the level of his.

"I see you have discovered something more fashionable to wear, after all, Miss MacTavish," he intoned dryly.

A firm brown hand enclosed hers as he assisted her in the final step, and did not let go as he gazed more fully on the splendid sight exposed before him.

Christina could feel the heat of his gaze as it caressed the nakedness of her scanty covering—or was it the heat of embarrassment? She had dared too much this time. Unaccustomed to any society but her own, she had grown too sure of herself, and now she faltered before her foolishness.

Seeing she had only one weapon in her small war, the earl graciously bowed out. "Unless you have come to surrender, Miss MacTavish, I suggest we find you a shawl to keep the chill off this evening. In case I did not make myself clear earlier, I have not had time for . . . the companionship . . . of ladies lately, and I am quite starved for more than food. Unless you mean to be the main course . . ." The remainder of his sentence dangled suggestively between them.

"You have made yourself most plainly clear even to the most innocent of ears, my lord," Christina replied irritably, rediscovering her tongue. She had thought to torment him, but had succeeded only in discomfiting herself. She should have known the Yankee's penchant for bluntness would permit no games. "I have only done as you ordered. Now that you can see how unsuitable I am for your guest, you must permit me to return to my room. I am too tired to eat under the circumstances."

A muscle jerked ever so slightly over one finely wrought cheekbone as Damien replied, "You are here as my guest for an entire fortnight, Miss MacTavish. Much as you may dislike my company, you will grant my wishes in this. Fetch your shawl and be quick about it."

Mutinously Christina glared back at him, but there was that in his eyes that reminded her of earlier threats, and she thought better of it. He had already proven his superior strength, and this was his house. She would do best to heed his warnings.

Cursing herself for a coward all the way up the stairs, she did not see the relief reflected in dark eyes below.

The earl made no attempt to keep her when Christina asked to be excused at meal's end, but politely rising and assisting her to do so, he continued holding her hand a moment longer than required, delaying her retreat.

"I am having a few friends to call on the morrow. I will need your assistance in seeing that the meal is properly prepared. You will be treated with all the respect a lady deserves, I promise. I am expecting your full cooperation."

His hand was warm and hard, completely enveloping her own, and Christina felt a tremor of some vague fear. Though she had kept her eyes demurely downcast throughout the meal, she had sensed the path his hungry gaze had taken more than once, and her skin burned with the fire of it. Still, he had promised respectability. Perhaps she could show him she deserved that right. Nodding silently, she withdrew her hand from his.

He let her go, and Christina flew gratefully from the room. She did not know what his command entailed, but she had no intention of lingering to quibble about it.

To her relief, his lordship had gone out before she rose, and Christina saw nothing of him the next day. As the day progressed, Mrs. Douglass deferred to her in matters of choice—which china should be taken down, which parlor should be cleaned—for the house was in a severely neglected state. Christina wandered through it bravely, ordering curtains stripped and shaken and moldering furniture removed from the best of the public rooms. Gentlemen would not notice if paint appeared faded and dingy, but they would certainly remark upon a cushion that exuded dust when they sat upon it.

By teatime there was still no sign of the young lord, and Christina relaxed and related the day's activities to her mother, bringing merriment to the sickroom as she described disintegrating draperies and mouse-shredded linens. Mrs. Douglass had discovered these atrocities with a fastidious horror that made Christina laugh the harder as she described it. In the end, the large housekeeper had retreated to a far room while Christina and the footmen emptied cabinets and drawers in search of the culprits.

Christina's fingers itched to put the tale to paper, but she had none with her and feared intruding on the Yankee's study in search of it. Besides, there was still more to be done and little time to be wasted on such frivolity. Christina returned downstairs to make certain all ran smoothly.

When the windows grew dark and the time for dinner grew near, Christina grew increasingly nervous. With one last sweep of the house, she ordered lamps and candles lit in the appropriate places, and then made a straight line for the safety of her room. Only the Yankee's absence had freed her from the impending sense of doom she had felt since their first encounter. His imminent return brought fear back in its proper place.

To her surprise, Mrs. Douglass awaited her, an expectant smile beaming across her face. Since smiles were not the stern Scotswoman's usual expression, Christina observed her with some awe. Before she could question, the housekeeper gestured toward a box upon the bed.

"It came for you just a wee bit ago. Shall I help you try it on?"

"Try it on?" With sudden foreboding Christina crossed the room and threw open the box lid.

Inside lay a summer gown of sprigged muslin, its low bodice meant to be concealed by the cross-draping of the lacy kerchief enclosed. As Christina lifted it out, she noted it lacked all need for panniers and hoops but required only a frilly chemise and petticoats. It was a gown of modest simplicity and extravagant fashionableness. Small violets decorated an otherwise white background, emphasized by blue ribbons and trim. Christina recognized immediately what her benefactor had done and did not know whether to cry for joy or throw it in his despicable face.

It was not a gown one would give to a mistress, but well suited to a young girl in her first season in London. Perfectly respectable for a guest in the house of the Earl of Westshipham, no one would have to know it was a highly improper gift from his lordship to his intended mistress.

The urge to cry became stronger, but beneath the housekeeper's beaming smile Christina dared not give way to the relief of tears. Stuttering a request to bathe first, she drove Mrs. Douglass away before allowing the wetness to run down her cheeks.

No one but her father had ever bought dresses for her. No one but a husband or her mother should buy them for her now. Her mother could not, and there would never be a husband, so why shouldn't she accept this outrageously expensive gift?

Christina knew why, but lacked conviction in her beliefs. She ached to hold the beautiful material against her skin, to feel the folds fall lightly about her hips, to know the bodice fit her as it was meant to do. She had seen the style in ladies' magazines and knew it was meant to be worn with cascades of curls down her back, curls she had in natural abundance. The gown was designed with her in mind, whether the designer knew it or not. She had denied herself much over the years, but never had she denied her femininity, and it cried out now for nourishment.

Carefully bathing away the day's grime, washing her hair until it squeaked clean, then drying it with great care before the fire, brushing it until it sparkled, Christina kept her eye on the vision of loveliness lying across her bed. She had scarcely noticed her surroundings until now, but the pink eyelet trappings of the canopied bed made an ideal setting for the violet gown.

Having already decided the safest course to tread with a madman was to obey his whims until she escaped, Christina argued herself into putting on the gown. It fell about her lightly like silk, and Christina marveled at its softness beneath her fingers. Not daring to show her mother the expensive gift, she rang for Mrs. Douglass, who miraculously appeared within seconds to fasten it.

With growing excitement, Christina showed the adept housekeeper how she wished to fix her curls, and between them they arranged it in a satisfactorily stylish coiffure. Mrs. Douglass murmured words of approval as Christina stepped back from the mirror, and amber eyes danced with delight as Christina observed her own image.

A golden cascade of curls fell down over creamy shoulders, tied back by blue ribbons, preventing all but a tiny curl at either ear from falling near her oval face. The hairstyle emphasized wide amber eyes and drew attention to the proud tilt of a slender neck, and from thence, to the provocative décolletage of the simple gown. The effect was both demure and exciting, and Christina could not believe the young woman in the mirror was herself.

"Ah, that Damien . . . his lordship, do know what it is a woman likes. I feared ye wouldna wear it, but no other could wear it so beautiful." The older woman sighed with satisfaction as she observed her handiwork.

The use of the earl's Christian name caused Christina's eyebrow to lift slightly, but she did not question it. Yankees were an ill-bred lot and the earl had no doubt never expected the title to fall to him. But it did seem to signify this was the Damien Drayton her mother spoke of. That meant little to her, however. Whoever he was, he still remained a beast of unnatural proportions and she must now walk willingly into his lair, dressed for the kill.

"Has his lordship left any other instructions for me?" Christina asked in a murmur, lowering her gaze from the false reflection in the mirror. She was no longer the innocent miss or elegant lady it showed there, and there was no use in pretending differently.

"Lord, no, miss. You're to do as you please. He did suggest you might enjoy the library while you wait. Of course, he didna notice the dust about," Mrs. Douglass snorted disdainfully.

Christina's eyes lit at this news, and within minutes

she had taken rag in hand and dusted off a suitable number of volumes for perusal.

Damien found her there sometime later, an ethereal figure in white in the candlelight, curled in an old and cracked leather chair before the dying embers of a small fire. If it were not for the voices of his companions behind him, he would have left her there undisturbed, but they recalled his duty, and he cleared his throat.

The book flew from Christina's hand, indicating the frazzled state of her nerves, and she glanced up at him with a dark, wide-eyed look akin to terror.

"I did not mean to terrify you, Miss MacTavish," he stated dryly. "I only meant to tell you we have arrived and to ask you to join us."

Christina allowed him to guide her from the room, his fingers gently at her elbow. He towered a head over her, though she knew herself to be considered tall, and his size alone was frightening. Still, he could do little in the presence of others.

Three young gentlemen waited in the parlor, sipping at some wine from the decanter on the table. As introductions were made, they were only a blur of staring faces to Christina, but she gradually sorted them out through their speech.

The youngest one, Viscount Something-or-other, had dark hair and paid her extravagant compliments which the others all ignored. The eldest seemed to be a man well over a score and ten, several years senior to the earl himself. This man had cold gray eyes and smilingly spoke flattery with double meaning that brought a black frown to Drayton's already forbidding features. The third guest captured Christina's attention with a slight stutter and a winning charm she could not deny.

"Jeremy, Miss MacTavish has just come from a countryside filled with young louts and old codgers. You do not need to turn on the full force of your charm to win her."

The blond, blue-eyed younger son of a marquis ignored his host's dry comments. "What amazes me,

Drayton, is that a m-man as s-selfish as yourself would even c-consider sharing the company of this beauteous damsel. C-can it be that you are f-finally growing a soft heart?"

"Or a soft head?" murmured his sharper-tongued companion. Gray-eyed Bothwell situated himself on Christina's right, despite Jeremy's attempt to outmaneuver him.

"Gentlemen, if you persist in making personal comments, I will have to remove myself from your company." Christina fended off Bothwell's overeager hand and moved discreetly to her host's side. She may have been raised in the country, but she had learned at an early age how to handle herself in any social situation. "My lord, I believe dinner is ready to be served whenever you desire."

No approval warmed those hard, dark eyes, but the earl nodded slightly and gestured to Lord Jeremy. "Standifer, if you would take the lady in . . ."

Christina waited until his lordship indicated the meal had ended before rising and hoping to excuse herself, but Damien quickly nipped all such hopes in the bud.

"Miss MacTavish, the evening is early yet. Your mother has indicated to me that you possess some knowledge of the spinet. Would you be so kind as to give my guests and me a bit of entertainment before we go out for the evening?"

Christina met his gaze with equanimity, hiding her despair and fury. He deliberately encouraged the worst in her, but she would not let him make a fool of her in front of these gentlemen. She gritted her teeth silently as she agreed.

Flashing the annoying Yankee a disdainful glare, Christina swept from the room, her skirts rustling crisply through the dim interior. As candles were lighted, she sorted nervously through the music on the bench and chose a few simple pieces that demanded little of her or the instrument. She had learned to play, as every lady must, but she had no talent for it.

Yet the gentlemen listened with interest and joined

in the chorus with gratifying pleasure, and Christina felt her spirits rise for the first time in months. She loved music, and the pleasure of lifting her voice in company with others was strong, but more than this created her feeling of well-being. She had stepped into a strange and frightening world and found herself at home in it, if only just for the moment. She could have friends here, if she wanted, and she threw the arrogant Yankee a glance of triumph, rippling the keys through a brief refrain of the satiric "Yankee Doodle" before launching into the next piece.

Arms crossed over his broad chest, Damien leaned against the mantel on the far side of the room, his dark gaze following the cozy scene carelessly while his lips twisted in a wry grimace at her taunt. He acknowledged Christina's challenge with a slight lift of his brow, but advanced no closer.

Exhausting her repertoire, Christina slid from the bench, ignoring all protests as she curtsied politely before her host.

"My lord, it grows late and my mother awaits me. Might I be excused now?"

A snort of derision came from behind her as Bothwell poured himself a glass of wine, but Christina ignored it. Before the earl could reply, Jeremy intruded with a plea of his own.

"Before you take your leave, you must give permission for my sister and me to call. You cannot confine yourself to this gloomy hall for the entire season."

Christina glanced worriedly to the earl's dark face, then back to the young lord's. It had never occurred to her that she might be considered part of polite society, and certainly not part of the exalted circles to which the Yankee had just introduced her. Yet they seemed to be accepting her as such. Was that what the Yankee had intended? She found no answer in his bored expression and answered of her own accord.

"I would love to meet your sister, my lord, but I fear I am confined here until my mother's health improves.

You would be doing me a kindness to call upon occasion."

"I trust that invitation extends to myself also, Miss MacTavish."

Christina did not need to turn to know that voice belonged to the gray-eyed Bothwell, and from the dry hint of sarcasm in his tone, she gathered he had his own opinions on this subject and many more.

"Only if you bring your sister, Mr. Bothwell," she replied airily. Accepting the Yankee's arm, she followed him to the door, ignoring any reaction behind her.

Instead of releasing her to flee to the safety of her room, the earl covered her hand against his arm and bowed slightly to his guests.

"Gentlemen, the carriage should be waiting outside. If you will excuse me a moment, I will escort Miss MacTavish to her chambers and say my good-nights to her mother."

Again that snort of disbelief from the rake Bothwell, but well plied with liquor, the three young gentlemen went eagerly, their boisterous jests ringing through the halls, once released from the confinement of female company.

The earl watched them depart, then carefully closed the parlor door, leaving just the two of them in the flickering light of the dying fire.

Uneasily aware of the dark fires behind jet eyes, Christina backed away, but he held her firmly, his hand warm and hard against hers.

"You behaved better than I conceived possible, Miss MacTavish."

"You still think me a scrub maid, then," she replied caustically, her fingers digging into the velvet cloth of his coat. The powerful arm beneath did not flinch.

"You acted the part well, at the time," Damien answered without a trace of chagrin. "A mistress to please my appetites was more than I expected to find in my uncle's house. One who can also rival the cream of London's demimonde was beyond all expectations. You are the most useful discovery I have made since setting foot on these shores."

"You filthy boor!" Christina cried, her eyes widening at this final outrage. She had tried so hard to impress her true status upon him, and he called her whore still! Without thought, her free hand rose to slap the smug look from his hard face, but Damien moved more swiftly than she.

Snatching her hand behind her back, the Yankee jerked her against his hard chest, his well-muscled arms holding her easily imprisoned against him. Before Christina could fight free, his warm, wine-scented breath caressed her cheek, and his lips settled hard against hers.

With a muffled scream of indignation, Christina attempted to turn her head away, but he held her firmly, his mouth making demands she had learned too well. Bent slightly in his embrace, her breasts crushed against his powerful chest, the heat of his loins pressed scandalously against her belly, Christina felt herself trapped with no hope of escape.

His mouth sampled hers casually at first, tasting of the sweetness of her lips before probing deeper. Christina fought the tingling sensations his touch brought upon her; she struggled in his grasp, concentrating on the unequal fight and not the surging heat that bound their bodies together. He had to be the devil himself to instill these feelings in her, and she fought herself as much as him.

Still, the moment came when all struggles proved futile. His kiss pressed home, slanting insistently against her mouth, demanding she surrender. As his hands freed hers to travel caressingly along her spine, pressing her closer into his embrace, Christina gave way beneath the compelling currents of need flowing between their bodies.

Her lips parted beneath his insistence, and his tongue swept her senses away, claiming her for his own as their breaths combined. She felt the Yankee's strength become hers for that instant, and she reveled in the feeling that blended her softness with his hardness.

Yet when he set her aside, her hand acted quicker than her tongue, and the sound of her palm smacking against the hard line of Damien's angular jaw echoed in the empty room.

"I am not your whore!" she cried, and before his stunned expression, she fled the room.

She heard the words, "You soon will be!" roar behind her, but she did not stop to challenge them.

Disgruntled, Damien held a hand to his stinging cheek. He should know better than to toy with young virgins. What he needed was a mature older woman who would keep her curiosity to herself and accept his attentions for what she could get. But what he needed and what he wanted were two entirely different things.

Remembering the warm taste of passion on honeyed lips, Damien regained some control of his temper. His single-minded sense of duty kept him from wavering from the path he had set. He would have her and pay the price of his indulgence, but there was no reason she should pay more than she already had. He would carry out his purpose here and be gone, leaving her better equipped to deal with the world than before. Or so he told himself. If the truth be told, he needed her as much as she did him.

The trick was not to let her know it.

7

Even the welcome assurance that she did not bear the Yankee's seed did not improve Christina's humor the next day. Her eyes wore the dark circles and red rims of a sleepless night and she refused to go belowstairs until she was assured the monster had left.

The extra precaution proved futile, however. Every room she entered bore some trace of him: the cigars on the mantel, the decanter on the sideboard, a book he had been reading lying carelessly on a chair. Even the servants conspired to mention his name in every other sentence, until she felt certain she would kill the next who allowed the words "his lordship" to slip past his lips.

She did not have the opportunity, for the earl's next surprise left her totally speechless.

Entering her room for some item her mother had requested, Christina encountered Mrs. Douglass sorting through her collection of outgrown silks and satins. A small pile of her best gowns lay upon the bed, and the Scotswoman held up another in critical examination as she entered.

Instead of starting guiltily, the housekeeper serenely turned the gown for Christina to see.

"It is a wee bit childish, is it not? Do you wish it to go to the maids or shall I send it up with the others?"

Bewildered, Christina stared at the assortment of outgrown gowns and shook her head. "What are you doing with them?"

The housekeeper registered surprise, then annoyance. "That man has the common sense of a gale storm. He didna tell ye?"

The slip of brogue indicated the extent of her annoyance, and Christina shook her head silently, knowing the folly of crossing the Scotswoman when her ire was raised.

"He has sent a seamstress to let them out. He says you will not allow him to buy you more—and very properly, I should say—but there should be no harm in improving what you already have. These are fine gowns and with a bit of lace and trimming . . ." Seeing Christina's frown, she hesitated. "Surely you cannot object? You cannot entertain his lordship's guests in that thing that is not fitting for the maids to wear."

Christina looked down at the brown woolen she wore, its seams showing her poor talent for needlework, its bulk hiding any claims she had to womanhood, and wrinkled her nose in disgust. She had never realized how much she detested the thing and how much she treasured her beautiful gowns until the Yankee had made her learn what it meant to be a woman. Now she looked at her brown rag with repugnance and, remembering Lord Jeremy's promise to call, reluctantly acquiesced to the seamstress's work.

How she *hated* the man! And she hated him more each time he showed her his thoughts. He forced her to remember she was not only a lady but also a woman, and she resented it with every fiber of her being. She had been content to bury herself in Cornwall with her books and papers, accepting spinsterhood and poverty in exchange for another crumb to eat. But he would not let her alone. Dressing her in fine gowns, introducing her to society, treating her as a woman—all ploys to accomplish his intent, and she followed meekly down the path he chose.

He hoped she would not be satisfied to return to Cornwall untouched and unfulfilled, but there he was wrong. She would take his gifts, enjoy this brief respite, and when her mother's health had recovered sufficiently, return whence she came. The thought of surrendering herself fully to that monster again made it easy to forget all else, even if she had not known the shock of it would in all probability kill her mother. She was quite safe from his ploys, for now.

Or so Christina told herself as she tried on a gold gown the seamstress had let out and trimmed with a contrasting French cambric bib that made it not only fit, but look fashionable. It had been one of her favorites, and Christina smoothed its skirts lovingly as she descended the stairs to answer some complaint in the kitchen. Even if she were not the lady of the house, she looked the part now.

Her thoughts were echoed by words from below.

"It suits you well, though I fancy it makes your eyes look darker than usual. Are you not feeling well?"

Damien stepped up on the stair beside her when she did not come down, his black eyes searching her face with care.

"For the first time in days, I am feeling extremely well, thank you. Now, will you let me pass?" Christina asked coldly. She had not counted on his early return and did not know how else to escape his unnerving proximity.

He did not move, but seemed to ponder her words carefully. "What do you mean? You have seemed healthy enough. If you have been . . ."

Something in her piercing glare answered his question, and for the first time since she had known him, a grin tugged at the corners of the Yankee's mouth.

"You mean, since our first . . . encounter? You needn't have worried, you know. I took precautions once I discovered my error. I saw no reason for you to bear the burden of my guilt, though your innocence is touching." His grin grew larger at her shocked expression.

As she realized he had once again read her thoughts and now knew even her most intimate secret, Christina slowly flushed scarlet. Without a word, she swung around and proceeded back up the stairs.

Damien caught her before she had gone two steps,

his long stride coming to a halt in front of her, blocking her path again.

"I know you better than you realize, Christina MacTavish, and far more than you'll ever admit. You were born and raised to be a lady, but there's that much of your father in you that keeps you from being wholly what you would like to seem. Now, declare a truce and come riding with me. I wish to show you the park."

Christina stared at his dark pirate's face with astonishment, a tumult of emotions preventing clear thought.

"You knew my father?" she finally asked stupidly, instantly regretting not having given a more forceful negative to his last demand.

"In a manner of speaking, yes, but I will not tell you more now. Fetch your mantle, the air is still quite chilly and the carriage is an open one."

Damn the man! Arrogant, presumptuous, close-mouthed, and altogether too dangerous for her own good. Yet he knew something of her father, and curiosity got the better of her.

The curricle held only two and the Yankee drove it with the style and expertise of an accomplished whip. Christina attempted to concentrate on the sights and sounds of London, but the man beside her had no intention of being ignored.

"It is a bit difficult for me to establish a reputation as a rake if my intended mistress looks bored to tears. I would appreciate a few smiles, or at least your rapt attention."

Christina's head jerked around and he bent a grim smile upon her.

"Well, I have your attention, anyway. We will work on the smiles as we go."

"You may go to hell in any manner you choose, my lord, but I do not intend to accompany you. I would suggest you begin looking for a more suitable companion in your pursuit of life's perversions." Large eyes glowed with an amber gleam from beneath her bonnet as Christina delivered this message.

His imperturbably black gaze followed the horses as they turned into the park entrance, but his thoughts never strayed from the subject at hand.

"You are admirably suited in more ways than I care to enumerate, Miss MacTavish. I regret that our relationship had such a catastrophic beginning for you, but I still feel I can offer more than the life of poverty and degradation you were left to live in Cornwall. You are accustomed to the life I am offering, not the one you left behind."

"I am accustomed to living honestly, and degradation is what you will bring me. I do not care to argue the point further." Changing the subject, Christina returned to his earlier remark. "Why do you wish to be a rake?"

Damien gave her a quick glance, then raised his whip in greeting to another carriage jolting along the roadway. The other couple waved back, stared openly at Christina, and continued on. The Yankee gave a grim smile of satisfaction.

"People notice you. If you would take off that godawful bonnet, they would come to a complete standstill. I do not wish to become a rake, Miss MacTavish, but appear as one. There is a difference."

"That point is debatable, my lord, but for the sake of the question, I will accept it. Why do you wish to *seem* a rake?"

The whip cracked in the air above the horses' heads, increasing their pace at a dangerous rate. The earl appeared impervious to the irate glares he drew from more sedate travelers.

"Not that you will believe me, but I seek peace and justice, and they can only be accomplished by secrecy. More than that I will not tell to a country miss who refuses to open her eyes to the world around her. Now, practice smiling. It is the least you can do in return for my hospitality."

His abrupt changes in subject always left her gasping, but his statement jarred all other thought from her head. Peace and justice? She had never heard anything so preposterous in all her life.

With a deliberately devastating smile of insincerity, Christina asked sweetly, "Is it current events you wish to discuss, my lord? Has the Lord High Admiral made another incredible *bon mot* upon the state of the navy? Or is it the foolish war over a colony of savages you wish to remark upon?"

Damien gave her a look of disgust. "The fact that your father should have been a Scots laird and your mother is of a noble family that dates back before the conquest gives you no right to call me and mine 'savages,' either. I have seen you wince over my accent and speak with disdain of 'Yankees.' Does place of birth merit more respect than titles?"

The harsh accusation of his tone surprised her little, a soft word would have surprised her more, but his knowledge of her family caused considerable consternation. Christina's head jerked up suspiciously.

"How do you know so much about my family? And knowing it, how can you treat me as you have? I have every right to call you savage when you behave as one!"

Damien snorted. "What would you have me do? Would you have been content if I had thrown you a purse full of gold and left you to wallow in the mire with your farmer and his friends? A lady in your position has two choices in this country—she may become a governess or companion in a wealthy house, or she may become a whore. Unprotected and beautiful as you are, they may be the same thing. With your manners and accent, you could not find a place anywhere else. No one would believe you as servant or tavern maid, though in the colonies, all manner of women hold these positions. They are not judged by their clothes as unfit for work, their accents do not bar them from becoming seamstresses or owning their own shops. And you call *me* the savage!"

"If I had been the daughter of a duke instead of a merchant, you would have married me after discovering you dishonored me. Do not preach class differences to me!" Christina retorted heatedly. She could not imagine a world where ladies owned taverns, and did not believe he would have looked twice at such a woman. Men married for wealth and titles, and a man with his own wealth and title married for breeding sons of more noble wealth and title.

"I would not have married you if you had been the Queen of England!" The earl's dark face closed into chiseled stone as he stared out above the horses. "You got what you asked for, and though I regret my haste, I have no intention of marrying you or any other woman. As I have tried to tell you, I am offering you the only means in my possession to make amends. Marriage would only be a worse punishment than you deserve."

Christina wrapped her mantle more tightly around her, thoroughly chilled by his words. She heartily agreed that marriage to him would be a punishment, but it struck her oddly for him to say it first. And to call her beautiful in one breath and to state emphatically in the next that he would never marry her presented a strange contradiction. Was it to her personally that he objected? Or marriage in general?

"I am glad we are in agreement on one point, my lord," she responded sarcastically, then fell silent.

He threw her a quick look, then, noting her chattering teeth and clenched wrap, urged the horses toward the exit.

"I do not hope to bring you to my point of view on all things, Miss MacTavish," he responded emotionlessly. "Only on the ones that count."

She threw him a disbelieving glare and they continued the ride home in silence.

He went out before dinner that evening and Christina ate her meal in relieved peace. Her mother seemed to be improving, the earl obviously meant to keep his word about not molesting her, and she had sent another letter to her uncle enclosing her new address. Anything could happen within a fortnight.

A long time after she had retired, as the tall clock on the landing tolled the wee hours of the morning, Christina heard the uncertain steps of heavy feet upon the stairway. She listened with bated breath as the feet found a more secure purchase and continued on without incident. His lordship had apparently indulged his attempts at being a rake to a remarkably authentic degree.

She went about her business the next day without inquiring into the earl's whereabouts. She could not spend her days living in fear, and if his words had any value, she had nothing to fear from him. That her heart lurched whenever Damien appeared and her breath constricted in her lungs did not mean she had any rational reason for these reactions. Her body had betrayed her before; she could not rely on it for having any sense.

She was upstairs trying on one of her newly refitted silks when Mrs. Douglass carried in Lord Jeremy's card on a silver platter.

"He be downstairs with his sister. Said you did not give him proper hours to visit, so he took his chances. Shall I tell him you are not at home?"

Mrs. Douglass watched her with no small amount of curiosity. More than the other servants, she knew Damien Drayton, and she found it hard to believe that gentleman took no interest in the blond, amber-eyed beauty he had installed as guest. Yet he made no attempt to court her, treated her with open disdain, and made no objections to her entertaining gentleman callers. Or at least, not yet.

Christina stared at the ornate card with wide-eyed wonder, then glancing hastily at her reflection in the mirror, hurried toward the stairs. She could not let her first callers go ungreeted.

Lord Jeremy rose instantly when she entered, his smile brightening the gloomy room. Not so tall as the earl, he still stood half a head taller than Christina, and his stocky frame moved with muscular grace as he took her hand.

"Y-you will allow me to p-present my sister, Seraphina."

In his eagerness the young lord ignored all social

etiquette, but neither girl appeared to mind as they cautiously made that first appraisal that so often decides a friendship.

Christina had feared a stiffly proper young aristocrat, but Lady Seraphina seemed as unaware of proper etiquette as her brother. They both exuded superb confidence in themselves and their positions and had no need of the artificial graces taught at Mrs. Grenoble's Academy. Christina liked them both immediately.

Jeremy sprawled in the chair indicated, scarcely taking his eyes off his hostess, though the faint pink of Christina's cheeks indicated her embarrassment.

Tea and cakes were produced, and the trio gradually drifted into less formal conversation, their enjoyment in each other's company rapidly dissipating all constraint. Young laughter rang through rooms long empty of all sounds of life.

The brief moment of relaxation ended all too soon, but not the links of friendship created in those moments. Lord Westshipham's butler—a phlegmatic, stalwart individual the exact opposite of his lecherous country counterpart—interrupted with an announcement of the arrival of Mr. Bothwell.

"Bothwell? Damme, but what is that rake doing here? Excuse me, ladies," Jeremy hastily amended at his sister's glare, "but Damien is sadly lacking in common sense if he allows that cad courtesy in his drawing rooms. Shall I send him packing, Miss MacTavish?"

The light in Jeremy's eyes indicated he relished the idea, but Christina did not possess the temerity to agree. With a reluctant shake of her head, she gestured for the butler to introduce their new arrival.

"He is Lord Westshipham's friend. I cannot send him away," she whispered hurriedly to her companions before Bothwell entered. Jeremy's frown indicated his thoughts on the matter, but she had no control of the situation.

Bothwell made a sweeping bow to the room, raising a mocking brow to Jeremy's disapproving frown before his smile fell upon Christina.

"Ahhh, Miss MacTavish, I regret I have no sister to act as chaperon, but perhaps Lady Seraphina will stand in for me. Surely that is proper enough for even the sternest of guardians?"

"I daresay that is for Lord Westshipham to decide, Mr. Bothwell. Do have a seat if you do not fear his disfavor." Christina met his bold stare bravely. She did not like this man with his boldly appraising glances and insinuating tones, but she had no authority to turn him away.

"Is it his lordship's favor I must seek to earn your company? How interesting."

His smirk indicated the path of his thoughts, but Christina blithely ignored it, returning the conversation to where it had been before his interruption. She might have to endure his company, but no one said she must be polite about it.

The proper time for visiting came and went, and reluctantly Lord Jeremy and his sister rose to leave. Forced to rise by Christina's doing so, Bothwell lingered in the room as if he meant to stay.

"Mother will love meeting you. The invitations are going out this week. You must persuade Damien to escort you. He has been away too long," Lady Seraphina whispered confidentially as they prepared to leave.

Confident his sister had the matter of the dance well in hand, Jeremy turned his attention to more immediate concerns. "Bothwell, aren't you coming with us?"

"I believe I am capable of finding my own way out, Standifer. Toddle along and I will catch up with you elsewhere." Bothwell lounged against the wall, fully prepared to wait them out.

Christina turned her back on the doorway where her friends stood, facing the culprit fully. "Why, Mr. Bothwell, has your sister arrived after all? Pray usher her in here at once so I might make her acquaintance." She stepped aside, gesturing toward the doorway in a motion that could not be taken in any other way.

Bothwell straightened his length upright, a frown

forming between his eyes at this witty dismissal. Before he could make any comment, a new voice intruded.

"Apologize for my lateness, ladies. Bothwell, Standifer, sorry you couldn't stay longer. You'll have to bring Lady Seraphina again sometime soon. Christina, I need to have a word with you."

Sweeping into the room like a sudden thunderstorm, throwing his hat and cloak into a corner, black eyes flashing dangerously as he maneuvered Bothwell from his place, Damien Drayton effectively brought an end to the visit. His brooding dark face, framed by the length of his sideburns, bore a stern expression preventing all argument.

Within minutes the parlor was cleared of all but Christina, and when she attempted to leave also, Damien slammed the door and barred the way. Dark eyes swept insultingly over her fashionable coiffure and respectable silk, stripping them of their respectability. Christina flushed, feeling naked beneath his glare.

"Your cleverness does not impress me, Miss MacTavish."

The fact that he had used her familiar name earlier had not gone unnoticed, and his return to formality now did not diminish the wrong done. Christina swung away, her skirts rustling angrily as she crossed to the far side of the room, out of his reach. She bit her tongue to keep the fury in, but could not keep totally silent.

"That was abominably *rude*, my lord. Was there some reason for that performance?"

"This is my house and I reserve the right to be as rude as I please. I did not bring you here for the purpose of auctioning off your services, and I resent having to fight off your suitors when I arrive home. It is high time we came to some understanding on a few matters."

Terror seized her as he advanced into the room, but he stopped halfway across to pour himself a drink from the decanter. Raising his glass to his lips, Damien casually observed her trembling figure in the corner, eyes like coals raking over her form-fitting bodice of emerald silk to the full sway of skirts over rounded hips. Cowardice chased away Christina's fury, leaving her incapable of response. The glare of those eyes paralyzed her, but no more so than the memory of what had been between them. She read it easily in the fire of his gaze, and stepped backward, out of his reach.

"Lost your tongue again? Or afraid to reveal your lies? I don't intend to eat you, not right away at least. Come here and let me prove a point." Damien indicated a spot in front of him.

Christina shook her head. "No, my lord, I'd rather not. Say what you have come to say and let me return to my room." There seemed no use in arguing with a madman. Her only hope was to keep out of his reach, but his masculine figure seemed to fill the room, fragmenting all other thought.

"I have little time or patience to waste, miss. I do not intend to hurt you. Now, quit cowering in that corner and come here."

The dark lightning had left the Yankee's eyes, but the impatient tone of his voice warned of the dangers of disobedience. Christina stepped hesitantly forward, stopping just out of reach of his long arms. Even so, the nearness of the lean grace of his masculine frame heightened her trembling.

"You slapped me the last time I kissed you, and perhaps rightly so, but you cannot deny you enjoyed it as much as I."

Christina did not dare look up, but concentrated on the starched white cravat above his crimson waistcoat. She could feel his dark gaze burning against her skin, and the tension between them thickened to an unbearable degree.

"I w-will d-deny it," she stated, not so stoutly as she could desire.

"And you are lying, too. Look at me, Christina, and tell me you dislike being kissed."

Slowly she raised her eyes to his and once more found herself trapped in those deep wells of hunger.

Though his stern features remained cold and aloof, she found the roots of his soul behind those dark hollows. She forgot the question and could not reply as dark fingers raised to touch her carefully pinned curls.

"I liked it better the other way. Your beauty is too natural to be disguised behind society's artifices. Don't ever powder it."

He seemed almost to startle himself with the warmth of these words, but there was nothing surprising in his next move.

Slowly, letting her know what he intended to do, the Yankee circled her waist with his large hands and drew her closer. Christina resisted only slightly, unable to tear her gaze away from the intoxicating promise of his eyes. When he bent his head carefully to hers, she sighed softly and closed her eyes, welcoming the touch of his lips upon hers.

He made no attempt to push further than she wanted to go. His lips moved exploringly across hers, awakening sensations that had little to do with passion, teaching her the pleasantness of this contact without the fear.

Christina drank it in eagerly, her hands daringly coming to rest on the smooth satin of his waistcoat as she lifted her head to his kiss. This was how she had imagined it that first time, before he had stripped all illusion away, and she breathed deeply with the relief of this loving touch. This was how she had hoped it would be, and her lips parted softly beneath his request.

Their tongues touched and his hands tightened convulsively about her waist. With a gentle sigh of regret, Damien released her mouth, but continued holding her tightly, his dark eyes searching her face.

Christina watched him questioningly, her heart thumping against her ribs. He had been gentle. She did not understand why, but wished it could go on forever.

"Have I proved my point yet, Christina?" he asked gently. "Or are you so damned innocent you do not realize what has happened?" At her wide-eyed stare Damien grimaced slightly, but did not let go. He must make her understand, for he was not certain he could tolerate it if she did not. "You are mine, lovely lady, in all the ways a woman belongs to a man, except the one way society requires. I cannot provide you with the marriage tie, but neither can your other suitors."

Christina stared at him blankly, too dazed to fully comprehend the depth of his words or the direction he was taking. "I do not understand, my lord," she finally admitted, stepping out of his embrace.

Damien's fingers slowly unfolded their grip, freeing her from his hold. In the room's deepening twilight his face was but a shadow of itself. Sorrow found a place in his heart. For her own good, he must continue to play this part, but it grew increasingly difficult to remain cold to her charms. It was the only sensible thing to do, however, and he replied with enigmatic aloofness.

"No, I see you do not. That is my fault, but it cannot be repaired. I presume you do understand that neither Bothwell nor Standifer looks upon you as marriage material?"

A crimson flush stained her cheeks before she turned away. "Even if they did, I realize I am not. Innocent I may be, in some ways, but I am neither unprincipled nor a fool. I only seek a small amount of friendship. Is that permissible?"

"For now, Christina." The Yankee's voice reverberated deep in his chest, filled with some meaning she had yet to grasp.

Reassured by the reasonableness of his reply, she turned to face him once again. "Then I have your permission to entertain guests upon occasion?"

"I did not mean to deny you that permission in the first place, only make you see the folly of it. I have made no secret of why I have brought you here, have I?"

Damien poured another glass, offering one to Christina and drinking it himself when she refused. He drank far too much these days, and at the moment he could find little reason to discontinue the practice.

"No, my lord, though I trust you have not made your

intent common knowledge. I think I have made my opinion quite clear also," Christina replied coolly, hurting that he had brought up such a subject just when she had hoped they were reaching some agreement.

"Unless your uncle appears, I do not think you have much choice in the matter," Damien replied measuredly, looking for words that would score his point. "You have already admitted a respectable marriage is out of the question. That poor besotted farmboy back in the village might be persuaded to accept you, but he will treat you roughly in retaliation. The knowledge of our affair is quite common."

He ignored her uneasy start as he revealed this piece of information. "Besides, you have your mother to support, and there are few willing to take both spoiled goods and an invalid parent. Employment as governess or companion is out of the question when your reputation becomes known, and you could not support or nurse an invalid with either of those occupations. You have no choice, Christina. I will make it as easy on you as possible, and because of my own circumstances, you will benefit more from remaining with me than with any other. Will you hear me out?"

Christina buried her face in her hands, hating the sound of those reasonable words, preferring he scream and curse and give her cause to close her mind and heart. But he did not, and every word pierced her with remarkable accuracy, making it impossible to avoid or ignore him any longer.

When she did not answer, Damien put a hand on her shoulder and firmly settled her into a high-backed wing chair. He next produced a glass of wine and forced it between her fingers before returning to the center of the room, where he paced restlessly up and down.

"I will not be in this country for long. In a few months I will be either dead or gone. I am telling you this in strictest privacy. I trust you can keep a secret?"

Christina nodded silently, gripped by a new horror. She knew the Yankee represented danger, but she had not realized the danger extended to him instead of herself. Dead or gone. The tone of his words echoed ominously in the heavily curtained room, strangely out of place in this fashionable abode. Yet she had sensed from the first that the Yankee was not the civilized gentleman he portrayed.

"How can you be so certain?" she finally asked when he did not immediately continue.

"Because, like you, I have no other choice. Once you agree to stay with me, I will have to explain some of it, for I may need your assistance, but until that time you are safer in ignorance." Damien's pacing slowed as he sought the words he needed.

"I have had time to think this out more fully since I first made my proposal. We need each other, but I have nothing to lose and you have everything. I have sought some way to make my wrongs right and have come up with the best solution possible under the circumstances."

Christina interrupted with irritation. "I thought we agreed there is only one honorable solution, my lord, and neither of us is prepared for it."

Damien turned on her, his dark face contorted with some emotion she had not yet learned to decipher.

"Dammit, Christina! Will you quit calling me by that despicable title? My name is Damien. Use it, and skip the formalities."

Silently vowing to call him nothing before admitting to the intimacy of his name, Christina nodded warily. Perhaps he was mad after all.

He returned to pacing. "The estate apparently includes an unencumbered terrace house just off St. James Square. I have found it to be in good repair and will have it cleaned and properly furnished. The house and an ample allowance for life will be yours once you consent to my proposal. In exchange for a few months of your time, you will be provided with a security and income sufficient to support yourself and your mother for so long as you both shall live. You can become another man's mistress or you can change your name and live in respectability and possibly pass yourself off as a widow and marry, if you so desire. I am offering you an entirely new life in exchange for what you can give me for a few short months of mine."

Damien came to a halt in front of her and stared down at her bent head. Christina closed her eyes and shook her head, praying the nightmare would go away, knowing it would not.

"You are the one who does not understand," she whispered brokenly, omitting "my lord" at the last moment. "I cannot be what you ask of me. I cannot . . ." She stopped, unable to find the words to describe her horror of what he had done to her, substituting another fear instead. "It would kill my mother."

"I have thought of that. She will be told we are secretly married. When I go, you will announce that you are a widow and that the only part of the estate not entailed is the house on St. James. She will believe that and be quite content."

The smug tone of his voice infuriated her and Christina glared up at him. "And what will I tell her if I am breeding your 'heir,' my lord? That the world must not know he is the true Earl of Westshipham? Will she believe that?"

Damien shrugged and walked off. "It is near enough to the truth, as you will find out later. I have an excellent solicitor who will be handling all these matters. If that should occur, you can go to him. He will see that it is handled in the best possible manner. I will not leave you totally bereft."

Fury raged through Christina's veins, making it easier to shake off the torpor he had induced in her with his factual listing of impossibilities. "It," he called the bastard he might breed. His own child was a "matter" to be "handled"! Of all the callous, unfeeling, degrading things she had ever heard . . .

"You are most kind," Christina stated coldly as she rose from the chair, "but the answer is still no. I will beg on the streets before I will accept such depravity."

Damien stepped in front of her, raising his hand to pluck a curl from its pin, his dark face enigmatic as he studied hers. "You are young and frightened, but you must grow up someday. You have not yet learned what it means to be a woman, but you are learning quickly. Give me the fortnight you promised, and if your uncle does not appear by that time . . ."

His hand completed the statement. With infinite gentleness Damien's fingers slid over the ivory column of her throat and down the modest neckline of her gown to dip caressingly beneath the silk and cup the warm mound of flesh pushed up by her bodice.

Christina bit back a gasp and shivered violently as his fingers stroked the sensitive crest to a tingling point. She had forced the memory of that day from her mind, but she could not hide it from her body. A vast aching chasm opened within her and she nearly groaned aloud as he released her.

As she dashed for the door, she heard him call out in a low voice behind her, "Sleep well, Christina."

Damien had no intention of sleeping that night or any other night. The fashionable of London did not encounter the day until darkness was almost upon them, and Damien's day began as Christina's country hours grew to an end.

The earl lounged in a velvet chair and listened to Bothwell's snide remarks with half an ear as his gaze wandered around the fashionable gaming house. The man he had come to meet had not yet arrived, but an old acquaintance caught his eye and he grimaced inwardly as she approached.

With hair upswept in a towering powdered pompadour adorned with butterflies with intricate gold chains about their tiny wire feet, flashing eyes of bold blue, lovely features powdered elegantly white to enhance her frailty, Lady Annabelle had once swept London with her astonishing beauty. A few years had passed since then and other *nonpareils* had taken her place, but Lady Annabelle's loveliness had not faded.

Only Damien had changed. Once he had found the lady an amusing companion and a fascinating mistress.

Watching her approach now, he wondered what he had ever seen in her artificial beauty and her cynical tongue. Another face came to mind, a fresh, young face of unadorned beauty framed by a golden halo of tumbling curls. The fact that this new face frowned at him with dislike while the lady's rouged lips smiled welcomingly in no way diminished his memory.

Still, he stood as Annabelle arrived, and took her in his arms as she so obviously expected. Their lips met as the lady pressed herself sensuously against his length, and Damien tested the heady wine of her mouth as their kiss deepened.

His long-starved body responded and Annabelle sighed with pleasure as Damien crushed her closer, revealing the extent of his desire. But a loud cough beside them quickly ended the embrace as Damien lifted his head to meet the amused gaze of his friend and solicitor, Ben Thomas.

"I apologize for intruding upon your reunion, Drayton, but I must have a word with you." From behind wire-rimmed spectacles, the short, stocky lawyer surveyed the young couple with sharp understanding.

Knowing the reason for Ben's intrusion, Damien grimaced with disgust at himself for being so easily side-tracked by his own hungers, and abruptly deposited his former mistress in his companion's lap.

"Here she is, Bothwell. I've warmed her up for you. Take advantage of the fire while it's still hot." Untangling himself from Annabelle's clinging embrace and ignoring her screech of fury, Damien continued in his worst Yankee drawl, "Nice seeing you again, Annie. We'll have to do it again sometime."

Shrugging his impeccably fitted coat back into place and smoothing out the wrinkles, Damien stalked off across the crowded room with Ben Thomas murmuring polite reproaches at his side. Damien knew the solicitor well enough to know nothing shocked him, but he had almost shocked himself at the ease with which the part of rake came to him. It served him well, however. Annabelle's mouth, as well as her favors, was easily bought. He had no intention of falling into that little trap.

"You're establishing your reputation as a damned cad quite effectively, Drayton. I trust you will apply subtler tactics on your next victim," Ben admonished.

"I'm not a fool, Ben. There is a little matter I need to discuss with you in the morning, but you had best disappear for now. Your association with me is dangerous enough without coming in on this end of it." Damien grabbed a drink from a passing tray and regarded his solicitor thoughtfully.

"I'm old and have little to risk, but if I'm to be around when you land yourself in the Tower, I suppose I must heed your advice. Take care, Damien. It is a dangerous game you play."

Damien nodded abstractedly, his attention already focused on the man he had come to see. The noted politician looked nervous and out-of-place in this gaming hell. He would have to get him out of here quickly.

Sipping his drink, he staggered slightly as he separated from Ben and made his way through the crowd. He wandered seemingly aimlessly, pounding the back of a casual acquaintance and pinching the plump arm of a pretty barmaid, until he arrived at the side of the nervous politician.

With a drunken stumble, Damien spilled the remainder of his drink down the man's waistcoat.

"So sorry, old chap. Damned crowded, wouldn't you say? Hey, ain't you Arbuthnot? Old Ben told me to look you up. Where's your drink? Can't allow you to go about without a drink."

The politician recoiled with disgust at this drunken monologue, but at the mention of the code words "Old Ben," he refrained from brushing off his inebriated companion.

With seemingly drunken abandon, Damien skillfully guided his contact into a private corner where they could sip their drinks and talk guardedly.

"Ben said you could help us." Damien deliberately refrained from mentioning Ben's surname. Both men knew he did not refer to the innocent solicitor, but any listener would not know.

"So he sends me a drunken lecher? How do I know I can rely on—"

Lounging idly against the wall, glass in hand, gaze wandering aimlessly about the room, Damien still managed to cut these hasty words off with abruptness.

"Not here. My ship's in the harbor. My driver is on your coach. He'll take you." As if he had just made a witty rejoinder with which he was well-pleased, Damien grinned, saluted his companion with his glass, and staggered away.

Having struggled from Bothwell's eager grip, Annabelle stood and glared across the room at her former lover. "Whoever warms his bed now certainly doesn't do a thorough job of it," she muttered maliciously.

Bothwell chuckled. "Thought you had him back, didn't you, Annie, dear? The chit between his covers now is some years younger than you, I venture, and not quite as experienced. Give her time."

Annabelle shot him a venomous glance. "Then that leaves the game to you, doesn't it? What will you do, seduce the girl or torture Drayton at knife point?"

Bothwell frowned. "That's none of your damned business. If you're smart, you can still win him back. Nicholas won't like it if you quit," he warned.

"I won't quit, but I like your job better. I wouldn't mind taking a sword to that devil for a change."

The sophisticated rake grinned wickedly as he watched Drayton move toward the door. The Yankee was playing right into his hands, and he intended to enjoy every minute of it. "I'll see that Nicholas lets you carve the girl. When the time comes, Drayton is mine."

And with that wicked leer still hovering about his lips, Bothwell followed his target from the room.

8

His lordship must have found some other outlet for his needs, Christina thought grimly as she descended the stairs some days later. He had come home in the wee hours of the morning each day, and his step had not been one of drunkenness.

This thought should have relieved her, but for some perverse reason it did not. Damien continued to court her patiently, appealing to her thirst for knowledge by combining trips of pleasure with sojourns into learning, but he made no further attempt to impose his physical desires upon her. This denial had become even more frustrating than his previous molestations.

Christina rubbed a smudge upon the polished sideboard. She had begun to admit she enjoyed being held and kissed. Surely that was natural? She had a need to be needed; it gave her a strength she did not possess, and she missed the feeling of power the mighty lord's hungry gaze gave to her.

The end of a sennight brought the Standifers' ball, and Christina allowed her excitement to rouse her from the doldrums. Lord Jeremy and Lady Seraphina had visited upon several occasions these past days, making her feel wanted as a friend, though she would know few others at the dance.

The amber silk had been remade to fit with some semblance of modesty, but the low décolletage still did little to hide Christina's high-breasted figure. The seamstress had insisted it was the fashion and refused to add more than the slightest trimming of lace.

Christina glanced at her image in the mirror now and feared to take a deep breath. The wooden stays in her bodice pushed her breasts up higher and fuller than they had any right to be. Her slender proportions appeared almost voluptuous in this gown, and Christina stared at the image in disbelief.

Despite Damien's opinions, Mrs. Douglass had dressed her hair in an upswept coiffure decorated with hothouse flowers. Without panniers or hoops, her full skirt fell in a widening circle over stiff petticoats, caught up in a froth of ruffles and lace to reveal glimpses of tiny slippers. She was without fashion, but even her critical eyes could tell the gown transcended it. Others might declare the wearer's beauty produced the effect.

Damien made no comment to either effect. Dark eyes swept over her as she approached, observing every detail, and offering no hint of his thoughts. Garbed in light blue with silver lapels, the long tails of the cutaway jacket falling formally over tightly tailored breeches of a matching hue, silver buttons shining with an extravagant gleam, he appeared every inch the fashionable lord he meant to portray. Russet hair powdered and clubbed neatly framed a bronzed face of sharp contrasts. Those hard angular features did not match the costume of the elegant gentleman.

"Miss MacTavish." He offered his arm formally.

She slipped her hand into the crook of his elbow, and for a moment his other hand covered it, crushing her fingers against the soft satin of his coat. Dark-lashed eyes swept upward to meet his implacable gaze, then retreated as he led her toward the door. Suddenly Christina felt as if she attended her own execution.

The drive to the Standifers' was a silent one, both occupants of the carriage totally engrossed in their own thoughts. There had been talk enough between them these past days, but not enough for Christina to venture the path of his thoughts. The silent Yankee had a character deeper than a bottomless well, and she feared delving into it.

Standifer House was one of the newer constructions in

Piccadilly. An enclosed courtyard set the grandeur of the Georgian structure off from the public road, and the imposing facade rose majestically above the carriage drive. Compared to the cramped, dark Drayton town house in Soho, this was a palace.

Christina was not allowed to gaze on it in awe. Damien swept her through the archway and into the wide receiving hall, and amidst the garden of silks and flounces around them, introduced her to their host and hostess.

The Standifers were an austere couple, their proud bearing and stern visages indicating their firm upbringing and beliefs. Still, they greeted Damien warmly and noticed Christina with approval, acknowledging their younger son's eager introduction with fondness. They seemed close and loving, an anomaly in a family of such wealth and proud heritage. Christina watched their warm camaraderie with wonder and a certain amount of wistfulness. Her highly improper family had once enjoyed this same coziness.

Lord Jeremy insisted on the first dance. Christina attempted to talk her way out of it, but on hearing her objections, his mother regally waved them aside.

"We are all friends here. There is no need to stand on such protocol. I am certain Lord Westshipham would not expect you to sit out your first ball, and if your mother approves . . ."

At Damien's nod of agreement, Jeremy promptly appropriated Christina's arm.

Ebony eyes gazed upon the fair couple thoughtfully for a moment; then with a slight bow to the Standifers, Damien turned to their lovely daughter.

"Lady Seraphina, would you allow me this dance?"

Cornflower-blue eyes lit with magical excitement and Seraphina's peach-and-cream complexion blushed delicately rosier. With a sidelong glance to her parents for approval, she accepted Damien's strong arm.

Christina sensed the sudden tensing of the arm beneath her hand and looked up questioningly to her escort. Jeremy's normally sunny expression had clouded over, and he watched Damien carry off his sister with brooding eyes.

When they had advanced out of the hearing of his parents, Christina queried, "What is wrong, milord? Surely there can be no harm in old friends sharing a dance?"

She had sensed the direction of his thoughts with great accuracy, and Jeremy returned his gaze to the lovely amber eyes beholding him. Pain haunted the inner depths of those gold-flecked wells, and he responded gently.

"No, there is no harm done, b-but my s-sister f-fancies herself in love with the cad, and I believe D-Drayton knows it. He has always d-discouraged her f-fancies in the past. I cannot think why tonight should be d-different."

Christina knew, and her lips tightened with irritation. Any fool could see Seraphina's impetuous crush on her brother's dashing friend. Damien's monumental ego could not be so blind as to ignore it. Unless he intended to court the lady, he had no business encouraging her, and Christina felt quite confident the reckless Yankee had no interest in courting the doll-like Seraphina. He paid her court only to irritate Jeremy, and Christina could guess the reason for that.

"He only means to be polite, I am certain," she whispered reassuringly as Jeremy led her into the formation of dancers.

He gave her a curious look but relaxed beneath her warm smile and fell into the elegant pattern of the dance with enjoyment.

As soon as the set ended, Damien immediately appeared at their side, his dark face reflecting none of his thoughts as he appropriated Christina's hand.

"My turn, I believe," he murmured expressionlessly.

"D-damn you, D-Drayton, what have you done with my s-sister?" Jeremy asked with laughter, but a certain uneasiness lingered in the shadows of his gentle blue eyes.

"Left her with Bothwell, of course," Damien replied with a shrug, commandeering Christina's hand and tucking it firmly beneath his arm.

At the alarm in Jeremy's expression Christina extended a hand to touch his coat, diverting his gaze to her and away from the scene across the room and behind him. She could see Seraphina extricating herself from Bothwell's dubious presence. A moment's delay would save Jeremy's peace of mind.

"H-he is j-jesting, m-milord. D-Damien has a s-strange sense of humor, upon o-occasion."

A look of consternation spread across Jeremy's features at this speech, and Christina felt the arm beneath her hand twitch unreasonably. Glancing up, she saw Damien fighting back a smile, his whole body tensing with the effort to keep from chuckling out loud.

"Do not concern yourself unduly, Standifer. She is lying, but give her no reason to lie, and she speaks with more precision than the queen. Have a good evening."

With these final words he swept Christina off into the crowd of dancers, leaving Jeremy to look alone and bewildered on the edge of the crowd.

"You are a despicable beast," Christina hissed through her teeth between the patterns of the dance.

"That will teach him to trespass on another man's claim," Damien replied calmly.

Christina's back went rigid as he held a firm hand to her waist and escorted her through the circle of dancers into position. "I am not yours to claim and he is your *friend*," she protested angrily.

"Friends can be dangerous when enamored of my intended mistress. If you will not discourage him, I must."

Christina gazed hastily around to see if any could hear this outrageous remark, but he was well accustomed to ballroom flirting and had timed his whisper well.

"You are a fool," she finally spat out, then sank into outraged silence for the remainder of the dance.

She could not avoid Jeremy throughout the evening, but made every effort to do so. Damien was a preoccupied escort at best, wandering off into serious conversations with other guests whenever another man claimed her hand, but she noticed he made a point to dance with Seraphina every time Jeremy came to claim her.

After one such encounter Damien casually sauntered to her side to guide her toward a curtain-covered anteroom. "Would you care for some refreshment? Perhaps if I hide you away I can be reasonably assured that young puppy does not come sniffing around again."

"So long as I do not have to speak with you again this evening, I will be more than happy to remain here until it is time to leave." Christina brushed by him and into the candlelit alcove. A window seat looking out over the garden called her attention, and turning her back on her escort, she appropriated it, pointedly ignoring him.

"Your wish is my command, my love," Damien retorted angrily, giving her proud back a furious glare. "I am growing quite tired of looking after a petulant spoiled brat. Enjoy yourself, mademoiselle." He stalked out, swearing to himself. He would be better off with Annabelle. She was a bitch, but at least he would not give a bloody damn if she danced with every man and infant in the room. How in hell was he going to protect this little brat from every damned lecherous male in the country but himself? And why should he?

The room became achingly empty after Damien left. Christina hated the man with every fiber of her being, but she could not deny that he was more alive than any other man she had ever met. His every movement bristled with a strength and vitality that created an almost palpable air of tension wherever he went. His absence created a gaping vacuum no one else could fill.

Christina pressed her forehead against the windowpane, letting the coolness of the glass relax her cascading thoughts.

A silent footstep behind her caused her to jump and

spin around, ready to commence the battle once again. To her surprise, it was Bothwell, not Damien, who dared intrude upon her privacy.

"If Drayton is such a fool as to neglect a treasure such as you, I can assure you I am not. It is time we became better acquainted, Miss MacTavish."

He was not as tall or athletic as Damien, but lithe and wiry, and his icy gray eyes hid a multitude of sins. Christina trusted him not at all, and attempted to brush past him. In this small room the attempt was futile. He caught her arm before she could skirt him.

"I merely sought some breathing space, Mr. Bothwell. It is not at all proper for you to single me out in this manner. Let us return to the ballroom," Christina stated frostily, giving his encroaching hand a look of contempt.

Bothwell chuckled rudely. "You play your part most convincingly, but once the Standifers discover your true role, you will not be allowed to consort with their likes again. It is a grand jest Drayton plays on the tedious bores, introducing his mistress at their society gala, but you must both know the truth will out soon enough. Once the jest is over, what will Drayton do with you? He tires of his women rather quickly, if I remember rightly."

Fury colored her cheeks, but Christina managed to maintain her haughty poise. After all, she had seen the snobs at Mrs. Grenoble's do it often enough.

"You are quite mad, sir. Please remove your hand before I scream for help. I can assure you, neither Lord Westshipham nor Lord Jeremy would look lightly upon this outrage."

The frost in his eyes grew colder. "And I assure you, madam, that the only one harmed by such a scene would be yourself. If Drayton cared one way or another what happened to you, he would never have left you here alone. Now, let's see what he finds so damned attractive about an ice princess like you."

Cruelly gripping her arms, Bothwell dragged her against him, his whiskey-flavored mouth coming down hard and heavy against hers. Christina's cries were gagged by his invading tongue and, realizing her mistake, she quickly clamped her teeth closed, causing him to curse as she fought silently. She had learned the folly of screaming once before; she would shred this devil to pieces before she let him destroy what name remained to her now.

Denied access to the succulent temptations of her lips, Bothwell bent his kiss to other pursuits, his rough stubble of beard scratching down her cheek and throat as his hand sought soft curves. Christina kicked at his shins, connecting sharply but causing little damage with her slipper-shod toes.

With another curse he shoved her backward onto the fainting couch positioned conveniently behind these curtains, and before Christina could disentangle her petticoats, he was upon her.

Beneath the lavish scent of his toilet water, Christina could smell the stink of his unwashed body, and her supper came up to lodge in her throat. Cruel hands groped at her breasts, ripping away the fragile bodice of amber silk, and she almost cried at this desecration of her lovely gown. She could not believe this was happening again, not in the midst of crowded London, with all society but on the other side of the curtain! It was just a nasty dream from which she would soon recover.

Bothwell's heavy weight held her pinned, but her fists beat furiously about his head and her feet kicked wildly beneath hampering petticoats. Christina found no temptation in his crude lovemaking, none of the desire the Yankee's kisses had generated, and she had no difficulty in putting up a full-scale war. Only her puny efforts seemed to have no effect on Bothwell's intentions.

As Bothwell's fingers closed wickedly about her bare breast, Christina's hand flew to her mouth, and closing her eyes, she bit deeply into the flesh to muffle her scream. When the urge to scream diverted into an increased will to fight, she opened her eyes again, only to discover dark fires flashing furiously over Bothwell's shoulder. Christina's heart scurried into a dark corner and cowered there beneath the force of the gale to follow.

"Bothwell, if you wish to live to see the morrow, you will remove yourself from my sight immediately."

The timbre of Damien's voice rang ominously quiet, like the roll of thunder before the coming storm, and Bothwell responded with alacrity. Jumping to his feet, he brushed himself off, gave Damien a look of disdain, and without a backward look to the weeping girl on the couch, stalked from the room.

Huddled on the hard cushion with her back turned toward the room, her sobs shuddering her shoulders, Christina clenched at the torn fragments of her bodice and pride, attempting uselessly to hide herself from those all-seeing black eyes.

Damien cursed in a string of epithets that would have done honors to a sailor; then, stripping off his elegant coat, he sat gingerly on the edge of the couch and attempted awkwardly to place it around Christina's shaking shoulders.

"If I did not have other uses for him, I would kill the bastard," Damien muttered darkly. Realizing this admission provided little comfort to anyone but himself, he bent gently over Christina's weeping form. The proud woman he had held on his arm had been reduced to a terrified child in a matter of minutes, and his heart could not bear the change.

Whispering hoarsely, he clasped her shoulders. "We must get you out of here, my love. Be a good girl and let me help you up."

The softness of those cultured tones drew tear-stained velvet eyes up to meet the black-lashed depths of the Yankee's. For a moment compassion flickered there, and then they shuttered closed again.

The strange familiarity of those soft tones roused Christina from her stupor. In dazed confusion she accepted Damien's hand and, clinging to the coat covering her shoulders, rose to her feet. His manly scent surrounded her, and she clasped the silver folds gratefully over her torn bodice. She had learned many things these past few minutes, but she was in no state to appreciate them.

"We cannot go out there with you looking like this." Damien glanced around, his gaze coming to rest on the window, then swerving back to Christina.

With a sudden growl he spied the injured hand clutching the lapels of his coat, and unfolded it gently. "What in hell is this?" He turned her hand up to reveal the blood running from the tiny puncture wounds of her teeth.

Christina said nothing, but attempted to pull away. Comprehension came instantly, and Damien's curses took a new bent as he wound the clean linen of his handkerchief around her hand.

"You learn quickly, but that's a damned good way to give yourself blood poisoning. I think I will kill him after all."

These words were said in the same emotionless tones she knew so well, but his touch was exceedingly gentle as he wrapped her hand and pulled the coat more firmly about her. She sensed the anger tensing his ramrod-straight body, but not an ounce of it reached her.

"If you do not mind a rather unladylike jump, I think we can go out through that window and leave by a less crowded route than the ballroom," he suggested gently, watching her appraisingly.

Christina nodded, willing to do anything to avoid facing that roomful of strangers again.

Damien threw open the double sash and stepped out from the window seat, then turned and lifted Christina carefully after him. His strong arms held her briefly against his chest, then released her to reach in and close the panes again.

They followed a circuitous route through the gardens and down a back hall, where Damien found a servant to carry his message of apology to their host and hostess. Their carriage had pulled up at the front step before Lord Jeremy rushed down the hall after them.

Blue eyes swept worriedly over Christina's trembling figure and unorthodox costume, then turned accusingly to Damien.

"What happened?" he demanded.

"Christina has been taken ill. You might send that pâté back to the kitchen. It had a decidedly off flavor, but this foolish miss has a fondness for it. Beg our excuses with your parents, we cannot linger."

The lies rolled glibly from his tongue as Damien maneuvered them past Jeremy's startled gaze and out into the night.

The coach door closed behind them and Christina collapsed wearily against the velvet cushions. Drained of all strength, she could not even return to the release of tears. She silently closed her eyes and tilted her head back against the cushions as Damien arranged his large frame on the seat opposite.

"Since you have never forgiven me for that first incident, I do not expect you to forgive me for what happened tonight, but I wish to offer my apology anyway."

There was nothing contrite in his tone, but the effort of his words spoke another tale. He seemed to speak his thoughts out loud, an occurrence so unusual, Christina could not help but listen.

"Until tonight, I did not realize how humiliating my treatment of you has been. Bothwell . . . Damn, but I wanted to kill him! this accursed . . ." He halted, stopping the flow of words before starting in another direction. Forced to consider her as a person in her own right and not the object of his own goals, Damien lost some of his usual eloquence. Fury raged through his veins, fury as much at his own stupidity as Bothwell's degeneracy. He had done no more nor less than Bothwell, but had excused his behavior by offering what he considered to be fair reparation. Convenient for him, perhaps, but at no time had he considered how Christina would view his offer. She was too young to look upon the relationship between men and women from his cynical but practical viewpoint, and he was scarcely in any position to offer any more. In fact, she would be better off to continue hating him. The point seemed moot now.

He continued slowly, searching for words to express his apology for all that had come before and would follow now. "If I can feel this way about Bothwell's callous assault, I do not wish to imagine how you must feel. I have selfishly ignored your feelings for too long. I see now you were not meant for the life I intended for you. You deserve to be treated as the lady you are, and not the whore Bothwell imagined you to be. Too late, perhaps, I see what you have been telling me all along, and I sincerely apologize for my blindness."

Christina did not think he fully understood the extent of her fears, but it helped to know he now realized there was little difference in his assault and Bothwell's. She enjoyed the privilege of being thought a lady, but that title mattered little when all around her thought it synonymous with "toy doll." She wished he would recognize her as a woman with the same thoughts and dreams and feelings as he, but that seemed a little much to ask.

She had to acknowledge his speech in some way, and having no wish to incite an argument, she murmured, "Thank you, milord," and fell silent again.

He followed suit and they traveled the dark streets in silence.

Ben Thomas gazed dispassionately at the not-quite-sober young man lounging carelessly in the leather chair beside the fireplace in his study. Somewhere during the evening Drayton had discarded his powdered wig, and his elegantly tailored coat now lay in a heap upon the floor, but even in this state he retained some semblance of the forceful, highly independent character the lawyer knew him to be. Ben waited patiently.

"Dammit all, Ben, I ruined her in Cornwall. What would you have me do with her?"

The question was obviously rhetorical under the circumstances, but Ben could not resist the reply lingering on his tongue. "You could marry her," he suggested.

Damien exploded. "Haven't you heard a thing I've said? She loathes the ground I walk on, and rightly so. Best damned thing for her." He threw back a swift gulp of the drink he held in his hand. "I've got enough on my mind without worrying about leaving weeping widows behind." He snorted, playing out the scenario in his mind. "Can't you imagine the horror of some genteel English lady learning what kind of criminal she has married? Use your imagination, Ben. What do you think would become of her and her invalid mother when they learn who I really am? Hell, what I need is a mistress, not a wife. Don't you have any suggestions?"

Ben poured himself a drink, prolonging his silence. He had known Damien Drayton since he was just a lad, knew better than most the earl's multiple talents and single-mindedness, and knew better than to argue. Once Drayton determined his goal, he would accomplish it or die trying. This time, the latter seemed the more likely occurrence. The fact that this girl had distracted him to this degree said much, for Damien had never been one to allow a woman to stand in his way. He had a singular aptitude for treating women like objects to be placed as he desired. Never before had one objected to this treatment. Ben wished he could meet the lass who had finally opened the boy's eyes, but he doubted that this rare introspection would last for long. Damien was one for action and not introspection.

Ben took a sip of his drink and gave his fully considered reply. "You had best find the girl's uncle. If you can keep him from calling you out or throttling you bare-handed . . ."

Damien rose from the chair and reached for the cigar box on the mantel. "He seems to have disappeared from the face of the earth, and I am running out of time. If I don't find him soon, I'll have to send her back to Cornwall."

Ben heard the reluctance in the younger man's voice and marveled at it. "Or make her your mistress?" he suggested softly.

Damien continued staring at the fire, remembering the sudden flare of eager hope in her amber eyes at the promise of a very uncertain freedom. He could do it, but he wouldn't. "She'd make some man a good wife, but a lousy mistress. Find her uncle for me, Ben."

9

Christina discovered Damien regaling her mother with the gaieties of the previous night's ball and gave a smile of relief. She had been avoiding her mother's eager questions, not knowing how she could hide the dismal outcome of the evening, but Damien had saved the day with his blithe lies again.

Eleanor MacTavish looked up at her daughter's entrance, her eyes bright and shining with pride as she gazed upon the handsome young couple. She felt better than she had in years, and the lines of worry were gradually fading from her brow.

"Damien has been telling me what a success you were last evening. I only wish I had been there to see it. Your father would have been so proud."

Christina cringed inwardly at this mention of her father, but managed to produce a weak smile. Damien's dark eyes observed her difficulty dispassionately, but a moment later he made their excuses.

"I do not wish to tire you, my lady, and I need to borrow your daughter for a while. Would you excuse us?"

Eleanor beamed her approval and Christina soon found herself back in their sitting room confronting the Yankee's frowning visage.

"My lord?" she inquired gently.

Damien's thoughts returned from whence they had wandered and his frown disappeared as his gaze rested on Christina's fragile grace. In her light muslin gown, golden curls cascading down her back in rich profusion, she seemed no more than a slim willow wand to bend easily under any burden. He had been insane to believe this ladylike girl could perform the duties at which more experienced women would have cringed. His desire had got the better of his senses. He would rectify the error immediately.

"I have taken the liberty of writing to your uncle myself," he stated calmly. "You need a guardian to look after you as I cannot. I am familiar with the story of your mother's family and their disapproval of Argus MacTavish, but I see no reason why the past should continue to maim the future."

Christina's eyes widened as she gazed upon this astonishing man. He knew everything about her, but revealed so little of himself. Who was he really? Some moment from the prior evening tugged frantically at her memory, but it continued to elude her as it had all morning. She shrugged it away and raised her chin proudly.

"Thank you for your concern, my lord, but I have looked after myself these past two years and can continue to do so. Now that my mother is improving, I can begin to look for a suitable position. You need not worry about me any longer."

Damien grimaced at the continued use of his title, but for once did not argue it. "I would prefer you not return to Cornwall. My reputation has irreparably damaged yours and only further harm can come of it. But we will discuss this later when your uncle arrives. I think he dare not ignore my summons."

Christina sighed and paced to the end of the room, staring out over the fog-laden streets below. "The country is my home, my lord. The city's excitements pall quickly. Perhaps you were right when you said I had too much of my father in me. He loved Cornwall and the sea and would not come to London unless begged. Now I understand why."

He moved so quietly she did not know he was there until he laid a brown hand on her shoulder. His fingers were long and sensitive, but callused by hard word. She had not taken time to notice that before.

"I can sympathize with that feeling. There are days when I long for a rolling deck beneath my feet and the salt wind in my face, but we all must do what our lives require of us."

Christina could not hide the astonishment in her eyes as she looked up at him, and Damien acknowledged her look with a tight smile.

"There are still some days left of our fortnight, Miss MacTavish. Would you do me the honor of touring the remainder of the city with me during that time?"

The tantalizing glimpses of the man behind the mask came and went too quickly; Christina found it hard to adjust. But the hand resting familiarly on her shoulder gave her a strange feeling of security. "I would enjoy that, my lord . . ." At his pained expression she hastily amended, "Damien. But if I am not too bold, I wonder if I could ask a favor of you?"

At his nod, she continued bravely. "I do not like to disturb your study, but when your maids packed my trunk, they did not include my writing paper. They could have left all my clothes behind, and I would not miss them as I do the paper."

Damien raised an eyebrow in surprise, but did not question her plea. "By all means, help yourself to whatever you find. I doubt if my uncle ever once put pen to paper, and when I am gone, all that remains will rot. There should be quantities at your disposal."

She bobbed her head gratefully and breathed a sigh of relief when he was gone. She did not understand what game this Yankee played, only that it was a dangerous one. His very presence made her tremble, even when he attempted to be kind.

Still, she had agreed willingly to accompany him in the afternoons, and she could not deny that she enjoyed these outings. Now that the tension between them had been lowered to a reasonable degree by his apology, Christina developed a fondness for the furious give-and-take of their conversation. She also learned a good deal more about London and the colonies than Mrs. Grenoble's Academy had ever thought to teach her.

Yet, when asked about this war the colonies had declared and his own part in it, Damien grew strangely silent. He more than willingly discussed the arbitrary taxing and shipping regulations that had forced the colonists into rebellion, described the present sorry state of affairs of both armies at present, but he carefully avoided giving his opinion or mentioning his family's part in the bitter war. She had heard there were many wealthy colonists who loyally aided the British troops, and she had assumed him to be among these, but a shadow of a doubt crept in as she examined the forcefulness of his arguments on the other side compared with those he gave for England.

As if realizing he had said too much, the Yankee retreated from the subject and for the rest of their outings contrived to keep their topics on less political grounds. He toured the city as one saying farewell, lingering in parks and pleasant shops and coffeehouses, but observing the darker side of the city with grim determination. Christina often wondered at his choice of destinations, but made no comment when they spent much time traversing the streets in and around Covent Garden.

He continued disappearing in the evenings, coming home at abominable hours of the morning. Christina grew accustomed to the sound of his heavy tread outside her door just as the dawn's light threw its gray shadows upon the room. Occasionally he seemed to linger momentarily, and she held her breath, but he always continued on, sometimes with more than a stagger to betray his condition.

Jeremy and his sister called frequently, but his lordship held no more dinners to entertain these or any other guests. Damien scarcely seemed aware that his friends continued to call, for he was seldom awake or present when they came. Christina felt a vague sense of relief at this development, and Seraphina's disappointed expression did not make her feel in the least guilty.

With the household achieving some semblance of order under Mrs. Douglass' heroic efforts, Christina found the time to steal away to the tall secretary in the library, where she had ferreted away a large supply of writing stock. Her journal had been sadly neglected these last weeks, and her mind teemed with scenes and characters that begged for cohesion.

The unexpected sight of that golden head bent industriously over the rosewood desk brought Damien to a halt in the shadowed doorway. The early-afternoon sun poured through the tall library casements, illuminating airborne dust motes in a surreal dance over the golden halo of Christina's curls. He watched, fascinated, as the old quill fairly flew over the vellum.

Just the other day he had found one of those sheets rumpled and discarded beside the wastebasket, and he had carefully smoothed it out until the simple script had become legible. The page contained no more than an imaginative description of a household incident, but her words had caught the characters involved with amazing accuracy until the scene had jumped from the page to play before him.

Damien longed to see the pages beneath that slender hand now, but he did not dare betray his longing. A sense of loss swept over him as his gaze focused upon Christina's slight figure. His own actions had destroyed all chance of any further knowledge of this proud creature, and a painful awareness of his own shortcomings gnawed at his heart. Always duty and country before personal gain. His fingers bit inward to stab his palm, and he straightened to leave, when Christina sensed his presence.

Glancing up, she found Damien standing in the doorway, the brown angles of his face strangely pensive as black eyes studied her. Unaware of the golden picture she created in the sunbeam, she tilted her chin up, revealing the golden flecks of amber eyes as she spoke.

"My lord?" she inquired gently.

He had stripped off coat and waistcoat and stood framed in the archway, strangely informal in his wide-sleeved shirt and snowy cravat, his wide shoulders straining at tailored seams. Resting one hand against the door frame, he seemed almost to be restraining himself as his dark gaze rested yearningly on the peaceful scene.

Her words intruded on his reverie, and Damien replied to them with difficulty. "I apologize. I was only contemplating the life I have chosen to forgo. Sometimes it becomes difficult to remember that the principle is more important than the man. I am sorry I disturbed you."

His dark face had a strange, haunted look as he turned away from the sunlit room, and Christina longed for the power to race after him for explanations. His exit left her with a disturbingly racing heartbeat.

Only a few days remained of their fortnight. Soon she would banish herself forever to the lonely life of Cornwall and penury, never to see this mysterious Yankee earl again. Once she had wanted that more than life itself, but now . . . Christina shook away the cobwebs of her mind. She still detested the man, but she had begun to understand there was more to him than readily met the eye.

Then, there was still the problem of her mother. Under the physician's support and guidance, with the careful diet he recommended, and the rest and relaxation of having nothing about which to worry, Mrs. MacTavish slowly recovered. Yet she still had not the strength to sit for long and needed constant attendance. How would she survive once returned to Cornwall?

Christina shied away from such thoughts. Her uncle must surely come soon. She need only be patient. Perhaps Damien would give them a little more time.

These thoughts persistently pursued themselves round and round in Christina's mind as she toyed with her dinner. Damien had grown strangely silent as they ate. She no longer felt nervous under his scrutiny, and she had come to enjoy the polite conversation they engaged in before he took himself off to whatever dissipated pastimes he had found to pursue in the evenings. Now they had both grown silent and the polite air of formality lagged.

Damien held the fragile stem of his goblet between strong fingers, swirling the wine and staring at it absently. From the corner of his eye he observed Christina's bent head, the golden curls pinned and stacked artistically above her nape. In the candlelight she seemed particularly young and vulnerable, and he wondered afresh at his audacity in propositioning her so crudely. Perhaps the colonies had a savaging effect on people. Still, he did not think her quite so weak as those society misses he was forced to attend. Though vulnerable, she did not weep or develop vapors to emphasize the fact. He admired her natural courage more than he dared admit.

"I have not heard you sing or play since that first night, Christina. The spinet has been tuned since then. Will you play for me after dinner?"

Amber eyes lifted solemnly to study him; then, deciding he did not jest, she nodded carefully. "If you wish. The spinet may be improved, but I doubt that I am."

Damien hid a small grin at this prickly modesty. She played better than many of the pampered maidens whose mothers crowed their prowess, but who was he to enlighten her?

"It is a pity you do not have such an instrument in Cornwall. Perhaps your uncle does. Music can be soothing as well as entertaining."

Christina stared at her plate. "I have not yet made any decision on returning to Cornwall," she murmured flatly.

The crystal stem snapped between Damien's fingers, spilling wine across the linen tablecloth. Hastily sopping up the growing stain with his napkin, Damien could not keep the thundering pounding of hope from his ears as he fought for words to fill the gap.

Treading delicately around the obvious, he offered,

"I will do my best to protect you from the likes of Bothwell if you stay, but you must know you will be scorned by polite society."

"That is the least of my worries," Christina replied grimly, refusing to meet his gaze. She had surprised herself with the words, but knew them to be true. Nothing awaited her in Cornwall. Why should she return? Simply to protect her nonexistent virtue? She had grown as cynical as he, it seemed.

Damien felt a cold chill of premonition at the hard edge her voice had taken, but if he had only months left to live, why should he not enjoy them to the fullest? She would be the better for it, after he was gone. Still, she was young, and he could not let her make such a decision blindly.

"Should you choose to stay, your name will be on every man's tongue, and not in a manner to which you are accustomed. I will expect you to accompany me when I go to the park or the theater or those houses where gentlemen are welcome with their mistresses. I am not talking about a quiet, back-street affair. For what I have in mind, we will be very, very public."

Christina choked down the last morsel of food and set down her fork. She felt her cheeks crimsoning and did not dare look at the stern man addressing her so calmly. She did not think the public humiliation he spoke of would be so difficult as the act that would lead to it. The humiliation she had already suffered at men's hands was much more personal and poisonous than flapping tongues and sly remarks.

"I have not yet made any decision," she stated quietly, folding her napkin and laying it on the table.

His ears still sang with the excitement of revived hope, but he was careful not to press too quickly. Rising, Damien offered his hand, and they retreated to the drawing room, where the newly repaired spinet beckoned.

Christina sat down and began riffling through the music at hand. To her surprise, Damien appropriated the seat beside her.

At her questioning look, he ran a scale with long, sensitive fingers. "I used to play a bit. I thought we might make a duet."

Nothing about this man shocked her any longer. She nodded agreement and produced a piece well adapted to accompaniment.

His deep baritone was surprisingly good and after they had worked their way through a piece or two, Christina began to accept his unnerving presence beside her. The challenge of conquering the melody and the words and creating harmony erased the differences between them, temporarily.

In a moment of irritation at his claim that she played a particular piece too slowly, Christina ran through a few bars of "Yankee Doodle" in retaliation. To her shock, Damien picked up the refrain, then sung a mocking verse she had never heard.

Not to be outdone, Christina followed it with a particularly insulting version she knew. Damien laughed and turned it into a suggestive verse, which caused her to blush furiously.

Together they pounded through the chorus until their laughter made mockery of singing, and then, before Christina quite understood what had happened, she was in his arms, their lips seeking each other's blindly.

She had no thought of fighting him, but held desperately to his lapels as their lips met and meshed and parted with a fierce need that terrified her. She felt his strong arms clench her possessively and welcomed their strength. She had need of it, for she felt herself fast melting into jelly. The clean, musky odor of his skin filled her senses, the hard line of his mouth held and plundered hers, and her heart beat wildly against his chest.

When his lips released hers, Christina continued to cling to his coat, burying her face against the reassuring warmth of the fine material, not ready to relinquish his hold quite yet.

"I have never heard you laugh before, lass," Damien

murmured against the fragrant upsweep of golden curls. Her supple young body pressed against his created electrifying currents needing diverting. "You are too young to be so solemn."

Christina thought about that and not the feel of his large hands molded against her back. She had thought the same of him, that he never laughed. This insight into how he saw her made her stop and think. How odd that the Yankee should notice something of herself that she had not.

Gently she extricated herself from his embrace. "Sometimes I feel a thousand years old. I used to laugh."

"Before your father died, you mean?" Dark eyes studied her face with absorption, reading every line and flutter of long lashes.

He held her hands and she took comfort in it. She never spoke of her father's death. It still brought tears to her eyes. She nodded, lashes hiding the depths of sorrow in her amber eyes.

He was not fooled. Tilting her chin up, Damien forced her to look at him. "I think I know the name of the man who killed him."

Christina clutched his hand tighter, her fingernails biting deep into his palm. She still did not dare speak, but her eyes spoke for her.

Damien shook his head. "To tell you would be dangerous. I suspect he is the same man responsible for my father's exile. While I am here, I intend to find him, but revenge will not return your father. You must decide what will make you happy again. Your father would have wanted that."

Christina stifled a sob, forcing her mind to focus on the importance of his words and not her sense of loss. She knew he would not tell her more about this unknown enemy, but she wanted to hear more of her father.

Amber eyes glistening with moisture, she asked hesitantly, "How do you know my father?"

He sifted his words carefully before replying.

"We had reason to correspond after my father's death.

I met him once. That is all. But from his letters and actions I knew him to be a good man, a man of character and determination. There is much of him in you, Christina, if you will just realize it."

Wonder sparkled behind the tears. How could this Yankee know anything of her or her father? Those cold, hard planes of his dark face revealed his arrogant self-centeredness. He saw her only as a toy to be fondled and played with. Or did he?

Could it be possible that these kind words meant he saw her as a woman in her own right? A person with character and intellience and not just a woman to be seduced?

Too late she saw the folly of such thoughts. She had reason to believe him a master of disguise, a man of many faces, and this was just another of his roles. He had guessed her weaknesses and played upon them successfully.

Christina's heart sank as she withdrew her hand from the protective shelter of his.

"My father pampered me as he pampered my mother. I see that now. But I will learn to make it on my own. I can do it."

Damien bit back a grin at the defiant tilt of her delectable chin. "So you can, if you put your mind to it, but will you do it frowning or laughing? You have only a few days in which to decide." At her troubled look, he added gently, "I think you know why I cannot keep you here if you decide against me."

Christina nodded and looked away again. The heat of his kiss still burned against her lips, and she had learned to recognize the gleam of hunger in his eyes. He had behaved as honorably as it was possible for him these last weeks. To ask him to continue longer would be an impossibility. And her own resistance was growing strangely weak.

Damien rose and kissed the top of her head. "I must be off. Sleep on it these next nights. I will accept whatever decision you make."

He might, but could she?"

* * *

In a room strangely elegant for a warehouse overlooking the filthy Thames, two men drew deeply on long pipes, filling the close air with a pungent fragrance. The elder, though reclining carelessly on a bed strewn with black satin pillows, covertly studied the younger through narrowed eyes.

"You say he lost how much at a hand of cards?" The speaker's flintlike eyes watched carefully as his companion settled himself more comfortably on the gold velvet divan.

"Thousand pounds or more, all told. Don't know where he gets it. The house is a shambles, but he drives some fancy cattle. And that wench of his can't be too cheap." The gray-eyed younger man drew deeply of the smoke and held it with a small smile of pleasure.

"Sure as hell didn't come from dear old dad. We milked the estate for all it was worth, and then some," Nicholas commented idly, while his shrewd mind followed another train of thought. "Perhaps he's following the family tradition. Old Anson wasn't doing too badly for a colonial."

His companion exhaled, blowing a ring of smoke into the already murky room. "Wouldn't mind having a share of it, or the wench, either."

"There's a woman, you say?" With the hard lines of his face relaxed in a speculative smile, Nicholas showed some of the striking handsomeness that had once been his before a dissolute life and cynical bitterness had ravaged the charm from his features.

"Some doxy he's found out in the country and is passing off as a lady. I think she almost believes it herself, the way he carts her around and introduces her to society. Very amusing, but I daresay he's promised her the world, and it will cost him, sooner or later."

"A whore?" Disappointed, Nicholas emptied his pipe atop a half-consumed meal. "Can't reach him that way. You'll have to do it for me, Bothwell." He smiled to himself at the younger man's suddenly cautious air.

"Do what?" The languorous effects of the pipe evaporated as Bothwell studied his host suspiciously.

"Nothing of which Pretty Patty won't approve. She's waiting for you in the other room, by the way." Nicholas drew a long thin-bladed dagger from his belt and began to pare nonchalantly at his nails. "You marked her rather harshly last time—she still has some of the bruises, and the cut on her lip will probably scar. Still, she says she likes that in a man. Whores like that are hard to come by."

Bothwell grunted uncommunicatively, but his icy eyes took on an expectant gleam. "They all like a little roughness. But Patty, now . . ."

The smile on his lips never touched his eyes as Nicholas began to speak. "Then let me tell you what we need to do. . . ."

10

Christina listened to the clock on the landing strike three times. She had retired shortly after Damien's departure, but she could not sleep.

She tossed once again, seeking a cool spot amid the sheets to soothe her heated skin. The blasted man had taught her the meaning of desire and left her to suffer its aches unassuaged. Would the memory of his fingers upon her skin never leave? Must she suffer forever after this craving for his penetrating kisses?

If only that would be enough to satisfy him! She might gladly parade herself as his mistress if all he asked in return were her kisses. But her body still cringed at the thought of his harsh invasion, and her fear of him did not diminish. It was a contradiction she could not come to terms with, and she lay sleeplessly contemplating the impossible.

The uneven stagger of running feet echoed through the window she had opened earlier. A cool miasma hung in the air, reminding her of Cornwall, and she considered rising to close it. London was not Cornwall. Who knew what horrors took place below?

The sound of running feet on the cobblestones became a frantic beat against a door. It seemed strangely weak, and Christina's ears strained to find the location. Before she could, a hauntingly familiar whistle pierced the night, sending a sudden shock of recognition to the pit of her stomach. With growing horror she realized the sound came from below, and jumping from the bed, she scrambled for a candle and her robe at the same time, not even hesitating to understand what she must have known all along.

Precious minutes were lost in lighting the elusive wick and wrapping the robe securely before hastening to the hall. Not for a second did she doubt the source of the sound. The pounding had switched to a frantic attempt at lifting the bar from the outside. An impossible feat.

Racing down the stairs, she reached the foyer out of breath and set the candle on the post. With pounding heartbeat she struggled to lift the heavy oak bar.

With relief she heard the heavy tread of footsteps behind her, and at the butler's sonorous "Allow me, miss," she stepped aside.

The door swung open magically and Lord Westshipham staggered through, his white linen stained with red, his dark face paled to gray. Jenkins caught him up and held him firmly while Christina shoved closed the door, ignoring the wretched bolt.

"Can you get him upstairs?" Frantic, Christina watched the seep of blood through long fingers as Damien clutched the linen over his shoulder.

"Dammit, no, hide me in the servants' quarters somewhere. They're right behind me," he muttered thickly.

For the first time Christina noticed the familiar dark cloak flung about his shoulders and the rapier dangling at his side. Comprehension came quickly, and she gestured to Jenkins.

"My room's at the top of the stairs. Take him there while I search for bandages."

Neither man questioned her decision. Damien had exhausted his strength and the butler had no comprehension of the problem.

Jenkins had dumped his master across the pink ruffled bed and now struggled with his boots as Christina returned to the room with bandages. She had forgotten Damien had worn boots that evening. With a wild swing of her thoughts, she wondered where the highwayman's stallion was.

With a sharp jerk on her wandering attention, Christina hastily returned to the mundane. With Jenkins' help, they propped up Damien's bleeding shoulder and cut away the jacket and linen beneath. Gradually Damien's bronzed torso emerged from the layers of clothing, and Christina choked back a cry of dismay.

The coarse threads of his linen had stanched some of the bleeding, but once they were pulled away, the wound bled copiously. Damien's lashes fluttered open at the sound of her gasp, and with a wry twist of his lips he greeted her.

"Damn bloody-lookin' mess, ain't it? Just patch it up some so I don't leave a trail, and I'll be gone."

"Not bloody likely," Christina replied caustically in his own language. To Jenkins she ordered, "Bring me a bottle of brandy, take away these rags, and bring another set of clothes for his lordship."

The butler departed and Damien closed his eyes against the pain as Christina set about cleaning the wound. Once she had washed away the blood, she could see it was a clean slice, nearly to the bone, but only muscle seemed harmed.

"Christina, they've got a Bow Street runner on my heels," he whispered through clenched teeth. "I reckon Bothwell has given them my name, and they'll be here any minute. You've got to get me out of here."

His accent seemed to blend Yankee twang with Oxford drawl, but Christina ignored this anomaly and his admonition. As Jenkins reappeared, she gave him further instructions.

"Soak the clothes with some of that brandy and give me the rest. Just scatter them about the floor there." She gestured toward the carpet. "If anyone comes to the door, make them wait as if you were still in bed. After you let them in, hold them off until I come down. Do you understand?"

The older man's nearly lashless eyes grew wide, but some inkling of the predicament entered his brain, and he bowed wordlessly. Loyalty prevented any other response.

As he departed, black eyes opened once again to observe Christina's pale face above her scanty dishabille. Tawny curls fell in disarray over a silken robe of palest gold, its clinging softness leaving little to the imagination. With a cynical lift to his eyebrows, Damien threw a glance to the masculine attire now scattered across the floor of this feminine bedroom. The reek of brandy rose to his nose even before she applied it to his wound.

"Do you know what you are doing?" he asked sardonically.

"Unfortunately, yes," she replied with equal cynicism.

Satisfied that she understood the full meaning of her deeds, Damien closed his eyes and allowed the waves of pain to wash over him as she applied the brandy generously to his torn shoulder.

A loud banging below jolted her nervous fingers, but Christina hurried to finish the dressing. It would not do to save his worthless neck from the gallows if he should bleed to death in the process. With care she cleaned and stanched the wound, but for what she had in mind, she dared not strap it yet.

"Damien, my lord, can you hear me?" she whispered as loud voices broke into the foyer below and echoed up the stairs.

His eyes opened again. Glazed with pain, they still held sharp intelligence, and she breathed a sigh of relief.

"You must turn over to hide the bandage. Can you do that?"

He nodded, and with her assistance sprawled across the rumpled linen of her pink ruffled bed. The powerful, half-naked masculine figure usurped an incongruous amount of room in the dainty bed, and Christina bit back a gulp of fear. She had to be as mad as he. There was no other explanation for it. She threw the covers to conceal his breeches, leaving only his naked torso exposed.

She could linger no longer. Praying the bandage

would hold until she returned, Christina descended the stairs into the fracas below.

As the golden figure of this slender goddess appeared above them, the men below grew quiet. All eyes followed her descent, and Christina felt her skin crawl beneath the sensuous silk as she recognized the icy eyes of Bothwell. The others were unfamiliar, but the rough garb of the Bow Street runner separated him from the gentlemen.

Ignoring them all, she turned to the butler. "What is the meaning of this, Jenkins?" she asked quietly.

The gentleman's gentleman observed this performance appreciatively and nodded solemn approval before replying. "These gentlemen seem to be under the misapprehension that they might disturb his lordship at any time of night, miss."

Christina's gaze swept over the trio of gentlemen, two of whom shifted nervously under her wide-eyed amazement. Bothwell watched her through half-closed eyes, a knowing smirk pulling the corners of his mouth.

The fourth man was of a smaller, more compact stature. His partially balding head was on a level with Christina's and his animated blue eyes made no secret of their inspection. Still, she found no maliciousness in his open admiration, and when he spoke, she listened intently.

"Jack Hastings, of Bow Street, ma'am," he introduced himself. "These 'ere gentlemen claim 'is lordship be the perpetrator of assault and murder in the vi-ci-nity of Covent Garden this evenin'. I'm 'ere to 'ave 'im answer to that charge."

He had obviously practiced this lovely formality with much deliberation and smiled with satisfaction at his delivery. He shoved his gnarled hands in the wide pockets of his loose brown homespun coat and gazed expectantly at the lovely lady.

Christina swung about to face the butler questioningly, as if uncertain she comprehended the words.

Jenkins' slow tones confirmed the impossible. "He

claims he is from the Bow Street court, miss, and has the power to search the house."

"Miss MacTavish, if you will just let the man follow the trail of Drayton's blood, there will be an end to this nonsense. I daresay he's bleeding like a stuck pig in some back room somewhere. Let us search him out."

Bothwell's arrogant tones rang jarringly against the respectable scene Christina's presence had forced upon them, and the others gave him looks ranging from disgust to disbelief.

Realizing every second spent would mean that much blood lost, Christina hastened to put an end to the scene before it grew uglier.

"These gentlemen have no power from the court, do they, Mr. Hastings?" she asked coldly.

"No, ma'am, but if we all search, or if you'll tell us where 'e is, we'll be out of the way that much faster, ma'am."

"Very well, Mr. Hastings. If you will come with me, I will prove the wrongfulness of these charges, but I must insist these gentlemen remain where they are." Her amber eyes rested coldly on the offending Bothwell. His two companions gave him murderous glances and stepped away, as if to disavow their acquaintance with him.

The officer of the law beamed appreciatively. "Right you are, ma'am—Miss MacTavish," he amended.

Jenkins eyed her disbelievingly as Christina led the rough little man up the broad mahogany stairs of Westshipham House. Her slender beauty and the runner's bow-legged figure reached the landing and disappeared out of sight.

Christina stopped outside her bedroom door, allowing the little man to catch up, his eyes wide and staring as he took in the elegance of polished paneling and silk drapings. His job seldom took him into the posh realms of the nobility.

"Mr. Hastings, do I have your word that what you see here tonight will go no further than this door?" she demanded imperiously.

"Well, ma'am, Miss MacTavish, if it comes to court . . ." He hesitated, fearful she would refuse but not wishing to compromise his duty.

"Under the circumstances, it should not. Lord Westshipham is scarcely guilty of such heinous crimes as you charge him with, but he is guilty of sins you must see frequently in your work, Mr. Hastings."

With these words Christina threw open the paneled door, giving a full view of the scandalous interior.

Damien's clothes lay rumpled and reeking in a trail across the floor, as if thrown there in haste. Partially covered by wrinkled sheets, his healthy, tanned torso lay sprawled across the feminine bed, his inebriated snores reverberating through the room. To all appearances the drunken lecher lay in a stupor after having spent himself in his lover's bed.

Clouded blue eyes turned back to Christina's slim young figure as if to confirm what they saw.

Christina held her chin defiantly high. "He has many faults, Mr. Hastings, b-but m-murder is not among them."

"'E been with you all evenin'?" The man could not hide his disappointment at her nod.

"And if the m-man you seek has been w-wounded, his l-lordship is obviously not the one." She allowed a note of disdain to creep in her voice, hiding her nervous stutter.

"No, ma'am, I suppose not."

As she pulled the door closed, her face developed a thoughtful frown, and she whispered conspiratorially, "You do not suppose those gentlemen were playing some kind of practical joke? His lordship jested the other day that he had put Mr. Bothwell in a stew. I did not inquire at the time, but could this be his idea of revenge?"

Hastings' blue eyes grew cold and stony as this possibility penetrated. The man in that bedroom had obviously not stirred for hours, as what man would, given the circumstances? Why would those arrogant gentlemen below say he was where he was not? One glance at Christina's anxious face answered that question.

"Do not worry yourself, Miss MacTavish. If that be the case, I'll put a 'alt to their lyin' days once and fer all."

And with that ominous warning the man departed, leaving Christina standing in the upper hall. She had no desire to meet those eager gazes below again, and with decision she opened the door and reentered her chambers.

Damien had thrown off the sheets and was already attempting to turn over when Christina entered. At her mild curse, he collapsed among the pillows and turned a devilishly wicked look upon her.

"Your lies are most transparent, Miss MacTavish. You think me a murderer."

"And your escapades are foolish enough to include murder, my lord. Lie there until they are gone. That Bothwell would raise a fury if he actually saw you at your deadly deeds."

Damien's face blackened. "He dared come here? I will have his heart out, the filthy blackguard."

As cool fingers rested against his feverish skin to check the bandage, his expression softened. "You realize what you have done, don't you?"

Christina nodded glumly. "I don't suppose even a Bow Street runner is capable of keeping his tongue from flapping, particularly with the likes of Bothwell breathing down his neck."

"There will be time enough to get you out of here," Damien responded roughly as he jerked his head away from her fingers.

"There seems little point in that, milord. The deed is done."

The downstairs door slammed closed and ponderous footsteps began their tired tread upward.

"Is this your decision, then?" he whispered anxiously.

Christina held the blood-soaked pad to Damien's shoulder as he rolled over, ebony eyes searching her face with care.

"It would seem so, milord," she answered miserably, downcast eyes on the wound she tended and not the formidable male figure beyond.

Jenkins knocked sharply and entered at Damien's call.

"Help me sit while she straps this damned bandage in place," he commanded the solemn butler.

A clean compress was applied and tied in place and Damien lowered gently against the pillows. Jenkins glanced nervously at the slight figure in gold, and back again to his employer.

"Shall I send for a physician, milord?"

Damien's gaze too followed the feminine figure as she moved about the room. "No. If they are watching the house, it would be dangerous. I'll go in the morning."

"Then shall I assist you back to your chambers, milord?"

Christina interrupted impatiently. "Leave him there, Jenkins. That wound must close if it is to stop bleeding. A physician is needed, but if he must be obstinate, he'd best not be moved again."

Uncertainly the older man looked to Damien for approval of this highly improper order.

Casting a dark gaze to Christina's averted face, Damien nodded slowly. "Go, Jenkins . . . and thank you."

Properly dismissed, the astonished butler bowed out, leaving the young couple alone.

"You are certain, Christina?"

Christina washed her trembling hands in the basin, avoiding those penetrating, deep-set eyes. "I am certain of nothing, Mr. Highwayman." Her voice shook and she took a deep gulp of air. "Will you tell me what happened?"

"Not now, Christina. In the morning. Come to bed, I cannot harm you like this." The commanding quality of his words was softened by his voice as he observed her trembling fingers. He found his good fortune at this moment of disaster to be difficult to believe, but he would do nothing to dissipate the dream.

Christina dried her hands and bolted the door carefully. She must learn to brave her fears sometime, and there would never be a more appropriate opportunity. If she continued to fear what happened between men and women, she would make no man a good wife, and she would never marry anyway. What did she have to lose, except the means of keeping her mother alive should she refuse?

It made things easier to know he was the highwayman and not just the cold earl he had showed to her these last weeks. Such reasoning was a kind of madness, she realized, but she could not help feeling relief at knowing there was another side to him. The highwayman had been kind and gentle when he had no need to be. She placed her trust in this very elusive memory.

Christina quietly returned to the bedside. Damien's eyes had closed in pain and weariness, and she gazed down upon his wounded male form with awe and trepidation. When his lashes flickered open again, she blew out the candle. The silk of her robe rustled to the floor before her weight bent the soft feather ticking lightly.

Damien's hand reached out to enfold hers, and Christina felt the heat of his large body just inches away. Beside his hard strength she felt lost and vulnerable, but he did no more than hold her hand.

"That was a courageous performance you staged, my love."

"And quick thinking," she added with dry sarcasm, ignoring his term of endearment.

"That too, but mostly courageous. I was not certain I could trust your loyalty or your bravery. Another would have sent me to Tyburn and laughed about it. There is more to you than readily meets the eye."

"I will take that as a compliment, my lord. Had it served my purpose to have you hanged, I would have allowed them to do so. Do not test my loyalty."

This whispered conversation with a strange man in her hitherto feminine bed had a disturbingly unsettling effect, and Christina hastened to end it. "Go to sleep, milord."

Damien chuckled in the darkness. "You expect me to sleep after that statement? I fear waking to find my throat slit. Good night, Christina."

The comforting rhythm of his soft snores soon filled the room and gradually Christina slept to the music of them.

11

She woke to find the bed beside her cold, but the pillow still dented where his head had rested. A blood spot on the sheets confirmed the night before had not been a dream, and her hand slowly drifted over the linen that had so recently covered his half-naked body. Her second night with a man had been much less fearsome than the first but no less eventful. What happened next?

Dreading that question, Christina rose and washed thoroughly. She feared calling for a bath, feared her fall from grace would already be known to the servants. How would she face the formidable Mrs. Douglass? The very thought made her quake. What had Damien called her last night? Courageous? She felt nothing akin to courage now.

Methodically she donned chemise and petticoats. She was in no hurry to face whatever awaited her below. Perhaps she should have let the Yankee hang. It certainly had a certain ring of justice to it, particularly now that she had learned of his dual role. The cad.

But he knew her father, knew her father's murderer, and offered a means of returning her mother to health. At the moment Damien was the only friend she had, if she could call him that. Lord Jeremy and Lady Seraphina were pleasant, but they knew nothing of her. The Yankee knew everything. It made a difference, although she was at a loss to discern why.

A sharp knock at the door startled her from her reverie. Grabbing a linen towel, she covered herself and called out, "Who is it?" but she knew that knock without being told.

Damien slipped through the door, dark eyes immediately finding her and raking her from half-covered bosom to unstockinged feet. A small smile crossed his lips as he made a more leisurely inspection in the other direction, beginning with a shapely turn of ankle, lingering on full curves pushed generously above the chemise.

Christina flushed crimson as much in anger as embarrassment. "Are you quite satisfied with your purchase, milord?"

"Under the circumstances, you really must become accustomed to calling me Damien, my dear. And I have not purchased you yet. As a matter of fact, that is why I have intruded so inopportunely, or opportunely, as the case may be."

He stepped forward, watching the play of fear and indecision cross her delicate features. This westerly room held little light at this time of day, but it was enough to enhance the golden beauty of the frightened creature before him. Creamy skin tinted with hues of rose beckoned to be touched, the tiny golden hairs along her bare arm begged to be stroked, but terrified amber eyes held him back with a power beyond his control.

With wicked deliberation Damien winced and brought his hand up to his injured shoulder.

Instantly Christina dropped the concealing towel and rushed to examine the wound, her fingers flying swiftly to the bulging outline of the bandage beneath his linen shirt.

Before she realized his trickery, Damien's arms were about her and his lips trailed searing fires down her face and throat.

Christina gasped and turned her head, but made no effort to escape his magnetic embrace. Her heart pounded painfully against his broad chest and her fingers clung with terror to the lapels of his blue superfine coat, but she could not flee the security of his arms.

Timidly she murmured, "Your shoulder. Have you seen a physician yet?"

"He has called me every sort of a fool, patched me up, and vowed silence. I am in no danger. Other than an abominable ache, it works quite well, as you can see."

Damien rode both hands down the yielding softness of her bodice to the tempting curves beneath, pulling her hips close to his without effort. Both hands held her equally firmly.

Christina felt her knees go weak and dared not meet his gaze. She had agreed to this intimacy and more, and, if she dared admit it, craved it with an unnatural longing. She actually enjoyed the possessive hold of those masculine hands and his insinuating position!

Reluctantly Damien loosed his hold, setting Christina from him so he might read her face, keeping his hands about her waist as if to prove her reality, or prevent her escape.

"You must call Mrs. Douglass and have her help you dress." At her embarrassed, inquiring glance, his dark craggy face grew grim. "You need not worry. Jenkins and I have been very discreet. Your reputation is substantially safe until Bothwell and his cronies hit the streets."

"Then what is the hurry, my . . . Damien?" Christina wondered if he could feel the erratic pounding of her heart beneath his fingers. It seemed to be shaking her insides with its violence.

Thin lips twitched in a sardonic grin. " 'My Damien.' I like that, a decided improvement, if a trifle eccentric." As her amber eyes threatened to turn stormy, he hastened to continue, "You have a visitor below. I think you had best talk to him."

Christina's eyebrows rose. "A visitor? This is a bit early for a formal call, is it not?"

"Not so early as you might think. Your hours have grown atrocious of late."

There it was, the mocking Oxford drawl she remembered too well. Christina desired heartily to smack that smirk from his face, but her curiosity had been whetted.

"And your accent has improved immensely, milord, but that is neither here nor there. Who is this visitor that you must break in here like this?"

Damien's grin disappeared and his hands dropped to his sides. Watching her closely, he spoke with a casualness belying the taut line of his jaw.

"He claims he is your cousin."

Christina's hand flew to her mouth and her eyes opened wide with dazed confusion and horror, searching his face to see if this was some form of jest. A cousin! She had no cousin. And to come now, at a time like this . . .

Relieved somewhat at this reaction, Damien shrugged lightly and walked to the door. "You have not heard from your uncle in years. He could have married. It is scarcely an odd occurrence. You had best come down and talk with him. There is yet time to change your mind."

And he was gone, leaving Christina to stare open-mouthed at the door.

Nervously smoothing the printed cambric of her gown, checking herself in the hall mirror to be certain no sign of last night's guilt lingered somehow in her face, Christina advanced upon the parlor door.

Damien rose leisurely as she entered, the bronzed angles of his face reflecting approval as his gaze wandered over her modest attire. With nervous relief Christina accepted his presence and turned to regard the room's other occupant.

Unremarkable eyes peered from a thin face of unhealthy hue and bland expression as the young fop across the room rose to greet his newly discovered cousin. Immense falls of slightly bedraggled lace adorned a coat of crimson fustian pulled back to reveal a waistcoat of garish yellow. Christina practically blushed at the appearance he made in this severe room of masculine bent, before the grim Yankee who always dressed in the height of good taste.

"Miss MacTavish . . . Christina . . . my father has spoken so well of you, I feel we have already met."

He wrung her hand eagerly, the soft flesh and light bones revealing a hand foreign to hard work. Christina quickly extricated her own and secretly wondered at the differences hands could reveal. Damien's hand was hard and strong, his grip firm and sure at all times. Her cousin's was as weak and uncertain as the line of his mouth. She hid a grimace of displeasure at this comparison.

"I am sorry. I cannot return the compliment, Mr. . . .?" She hesitated inquiringly.

"Thaddeus Adderly, my dear." Damien took the introduction upon himself. "It seems your uncle is ill and has sent his son to protect your virtue."

Christina threw the Yankee a sharp glance. He had returned to the bitter, sardonic tone that had marked their first meeting, but no dangerous storms clouded his black eyes. He sat placidly, fingertips touching, as he regarded the tableau of long-lost cousins united.

"Mr. Adderly," she acknowledged, seating herself uneasily at the edge of a chair while she studied her savior.

Thaddeus Adderly twisted his finger in the collar of his cravat at Damien's caustic words, but when no other comment was forthcoming, he launched into eager explanations.

"My father travels extensively, as you certainly must be aware. He has been taken ill on the Continent, and your letters have only just recently reached him. He sent an urgent message ordering me to find you and ascertain your well-being. It has been a pleasure to discover you have fallen into such good hands. His lordship has been explaining the circumstances of your presence here. I most sincerely regret the news of my aunt's illness, but you are most fortunate in your choice of benefactors. My father could not have chosen better. However . . ."

He gave Damien a doubtful glance and turned back

to speak to Christina, but she had already grabbed at this break in his soliloquy.

"My uncle is ill, Mr. Adderly? I trust it is not serious? My mother would be most grieved—"

He interrupted with an impatient wave of his hand. "Not at all, but it has prevented him from responding as quickly as he would like. Unfortunately, the climate in Cornwall is not to his advantage, and the manor house there has been closed for some time. He finds it more convenient to reside in Italy. Perhaps when your mother is well enough to travel again, we will be able to reunite them and make a happy family once again."

In disgust, Christina deliberately interrupted his speech. "What does my uncle suggest we do in the meantime?" A trace of bitterness edged her question and she heard Damien's grunt of approval behind her. She did not dare meet his sharp gaze for fear of the mockery she would find there. This cousin offered no rescue, she sensed it at once. The damn Yankee must have known it before he went to find her.

At this pointed questioning Thaddeus squirmed uneasily, his gaze flickering to the earl and back to Christina. He had obviously not expected the august presence of his lordship at this conference.

"He made no actual suggestion, just asked that I see if you are well and in good hands. I can see that you are in the best of care. However . . ." Again the nervous glance to the earl's cynical expression, but Christina's wide-eyed innocence seemed to restore his confidence, and he continued. "It might be construed as improper for you to be residing with a gentleman not your relative, particularly with your mother being bedridden . . ." He hesitated again, waiting for an explosion. When it did not come, he finished hurriedly. "For the sake of propriety, I must insist that I lend some credence to your residence here."

At Christina's bewildered look, Damien explained crudely. "He wishes to stay here and act as your chaperon. Is that not right, Mr. Adderly?"

The youth fidgeted, coughed lightly into his handkerchief, cast Christina a quick glance, and nodded hastily at his lordship's wisdom.

"That should be most amusing. Christina, have Mrs. Douglass prepare a room for this gentleman. We would not wish to flout propriety, would we?"

Ignoring Christina's startled expression, Damien continued. "You will need to retrieve your belongings from your lodgings, Mr. Adderly, and I am certain you will need a rest after your long journey. Mrs. MacTavish does not entertain visitors until teatime, so there will be sufficient time for you to settle in and make yourself known to your aunt. I trust your stay will be a pleasant one."

Damien stood, making it clear the visit had come to an end.

Totally bemused by this fast turn of events, the slender young fop rose, switched his walking stick from one hand to the other and back again, gave Christina a hasty bow, began to offer his hand to the earl, who continued to stare at him coldly, thought better of it, and departed.

Christina sat with eyes downcast, hands folded in her lap, her stomach fluttering. This mad Yankee had managed to throw out her only known relative while at the same time inviting him to stay. She had never seen such a performance in her life. Any honorable gentleman would have been thoroughly insulted. But Thaddeus Adderly did not strike her as a particularly honorable gentleman. At that thought she raised her eyes and met Damien's impenetrable gaze.

"What now, my lord?" she asked with a trace of sarcasm.

"I hoped you would tell me that," Damien replied, dark eyes watching her carefully. He kept the width of the room between them, but he read easily every thought on her expressive face.

Christina's lips curled up in a mocking smile. "I think my uncle has as little use for his son as he does me. Why did you invite him?"

"Before I answer that, tell me if this changes your

decision. You might possibly force your charming cousin to open up the moldering manor at Adderly. You have certainly worked wonders with this one. Once installed, your uncle would have to pick up the bills or find some other situation for you."

Christina scarcely needed to contemplate the possibility. She had made her decision and saw no reason to change it. She shrugged nonchalantly. "I would prefer to stay where I am wanted. It has become quite obvious my uncle does not want me, and I have no intention of forcing myself upon him as his son does on you. The only question remaining is, do you want me?"

Dark fires burned deeply, changing his impenetrable mask to a blaze of intense heat. Still Damien constrained himself.

"You know the answer to that question."

The deep baritone of the Yankee's reply met a resonating chord in her heart, and Christina quivered beneath his stare, the hungry heat of his gaze raising color to her cheeks and setting her body trembling.

"Then, my lord . . . Damien, my decision has not changed. Only . . . my cousin's presence makes things a little awkward."

No smile flickered across his features at this confirmation of her surrender. Damien contemplated her youthful fairness a moment longer, weighing the courage with which she made this decision against the frailness of her appearance.

Remembering last night's performance and other episodes when those deceiving amber eyes had flashed hot fires or hurled icy shards, he decided that in this case, appearances were deceptive. She was young, but she was a MacTavish: strong and fiercely independent.

As if suddenly relieved of an invisible burden, Damien swung his broad shoulders loosely within his confining coat, stepped across the room in two great strides, and swallowed up her slender figure in his embrace.

His fierce kiss left Christina dizzy and beyond thought as she floated in his arms, caught up in the intensity of his needs. If she still harbored doubts, the strength of his embrace erased them. She needed this Yankee as he did her; together they could conquer all.

Still swimming dizzily in waters way over her head, Christina rested her head against his chest when he returned her to the floor. All manner of treacherous shoals surrounded her, but so long as she remained in Damien's arms she felt safe.

What an insane thing to think of this demented monster who had raped her, drugged her, and intended to make a whore of her! Christina shut her eyes and tried to think rationally, but could not. He had put a spell on her as surely as any witch or warlock.

"If your decision is final, my love, you and I must sit and talk awhile. I would have you understand fully what you are undertaking before either of us puts pen to paper." Damien ran his hands into the soft coils of tawny hair, tilting her face back until amber eyes met his.

"Paper?" she questioned dazedly, still not certain how she came to be here or why.

"My departure, whether by ship or otherwise, is quite likely to be very abrupt. I would have your future ensured before I go. You must think of this as a business transaction, Christina, and nothing more. We will put our promises to legal papers drawn up by my solicitors."

A business transaction. Legal papers. Christina's head quickly came down out of the clouds. She shoved from his embrace and stepped back, watching him warily. He was right to remind her. In his arms she had foolish visions of impossible nature. Out of them she could see the cold Yankee with his rigidly stern demeanor. A business transaction. A cold chill took root in her bones.

"Of course. How much are my services worth, exactly? Will I be paid for each tumble in bed, and extra if you require more than a tumble? How does one go about drawing up such a transaction?"

At her violent sarcasm Damien's brows drew down in a frightening frown and his fists clenched at his sides. Christina could see him visibly fighting to quell his temper, and she quailed before her foolishness. He brought out the worst in her, that was a certainty.

As her furious gaze wavered and her defiant chin trembled beneath his glare, Damien's lips began to twitch and his eyes crinkled in the corners with the humor of their argument. They fought even when they were in agreement. These next weeks or months should be merry ones.

"Every time I have to spank you to make you behave, I take away a shilling. Do you have any more pertinent questions?" He grasped his hands behind his back to keep them from straying elsewhere, but he could not prevent his gaze from absorbing the lovely sight he would soon possess. Even in her modest country gown she was the most beautiful woman he had ever seen.

Christina felt naked beneath his gaze but held her ground. "My cousin. How can you invite him here and dishonor me beneath his nose? I cannot risk upsetting my mother if he chooses to call you out."

Damien nodded approval at this more sensible questioning. "Come, let me order some breakfast for you and we will retire to my study. You will have more questions than this before long."

Damien sat behind his desk and watched as Christina delicately picked at the monstrously large breakfast provided. He had no notion where to begin or end, but, in all fairness, he must give her some inkling of what to expect. That she could easily see him hanged with the knowledge, he knew, but he had trusted her father and learned to trust her. He must go with his instincts.

"What is your opinion of your newfound cousin?" he asked idly, playing with his quill.

Christina made a moue of distaste and wrinkled her nose. "I think I preferred it when I thought I had no relatives at all. It is rather embarrassing to think my family's bloodlines can produce that."

Damien shot her a wry glance. "Do not be so harsh on your bloodlines. All families have their flaws, some worse than others."

He fell silent and Christina wondered if he spoke of

his uncle. She supposed he must, but the thoughtful frown upon his face made her uneasy.

He stirred from his reverie and returned to his questioning. "Aside from that, what is your opinion of him? You were obviously not impressed, since you chose me over him, and I have some idea of your opinion of me."

Christina's grin broke the gloom of the curtained study at his admission. "I suppose I must rate slugs below monsters. At least you are honest in your villainy. This Mr. Adderly is a toad pretending to be a man. I cannot trust a creature such as that."

Damien nodded agreement. "My thoughts exactly. I find it odd that he turned up at this particular moment. I wish to keep my eye on him and I do not give a damn what he thinks of our relationship. I do not think I am in danger of his calling me out, and if the truth be known, I do not believe he will notify your uncle of your circumstances so long as he is receiving free room and board from me."

Christina looked shocked, then thoughtful. "Why? I do not understand."

Damien crossed his fingers and stared at them, his brow drawing down in a frown. "I have many enemies, Christina, and when you hear my purpose here, you will understand why. I only trust that what I say to you now will go no further than this room. I know I cannot buy your loyalty, but as you trusted and aided the highwayman, I trust you will do the same for the earl."

Christina laid aside her fork and studied the dark, intense man behind the desk. He had lifted his eyes to meet her gaze, and those strange black pools pierced her with the emotions that his face never betrayed. In their depths she saw a need he would never admit, and a pride that would mock at death. A man like that inspired fear, and also a fierce loyalty that none would ever forget. Somehow her fate had become inexplicably tangled with his. She knew she would never carry out her threats to have this man hanged.

"The highwayman helped me when no one else would,

treated me with kindness and respect, and made no demands of me. I cannot say the same of the earl. I cannot fathom how you can be both men, yet I am a MacTavish. If I am bound to you, I will support you until my dying day. I have no other choice."

Damien's gaze softened as it rested on her defiant expression. For all he knew, the MacTavishes were a rebellious, cantankerous lot, but he had made his choice, too.

"You have other choices, and one day you may have to make them. For now, I will be satisfied with your word. You are disarmingly honest. Not a trait to be admired in my business, but you seem to circumnavigate its difficulties admirably."

His grin grew and the highwayman returned. Christina relaxed and sat back in her leather chair. "Just exactly what is your business, my lord? If you say you are the devil himself, I will not doubt it."

"I am just what everybody calls me, a Yankee. Except, of course, everyone assumes my title makes me a Tory. I am not. I am a rebel, a traitor, a spy, if you will. I am carrying papers on me that could have me hanged in an instant. A few years ago they would have placed my head on a pole at Temple Bar. I do not know what atrocity they save now for someone like me."

Damien callously watched her grow pale. He lived with this knowledge every day. She must come to accept it. It certainly helped that she hated him now and would hate him worse as time wore on.

Christina felt the remains of her breakfast rise in her throat as she imagined that handsome, cold visage cut off at the neck, and she hastily covered her mouth with her hand and forced the image away. She must concentrate on his words and not her imagination. This was a business transaction, he had said. Coldhearted, impersonal business.

Still pale, she finally managed to stutter, "Why? You have everything. Why would you be a spy?"

Damien shrugged and rocked back in his chair, running one hand through thick locks of russet hair as he formed his reply. "I do not relish the role, I can assure you. I would much prefer being back in the colonies with a sword and rifle in hand, defending my home as I know best. I have just received disturbing reports that that foul traitor Arnold is attacking my home state of Virginia, and I fear for the lives of my family. Instead I am here playing at intrigue because it was asked of me and the circumstances warranted it."

Christina could hear the anguish in his voice as he spoke of his family, the first genuine emotion that had been drawn from him, and she felt a tug of sympathy for his conflict. Still, she did not understand his choice.

"I do not understand, my . . . Damien. Why did you not bring your family here?"

He leaned back and stared at the ceiling. That was an easy one. "They would not come. My mother has no wish to return to a home where she was treated so cruelly. My father's grave is in Virginia, her life began in Virginia, she claims, and so she will stay. My brother and sister, of course, grew up there and have never been to England. They express interest in London, but not while a war is going on. They have their duties there, and I can only wish I were with them."

"But you have been here before?" she encouraged him when he hesitated.

"Yes. I was educated here. My father always knew the earldom would fall upon me, and he saw to it that I was able to uphold my responsibilities should it become necessary. He did not foresee this war. Nor did he foresee the destruction his brother would leave behind. My uncle has made the title one of shame and left the estate in debt so deep it has bankrupted many of his creditors. I have arranged to sell off all that is not entailed except the house off St. James. That scarcely puts a dent in the debt, but I have done what I could. I wish to leave here feeling as if I owe England nothing."

Damien rose and stalked to the window, his fists clenched as he recited his tale.

"Going through my uncle's ledgers, I discovered a great deal of money lost to certain gentlemen who will remain nameless. Knowing my uncle's penchant for gambling and the reputations of these gentlemen, I tested my theory soon after my arrival here. The gentlemen are cheats, and not particularly good ones at that. My uncle's brain had rotted to a particularly decadent state to have fallen for their trickeries. Syphilis is not a very pretty disease, I understand."

He swung around to catch the look of horror on Christina's face. "It is a disease of the corrupt, my dear, but I will spare you the details."

He stepped to the liquor cabinet and reached for a bottle, but halted himself and returned to his chair.

"I came to England with three definite purposes—to settle my uncle's estate, to kill the man who drove my father from his home, and to carry out my mission for the Continental Congress. I needed funds with which to accomplish any of them. My own money is tied up in Virginia, and there is little ready cash over there now. The estate I had counted on was gone. There seemed only one alternative."

"Take the money back from the cheats," Christina breathed in awe. It made sense. How she wished she'd had the ability to do the same!

Damien granted her a brief grin. "Of course. They wagered wildly at first, but grew cautious when I won too much. So what I could not win, I took. The highwayman kept very accurate books. I never stole more than I figured they owed the estate."

"That is what we are living on now?" Christina asked incredulously.

"Most certainly. Tainted money, all of it. It seemed somehow fitting." Amused dark eyes watched her reaction.

"And the income you promised . . .?"

"To you? The same source, I fear. It seems my uncle cheated you out of some rather large sums." At her startled expression, Damien explained. "I did not think it like your father to leave you impoverished, so I made inquiries. The signatures on those notes were forgeries. My uncle stole that money from you just as surely as his gambling cronies stole it from him. I simply stole it back again."

The look of horror on her face quickly turned to indignation. "Then the money is mine! How dare you make me earn it in such a manner!"

Damien laughed and propped his buckled shoes upon the desk. "I became a thief to obtain it. At least you will not hang for your offense. You will have to lose that haughty air, my dear—the likes of you and me cannot afford it."

The last of her innocence died and grew hard as she swallowed her fury. He had every right to classify her on the same level with him now. Prostituting herself was as much a sin as theft. They should make good companions. She made a wry face as she swallowed her pride.

Damien grew serious as he watched the play of emotion cross her face. It scarcely seemed fair to dump such a burden on one so young, but life had never been fair. She would do better to learn that now while he could still protect her from the worst of it.

"You're a despicable fiend," Christina stated calmly, accepting the worst. What other choice had she?

He nodded approvingly. "It is best you continue thinking that. I want no romantic illusions between us. I have treated you roughly as it is. If I thought I would be breaking a romantic young heart, I would send you back to Cornwall at once."

Christina shoved her breakfast tray away with a look of disgust. "Then be certain you have chosen wisely, my lord. I have no such illusions."

"I rather thought not," he said with grim satisfaction. "Your declaration that first time that you would never marry me made a distinct impression. At a time like that a man has visions of being forced to the altar with a gun at his head. You relieved that fear quickly enough. Any wife of mine would be in as grave danger as I."

At Christina's questioning look, Damien sank his head between his hands and searched for words of explanation.

"I need not point out the fact that should I be caught with these papers in my possession, I would be hanged for a traitor and probably drawn and quartered for good measure. The wife of a traitor would be under constant suspicion and would not be allowed in decent society again. That is minor compared to the other evil I have sworn to commit.

"You know the story of my father's exile?"

He looked up then, catching Christina's slight nod. With a flicker of relief, he skipped over that part of his tale.

"My father never killed a soul in his life. He was a gentle, amiable man. The duel was forced upon him as a matter of honor, but he had no intention of killing. He aimed above his opponent's head. The gun exploded in his hand, literally exploded, and the other man fell dead. My father knew nothing of firearms, but I know enough to realize that gun was intentionally packed with more powder than it could hold. With luck, both men might have been killed. I cannot be certain if that was the bastard's intent, but the effect was the same. My father became a wanted man and had to flee the country, leaving the estate free to be plundered by my uncle and his bastard son."

The final two words exploded in the dusky gloom of the study in much the same manner as the pistol must have done that murky dawn. Christina shrank back from the force of his glare, fearing the furious lightning of the Yankee's eyes.

Damien's chair dropped back to the floor with a thud and he rose from the desk, coming forward to stand before Christina. His was an awesome figure of broad shoulders and narrow hips, well displayed in tailored tailcoat and tight breeches. Christina gulped as she remembered the steeled musculature beneath that civilized linen. She would hate to be this man's enemy.

Crossing his arms across his chest, he leaned back against the desk and gazed thoughtfully upon the fair face before him. "My bastard cousin made one attempt on my life last night. There will be others. But so long as he thinks of you as a whore, you should be safe. Only as a possible mother of my legal heir would he consider you a danger. Like his father, he possesses a singular disrespect for women. He tends to consider all women whores and ignores them except as suits his needs. You could be most helpful to me under such circumstances."

Christina twisted her hands nervously beneath his unswerving gaze. "I am not certain I understand."

"You do not need to. I'm not certain he does. Though I have never met the man, I have learned much about him. His is a twisted mind—whether from birth or circumstances, I cannot tell. His mother was a maid at the hall for whom my uncle developed an uncontrollable passion at an early age. Of course, marriage could not be considered, but I believe the affair continued until her death in childbirth. Nicholas is the only surviving child of the affair and my uncle seems to have raised him with foolish notions of the estate belonging to him one day."

Damien shrugged and with a sudden movement drew Christina from her chair. Capturing her waist with one arm, he pulled her between his legs as he sat on the desk's edge. His other hand absently trailed through loosened tawny curls, enhancing their disarray.

Christina rested her hands against his chest to keep from trembling. The familiar outline of the heavy bandage seemed strangely reassuring against her palms. Flashing dark fires had grown dim and thoughtful and he scarcely seemed to realize he held her as he completed his tale.

"I suppose Nicholas must have one day grown old enough to realize the difference between legitimate and illegitimate heirs, but by then he was too warped with hatred to care. My father stood in his way and he thought to remove him. It was Nicholas who loaded the guns that day. I cannot be certain how my grandfather died, but it was soon after my father fled to the colonies. My uncle and Nicholas took full control of the estate thenceforth."

Christina curled up closer against his chest, resting her head against his lace cravat and hearing his words rumble against her ear. He spoke calmly, without any hint of hatred, yet he had stated earlier that he had returned to England to kill this cousin. He had a strength of purpose she could not deny, but her instinct was to comfort him.

Damien buried his face in the soft scents of her stacked curls. "Nicholas is an evil man, Christina. I will not repeat the debaucheries committed in my bastard cousin's name. He owns gambling dens and whorehouses throughout London, bought with money drained from Westshipham. Everyone knows of him, but few know he is any relation, and none are able to tell me how to find him.That is why I must haunt the gutters of the city, the filth of humanity, until I fall far enough to reach his lair."

"You are mad, my lord," she whispered against his shirt.

"No, I simply seek justice. If any man deserves to die, it is he, but it is a matter of self-preservation also. So long as I am alive, he cannot trump up an excuse to claim the estate. It seems to be an obsession with him. So to protect myself and my family, I must rid the world of him."

He shrugged again and Christina looked up to meet his gaze. A wry half-smile played about his lips.

"Besides, it makes good cover for my other purpose here. Who would suspect a rakehell lord to be carrying papers asking terms for England's surrender?"

12

Christina crossed and recrossed her gloved fingers while casting sidelong glances at the stiffly upright man beside her. The carriage bumped and jolted along rutted city streets, but he scarcely seemed to notice the discomfort.

Since their discussion earlier, Damien had retreated behind the grave demeanor of the taciturn Yankee, and she did not know what to make of the change. Did he regret revealing so much of himself to her? Had she displeased him in some manner? Would he change his mind?

This last set up a clamor of alarm within her head. Now that she had made up her mind to accept his audacious proposition, she could not imagine doing otherwise. Her reputation was destroyed both here and in Cornwall, her mother was still ill, and they were penniless. How would they survive without the Yankee's ill-gotten gold?

It was as much her money as his, and she would have it, one way or another. Christina set her chin determinedly and refused to admit despair.

As if following the path of her thoughts, Damien finally broke his silence.

"We are almost at the solicitor's. Do you have any questions or requests you would make before we set this arrangement to paper?"

He spared a smile as he gazed down upon the golden head beside him. She had apparently been at great pains to arrange her hair in a fashionably intricate stack of curls, but before this day ended, he intended to loose it in the wanton abandonment he preferred. Damien's smile grew broader at this thought.

Christina gave his smile a suspicious glare, then turned her gaze back to nervous fingers. She had one wish, but did not know how to phrase it without being laughed at as romantically foolish.

Sensing her reluctance, Damien captured her fingers and held them still until she turned golden-brown eyes back to him.

"You have as much right to make demands as I do, Christina. We are equal partners in this. Do not be shy with me."

Her eyes widened. Equal partners with an earl? But a whore and a highwayman . . . A golden gleam of understanding ignited and grew brighter as her horizons widened. They were truly equal partners. He needed her as much as she did him, and her smile became a little brighter. A Yankee thief. And she had once scorned an illiterate farmer. How ironic!

Still, her wish remained foolish, and she did not like to be scorned. She looked down at their intertwined fingers and sought for words.

"My family raised me as a lady, expecting one day I would make a good marriage. I had no thoughts otherwise and was prepared to submit to the duties of a wife as expected of me. Now, there will be no marriage, no ceremony, no pride in my position. Only the duties remain. If only I could feel as a bride for one day, it would make what must follow come easier."

A hint of tears spoiled this calm recitation, but it had to be said. The thought of the night to come held a horror for her she could not explain in any other way.

Damien understood at once. With a thoughtful frown he contemplated the obstacles, found them easily surmountable, and grinned confidently.

"As you wish, my dear. It will be a hasty betrothal, but we can pretend this is Gretna Green if you prefer. I do believe we have already exchanged our betrothal kiss. Does this mean I must treat you with proper respect for the remainder of the day until our vows are signed?"

Christina stared at dancing black eyes as if he had gone quite mad; then, beginning to understand his game, she gave a cautious smile. "I do believe it is expected of an engaged couple to occasionally indulge in some sort of passionate fondling when others are not looking. I am supposed to take great care that we are not too far from discovery, however, so you had best beware."

Damien quickly drew the curtains, gave her a wicked leer, and slid his arm about her waist, drawing her close enough to trace a line of fervent kisses down her cheek. When his mouth finally reached hers, Christina gasped with the pleasure of it, and surrendered gladly to his madness.

The carriage drew to a halt too soon. His fingers had just begun to trace the fine line of her throat, and her breast burned for the heat of his touch. Already he had taught her body what to expect, and she found herself eager for the next lesson.

As the footman opened the door, throwing the interior into full daylight, Damien smiled regretfully. "If I had to play this game for a long betrothal, my dear, you would find yourself well ravished long before the proper time. I think an elopement is the wisest choice."

The corners of Christina's lips turned slightly upward. "How brash you are, sir! And la, what you must think of me! We must stop meeting like this at once!"

She fluttered her lashes coyly and the footman's mouth fell open as the stern earl broke into a paroxysm of laughter and roared until passersby stopped to gape.

Christina nudged him sharply, and Damien sobered enough to climb out, but the dancing gleam in his eye as he helped her out warned her that the dangerous highwayman had returned.

They arrived in the lawyer's office without further flights of fancy, however, and the businesslike Yankee again came into play. Introducing the older bespectacled gentleman behind the desk as Ben Thomas, Damien saw them seated and commenced negotiations immediately.

"Ben, Miss MacTavish is the lady about whom I have spoken. She has finally agreed to my proposal and I would like the papers completed and finalized today, if at all possible."

Christina felt the keen gray eyes behind the spectacles turn on her with surprise and suspicion, and she did not dare raise her eyes to meet his. Damien had obviously already explained his intention of taking a mistress. Last night it had been easy to play the part of whore because she was not one. This man would know her one of a certainty.

"Damien, by gad, she is no experienced courtesan! All the women in London you have to choose from and you must choose an innocent straight from her mother's arms?"

The solicitor did not attempt to hide his astonishment and disapproval. Christina looked up with surprise. She had watched lesser men fawn over his lordship and agree with his every word without thought. How had this lowly solicitor the temerity to stand up to a lord?

She half-expected Damien to explode in fury, but he only sat back in his chair and crossed his booted leg over his knee, his thin lips slightly upturned. His stout opponent glared at the young lord's impertinent grin, then turned in appeal to Christina.

"Miss MacTavish, I do not know what fine words this arrogant scamp has used to woo you, but you must realize fully he has no intentions of marrying you and will most certainly leave you to your own devices within a few months at best. Do not, I pray, let romantic notions get the better of common sense."

Amber eyes met penetrating gray ones coolly. "Common sense tells me Lord Westshipham is a rake and a scoundrel and I will be better off once he is gone. It also tells me starvation is a poor way to die. There is no argument I have not already used myself, Mr. Thomas. I ask nothing but that you draw the terms fairly."

The lawyer looked mildly bemused at this amazing statement from a fresh-faced lass and turned a look of consternation to his client.

Damien shrugged nonchalantly. "I thought her one of my uncle's whores and raped her. I have ruined what little chance she had of marriage, and her only family seems disinclined to take her in. This is the only way I know to make amends."

"Amends!" Ben Thomas snorted, removing his spectacles and cleaning them with his handkerchief before returning them to his nose and staring back at the young couple. "You will become as much a bastard as your cousin if you continue on this path, Drayton."

"Ben, if you will not draw up the papers, I will go to someone else who will, but the trust is all the money Christina will have, and I would rather you handled it than some unscrupulous character. You helped my father and now I ask you to help me. You know how my hands are tied."

The two men exchanged meaningful glances and Ben sighed in surrender, turning back to Christina.

"You know the terms he is asking? You are to be at his command day and night until such time as his lordship or circumstances terminate the relationship. In return, his lordship will present you with the deed to his property off St. James Square and a trust income sufficient to meet your daily needs and support you and your mother and any offspring of this arrangement for the rest of your lives. The house will be yours outright, to do with as you will. The principal of the trust cannot be touched, but reverts to your offspring or his lordship's estate in the event of your demise. The income, however, is yours to do with as you will."

The monotonous legal verbiage made it easy to restrain all emotion, and Christina nodded agreement without revealing the frantic beat of her heart. Offspring! Why did he not just say "bastards" and be done with it? As if to compound the agony, the lawyer had more to say.

"Of course, should you choose not to keep any offspring of this relationship, as executor of this estate I must be notified at once. Not to do so would jeopardize the trust and your income. You do understand that fully, Miss MacTavish?"

Anguished amber eyes darted from those cold gray ones to Damien's impenetrable obsidian. To bear his child would be hell on earth! How could she possibly place herself in this position?

Seeing her terror, Damien hastened to take her hand and speak reassuringly. "It is not a likely occurrence, Christina, and Ben will guide you wisely should it happen. Do not torment yourself with what has not yet occurred."

Ben snorted inelegantly but kept his silence, watching Christina's fair face pale a shade lighter. He did not think the chit as hard as she pretended, and he did not for a moment believe she possessed no romantic fancies. For that matter, he was none too certain about his lordship, either. The two of them seemed lost in their own little world while they stared wordlessly at each other, their gazes speaking words without sound.

Biting her lip to hold back a sob, Christina turned a moist amber gaze back to the solicitor and nodded solemnly. "I understand."

At the obvious distress in Christina's eyes, the lawyer sent Damien a look of fury, but the young lord remained coldly dispassionate. Sighing, Mr. Thomas shuffled some papers and leaned back in his chair.

"You're a pair of fools, but then, what is the opinion of an old man? The papers will be ready this evening."

Damien met his gaze calmly. "You're not old, Ben, just set in your ways. Bring the papers to the house this evening and stay to eat. We're having a small celebration."

At the lawyer's sharp glance, the earl grinned, captured Christina's hand, and rose. With a jaunty salute to his friend's disapproving frown, Damien gallantly escorted Christina from the room.

The remainder of the afternoon slid and jolted along like a snowball downhill, rapidly gaining speed and losing control.

In Madame Alexander's they found a partially constructed gown of gold satin and ivory lace that the seamstress swore could be fitted and finished before the day ended. While Christina found herself strapped in measuring tapes and pins, Damien made a tour of the shop, an eager clerk following at his heels and hastily scribbling his peremptory orders for everything from undergarments to ball gowns. Christina's protests were blithely ignored and soon dwindled to a halt beneath the avalanche of his purchases. He evidently intended her to be the best-dressed whore in town.

Exhausting this shop, he carried Christina back to the street and contemplated several more, but with sudden decision he swung her back into the waiting carriage and ordered the horses turned toward home.

Christina breathed easier until they entered the town house and met Mrs. Douglass' stony glare. Apparently well aware of the cause of the housekeeper's dour expression, Damien swept by without inquiring, dragging Christina in his wake.

As they entered the upper hall, Christina developed some understanding of the reason for her maid's stern demeanor, and she felt the heat rise to her cheeks. An army of maids was systematically emptying the pink bedroom she had called her own, carrying her few precious belongings down the corridor into the nether regions on which she had never dared trespass. It had not occurred to her that she would not be allowed the privacy of her own chambers.

Meeting anguished amber eyes with cool aplomb, Damien steered her toward the sitting room between her room and her mother's.

Mrs. MacTavish greeted them with a joyous smile of welcome, her swift gaze darting from their joined hands to Damien's assured stance and strong face. A vague uneasiness flitted behind normally vivid blue eyes, but her words reflected none of it.

"Come in, come in, and tell me what you two have been up to lately. The doctor says I might soon be well enough to go downstairs, and then I will be able to find out on my own, so 'fess up, you two. Has my daughter been behaving shockingly, Damien?"

Christina sensed her mother's anxiety beneath the gay chatter and her fingers trembled within the warm strength of the Yankee's. Her tongue refused to function, but Damien's had no such trouble.

Smoothly drawing Christina's trembling hand under the protection of his arm, he bowed lightly before Eleanor's seated figure, then met her gaze with serious intent.

"The truth of the matter is, ma'am, that I have been the one behaving shockingly. I have worn down your daughter's resistance until she had no choice but to surrender to my pleas."

He deliberately chose insinuating phrases, but Christina watched her mother's guileless eyes light with joy and knew her romantic fantasies had flown to the best possible interpretations. Damien had gauged her mother correctly, and though furious at these deliberate deceptions, she admitted the wisdom of his methods.

At the expectant gleam in the lovely eyes of the frail woman before him, Damien felt his first twinge of guilt, but roughly shoved it aside. He had no time for moral sermonizing. His decisions had been made long before he sailed to England.

"Mrs. MacTavish, your daughter has consented to take my hand in marriage." Before his listener could break into excited speech, he waved her words aside. "Do not offer us congratulations yet, my lady, until you hear all. Due to the delicate nature of my mission here, our nuptials cannot be immediately announced, but I cannot wait for the niceties. If you will forgive my haste, the service takes place this evening in the company of a few close friends who will keep our secret. Christina has agreed to this secrecy, if you will acquiesce."

Damien's solemn manner provided the perfect foil to Eleanor's ecstasy. As she bit back cries of joy, her gaze danced from her daughter's anxious face to the lord's intense dark stare, and her smile spread wide with excitement. She controlled it dutifully.

"Christina, this is what you want? You will not be unhappy keeping such a secret?" Eleanor knew her part as parent well, but romantic hopes filled her heart and head, and she would have taken only one answer to her question. She waited expectantly.

Seeing her mother's happiness, Christina smiled softly and clung to Damien's arm for support as she found the words to seal her fate. "It would make me happy, Mother."

Freeing herself from Damien's embrace, she knelt before her mother, throwing her arms around the frail figure of the woman she loved. This was all the family she had left in this world. She must protect her with all she had. Tears streaked down her cheeks as her mother kissed her bent head.

A knock at the door intruded on this scene, jarring the participants from their separate thoughts. Damien stepped to the door and threw it open, his immediate frown revealing his opinion of the interloper.

Apparently thinking better of his first reaction, he gestured for the intruder to enter. "It is time you met your aunt, Mr. Adderly. Come in."

Christina jumped to her feet, wrenching her mind back to the present. Had it only been this morning that she had met this reprehensible creature she must call cousin? It seemed another lifetime, and she had no desire to remember it.

However, Eleanor's puzzled expression demanded answering, and introductions were hastily accomplished. Thaddeus' explanations did not clear her bemused brow.

"Thomas had a son? How odd. I should have thought I would have heard of such a thing. Come here, boy, and let me have a look at you."

Her voice took on a curiously commanding quality and Christina watched with amazement as her gangling cousin straightened and came to attention beneath her mother's direct gaze.

"I was born abroad, madam, and schooled on the Continent. My father never stayed in one place long."

"Of course, that would explain it. Come, sit down

beside me and tell me of my brother. You say he is ill?" Turning to the young couple who still remained standing, she made a peremptory wave of dismissal. "You two will have much to do. Leave Thaddeus with me and go with my blessings."

The twinkle of her eye declared their secret safe with her, and they bowed out, leaving the awkward Thaddeus hemming and hawing on the settee beneath Eleanor's inquisitive gaze.

Christina collapsed against the wall outside the door. "How can I go through with this? If she should ever discover the truth, it would kill her!"

Damien stood before her, keeping his hands to his side. "On the contrary, you have just made her very happy, relieved her of a terrible burden, and she will never believe anyone who tells her otherwise. In a few months I will be gone and you can play the grieved widow for a while and she will be none the wiser. To have returned her to Cornwall and poverty would have been criminal."

Drawing a deep breath, Christina closed her eyes and leaned her head back against the hard support of the wall, trying to calm her frazzled nerves. Logically, he was right, but she had a hard time looking at this cruel deceit with logic.

"I must leave you for a few hours. The seamstress will be here shortly with your gown. Will you be all right while I am gone?"

His absence would be a balm to her shattered soul. Without opening her eyes, Christina nodded wordlessly. She felt him hesitate and prayed for his speedy departure. As if sensing her need for privacy, Damien spun on his heels and clattered down the uncarpeted stairs.

But privacy eluded her. Though Lorna Douglass avoided her, the army of maids still paraded through the upper rooms under their master's orders, and Christina found no shelter there. Downstairs she would be subject to Lorna's disapproving frown or her cousin's inopportune questioning. And then the seamstress arrived with a bevy of helpers, and any hope of choice escaped.

Surrounded by pins and needles and chattering voices, Christina gave in to numb despair. Events carried her along in their relentless grip, bringing the evening's inevitable culmination diabolically closer.

The gown slid silkily across her skin, rustling pleasingly across small wire panniers and crisp petticoats before falling in graceful swathes about her ankles. The various maids and attendants uttered exclamations of delight as the hooks fastened tightly, expertly and effectively revealing the slender curves rising from the tide of golden satin. The gown fit more perfectly than any Christina had ever owned, and tears of mixed emotion moistened her eyes as she fingered the fine material. A more beautiful bridal gown had never been made. If only it could be sanctified with marriage.

An insane notion. Christina's lips tightened with a willful surge of determination. Facing the mirror the seamstress placed before her, she gazed grimly at the woman reflected in the glass. The froth of ivory lace at her neckline teased delicately along the uppermost swells of her high, firm bosom, provocatively revealing a generous amount of cleavage and promising more before plunging in a waterfall of lace to her waist. The gold satin peered from beneath the cascade, scarcely covering the tips of her breasts, held skillfully in place by wire stays. Elbow-length sleeves erupted in a matching explosion of expensive lace sweeping to her wrists, completing the image of elegance.

The seamstress obviously knew what she was doing. Surface innocence concealed a sensual display of a sophistication Christina's imagination could not hope to match. She stared at this unknown woman in the mirror with perplexity. Tawny gold hair stacked in casual disarray emphasized the slim line of a slender throat curving gently to full, young breasts which sloped downward to a tiny waistline before blossoming out in wide, swaying skirts. Was that the reflection of a whore or a virgin?

He had done away with one, he might as well have the other. As Christina lifted her chin in grim defiance, her gaze suddenly encountered the wintry blue of the housekeeper's.

Christina swung around, facing the dour Scotswoman with a determination that she did not feel. If she must be a whore, she must learn to carry the name with pride. Lorna Douglass had been more than kind to her these past weeks, but Christina refused to be looked down upon by anyone, for any reason.

"Do you think his lordship will be pleased?" she demanded, smoothing the fine satin beneath caressing fingers.

"He will be more than pleased, I should imagine," Lorna replied with a touch of sarcasm. Then, relenting, remembering her purpose there, she asked coolly, "Shall I fix your hair?"

Christina searched that dour visage for scorn, and finding none, breathed a sigh of relief. She needed an ally of some sort, someone she did not fear, and Lorna Douglass would make a stalwart companion of the best kind.

"If you would, please. I can do nothing with it."

Gemlike amber eyes softened to velvet brown and Lorna fell before their innocence. Sending the flurry of maids and mantuamakers packing, she cleared the room with relieving efficiency. Christina felt some of the tension drain away as the army of prying eyes disappeared.

Beneath Lorna's skillful fingers tawny curls shaped themselves artistically in an elegant coiffure that added inches to Christina's height. Several curls dangled enticingly about shell-like ears, softening the bare expanse of neckline revealed by the gown.

Gazing worriedly at pale cheeks and overlarge dark eyes in the drawn face of her reflection, Christina asked hesitantly, "Do you think he would wish me to wear paint or powder? I look like a ghost no one will notice."

Lorna harrumphed with disgust. "If he's that blind, we will buy him spectacles. Don't you dare spoil your face with paint. Spoil your innocence if you must, but leave the appearance of it for your poor mother's sake."

"He has already spoiled my innocence. If that does not show, I suppose naught else will either." Sadly Christina contemplated her reflection. Did anything of her surrender show in her eyes? In the set of her lips? Would all who looked upon her know her as she was?

Lorna tugged painfully at a recalcitrant curl. "So that is it. He has taken you once and you think yourself spoiled for all others. That is a foolish notion put about by selfish men to gain their own pleasure. There isn't a man in this world wouldn't fall at your feet if you would but notice him."

Christina made a wry grimace. "After what I have learned of the male of the species, I do not want any of them, at my feet or otherwise. The earl has promised to go away and leave me alone within a few months. That is the best offer I know."

Lorna snorted. "Then you are a bigger fool than I thought."

She stepped back to admire her handiwork, giving Christina no further chance to question.

Damien stopped before the window of the goldsmith's and stared in at the glittering display of wealth. Any one of those expensive gewgaws would rest splendidly against the setting he had in mind. He would never have thought twice about using the highwayman's ill-gotten gains or the earl's dubious credit to present a handful of that dazzling display to any other mistress, but he hesitated now. The money meant nothing to him, but could he say the same of Christina?

Pulling a delicate, carved band of gold and diamonds from his breast pocket, Damien examined it thoughtfully. He was a practical man. The chances of his ever surviving to find a wife and raise a family were very slim indeed. His priorities were elsewhere, and the means of attaining them extremely risky. So why should he not indulge himself for a few months' time? To become romantically involved would be the height of foolishness and exceedingly dangerous for both of them, but where was the harm in showing a small gesture of appreciation?

Containing the rush of pleasure he felt at the thought of placing this band on Christina's hand, proclaiming her as his own for all the world to see, Damien slid the gold band back into his pocket and turned determinedly from the glittering temptation of the window. War might have made a cynical criminal out of him, but he retained enough sense to know better than to tarnish fine gold with cheap paste. He did not know Christina well enough to know whether she would appreciate the difference, but he would offer what little respect he could, for his conscience' sake.

13

At Lorna's insistence, Christina followed her down the dim corridors to the earl's wing of the house. The short distance from her mother's suite to her new home threatened to become an insurmountable chasm as her footsteps reluctantly followed in the housekeeper's path.

Lorna threw open the door and gestured for Christina to enter. With hesitant step she crossed the portal to the chamber the Yankee had appointed to her.

In a glance she could tell it was not his room, and she nearly gasped with relief. Although the massive tester bed and highboy were sturdy enough for a masculine room, the golden draperies and canopy with fringes of lace and eyelet were definitely not suited to Damien's spartan nature. He might don the mask of rakish fop, but she had learned enough of his character to know he preferred simplicity and practicality. This room would be hers.

Anxiously her gaze swept the spacious interior, at once locating the door that would undoubtedly lead to the Yankee's chambers. There would be no sneaking back and forth down darkened corridors at dawn. He could come and go from her bed as he pleased.

Shaken by this thought, she averted her gaze from the door and, lifting her chin, strode boldly to the wide window casement, throwing back the draperies to look out over the garden. She had made her bed; now she would lie in it.

"Thank you, Lorna. I know you must have worked hard to clean it so quickly. It is the most beautiful room in the house." And it would be, with the morning sun streaming through the windows, if she could only survive the night.

"His lordship had us clean it out when you first arrived. He ordered the hangings special made. If thanks you wish to give, it be to him."

The housekeeper spoke gruffly, but Christina sensed it was not in anger and hid her shock at this evidence of Damien's confidence in her surrender. Damien had told her the Scotswoman had been with his family since before his birth and had traveled with his mother to America. She had returned to revisit her old home and to keep his house, but she apparently disapproved of the new lord's actions. Perhaps men didn't keep mistresses in America.

Turning to ask, Christina found the housekeeper gone, the door shut silently behind her. The feeling of aloneness almost overwhelmed her, but she fought it. She needed this time to gather her strength for the evening to come.

There was still time to back out of this. She did not think Damien would force her if she should change her mind, but he would most certainly return her to Cornwall as quickly as she could pack her bags.

It was that thought which kept her motionless at the window, staring out into the rain-blurred kitchen garden. She had no desire to return to Cornwall and the life of poverty and illness she and her mother had shared there, but those were not the only reasons. The thought of returning without ever seeing the Yankee again stayed her hand. May the good Lord forgive her, but she could not leave. She did not understand why, but she could not do it.

There was no rhyme, no reason, no logic for her decision. She could make excuses, and very good ones—her mother's health depended on staying here, they would starve in Cornwall, the Yankee had the money that was rightfully hers—but excuses they remained. From the moment she had discovered the slim edge of danger Damien lived upon, whether as earl or highwayman, she had been incapable of returning to Cornwall without him. And that was that.

When Damien entered the room sometime later, he found only a single candle burning, and his eyes had to search before locating the still figure in the window seat. He hesitated in the doorway, but upon seeing him, Christina rose gracefully, her skirts swirling about her feet as she approached, no sign of hesitation or reluctance upon her serene features.

"Is it not bad luck to see the bride before the wedding?" she asked calmly, offering no other protest to this invasion of her privacy.

"I think there are special dispensations for elopements," he returned with equal gravity, but his eyes gave him away. They softened to black velvet as they observed the golden girl against the golden backdrop of this bedroom he had created for her.

Tawny hair flickered with white-gold highlights in the candlelight, and the ivory perfection of her skin complemented the gilded glitter of her gown. His gaze rested on the full swell of ripe breasts above the ivory lace, and Christina's breath caught in her lungs at the hunger flaring behind his shadowed gaze.

"I wished you to wear this, this evening. I thought it suited the gown and the occasion." Damien withdrew a velvet box from his coat pocket, his chiseled features shadowed and unfathomable in the poor light.

Christina wished for some warmth, some show of affection to ease her fears, but this gesture did not meet her needs. Hiding her disappointment, she accepted the box, opening its lid gingerly.

Inside, against a satin bed, lay a finely wrought necklace of pearls and gold. The delicate chain wound into a filigree of gold intertwined with dainty pearls, dropping to a single dangling seed of immaculate luster. No ostentatiously extravagant gift this, it reflected the giver's impeccable good taste and was intended to enhance and not overwhelm the wearer's beauty.

With a stunning smile of surprised delight, Christina held the chain against her throat, admiring the play of candlelight against its gleaming gold, before glancing shyly back to the giver.

"It is much too beautiful. The highwayman must have risked much for the wealth to buy this."

Damien's strong brown fingers grasped the clasp and lifted it about her neck. "This is from me. The highwayman and the earl had nothing to do with it."

As long dark lashes swept upward, startled by the warmth of his tone as much as by his declaration, Damien completed the fastening, and with firm, sure grip upon her shoulders, bent his lips to hers.

Hunger lay just beneath the surface of his ardent kiss, hunger and an almost violent passion, but he allowed neither to come between them now. He claimed her with his kiss, commanded her with his caress, and Christina surrendered to his demands without protest. Her lips parted to welcome him, and their breaths mixed in a molten fire of incredible sweetness.

Eyes closed, Christina clung to Damien's wide shoulders as his mouth devoured hers. It seemed she should be lost and disappear within his overpowering embrace, but she felt herself growing and expanding to meet him. The headiness of this sensation nearly swept her from her feet, and when their lips separated, she continued to cling to him, her head resting against his shoulder as his arms wrapped about her waist and held her close. His breath murmured along the bare nape of her neck, and their hearts pounded as one.

"I can feel your heart beating like a wild thing," Damien murmured. "Do I frighten you that much?"

Lashes moist with tears, Christina smiled slightly, but did not look up. "I am terrified, but not of you any longer. Thank you for the gift. I know a man is supposed to give his mistress jewels, but I would like to think of these as special. They are so perfect . . ."

Damien kissed the slight curve of her neck, then gripping her chin with firm brown fingers, lifted her face until their eyes met. The stern lineaments of his face remained as remote as ever, but the tone of his voice held a hint of warmth.

"They are special. I may dress you in diamonds and silks from the highwayman's thievery or the earl's credit, but these are from me. Not to my mistress, but to Christina MacTavish, my friend and accomplice. You have already given me more than their value. I wished you to possess something equally untainted in return."

Christina read his meaning in the intonations of his words and the look in his eyes. He could not offer love or marriage in return for her lost virtue, but he wished to offer friendship. A week ago she would have laughed in his face. Now, understanding he was a man facing death alone, without friends or family to comfort him, she accepted his offer. Love was an ephemeral thing, but respect could be relied on. If she could still command his respect, she would be content.

Rose lips tilted upward. "You have gained a loyal accomplice, Mr. Drayton. Treat me with some measure of kindness tonight, and you may even have a friend."

Damien's hands returned to his sides, and Christina noticed he had donned a new coat of midnight blue with gold braiding for the occasion. The muscular curve of shoulders and chest strained at the tightly tailored seams, and remembering the brawny strength they covered, she flushed slightly. The elaborate lace of snowy cravat and shirt sleeves could not detract from the masculinity of his solid figure, and she felt a faint stirring of desire to see the man beneath again. She knew better than to allow her gaze to stray down the narrow hips and powerful thighs encased in tight cream-colored breeches. She had no need to confirm his virility.

With an amused lift to his lips as he watched the color rising to her cheeks, Damien replied, "After tonight, I will have a lover, Miss MacTavish. I am looking forward to teaching you the meaning of the words. Now, our guests are waiting. Shall we proceed?"

The color drained from Christina's face as she realized the time had come to seal her fate, but bravely she met his gaze and took his arm.

They descended the stairway as a couple, Damien proudly displaying the golden jewel on his arm to the audience waiting below. Christina caught her breath as she recognized Lord Jeremy and her cousin standing with the solicitor, but she had rather it be these few friends and family than the arrogant strangers like Bothwell and his rakish companions.

She met Jeremy's puzzled gaze with a cool aplomb she did not feel. Another man would immediately guess why the poor country mouse had suddenly gained silks and jewels, but Jeremy would not believe it until told. A stab of misery accompanied this knowledge. Why could she not have been an heiress and gentle Jeremy be the man to whom she gave herself? Surely she could learn to love a man as honest and kind as she knew this young lord to be. But she was not an heiress, and she must destroy all such illusions with the blackhearted Yankee at her side. She feared the power Damien held over her desires, knew next to nothing of the man behind the icy mask, but he required only her looks without wealth, and so won the battle.

As they reached the last step, Jeremy took her hand and lifted it to his lips, his gaze wordlessly expressing his adoration as their eyes met. But the touch of his lips upon her hand disturbed no part of her as Damien's black look did when he noted this greeting. She trembled beneath that obsidian glare, but no anger tinged his voice when he spoke.

"I'm glad you could make it, Standifer." His deep voice rumbled in his chest as Jeremy switched his gaze away from Christina.

"Is there some special occasion for celebrating?" Jeremy inquired lightly, though the crystal clearness of his blue eyes could not hide his uneasiness.

"Quite so. A victory of sorts, but I believe Ben here has some papers that must be signed before the celebration begins." Damien gestured to the elderly solicitor, who dipped his head in reluctant acquiescence. Then, turning to the garishly dressed young fop lounging against the newel post, his interested gaze riveted on Christina's resplendent bosom, Damien inquired,

"Mr. Adderly, have you been properly introduced to the other guests?"

Christina had scarcely noticed her cousin's presence until this remark drew her attention, and her skin crawled at his smirking expression. She did not know how much this young fool knew or guessed about her position here, but he certainly seemed to have no objection to it at the moment as Damien nonchalantly made the introductions.

At learning this flaccid youth to be the sole protection provided by Christina's absent uncle, Jeremy's look of uneasiness became one of alarm. His gaze darted from Damien's possessive hold on Christina's waist to the unconcerned smirk of Thaddeus' bony features, then shifted to Ben Thomas' sympathetic gaze. That look, more than any other, crushed all but one hope. In desperation Jeremy turned to Christina.

Damien gave no time for any communication between his childhood friend and his intended mistress. With a gesture of impatience he indicated the study.

"Mr. Thomas, if you will lead the way, we are prepared to set the ceremony in motion. I believe you stipulated two witnesses?"

Thaddeus immediately became alert, and hope flared anew in Jeremy's eyes, but Christina's calm look of resignation as she entered the study on Damien's arm quelled any instant happiness.

"Drayton, are you going to tell us what this is about?" the young lord finally demanded as the lawyer spread papers and writing utensils across the desk.

"Christina and I simply have come to an agreement and Ben has been kind enough to formalize it for us. Christina wished for a bit of ceremony and I wanted a celebration, so we gathered you here now and a few others later for a night of revelry, as it were. Have you some objection?" The dry tone of his voice said he expected none, but Damien waited for some reply.

Before Jeremy could put together the words, Thaddeus interrupted with an interested drawl. "I say, does this mean I will be calling my cousin countess?"

Christina's fingers curled nervously into her palm. Perhaps the tension in the room was all hers, but she did not like the way this scene was developing.

Damien gave the impudent interloper an amused flicker of his eyelids. "If that amuses you, by all means, call her anything you like, but generally she prefers to be called Christina."

Jeremy attempted to stutter out another objection, but tired of Damien's toying, Christina rested her hand gently against his arm.

"Don't, milord. Stand by me as my friend now and forgive me for my faults later. I know full well what I am about, and nothing will change our minds."

Damien noted this quiet interchange with hooded gaze, but taking it as an end to his little game, he turned a stern eye on the solicitor.

"Is everything ready, Ben? You have the deed as well as the contract?"

"You know I do. If you wish to have another solicitor go over it, please feel free to do so. I will tell you right now, I drew them up with Miss MacTavish's interest in mind." Wintry gray eyes glared over the top of his spectacles as he challenged Damien's black gaze.

"That suits my purpose, Ben. Let me see them."

The Yankee quietly took the offered papers and skimmed them quickly, offering them to Christina when he finished. She glanced over the legal verbiage, noted the deed made out in her name, and shook her head, returning them to the lawyer.

"I will trust in Mr. Thomas," she answered his questioning gaze quietly.

"Don't you think a more experienced member of the family ought to take a look at them, cousin?" Thaddeus had watched the entire performance with undisguised interest and now intervened when it became obvious he was not to be consulted.

The lawyer threw him a thinly veiled look of disgust but said nothing, leaving the decision to his clients.

Christina had no desire for anyone to see those papers, could barely look at them herself, and she knew

Damien would never reveal them without her consent. Yet if he were the one to refuse her cousin's request, it would seem he had something to hide. He lifted a questioning brow to her now, and Christina shook her head negatively and took the initiative.

"The papers are of little importance to anyone but myself, cousin. I am satisfied with them. That should be sufficient." She spoke firmly, with just enough authority to cause the men to stare at her with some surprise. They thought her a docile innocent, but she would teach them better.

Jeremy had remained in the shadows, waiting for some objection to come forth, but when it became apparent Christina would carry the day, he stepped forward into the lamplight.

"Christina." His voice was soft and low, urgent, and his gaze transferred warningly to Damien before capturing amber eyes.

Christina clung to Damien's arm, knowing Jeremy came closer than any other to understanding what she did and had the best chance of dissuading her. She said nothing as she met his gaze.

"Will offering my protection and that of my family change your mind in any way?" he asked softly, as if to her ears alone. The intensity of his gaze spoke more than his words, and no hint of a stutter marred his meaning.

It might have meant something yesterday, but it was meaningless now. Bothwell would be carrying the rumors all over town. The marquis would never extend his protection to such as her after that. She shook her head sadly.

"No, Jeremy, it is much too late for that. You need not witness this if you do not wish. It is only a formality."

Christina felt Damien's hand tighten reassuringly over hers as she spoke, and was grateful for the reminder. Jeremy's protection was much too late.

"No, I will stand by your side." Jeremy did not even look at his friend, but took his place beside Christina.

With a grim nod Damien reached for the first document. Sweeping it off the desk, he held it in his hand without signing it, turning to Christina.

"Nothing in this paper mentions love, honor, or obeying. They are words that have no place in my life right now. But I can promise to cherish and protect you for so long as I am able. I would rather it not be until death do us part." A grim smile crossed his face, mocking his own longevity.

Perhaps it was that mirthless, cynical smile that was her undoing. He had no illusions about what he had to offer, but offered all he could. Christina felt an inexplicable stabbing pang in her heart and suddenly wished they were alone so she dared reach out to touch that stony face. Instead, she could only echo his vow.

"Then, till success do us part, Mr. Drayton," she murmured with a hint of an impish smile, her hand reaching to take the papers from him.

He set the papers back on the desk and captured her hand instead. The brown of his hardened fingers contrasted strikingly with her slender white ones. "Your promise is more important than any piece of paper, Miss MacTavish. You promise to be mine, and no other's?"

The intensity of his dark gaze warned her of all that promise meant. Just as a bride, she must surrender friends and family and give herself up to him. Though she had no vow of marriage to bind her, she could not give her heart to another, neither could she expose his traitorous intent or his ill-gotten gains. She promised to respect his secrets, thus cutting her off from all she knew. He demanded much of her, but twice as much of himself.

Christina's fingers curled warmly about his hand. "I do, my lord."

A sigh whispered behind her, but Christina scarcely heard it. The bright flame of light in Damien's dark eyes held her enthralled, and she scarcely knew how or when he removed the ring from his pocket and slid it over her captive finger.

"To success then, my love," he murmured as he

pressed the ring home. Then, bowing his head until his lips brushed lightly across hers, he sealed their vows with another promise that only she could know.

Christina quivered beneath that swift, tingly touch, all her nerve endings aroused to a feverish pitch with that gentle reminder of what was to come. In a matter of hours his possession would be complete.

The actual signing of the papers was an anticlimax of which Christina was scarcely aware. All her senses were dominated by the masculine figure at her side, the sound of his deep voice murmuring instructions, the pressure of his hand squeezing the ring into her flesh, the proximity of his broad shoulders as he leaned beside her to point the line for her signature. She had no room for any other thought so long as he stood by her side.

Of course, the ceremony could not last forever. As the two witnesses scribbled their titles across the pages, Christina became gradually aware of the chatter of voices in the adjoining room. She glanced anxiously at Damien, but he had trained his gaze on the desk, making certain neither man had the opportunity to inspect the documents he signed. Not until he was satisfied the papers were safely signed and in the solicitor's hands did he relax and return his attention to his companion.

"Are you prepared for the reception, Miss MacTavish?"

"Or would it be better styled as a coming-out party?" Christina asked with a slightly bitter twist of the lips.

"Both, perhaps. It is better to do it here than elsewhere. At least you can escape whenever you are ready." He watched her quizzically, waiting for an angry outburst or a bout of tears.

He received neither. Christina only nodded her acceptance of his choice and steeled herself to endure the shame of the hours yet to come.

Before they could cross the portal and join the company, Thaddeus placed himself between them and the door. Arms crossed over his chest, he regarded Damien with a half-reproachful, half-cynical stare.

"You're not about to commit something for which I

will be forced to call you out, are you? For all the pretty words, that is hardly what I'd call a wedding ceremony I just observed."

Damien gave him an impatient glance of irritation. "Your cousin has made her choice; now you may make yours. Call me out and I will meet you gladly; otherwise keep your mincing little mouth to yourself. You invited yourself here; you are free to take your leave whenever you please."

Thaddeus took a deep breath of injured silence and cast Christina a furious glance, but Jeremy intruded before words of anger could lead to further foolishness.

"His lordship keeps a wicked wine cellar. Let us go explore its depths for the evening. I hear there is a place just outside Covent Garden where the women . . ." Jeremy's words faded with distance as he guided the irresolute young rake from the study. Temptation proved the better part of her cousin's valor, Christina observed without rancor.

With his hand purposefully at the small of Christina's slender back, Damien marched into the large salon of waiting guests.

Heads turned as they entered, eyebrows raised, knowing looks were exchanged, but few smirks crossed the faces of the earl's chosen party. Christina sensed jealousy, envy, and spite in the eyes of many of the women, but no condemnation, no horror at being forced to associate with a harlot.

At first she assumed they thought her still his lordship's houseguest, that her change of status was not so obvious as she felt it to be. But it did not take long for her to hear the insinuating suggestions and sly jests murmured around her and to see the knowing digs of elbows and slaps on the back as Damien presented her with obvious relish. Everyone present knew she would grace the earl's bed before this night ended and probably assumed she had been spreading her legs to him all along. And they didn't care.

This observation brought her up short, and Christina began watching this motley assemblage through eyes opened by a new cynicism. Several of the men had apparently come unaccompanied and these few spent much time by the punch bowl and supper table, exchanging ribald jokes while keeping one eye on the various physical attributes of the female company. But in the majority, the guests had arrived in pairs and it was to these couples Christina's reflections reverted.

The men were gentlemen of the sort she had met throughout her London stay: wealthy, for the most part; titled, in many cases; even powerful, in some. Some she knew to be married, but not to the women they escorted, and therein lay her explanation.

Though many of the women could very well be ladies of quality and most of the men were gentlemen of society, not one had arrived with his or her spouse. These were fashionable ladies of the evening, high-class whores, and in some cases, wives who chose to appear publicly with their lovers. Christina's eyes nearly fell from her head as she recognized the company to which she was being introduced.

"Does all London flout the vows of marriage?" she whispered in shock as she watched a perfectly respectable gentleman of the court slide his hand beneath the bodice of a very well-endowed lady married to a well-known baronet. What was even more shocking was that the woman continued her conversation with another couple as if he merely held her hand.

"Not all, but most." Damien shrugged sardonically. "They marry for money or title or convenience, and dally for pleasure. This crowd is an idle lot for the most part, with more time and wealth than they know how to handle. Still, when they wish something done, they have the power to do it. It pays to cultivate them."

The cynical tone of his voice was not reassuring, and Christina's skin prickled as he ran his hand up and down her arm. His gaze had found what had prompted her remark, and she sensed the path of his thoughts.

"Treat me like that, and I will jerk your arm out of its socket, my lord," she murmured sweetly when his dark gaze fell speculatively on the ivory curves rising above her silken bodice.

Damien pulled her closer, his grip holding her arm to her side, placing his hand in a daringly provocative position. She felt his thumb slide along the silken curve of her breast, and held her breath.

"Don't tempt me, my sweet. Every man in this room knows you're my mistress and is contemplating when he might move in on you. Just show some sign of dissatisfaction with my attentions and they will surround you in droves."

Christina swallowed this piece of knowledge with horror. It had the ring of truth to it, leaving her wondering how often he had employed this tactic to win away another man's mistress. She gave him a sharp glance that Damien blithely ignored.

As the hours passed and the tension of smiling politely beneath lascivious gazes grew, Christina began to dread the prospect of the bed upstairs less than the prospect of remaining down here any longer. She felt unclean, as if their looks were filthy hands touching her all over, and when someone did reach out and actually lay a hand on her, she flinched abruptly.

Damien quickly swept her out of reach of the amorous drunk, finding a quiet corner before grasping Christina's arms and searching her tired face with care.

"We have played our part down here. If you are ready to retire, I will call Lorna to take you upstairs."

The moment had come. Christina stiffened beneath his searching gaze, but her tired eyes melted wearily under his relentless stare. She could not fight it any longer. Other women endured it; surely she could. He had made it a wedding night of sorts, and she must honor her vows.

Reluctantly she nodded acquiescence. "I am ready."

14

Lorna bustled about, tidying away gown and other garments, while Christina sat before the mirror brushing long golden tresses to a luxurious gleam. She did it idly, without thinking, avoiding the reflection of her scantily attired figure in the mirror. The lace chemise was a gift from his lordship; she would have known it without being told. Though she had drawn in the fine ribbon of the drawstring, it still fell in clinging folds to just the top of her bosom, barely concealing anything but the tips. The material was of a weave so fine as to be almost gauze, and she knew her figure would be outlined with indecent clarity through it.

Lorna helped her to tie a matching ribbon in her hair, pulling the long curls back out of her face, leaving only one thick tendril to wind provocatively over her shoulder.

"There, lass, you do make a pretty bride. He'll not find another fairer should he search the world over."

"But another he will have when he returns to the colonies, will he not?" Christina asked with a wry twist of pale pink lips.

Lorna's expression grew sorrowful as she gazed upon the fair reflection of the young girl in the mirror. "So ye know that too, and cannot be dissuaded? Ye were not meant for the colonies, and he is not meant for this fancy life. It is foolishness what you do."

The housekeeper's Scot's burr grew more noticeable, giving evidence of her agitation, but Christina was beyond reaching. She squeezed the older woman's hand reassuringly, though this confirmation of Christina's suspicions about the woman waiting in Virginia had created an even greater turmoil. Perhaps the cad thought he did his intended a favor by taking only one mistress in her absence instead of many. Men were such fools.

Dismissing the housekeeper, Christina rose and drifted about the room. She could hear sounds of the party below dispersing; he would be here shortly. She snuffed all the candles but one. How had she come to this, waiting for her lover to take her to bed? She remembered the time she first woke in his bed, the pain and fear of the experience, and wondered how she could still be the same person she had been then. Had she learned nothing? Or did she enjoy the shame and humiliation?

When she could find nothing else to occupy her hands, Christina slid between the cool sheets, propping the pillows behind her so she could sit comfortably. One long curl fell over the nakedness of her bosom and she knew her nipples pushed suggestively against the thin cloth, but she could not disguise what she had become. Her heart beat fiercely in memory of his earlier kiss and she tried to imagine what it would be like without the protection of wooden stays and wire panniers. Her imagination needed little priming, and a flush of rose colored her cheeks.

Damien entered noiselessly. One moment the room was empty, and the next he leaned against the door, ebony gaze burning darkly in the shadows as he observed her waiting figure in the bed.

Suffocating, unable to breathe beneath his stare, Christina defended herself by boldly returning his observation. He had cast aside coat and waistcoat and cravat and stood before her now in partially open linen shirt and form-fitting breeches. He had obviously disdained the brocaded robes of fashionable gentlemen, just as he ignored the customary use of periwig. She could see the Yankee in him now as he stood there tall and straight as any Indian, the chiseled features of his bronzed visage stern and unmoving. A creature of the wild, almost animallike in his masculinity, he had no peer in this jaded society.

Christina stifled a cry of alarm when he finally moved, never once taking his gaze away from her. He carried a bottle of champagne and two goblets, and set them carelessly on the bedside table as he stared down at her.

"I have dreamed of this night until I am almost sick from the wanting of it. Now I fear doing the wrong thing and destroying the illusion."

Her eyes widened at this disturbing admission. What illusion could there be to the animal act he had carried out with such ease the first time? Nervously Christina watched as Damien filled the glasses, then sat beside her on the bed, offering the champagne.

"Surely you could have found ease with some of those willing women I saw tonight?" she offered timidly, sipping the bubbly wine and wrinkling her nose at the tingling sensation.

A small smile lifted the corner of his mouth as he observed this image of innocence. "I believe you made such an offer before. If I have only a few months in which to live, can I not fill them with all my worldly desires? I desire you, and no other. I wish a willing bride, a lovely wife, a passionate mistress, and I believe you can fulfill all those dreams. Surely we can hold such an illusion for a few short months."

Damien refilled her glass when she emptied it and Christina eyed the bubbling liquid dubiously. "Will I be all those things to you only if I am inebriated? Or does your taste still run to drugs?"

"Don't, Christina," he admonished gently, setting aside his own glass. "I regret that act as much as you, and have paid for it dearly, I believe. You have tormented me almost beyond the limits of endurance, knowing what I could have had and thinking it lost. The champagne is traditional, to ease the bride's fears on her wedding night."

She could not believe these words he uttered. She had known his desire, caught the look of hunger in his gaze, but that it could be any more than masculine lust she refused to believe. Any woman could have satiated it, but because she had denied him, his obstinacy demanded that it be her. Perhaps with this surrender, he would tire of her quickly.

Gently setting the empty glass aside, feeling the liquid bubbles effervescing through her veins, Christina turned the golden lights of her eyes back to his dark face and boldly met her fate.

"Tell me what I must do."

Damien's ebony eyes took on an almost purple iridescence as he reached long, hard fingers to touch the delicate line of her jaw. He traced the fine line of bone to gently rounded chin, then lightly stroking the underside, lifted her face to meet his bold gaze.

"Kiss me, love."

It seemed the most natural thing in the world. His arm provided the bridge between them, and Christina slipped along it easily, her fingers caressing the fine linen of his shirt as they wove their way around his neck. The hot masculine scent of his flesh had become familiar to her, and she drank it in eagerly as her lips pressed hesitantly against the unyielding angle of Damien's cheek.

And then her mouth found the hungry pressure of his and hesitancy fled. His lips held her for long intoxicating minutes, refusing to let go until she came fully into his arms. With her breasts pressed against his chest and her arms entwined behind his neck, he plied her mouth with gentle kisses, driving her mad with the desire for more.

She finally yielded to his persistence, parting her lips so that their breaths intermingled in a heady drug of their own. He kissed her deeply, drawing out a quivering response that marked the beginnings of passion, and Christina was lost.

Damien's hands traveled the length of her back, molding her closer to his hardness, and Christina melted against him eagerly. He bent her backward in his embrace, the urging of his kiss sapping any remaining resistance. Her hands slipped beneath his arms and her fingers clenched the rippling strength of his back as Damien lowered her to the pillow.

His kiss found new paths to follow now, and Christina moaned with the pain of it as his lips seared trails along her skin and she could not reach them. His hand lowered her chemise over her shoulder and his kisses gradually found their way over satin skin.

When he had explored that territory sufficiently, he moved back in the other direction, and Christina gasped with the hot fire of pleasure that shot through her when he reached the soft swells of flesh above her bodice and lingered in the valley between. With a deft movement he pulled the drawstring and the gown fell loose, freeing her breasts to his pleasure. The touch of his lips upon a tender nipple sent Christina into a whirlwind from which there was no escape.

She had fought him once when he had done this, but Christina could no longer imagine why. She strained against him, and he suckled greedily, drawing her trembling flesh into the searing heat of his mouth and incinerating all reluctance.

When his mouth finally returned to hers, Christina clung to him gratefully, her hands sliding beneath the open collar of his shirt and reveling in the hard smoothness of his skin while his lips twisted savagely across hers. She met his hunger with a need of her own, and it was Damien's turn to groan as she pressed her bared breasts against the furred mat of his chest.

"My little kitten is a lioness," he murmured against her ear, tumbling full length against the bed and pulling her with him. With one swift move he divested her of the chemise, and she lay naked against him.

Amber eyes glinted dangerously above him, but white teeth flashed happily against dark features. "A wildcat is much more entertaining than a purring kitten. Unfasten these damned breeches and let me feel all of you against me."

Lying on top of him like this, Christina found herself free to indulge her own desires, and did so with wicked wantonness. As her lips teased the hard muscles of his ribs, her fingers struggled with the fastenings of his breeches.

Damien aided her inexperienced efforts and soon she found herself grasping a handful of coarse hair where once there had been cloth. She quickly withdrew from this dangerous field and returned to the more familiar pleasures along the planes of his chest, but Damien had had enough of this teasing.

With a chuckle at this innocent limit to her daring, he rolled Christina beneath him, trapping her narrow hips with his muscular thighs while pinning her shoulders between the trunks of his arms. Christina gazed upward into dark-carved features, his bronzed torso filling her field of vision, and felt no fear. His strength might be greater, but she had the same power as he to induce this craving to be consumed.

"I am going to make you mine, Christina," he warned. "I intend to possess you in the same way I possess Westshipham Hall, my ship, or my plantations. If any man dare steal what is mine, I will kill him. Do you understand what I am saying?"

His heavy weight pressed her against the mattress, and in her heightened state of sexual awareness Christina was acutely conscious of the point where his masculine hips rubbed hotly against her belly, and her frenzied desire blurred his words to a siren song. But she understood and rejoiced in the understanding. She wanted to be his and no other's, wanted the security of his protection and not the loose freedom of a whore. And she knew that with her possession, she gained a victory of sorts over his arrogant coldness.

"To success, my lord," Christina murmured ambiguously, lifting her arms to pull him down to her kiss.

As if sensing the ambiguity of her submission, Damien fastened his lips to hers with a savage need that left them both gasping. His fingers curled around the vulnerability of her bare breasts, crushing them in his grip, teasing the crests to aching needlepoints of desire. His hand slid lower, encountering the moistness of her womanhood and caressing her until Christina wished to scream with the frustration of unfulfillment.

Satisified he had driven her beyond the point of no return, Damien casually rolled over and removed the remainder of his clothing.

In the flickering of one candle behind the draping of bed curtains, Christina could see little of the man revealed, but just the silhouette of the flat-stomached, lean-hipped man beside her set her legs to trembling. Undressed, he leaned over her, the hair-roughened skin of his legs brushing against the satin softness of hers as his hand traveled over the length of her curves, charting his territory.

Then he spread her legs with gentleness and knelt between them, and her aching readiness became one of fear. Christina's fingers gripped his shoulders convulsively, weakly holding him back. She could feel the throbbing heat of his hardness at the entrance to her body, and felt suddenly naked and defenseless beneath his strength.

She uttered no words, but Damien seemed to understand. His hand brushed the tousled hair from her forehead and his lips planted a light kiss there, then continued downward until they reached her mouth. With skill and a driving hunger he stoked the fires of her desire to an even higher flame, until the touch of his masculinity between her thighs created a raw, aching chasm that left her begging for his filling.

"Damien, please," she pleaded as his kisses covered her lips and face. Her hands slid daringly down his broad back, pressing him closer.

He needed no further persuasion. Christina cried out her joy as he eased into her. No pain marred this joining—she felt only the sweet bliss of completion and now understood she could only be whole like this, in his arms.

As his body began pumping into hers, she surrendered herself totally to his demands. Damien groaned with delight as she rose to meet his thrust, and cupped her rounded bottom in his large hands to guide her motion.

The exquisite torment of this impalement swiftly became a mad ride over which she had no control. They raced wildly along a precipice of dangerous heights, Damien carrying her higher and higher until the dizzying peaks brought convulsions of breathtaking magnitude. Then Christina felt his explosion deep inside her and she hung on for dear life as their bodies quaked and shuddered and became one forever.

She knew it would be forever. She could not imagine any other man in his place possessing her as intimately and knowledgeably as he. She had not known what her full surrender meant, nor understood how this joining tied and bound her body and soul. He had become a part of her, and a silent tear crept along her cheek. He had done what he had promised. She had been foolish to take his words lightly.

Damien found the tear with his lips, drank of its saltiness, and gathered her close, relieving her of his weight by rolling over and tucking her securely against his chest.

"I did not hurt you this time, did I?" he murmured throatily against her ear.

Christina shook her head against his shoulder.

He contemplated this silent reply and did not question further.

Although he offered food and shelter and security of a sort, they both knew he did not offer what she really needed. Silence seemed the only reasonable reply.

15

They woke and made love again during the night after the candle had guttered out, their bodies reaching instinctively for each other in the darkness. Damien's passion seemed less controlled, more ruthless with this joining, but Christina welcomed his wildness and held him tightly afterward.

Not until the morning sun had gilded the room with its light did they wake again. The covers had slid to the floor during the night and the dawn chill had not yet left the room when Christina shivered and moved closer to the heat of the man beside her. His large palm came to rest on her breast, then slid down the valley of her waist and pulled her closer upon discovering the chill of her fine skin.

Christina's eyes immediately flew wide as she found her nakedness held full length against his. The night before had seemed a dream, but daylight brought harsh reality. Meeting amused dark eyes, she groaned and buried her face against his shoulder. She had done it. She had become a whore, a harlot, the mistress of this Yankee thief. What madness had possessed her?

But she knew very well what madness it was. Even as she averted her eyes, she drew closer to his masculine strength, the wild rush of heat stirred by his caress sending the blood careening through her veins.

"Good morning, my love." Amusement threaded his voice at her ostrich act, but the memory of the previous night's pleasures kept him confident of her compliance. "Are you cold? Shall I warm you?"

At the insinuating tone of his voice, Christina looked up with alarm. "It must be almost noon. Mrs. Douglass will be coming in . . ."

"Not if she has any sense at all, and Lorna is a remarkably sensible woman. Surely my lioness does not grow shy with the dawn?"

His lips began to trace a teasing pattern along her hair while his hands sought and found the soft purchases he preferred.

Christina smothered a gasp as she felt his rising ardor between her thighs. "Surely we cannot . . . Not during the day . . ." Her eyes widened with amazement as he disproved this fallacy with amazing ease, slipping his hand between her thighs and parting them just enough to allow his entrance.

"What was that you were saying, my dear?" he murmured wickedly against her ear, before tumbling her back against the mattress and making his point even clearer.

Damien took her gently, sensitive to the bruising and chafing he had inflicted upon her earlier, and Christina warmed rapidly to this new aspect of lovemaking. When she reached the same heights as he, he took her quickly and firmly, his seed filling her with its thick heat as they shuddered together, making his possession complete.

In the daylight she could explore the hard contours of his body more fully, and she did so now, hesitantly at first, but growing more sure of herself when he made no objection. Her fingers traced the bandage on his shoulder, and when he winced slightly, she frowned worriedly.

"You have not strained it overmuch? Perhaps I should look at it."

Reluctantly leaving the haven of her arms, Damien rolled to one side, his ebony gaze drinking in the sight of smooth flesh and rounded curves that were now his to possess at will.

"It is healing. Do not pamper me," he commanded almost curtly. His hand circled the proud tilt of her breast, and he watched thoughtfully as the rosy crest hardened with his casual manipulations.

Though he had just taken her, Christina could feel a renewed surge of desire in her belly, but his curt words prevented her from reaching out to caress the long, hard planes of the bronzed body beside her.

"Is your illusion shattered, then?" she asked proudly, not allowing his words to touch her.

The hardness melted from Damien's face as he smiled. "Not even in my wildest dreams could I have imagined the lovely illusion you gave to me last night. I craved your beauty and your softness and meant to take the lady to my bed and make her cry out to be my whore, but I had no idea the lady was a disguise more effective than the earl. I think I like the wildcat as much as the lady. Where do you keep her when you are so demurely purring over teacups?"

Christina blushed beneath his bold gaze. She must have behaved like a brazen hussy for him to regard her like that. Yet how did a lady act under such circumstances?

"I was taught the manners of a lady, but my teaching did not extend behind bedroom doors. You must teach me the proper behavior if you are displeased."

"Displeased?!" Damien roared, swinging from the bed, his male nudity awesome in its magnificence. He stared down at her with mixed amusement and incredulity. "What makes you think I am displeased?"

Christina could scarcely think at all with him standing over her like that. The stern lineaments of the Yankee earl had blurred somewhat with the night's pleasure, and russet hair curled in a disconcerting fashion about his face. Those powerful athletic shoulders still seemed frightening in their immensity, yet now she knew they could hold her with tenderness, and she lost some of her fear. Altogether, she found him incredibly handsome and terrifyingly attractive, and she could scarce loosen her tongue to reply.

"You said you desired a lady in your bed. I didn't think a wildcat a very complimentary substitute."

Damien laughed and reached to pull her from the bed. "Fool. A man enjoys a lady during the day, easing his mind and softening his surroundings." Succeeding in bringing Christina to her feet, he loosed the last remaining ribbon from her hair and watched with satisfaction as it fell in a golden cascade about breasts and shoulders. "But a lady in bed is a deadly bore. She lies there and endures her husband's attentions simply for the sake of begetting sons and expects him to go elsewhere the rest of the time for his pleasures."

Christina stared up at him with amazement. He spoke jovially, with no hint of his usual grim cynicism, and his words were startling to an extreme.

"You mean, if I were to be a proper wife and lady, I must lie still and not respond to your caress and actually encourage you to go to another woman's arms?"

His grin tilted crookedly. "I believe you said as much just last night, if memory serves me rightly."

Christina searched her memory and had the grace to blush. "That was different. I am not your wife. I have no right to expect you to be faithful, but if I should ever have a husband . . ."

The amusement left his face and he gripped her arms hard, forcing her to look up to him. "You can consider husbands after I am dead and gone. Until then you are mine and you will do what pleases me. I have no use for whores, and any man who treats you as one will find the point of my sword at his throat. Flaunting a mistress gives my name the reputation I seek, but do not let the society I introduce you to give you ideas. You are here solely for my pleasure, and I will demand your complete loyalty until I am gone."

Christina stared at him with some bewilderment but nodded agreement. "I am not accustomed to lying, nor to whoring, my lord. I gave you my vow and I fully intend to honor it. I only sought understanding. I will not mention the subject again."

He relaxed and let her go. "I prefer you mention a subject than ponder it without my knowledge. I will not take you out into London's seamy side without removing some of your innocence and ignorance."

He picked up his discarded clothes from the night before, then gave her lovely figure another appreciative stare. "Although I rather prefer you as you are. It seems a shame to show you the glitter that can be yours for the asking. I would rather think of you as returning to the country after I am gone, but I cannot expect to direct your actions then. You will soon see how the other half lives and make your choice on your own."

With that, he strode through the connecting door, leaving Christina to stare after him, alone and bewildered.

She entered her mother's suite later that morning, nervously fingering the delicate ring of gold and diamonds Damien had given her the night before. She had scarcely been aware of its presence until Lorna had admonished her for wearing it on her right hand, where Damien had placed it. A wedding band must go on the left if she wished to fool her mother.

Eleanor MacTavish greeted her daughter with a smile, anxious eyes sweeping Christina's pale face and nervous hands. Her smile did not falter as she gestured for Christina to sit by her side.

"It is done, then? Damien has taken you for his bride?" she asked eagerly, unable to disguise her hope and happiness.

Christina nodded, unable to lie as glibly as Damien, but desiring her mother's happiness more than anything.

"Then why so pale? Surely Damien could not be so crude as to use you harshly on your wedding night? Or is it the secrecy bothering you?"

Christina closed her eyes and took a deep breath. Her mother could be as blind to reality as a babe in the woods, but at other times she displayed an amazing perceptiveness. Christina had feared her mother would not expect the marriage to be consummated until publicly announced, but her mother was no fool. She must have realized Damien's nature would never allow such a delay. Christina allowed a genuine smile of delight to spread across her face.

"Damien has been more than kind. I never expected . . . I never dreamed . . ." She stopped, at a loss for words for the passion-filled night he had shown her.

Eleanor nodded understandingly. "I know. It was like that with your father. I am so glad for you." She hugged her daughter, then sat back and watched the tears of joy slide down Christina's fair cheeks.

"I feared your Yankee might be too harsh for you. I suspect his is of a passionate and possibly dangerous nature, not so gentle as his father's. Watching the two of you together is like watching a thrush attack a thundercloud. Perhaps with time your gentler nature can tame his wild spirit. You have much of your father in you. He had patience and strength aplenty, and a pride that would allow him to bow to no man. You are your father's daughter, Christina. No matter how strong a man he is, you will not let Damien get the better of you. That is good. He needs to be reminded he is not invincible, I think."

Christina wished to laugh and cry at this ingenuous speech. How could her mother understand their characters so well and still be blind to the inevitable? The Lord of Westshipham would never marry a merchant's daughter in any fantasy world anyone ever lived in. But her mother was still lost in daydreams of her own youth, when she might have had the earl's younger son, and did not realize the difference a title makes.

Before she left, her mother caught her hand and admired the intricate wreath of delicate gold about her third finger.

"It is beautiful, Christina. It looks old and somehow familiar. Is it part of his mother's jewels?" she asked quizzically, straining to remember where she might have seen the ring before.

Harboring a strong suspicion that it might be part of the highwayman's loot, Christina did not attempt to look at the gift too closely. "I doubt it, Mother. He did not come here prepared to marry. I daresay he saw it in a shop and liked it. It suits his taste."

Eleanor looked dubious, but did not argue. Helpfully she suggested, "You had best wear it on the other hand or your marriage will soon be a public one."

Christina bit back a hysterical laugh and did as told. She seemed to have acquired two mothers these past days. It might grow a trifle difficult to anticipate and please them both.

She did not have long to ponder her mother's eccentricities. A maid announced a caller in the parlor and produced a tray with Lord Jeremy's card. Christina stared at it with helplessness, wished for Damien's presence, and resignedly agreed to accept the call. He had stood by her last night; she could not deny him now.

Jeremy had not changed his clothes from the night before. Indeed, it appeared as if he had never gone home. His pale blue coat was wrinkled and soiled, the lace at his wrists and neck a disgrace, and his normally affable features had grown dark hollows and lines. He glanced up at Christina's entrance, and the muddied look of usually sparkling blue pierced her to the heart.

His gaze slowly took in her fresh appearance, the high color of porcelain cheeks, the shining gold light of amber eyes, the simple innocence of her muslin gown, and his face seemed to draw together in resignation.

He had lost his hat somewhere in the night's revels and his hands hung awkwardly at his sides as she advanced. "I shouldn't have come, but I could not stay away. Jenkins just carried your cousin to his room, but I could not seem to reach the same blissful state of oblivion."

"Jeremy, you are punishing yourself for something over which you have no control. Why?" Christina wished for the means to reassure him, but did not know how.

"Tell me, do you love Damien?" he demanded, ignoring her question but answering her thought.

Christina stared at him, eyes wide with thought. She could lie if it would ease his mind, but there seemed little point in it. "He would destroy me if I should be so foolish," she replied honestly.

Jeremy gazed hard upon her, trying to see beneath fragile features to the woman beneath. "Then why?"

She heard the hurt and recrimination in his voice, but shrugged them off. "He would have sent me back to Cornwall and that would have killed my mother. It is not your duty to worry over me."

"You could have come to me," he reminded her.

Annoyed at his persistence on a subject she would rather not discuss, Christina answered tartly, "I take it you have not been listening to Bothwell, then. All the company last night knew—your family would certainly have heard. Don't be ridiculous, Jeremy."

His face saddened. "Then it is true. I hoped perhaps you would change your mind, but he claimed you long before last night, didn't he? The papers were just a formality. I cannot decide whether to call him out and carve that black heart of his from his chest, or give up on both of you."

His harsh words hurt, and Christina choked back a sob of dismay. She had known she must cast aside all respectable society with this step she took, but to be torn abruptly from this one true friend caused a pain she had not expected. Holding on to her pride and her love for this young lord and his sister, she responded with tears in her eyes.

"If those are the choices, I would suggest the latter, my lord. Damien has been known to live by his sword, and much as I hate to lose your friendship, I prefer to preserve your life."

A bitter quirk turned a corner of Jeremy's mouth upward. "I should know better than you his skill with a rapier. I was Damien's fencing partner back in school, until he outpaced the masters and none could best him. Even then he seemed to have some fierce purpose in his learning. Pistols are more popular, but I daresay he has mastered them also. Damn the man, he gives no quarter."

The tears threatened to brim over in Christina's eyes

at these words. She admired Jeremy's gentle, amiable nature, the strength of his honesty and character, and she could not bear to see the bitter turn Damien's betrayal had taken. Yet some sense of wry humor remained at his own deficiencies, and she prayed the hurt would mend with time. If only she could say the same of his sister.

Restraining the urge to reach out to him, she murmured, "At least this should preserve Seraphina. I cannot bear to imagine what she must think of me, but I trust she will think less of Damien now." Then with barely concealed anguish, Christina poured out her heart. "She is the first friend I have ever known, Jeremy. Please make her understand what has happened. Do not let her think too harshly of me. It is breaking my heart to think she will feel I have misused our friendship."

Gulping back a sob, unable to control her tears any longer, Christina turned to flee, but Jeremy caught her, encircling her fiercely in his embrace until she wept freely on his shoulder.

"Drayton would have swallowed Seraphina whole and gone looking for more, only she is too foolish to understand that. But you are not a fool, Christina. I do not know what hold he has on you, but if you ever feel the need to escape it, come to me," Jeremy demanded earnestly. "I do not have Drayton's power or wealth, but I will be your friend and offer whatever is within my reach. Do you hear me, Christina?"

Jeremy murmured these last words against Christina's hair, holding her comfortingly until her sobs subsided and she nodded silently. Then, gently releasing her, he stepped away from temptation.

"Thank you, my lord. Tell Seraphina farewell for me." Christina fled the room then, leaving a heartbroken Jeremy to find his own way out.

Christina sat at the desk in the library, scribbling furiously across the paper, when Damien entered it later that evening. The glow of the soft lamp beside her and a small fire in the grate were the room's only illumination, and he hesitated in the shadows, watching the intensity of her expression as she attempted to put her thoughts to paper. Golden hair fell in deceptively delicate ringlets about features feminine in their softness, the straight line of her nose blending harmoniously with the full rosy bows of her mouth and the golden accent of her eyes. Yet the lamp threw into sharp relief the shadowed hollows of strong cheekbones and determined chin and he knew her fairness a disguise fashioned by nature. He strode confidently into the room, awaiting her reaction.

At his approach Christina threw down her quill and rose from the chair, stepping forward to greet him. Granite features softened slightly at this response, and he took her hands in his, holding them gently while he searched the shadows of her eyes.

"You're home early, Damien." She still had difficulty voicing his name and not his title, but she practiced it deliberately to please him.

"I decided to devote one evening to the tutelage of my new student. A man has a right to an evening's pleasure when he takes a wife." He released one hand to throw his tricorne across the room, then used it to brush lightly the golden gleam of her hair.

This game of calling her "wife" pleased her, and Christina smiled saucily at the obvious twinkle in his eye. "Do you mean all these evenings you spend away from home are not for pleasure?"

A small frown puckered the bridge of his nose, but Damien slid his hands about her waist, neatly encircling it. "Not my idea of pleasure. Tomorrow you will begin accompanying me. Then you will see."

Christina felt a tremor of fear at the way he said that. He had voiced his reluctance at taking her out on the town before, and his tone now indicated some underlying unpleasantness in it, but she chose to accept his words at face value.

"I am to be introduced to the gambling dens of London, then?"

He regarded her quizzically. "And worse. This pleases you?"

"You will be with me, will you not?" At the affirmation in his expression, Christina shrugged nonchalantly. "Then I have no objection. Gambling is not one of my afflictions."

A mocking look lit his obsidian eyes. "But I am?"

A small grin tilted Christina's rosy lips and she reached to play with the lace of his cravat, avoiding his eyes as her fingers came in contact with the hardness of his chest. "Most certainly."

A grin flitted across his features at this flirtation, but he controlled it before lifting her chin so that their gazes met. "You saw Jeremy today. Why?"

Christina sighed and flattened her hands beneath his waistcoat, seeking reassurance from the steady beat of his heart. He did not speak with anger, she saw none of the grim distrust she had seen frequently before, but he still demanded explanations. He trusted no one.

"He is my friend, Damien. You have placed me in a position where I can entertain no women friends. Allow me this one relationship."

For a moment he hesitated, his hands biting tightly into the folds of material at her waist. But when she raised eyes of innocent amber to his face, he relaxed and released his hold.

With firm deftness his fingers unknotted the bow holding her kerchief, and his hands slid below the fine linen to push it from her shoulders. Ivory breasts rose enticingly above the ruffle of lace at her neckline, the valley between shadowed with promise, and he gazed upon this loveliness with appreciation.

"Just so long as I am the only one allowed to do this," Damien murmured warningly. "I am glad to see you wear the new chemise. I grew most tired of those high-necked ones."

His fingers caressed the line where lace met flesh, and Christina trembled with the longing he never failed to stir within her. She had given her soul to a devil. This must be her punishment.

She moaned slightly as he found the covered hook between her breasts and unfastened it, giving him the freedom to invade her bodice with impunity. Strong brown fingers closed about the nipple thus exposed, and Christina's hand dug into the cloth of his shirt.

"Don't, Damien. Someone will enter," she protested weakly, her head dropping to his shoulder as he calmly pushed aside her chemise and lifted the heavy weight of her breast in his palm.

"No one will dare enter without knocking, and I am in no mood to wait for bedtime. We will begin your lessons now, I think. If your ambitions are to become a high-class whore, you must learn to accept the attentions of your lover without protest. Men have wives to complain of headaches and watching servants, so they want mistresses who greet them warmly and with affection."

Christina cast him an anxious glance, her flesh chilled by his calm instructions, but his expression remained impassive. She felt a surge of anger but controlled it. He wanted an obedient mistress and she would be one or die trying.

With deliberation her fingers crept below his cravat and linen to slide provocatively along warm, hair-roughened skin. "If that is your desire, my lord, then I am at your command."

If his lips thinned harshly at these words, she took no notice, and a moment later neither cared. As Damien's hands slid along her shoulders, shoving aside bodice and chemise to expose the fullness of her flesh, he bent to stop her words with his kiss. The sudden flare of desire between them melted all else, soldering them in a molten steel of exquisite brilliance.

He undressed her effortlessly, his nimble fingers finding all the feminine hooks and ties and ribbons until Christina's skirts and petticoats and chemise slowly slipped to the floor at her feet. The fire's golden light flickered along ivory skin, sending shivering shadows over shapely long legs, silhouetting the roundness of soft buttocks, leaping higher to accent proud breasts and gleam softly in golden tresses. Against the staid bleakness of the stiff library, she shimmered like a candle flame, and Damien admired the contrast openly.

He seemed fascinated by her state of undress in this cold room of moldering books and old leather and dusty carpets, and Christina encouraged his fascination. She lifted her arms to unpin her hair, well aware of how the action lifted her breasts and displayed them to advantage. The hunger behind his eyes burned brighter, and she felt a surge of satisfaction at this small power she held over him.

Hair tumbling about her shoulders, Christina came into his arms willingly. The crispness of his cravat crushed against her breasts as her hands slid along his brocade waistcoat, pushing aside his collarless jacket as he had done her chemise earlier.

Shrugging off the cumbersome coat, Damien captured her waist and held her with his kiss, his hands running slowly along slender curves as their breaths joined and intermingled and she melted against him. With russet hair tied back in a velvet bow, his white brocade waistcoat glimmering in the firelight, his powerful legs encased in buckskin breeches, he was every inch the aristocratic gentleman he purported to be, but his savage kiss told another story.

When he pressed her hips against the place where his maleness strained against the tightness of soft leather, Christina groaned deep in her throat and rubbed instinctively against this welcome hardness. She was as wanton as he claimed her to be. Without bed or champagne or whispers of love, she desired him, and made no secret of that desire. Her fingers slid to unfasten his shirt, seeking the warmth of his flesh within.

With her bared flesh against his, Damien could control himself no longer. Knocking a stack of pillows from the decrepit leather couch onto the floor, he lifted her gently and laid her back against the pillows. Standing over her, his mighty legs planted firmly on either side of her slender frame, he became the savage warrior again, but Christina felt no fear.

Damien divested himself of breeches and boots and Christina gazed upon his masculine physique with no small measure of awe. An old sword wound marred the bronzed flesh along his ribs and the new one showed angry and red, but his towering frame was otherwise faultless, like a fine honed weapon of devastating ability.

He wasted no further time on the niceties. Propping the pillows beneath her rounded bottom and the small of her back, Damien knelt between her legs, poising there until Christina's eyes were drawn to meet his. She caught her breath at the burning intensity she found there. He meant to consume her, possess her body and soul, make it impossible to erase the brand of his flesh on hers. And he was succeeding.

As her eyes filmed over with the desire he aroused in her, Damien's granite face set in grim satisfaction. She moaned softly, thrusting her hips forward to beckon him, and he obliged.

Christina bit back a scream as he pierced her fiercely, filling her completely, until she thought he would surely split her asunder. He impaled her thoroughly with his maleness, making certain she understood his mastery, before easing his thrust and forcing her to learn patience while he plundered the ripeness of her mouth and breasts with his lips.

She scarcely needed his rhythmic thrusts to bring her to the shuddering cataclysms of the night before. He had prepared her well, and all control she might once have possessed took flight, dashing her from the precipices with his first motions and erupting over and over again as he took his pleasure from hers. His seed poured deep within her womb, possessing her with a life of its own as they shuddered together, his hard flat belly pressing down into hers.

With awe Christina began to understand the magnitude of this joining of their bodies. It brought pleasure, but it brought a good deal more. She could feel the life within her as clearly as she felt his maleness rubbing against her belly. Perhaps not now, perhaps not for days or weeks, but soon that life would take root. She knew it with the age-old wisdom of her woman's body. He would plant his seed and linger to watch it take root, and then he would be gone, leaving it to grow and flower and bear fruit within the fertile ground he had chosen.

Tears filled her eyes as she gazed up into the handsome, dark-carved visage above her, tears of joy at this miracle he had wrought. Did he know what he did, then? Did he know he passed on future generations through her? Had he chosen her for that purpose, knowing he might not live to have another child?

Christina did not dare question. When Damien wrapped her carefully in the soft linen of his long shirt, she snuggled gratefully within its man-scented warmth. And when he lifted her and carried her from the room as if she were no weight at all, she rested her head against the security of his shoulder and felt his arms tightening protectively about her and slept.

16

Warning Christina to be dressed for the evening's excursion, Damien departed for his daily tour of the coffeehouses. Most of the male population of London's gentility gathered in these spots daily, and any news worth knowing first appeared there.

Sitting in her bath of soapsuds, Christina watched sadly as he put on his hat and left without a backward look. Except when the mood took him, he did not even know she existed. She was a convenience like an efficient housekeeper or a good cook, someone to make his life more pleasant but never actually a part of it.

Shrugging, she stepped from the wooden tub and dried herself. He had never promised anything more, and she had not expected otherwise. He indulged himself and not her when he bought her satins and jewels and spent long evenings removing them. If she could just remember that, she would be safe.

She found Thaddeus at the sideboard, helping himself to a platter full of breakfast, when she entered for her morning cup of chocolate. He gave her a sidelong glance that took in the fashionable drape of her low-cut gown, the elegant and costly circle of gold about her finger, and the obvious frown on her fair forehead.

"Good morning, cousin . . . or should I say, good afternoon? His lordship must keep you well occupied in the evenings for you to rise so late."

The idea that this fatuous young fop was any relation to her made Christina nauseated. The striped silk waistcoat he had on looked like a carnival tent and she hoped he would choke on the impossibly high wrapping of his cravat. The effeminate outlines of his dissipated face seemed more distinct than ever this morning, and the narrow eyes hidden beneath a heavy fold of flesh had a decidedly ratlike cast to them.

Remarking this fact with a smile of satisfaction, Christina helped herself to the pot of chocolate and pointedly ignored his greeting. Seating herself at the head of the table, she frowned with displeasure when he pulled out a chair at her side.

"I think it is time we chatted, Cousin Christina. Perhaps we have more in common than you know."

"That is highly unlikely, Mr. Adderly." Her icy tones would have frosted windows, but her cousin had the sensitivity of an elephant, she observed.

"Your mother is a lovely lady, delicate, and probably as old-fashioned in her thinking as my father. I daresay neither would look approvingly upon the manner in which we spend our time."

His insinuating tone told her in what direction this talk led, but Christina refused to acknowledge his meaning. She would not let the termite disturb her. She would need to develop a thick carapace if she wished to survive in Damien's world.

"I have no idea how you spend your time, Mr. Adderly," she answered idly, helping herself to jam for her toast.

"But his lordship has left no doubt as to how you spend yours. What would our elders think if they learned your position in this house is flat on your back with your legs spread in his lordship's bed?"

His crudity brought a violent spurt of anger, and Christina's lips tightened against the phrases she would use on him. She must consider the source and act accordingly. Her nonchalance obviously irritated him or he would never have taken this tack to get under her skin. If she could maintain her own control, it should be amusing to see what happened to his.

"Have you been peeping through windows, Mr. Adderly?" she inquired with boredom.

His narrow face seemed to acquire a mottled look, but he repressed any display of temper. "The way you two behave, one does not need to peep through windows. I cannot imagine how you've hidden your secret from your mother, but I think she will believe me if I bring my father back to tell her what all London knows."

Alarm prickled along her veins, but Christina knew now it would be dangerous to display any such emotion. Carefully she drew him out.

"Why should you go to all that trouble, Mr. Adderly? Neither of them would appreciate it, I am certain, and the earl would most likely sever your tongue from your head for returning his hospitality in such a manner."

Her cousin's face cleared at this opening, and he continued much more confidently. "I can assure you, that would be my last resort. I have no desire to disrupt the path of true love; I am most enlightened about these matters. Of course, the earl cannot marry the daughter of the town clown, or whatever, but I do not think you so foolish as to accept a substitute without some recompense. His lordship made it quite clear the other night that you are bought and paid for. I merely wished to share in the bounty until I have increased my holdings somewhat. My allowance is minuscule at best and London is a dread bore without a bit of the ready. A pittance from time to time would prevent guilt from overcoming pleasure and forcing me to notify my father of your present unhappy position."

So that was it. Blackmail. At least she had judged the character of this toad rightly. Short of having Damien skewer him to the wall, Christina did not know how to get rid of him. He would scream to his father if she had him thrown out. And there was every chance her mother would believe the words of her long-lost brother over Christina's. She couldn't allow that in any case. It would be pleasant to have Damien run Thaddeus through with a sword—until they arrested the Yankee for murder or some such triviality. No, she had best keep Damien out of this for now. His temper was precarious at best.

"I presume you are asking for money?" Christina asked coldly, not even bothering to glance at the poisonous spider beside her.

"Just some spending cash to keep me in clean cravats and occasionally bankroll a wager or two. Playing at chaperon is most tedious when everyone laughs behind your back. I figure you owe me something for the humiliation."

"You are receiving room and board, Mr. Adderly. I cannot imagine what more you expect." Christina lowered her gaze from the ceiling to freeze directly on his pale face and ratlike eyes.

Thaddeus shrugged. "I expect a share in your good fortune or a release from this odious position. The latter would necessitate writing my father, of course."

"My good fortune, as you style it, keeps my mother and me from starvation and gives us a roof over our heads. It does not extend to ready cash."

That was a lie and she had told it boldly! A milestone of some sort. Damien had left coins in a drawer for her needs, and she had only to call on the solicitor to begin drawing the funds Damien had provided for her. But Christina had no intention of encouraging this leech with such news.

Thaddeus shrugged, unconcerned. "There are numerous ways of supplying that lack. That ring, for instance, could easily be replaced with paste, and we could split the difference. Speak to the merchants who supply your gowns and whatever. They will gladly pay you for your order and bill his lordship for the difference. Use your imagination, cousin. Your beauty will not last forever, and a tidy nest egg will serve you well."

Christina had not heard anything so crass in all her life and realized Damien opened a new life even he could not have imagined. Or had he? He trusted no one and she did not doubt that he would count her jewels and gowns accordingly. Disgust was the aftermath of shock. If even her idle cousin knew these ploys, must it not be common practice? Had no one in this world any morals or honesty?

Deciding what she lacked in morals she would supply in integrity, Christina vowed to starve before she committed such monstrosities. But there was no need to tell her cousin that.

"He would notice the ring. It is too obvious. The others will take time. Damien is not overly generous with his credit, if you have not noticed."

No lies, and she carried out this act with a finesse Damien would appreciate. Christina hid her smug grin behind her cup.

"My funds are growing low and I have run out of credit. Do not take too long, Christina," Thaddeus warned.

Christina cast him a scathing look, drained her chocolate, and strode gracefully from the room.

She had succeeded in wiping the encounter from her mind by the time Damien arrived to escort her out for the evening. She dared not contemplate the company they would be keeping now that she had fallen to a level below society's notice. Other courtesans flaunted their outcast position, but Christina had no desire to make that kind of scandal. She would prefer to stay at home and not face society at all, but that did not suit Damien's purpose.

She glanced at the daring cleavage exposed by her carefully pinned gauze kerchief. The silk bodice of her gown followed a Parisian design, shamefully covering only her waist to the undercurve of her breasts. Above the rose silk, only her chemise and kerchief hid her nudity, and their fine lace and gauze did not conceal the pointed ripe crests beneath. Christina felt scandalously naked and fingered the kerchief nervously, praying it would not come loose from its mooring.

Damien's entrance drew her away from these contemplations. He entered through their connecting door, evidently having returned home earlier to wash and shave and change, for she could smell the faint scent of his shaving lotion, and his elegant suit of forest green seemed freshly pressed.

Ebony eyes swept over her attire approvingly, coming back to rest with interest on the full curves pushed up and outward by the gown's design.

"Madame Alexander did not warn me I would need my sword when you wore that gown. It is a good thing I planned on taking it."

Christina glanced quickly to his hip, noting with horror that he had indeed donned sheath and sword. Her gaze swiftly returned to his dark visage, searching for explanation.

As usual, she found none. Damien's expression remained impassive as bronzed fingers raised to fondle the daring crests pressing against the gauze of her kerchief. The sensitive nipples rose and hardened beneath his touch, sending shivers of anticipation to the pit of Christina's stomach, and he smiled with satisfaction as he gazed down into bewildered amber eyes.

Christina's breath shortened as she lost herself in murky black pools, and she knew for the remainder of the evening she would ache for a repetition of that touch, pray for the moment when he would shove the hindering material aside and lift her into the searing heat of his mouth.

And he knew it, too. She could see the grim satisfaction in the set of his jaw as he slid his fingers along the edge of her kerchief and watched the flare of desire in her gaze. He knew he had not only paid for her services, but owned her in the only way a man could own a woman.

Christina shuddered with relief as Damien let her go with just that reminder. She still felt shame that this man was the one who raised such insatiable longings in her. Why could it not have been gentle Jeremy or even the ignorant farmer Thomas? But it had to be this man who looked on her as a plaything, a toy to be discarded when the time came. Pure shame scalded her veins as he led her through decrepitly elegant halls to the waiting carriage.

The gambling parlor he led her to was one of the more respectable ones, and Christina breathed easier as she recognized much of the company of their earlier party. At least he would not introduce her to the smoke-filled filth of the East End this first time.

Still, her education expanded another notch as she watched fortunes won and lost over the turn of a card or the spin of a wheel. Some of the amounts wagered doubled or tripled the amount Damien had set aside for her, and she could easily live a lifetime off just the interest on such a sum! Such insanity scandalized Christina's Scots frugality. The passion wasted on such a pastime seemed worthless to an extreme.

In the nights that followed, she learned to recognize the men who made their living off this sickness and the women who encouraged their spendthrift habits. She watched as the winners wandered off to upstairs rooms with women of dubious reputation or into the streets where thugs and thieves awaited drunken victims. These scavengers made the daring thieves who were known to rob by daylight seem almost heroic in comparison.

Damien folded his last card and leaned back in his chair to glance around the smoke-filled room. Without hesitation his gaze came to rest on the slim golden girl caught up in a conversation in one corner. It was seldom he had a chance to catch her unaware like this, and he watched with interest.

His lips twisted wryly as he realized Christina conversed with equal animation to a duke of the royal house and his companion, a woman blatantly off the streets of Covent Garden. He had been worried about lowering her to the status of his mistress, but he should have known better. Not only did the position of an earl's mistress raise her above that of country miss, but Christina possessed a quality that set her apart from all others in any situation. She seemed to have raised herself to the status of his peers. When he was gone, she would be able to move in exalted circles with ease, if she so desired.

Instead of pleasing him, that thought irritated Damien irrationally. He had done everything within his power to make her despise him so that the break, when it came, would be an easy one. He knew there was no chance of transplanting an English rose like Christina into the wilderness of his home even if she would be willing to part from her mother, which she would not. He had always known he must leave her here, but something within him resisted this irrefutable logic. He had come to fulfill the duties required by his country, and when they were done, he knew he must return to his home and the war. Christina and her invalid mother must stay behind, but Damien's usually practical mind could not quite grasp the concept.

As he watched, a viscount of their acquaintance came to stand beside Christina, his arm daringly sliding around her supple waist. With a savage snarl Damien shoved back his chair, glad for this excuse to vent the anger boiling up within him.

To no avail! By the time Damien had crossed the room with furious intentions, Christina had efficiently extricated herself from the unwanted embrace and came forward to greet him with a welcoming smile. The smile faded as he grasped her arm harshly and dragged her from the room, and his fury lost itself in her confusion.

But the frustration remained, with no outlet to vent it.

As the weeks wore on and Damien worked his way down into the seedier depths of London's pits, Christina came to know a good deal more than she had ever wished to know about London life. While the men gambled, she found herself in conversation with other women in the same position as she, women who had been the rounds and knew the ups and downs and ins and outs of this life, and their warnings horrified her.

She had known many of the upper rooms in and about Covent Garden were trysting places for illicit lovers during the day and whorehouses in the evening. But with shock she learned the upper rooms in many of these lower-class dens harbored the dregs of society who catered to every perverse need known to mankind. The screams she heard above the cacophony of drunken gambling and singing were not necessarily the results of argument or delight. They had an equal chance of being the screams of those who sought their own punishment or punishment of others with whips and other instruments of torture, or the cries of a helpless innocent imported for someone's salacious needs. Christina grew to dread the sound, and from there, to dread these evenings altogether.

Her obvious reluctance began to draw black frowns from Damien as she dawdled over dressing and primping, delaying their inevitable departure for as long as possible. As she debated over several paste necklaces and earrings and then the appropriate adornment for her hair, his scowl deepened.

"Christina, both my time and my patience are limited. I realize you are not comfortable with my choice of entertainments, but you knew what to expect when we made the agreement. Now leave your hair and let us go."

Reluctantly Christina rose. She had grown accustomed to the gawdy jewels and scandalous gowns; she had seen much worse on others. She could not grow accustomed to the open leers directed at her barely covered bosom, but Damien had taken to keeping her close to his side, and the threat of his sword kept all but the most reckless at bay. Those few soon learned their folly, and Christina now felt quite secure from unwelcome advances, and he knew it. Thus his impatience at her reluctance.

As he helped her don her mantle, Christina attempted to voice her apprehensions. "I do not see what we are accomplishing by this nightly foray into depravity. Of what use am I to you? What difference would it make if you went alone?"

Strong hands placed the silver cloth around her bare shoulders and lingered caressingly. Increasingly Damien found himself torn between two roles, but practicality always prevailed. She was a tool he had purchased for his use. He could not allow her to be anything more, and she must realize it, for now, at least.

"Two pairs of eyes and ears are better than one. I

can relax and devote my full attention to what I am doing, knowing you will warn me of any unexpected approach. At the same time, you are hearing and observing things that might have missed my attention while I concentrated elsewhere. My task is shortened and made easier with your help. You do not know what beneficial information you have given me already."

Christina remained skeptical. "Such as?"

"You remember the man you pointed out to me as a cheat last week? And the pickpocket you warned me of?"

Christina nodded. Damien stood behind her and she could not see his face, but she had come to learn his every expression. He was speaking thoughtfully now and his eyes would not be on her, but lost in the phrases that would give explanations without telling too much.

"I had not noticed them until you brought them to my attention. A little blackmail goes a long way, and between them I learned a great deal. I have a fairly good idea now which houses Nicholas owns and operates. I have only to narrow them down until I know in which he lives. He does not show himself, but he must know I am getting closer. Sooner or later, he must make up his mind what he intends to do."

The rough grating of hatred in his voice made Christina shudder. She would hate to be this man's enemy, hunted and hounded until flushed out for the kill. She did not doubt for a moment his ability to do so, but she feared the consequences with all her heart and soul.

"Is it so necessary, Damien?" she whispered sadly. "Could you not get your papers signed and sail back to the colonies and leave this man his dreams of glory? Surely he would not come looking for you across an ocean."

"He came for my father and yours, he has come for me, and he will come for my brother and my sons. He must be stopped, Christina, and I will not leave England until I stop him."

"My father? Why do you say my father?" Christina's heart lurched at this unexpected reference.

"I told you I corresponded with him. I found correspondence between Argus and my father after my father's death, and I wrote to let him know. He was most anxious to be assured my father died naturally, since he had been informed Nicholas had sailed for the colonies some months earlier."

The silence that fell then seemed unbreachable. Christina knew he waited until she understood the full implications of the words. Her father had been the first to notify the young lord of his bastard cousin's danger. And her father had been murdered. She bowed her head in acceptance.

Damien turned her around and held her in his arms, smoothing golden curls against his chest. "I can prove nothing, Christina. No court of law would hold him. My father broke his neck in a fall from a horse. He was an expert equestrian. I was at sea at the time, but my brother nearly suffered the same fate. Only at the last moment, he changed horses, and the broken saddle strap threw another. The chain of incidents is too long, Christina. My father's desk was rifled before I returned home to inspect it. I suspect your father's letters were read by someone besides me."

Christina's tears had long since dried; she had not cried again since surrendering Jeremy and Seraphina for this man who held her now. She would have liked the relief of tears, but they did not come. Her father had sought to do what was right, and so in the process had died, leaving his wife and daughter bereft. Now she must follow the same course.

"The man intends to kill you, then, and you are making it easier by standing in his path. What happens to your other mission if you should die before it is completed? Is this personal vendetta more important than your country?"

Damien smiled slightly at the serious expression lining such a pretty face. He could see the tears glittering just below the surface, but she had matured too much to let them fall. Soon his country maiden would be as worldly and sophisticated as the jaded society to which he had introduced her. It was a pity, but was her only protection once cast out into the world on her own, as she had been before and would be again soon.

"I have obtained most of the signatures requested. There are only a few vacillating, and one who has been unreachable. The men who signed it are as aware as I of the danger of its falling into the wrong hands. The papers are well hidden and will go to Paris without me, should I fall."

"Paris?"

"You will know all my secrets if you continue questioning, my dear. We will tarry no longer."

As Damien smoothed back a stray hair in her coiffure, Christina became aware of a movement beyond his shoulder, and her brow wrinkled with puzzlement. Surely the door had been closed when Damien entered? Yet it stood slightly ajar now.

She glanced around as they stepped into the hall, but she saw no one. It must have been her imagination. Her nerves had grown much too edgy lately. She would go mad if she thought someone always watching.

17

Thaddeus had grown more than impatient with Christina's promises and delays. His threats became increasingly ominous, and when she found him entertaining her mother on her first day downstairs, Christina's alarm grew proportionately. Mrs. MacTavish still had to be carried up and down the stairs, but her public availability made Thaddeus' threats more real. Christina began to delve into her pockets for small coins to appease his greed, knowing only a matter of time kept him from demanding more.

She knew she must tell Damien, but he had become increasingly preoccupied now that all his goals were almost at hand. The estate had been portioned out to meet its debtors to the best of his ability, and they lived on what remained of the highwayman's loot and his winnings at the gaming tables. Judging by the depraved surroundings they found themselves in most evenings, he must have narrowed his search for his bastard cousin, and from hints he let slip, Christina knew his traitorous papers were almost signed and ready. Their time together was almost at an end.

The thought of this alone kept Christina's stomach in a turmoil that knew no relief. Thaddeus' blackmail scarcely compared as a source of torment. She had thought the months would last an eternity, but they had flown by so rapidly he could scarcely believe Jeremy when he informed her his family would be leaving for the summer shortly. May had almost escaped without her notice.

With troubled gaze Christina watched as Damien reached across the card-covered table for his winnings. His angular face had grown harder and more drawn these past weeks, and she knew his suffering to be more than her own, although of a different nature. His plans relied on skill and timing and an element of luck. If any failed, his life would be forfeit. She shuddered and looked away. How could she bother him with the mundane problems of her cousin's blackmail or her own confused emotions?

For confused they had certainly grown. It had been difficult enough to juggle her hatred and her desire for this man who had made a whore of her, but hatred had become something else, much less distinct, and desire had become an overwhelming passion. Christina could no longer imagine days without him, and nights would cease to exist without the Yankee's hard, lean body beside her, caressing her with tenderness or simply holding her thoughtfully. What would become of her when he was gone?

Christina grimaced as she noted Bothwell weaving a path through the crowded room toward them. They had encountered him infrequently these past weeks, but rumor had it he had been losing heavily at the tables. His misfortune did not make him any less disagreeable, and Christina sought some means of avoiding him.

But the smoke-filled crib, dense with unsavory characters from every walk of life, left little in the way of protection. Resignedly she clung to Damiens chair and waited for Bothwell's usual cynical opening remarks.

Instead he sidled up behind her, out of Damien's hearing, and produced a hastily scribbled note.

"Have you any money with you?" he whispered cautiously as Christina hastily scanned the note.

She crumpled the paper with disdain and threw it to the floor. "I have a gold piece Damien gave me for luck. I take it that is insufficient to save his fool neck."

"I have a purse with me. I'll loan you the difference.

I'm sure Drayton's good for it. Come, we'd best hurry or there will be nothing left of your cousin to save."

Christina glared into his cold gray eyes with scorn. "He is my cousin, and I suppose this once I must bail him out before making his disgrace known and sending him back to Cornwall, but I see no reason why I must do it publicly. I will give you my paper for the amount owed and pay you back on the morrow, but I have no wish to see the wretch."

Bothwell threw her an impatient and furious glare. "Do you not think I have already tried that? He played for high stakes with forged notes, so they are prepared to carve him into little pieces and throw him in the river as a lesson to others. They may listen to your pleas, but they damn sure won't listen to mine."

Christina paled slightly and gazed anxiously at Damien. He was engrossed in a conversation at the table while seemingly tallying cards; she could not interrupt with this piece of foolishness on Thaddeus' part. Her cousin deserved a beating, but she knew the reputation of the gamblers in these places and did not doubt they would kill him.

"Where is he?" she whispered, and followed Bothwell's nod to an adjacent room. Not too distant; she could be back within minutes.

Accepting Bothwell's arm with instinctive distrust, Christina followed him to the back rooms of the gambling hall.

The noise from the main hall suddenly deadened behind the thick oaken partition, and Christina glanced around hurriedly. Above her, carried by the open stairwell, came cries of dubious and ominous origin, and she chose to ignore them. With relief she spied Thaddeus, bound and battered, but alive. At least Bothwell had told this much truth.

Her cousin's pale face offered a grimace of acknowledgment through torn lip and purpling bruises. "Thank God, you have come," he muttered thickly. "Talk to them. Make them listen to reason, Christina."

He pleaded with her, but his eyes shifted uneasily,

never looking her in the face, and Christina's nervousness mounted.

"Plead with whom? I see no one. Bothwell, untie the wretch and let us get out of here." She tapped her toe edgily, disdaining to soil her hands on the fool at her feet. She held no sympathy for blackmailers and cheats.

Bothwell threw her a look of scorn. "Where would we go? There is no back door and I can assure you the front is well guarded. The men we must talk to are upstairs. They must be amenable to reason if they have not killed him yet."

He caught her hand and tugged her toward the stairwell, but Christina resisted. "I refuse to go farther. If they want their money, they will come here for it."

"Christina!" He cousin's cry of despair became a shriek of terror.

The sudden flare of malice in Bothwell's eyes told more than she wished to know, and Christina spun swiftly for the exit.

In an instant, powerful fists clamped her arms behind her back and a rough hand shoved a filthy rag between her teeth as she opened her mouth to scream.

"I told you the bitch would not fall for such stupidity."

Christina's eyes swung with horror to Thaddeus as he rose to his feet and threw off his shackles. Dissolute blue eyes regarded her with malevolence as she fought her unseen foe. He strode out without another word.

She tried to scream, but could not. Harsh ropes wrapped around her wrists as she wriggled and struggled against her captor. She knew Bothwell held her, but some other had joined him. A stink of sewage and dead fish filled her nostrils and the callused hands binding her were not Bothwell's effeminately soft ones. Those crept to pinch her breast as she was roughly heaved over a brawny shoulder.

"I will see you soon, my sweet." Stony gray eyes gleamed coldly up at her as, bound and trussed, Christina was carried up the stairs.

Still struggling futilely, she was hauled down a narrow corridor of closed doors and dumped unceremoniously on a hard cot in a small room behind a door similar to all the others. The door closed and the sound of a bar snapping in place sealed her fate.

The filthy gag stifled her cries and dried her mouth. Rope tore delicate skin. Darkness deprived her of sight. In some far room she could hear whimpers and sobs, and closer, she could hear the unmistakable noises of passion. A brothel beyond a doubt, and one of the most unsavory sort for a certainty.

Christina remembered well the horror stories she had heard of these riverfront houses, of the brawls and murders of roistering sailors, of the damages inflicted upon the trollops who welcomed their drunken advances. Only the dregs of the streets, desperate for coins for ale or worse, worked these houses. What was she doing here?

Panic rolled in cold droplets across Christina's skin even though the rancid heat of this airless prison was almost stifling. What did they want with her? And who were "they"? Bothwell's warning ran alarmingly in her ears, but she could not believe he had arranged this kidnapping just to finish what he had once started. If so, he would be in here now.

Christina's mind sought frantically for reasons and for means of escape, finding neither. She scrambled awkwardly to her feet and backed against the door, feeling for the latch. It was locked, as she had expected, and examining the door's hinges, she surmised it had been bolted on the outside. No escape.

In a fury of helplessness, Christina kicked and battered at door and walls for what seemed hours, until, exhausted, she collapsed in a miserable huddle upon the bed.

Below, Damien felt Christina's absence like a cold draft upon his skin, but he played his cards cautiously, not daring to rouse suspicion. She could have wandered off on her own, but her absence triggered dark imaginings. His attention no longer remained on the game or the gossip, but fastened intently on his surroundings.

The discarded wad of paper on the floor became a wealth he coveted greedily. It took cautious maneuvering to retrieve it without notice. He gathered it up with a "lost" card and read it hastily, just as a slight commotion arose at the back of the room.

Damien wadded the scrap in his palm and with his eyes followed the path of a badly bedraggled but strangely triumphant Thaddeus as he stalked around the room's edge. A minor tough who acted as a collector sidled his way into Thaddeus' path, and Damien watched through narrowed eyes as the young fop paid his debt in gold. The paper in Damien's hand burned like a branding iron.

Hastily concluding his game, Damien rose and began shoving his way through the crowd. An inexplicable nausea choked at his gullet, and for the first time in his life, fear became a palpable reality.

Nightmares haunted Christina's exhausted unconsciousness. Rats rattled the rafters and perspiration rolled down her back into the stinking covers. Binding ropes irritated chafed wrists each time she tossed or turned. The noise of the door scraping against the floor sometime later brought instant wakefulness, but cautiously Christina kept silent.

It did not matter. The broad figure outlined in the doorway seemed to sense her wakefulness, and he spoke accordingly.

"You are not stupid, so listen well. My cousin's arrogant confidence will not allow him to leave you here. When he comes for you, I will kill him, as I have every right to do to protect my merchandise. When the Bow Street runners come, as they surely will when an earl is murdered, you may tell them you have been kidnapped and held against your will and your lover murdered. Do so, and I promise, within the week you will be in the hold of the next slaver out of here, your fine white body pawed and violated by every perverted diseased sailor on board day and night until you die."

His deep, resonant voice seemed to linger sensuously

on the threat, as if it was already being carried out and he was enjoying the result. Christina's skin crawled as she realized this must be the bastard Nicholas, her father's murderer, and he undoubtedly meant every word he said.

Nicholas closed the door and stepped forward, bringing with him the scent of musky cologne and fine wine. In the darkness he seemed larger than life, and with a shudder Christina realized Damien had met his physical match. Though this man must be much older, he moved with muscular stealth and sureness, and she doubted not that his physical prowess equaled his younger cousin's.

A cold hand stole along her lightly covered bosom and Christina caught her breath as icy fingers slid expertly beneath her bodice to nip at tender crests. She bit back a cry of pain as he twisted his fingers cruelly. Horror held her paralyzed as she realized her vulnerability in this perverted creature's hands.

Nicholas chuckled and withdrew his hand to ride it knowledgeably over the curve of her waistline and hip as if testing the strength and lines of a horse's flanks.

"Do not cringe so. My tastes do not run to youth or innocence, though your beauty is tempting. Mayhap, with a bit of teaching, you might win the honor of my bed. In the meantime I offer you your second choice."

His hand left her and came back with a ghostly flash of silver. "You will tell the runners the dead earl tried to kidnap you, that you are actually my property. They will believe you when you display the mark that brands all my girls."

The icy knife slid in a flourish along her bare breast. The letter N seared across her skin as if already branded, though the point did not nick her skin. The blade withdrew, but the violent shivering it had initiated could not be so easily halted. Christina gritted her teeth painfully to keep from crying out her terror.

"Of course, as one of my girls you must earn your place, but that should not be too difficult with your looks. I have promised you to Bothwell first. He has a tendency to be a little rough. You will have to learn quickly how to handle that kind of customer if you are to leave your looks unmarred. But the pay is good, and as I said, once you are properly trained, you might serve me. I think I might know one or two things more than my cousin."

His chuckle was not lewd but self-confident. He had all surety that she would choose his bed to that of multiple rape and death at the brutal hands of diseased sailors. But her fate seemed far distant to the more immediate one of Damien's. Would he come? Christina was not as certain as this bastard.

With a shock she felt the ties at her wrists severed with a single stroke. Before she could move her lifeless hands, the large shadow at her bedside disappeared as if he had never been there. Again the lock clicked and the bolt slammed home.

Christina jerked the gag from her mouth and rubbed frantically at aching wrists. She now understood what Damien had feared for her. This Nicholas was a ruthless animal who would stop at nothing, had no conscience whatsoever. He treated her as a whore because he thought her one. If he had thought her Damien's wife . . . The thought did not bear considering.

What if Damien did not come? It did not matter. Her fate would be the same in either case. If he came, he would die. Without Damien she had no protection. Bothwell would claim his due, and if she survived that, another man would take his place, and another, and another, until she had learned the tricks the perverted Nicholas needed to slake his lusts.

She would rather die first. With that thought in mind, Christina began to search the room systematically. She had a vague awareness that the sounds in the next room had changed, that the cries of passion had grown strangely quiet and that the cacophony of the gambling hell carried louder now, but her only concern lay within this room. She must find a weapon, a way out.

Only the wooden bars of the disreputable cot offered any hope. With patience she broke her fingernails and tore her hands at the unyielding wood, searching for some means of dismantling it. With a cry of triumph she pried loose an oak slat, and she stood uncertainly, looking for some means to employ it.

With no other fate to look forward to but death, Christina was fearless. Her throat and mouth were parched, but she summoned the strength to scream with all the fury she had stored for the weeks and years since her father's death. She would bring the house down around the ears of this madman who threatened all she knew and loved!

When her screams had no immediate effect, she began pounding floors and walls and door with her wooden mallet. Nicholas might come and throttle her, but even that was preferable to her ultimate fate. With luck she might warn Damien or start a riot. If anyone dared open that door, he would surely feel the weight of her fury.

A wild surge of hope renewed Christina's frenzy as she sensed an increase in the riotous noises in the corridor. Women screamed, men cursed, and if she heard rightly over the racket she raised, steel clanged against steel. A thunderous roar brought the smell of sulfur, but she did not desist. She would be heard, whatever pandemonium reigned out there!

Damien threw aside his smoking pistols and strode through the opening they had created in the riotous crowd of the upper hall. With his black cloak billowing from broad shoulders, the deadly rapier at his side, and his stern features set in a fierce expression, he appeared as a demon straight from hell to the other occupants of the smoke-filled hall.

A sailor leapt through the upper-story window with an ear-shattering battle cry, landing straight in the path of a knife-wielding thug running up behind Damien's unprotected back. Damien ignored the piercing cry that ensued, ebony eyes fastened upon a place well beyond the shoulders of the men around him.

Another sailor grappled with a half-dressed woman in the doorway to one of the rooms, but the grin on his unshaven face indicated he had no need of assistance. The echoing racket of a woman's screams at the far end of the hall continued to hold Damien's undivided attention.

A gentleman grasping at his partially buttoned breeches drew his sword in fear upon sight of the grim specter in black bearing down upon him. Damien whipped his rapier from his side and with a few swift strokes disarmed his hapless opponent. He had no time to uphold the honor of idle gentlemen.

A path through the melee began to open before him, and Damien hastened through it, his heart pounding so fiercely in his ears that it drowned out the screams around him, but not the ones from behind that barred door. The deadly expression in his coal-black eyes prevented any other man from inhibiting his stride—that, and the two bodies lying on the staircase behind him.

The splintering crash of an ax against the wooden door sent Christina reeling backward. Her hands stung and her throat ached and a thousand terrors rocked her insides, but she clung desperately to her wooden staff. No man would take her against her will ever again! Murder sang through her veins and her fingers clutched the rigid bar tighter.

The door crashed open, and instantly Christina leapt to her feet, her one weapon arcing downward toward the head of the intruder. A hard hand seized her wrist and sent her weapon flying before she could distinguish the outline of her cloaked assailant. Without a word of warning, she found herself crushed triumphantly in his tight embrace.

"Damien! oh, my God . . . Damien!" Christina flung her arms around his welcoming figure, tears of joy and fear streaking her face as she clung to him and he rocked her protectively in his arms. She could feel his heart thudding beneath hers and his arms held her fiercely, as if never to let go, but his words came with cool authority.

"If you must brain someone, let it be one of those thugs in the hall. Come, let us get out of here."

Damien grasped her waist tightly and led her into the melee of the corridor. Christina gaped in confusion at the mass of screaming half-dressed women fighting off roughly garbed and armed sailors while bemused men of every walk of life and in various states of undress either fought or sought to escape the riot. A path seemed to open before them and close protectively as they passed, and no one made any attempt to check their flight.

Downstairs the pandemonium of hell reigned. The smoke of candles and tobacco had become a thicker stench of burning wood that encompassed the room in darkness. Screams of terror split the air as the crowd sought windows and doors of escape. With calm certainty Damien smashed his boot through a half-papered, half-boarded window, tearing the hole he made until it opened enough to allow them passage.

Without a word he swept Christina up in his arms and carried her through the splintered shards, out into the fog-laden night air.

A shrill whistle produced a clatter of hooves in the narrow alley and a carriage loomed recklessly against the patch of sky between the buildings. At the same time a mass exodus began from the windows above. Even as Damien threw open the coach door, Christina watched with amazement as agile sailors scurried down previously unseen ropes, disappearing into the London fog as phantoms in the night.

Damien gave her no chance to question. Before they were firmly seated, the coach lurched forward, scattering all and sundry in its path, its unseen driver shrieking and snapping his whip to drive the horses on.

Gradually, as terror subsided into less threatening, shuddering fear, Christina became aware she still rested in Damien's arms, her head against his shoulder while powerful muscles clamped her firmly in place. She could not see his face, but the grim tension of his hold told her his jaw would be set in fury and his eyes lit by black lightning. She had learned his moods well these past months.

His hand drifted along the curve of her waist and Christina pressed herself closer to the security of his warmth. She feared his anger centered on her, but she was reluctant to leave this one haven of safety in a fearsome world.

"I feared you would not come, milord," she whispered forlornly, "and I feared worse that you would. He promised to kill you."

In the darkness she felt Damien's attention turn outward, away from himself and his own private pain. His lips brushed against her hair and his grip lightened, becoming more caressing. When she nestled closer against him, some of the tension holding him rigid relaxed.

"I should have thought that would have met your approval. You have wished me dead often enough."

The mockery was aimed at himself as much as at her, and Christina refused to rise to the bait. She had quit hating him long ago. She did not know what she felt for this dangerous Yankee, but she did not wish him dead. Her hand came to rest on the broad expanse of his linen-covered chest and her fingers played idly at the fastenings she found there. He had saved her from hell, though he himself had placed her within its reaches. The complexity of her emotions could not deal with all these facts at once.

"No, Damien. To wish you dead would be to wish the same for myself. Do not taunt my weakness any longer."

Damien's breath caught in his throat at this admission, but he refused to believe its truth. She had been badly frightened and did not know what she said. Like a terrified child, she clung to him for reassurance. Slowly he expelled his breath and answered with amusement.

"Weakness? I saw no sign of weakness back there. The only time I feared for my life was when you threatened to bash my skull with your cudgel. Had you been a fraction stronger or swifter, you would have accomplished my cousin's task for him. As it was, the commotion you made was sufficient to cover the approach of my men."

Christina gazed at him in wonder. He spoke with a warmth and humor he most often kept hidden, and his words were strange to a degree. She had no bravery, she had only sought her choice of deaths. And what else had he said?

"Men? What men? How did you reach me without meeting Nicholas?" she demanded almost angrily. He spoke as if it had all been an amusing episode! Perhaps, to him, it had been.

"It is not the first time a shipload of angry sailors has torn apart a house of ill repute. Do not concern yourself over the matter," Damien replied abruptly.

Christina let these words tease the corners of her mind, not daring to follow them further. A shipload of sailors! What else did he hide from her?

He did not give her time to ponder more. Bending his head to meet hers, Damien plied her lips gently, asking, not taking. Christina absorbed the sweetness of this pleasure with gratitude, needing the reassurance of his caress, but she could not be long satisfied with these butterfly touches. Her lips craved more, and Damien gladly supplied it.

It seemed suddenly urgent that he hold her, love her, possess her as he had not before, and their kiss melted to a molten lava that threatened to erupt if bottled too long. Christina clung to the urgency of Damien's fiery embrace, wanting to believe it held more, much, much more, than the heat of passion. She yielded to its promise.

18

Damien carried her past the gaping Jenkins, oblivious of the silence of the darkened house and its sleeping occupants. With determined tread he traversed the long hallway until they reached the suite of rooms they had shared separately these past months. Ignoring the door to Christina's chamber, he swept through into his own, laying her against the heavy velvet coverings of the massive mahogany bed.

Tawny gold curls fell in disheveled array over maroon velvet as he set the tinder to the oil lamp. Its light flickered across porcelain features pale with fatigue but coloring rapidly beneath his burning gaze. Amber eyes flecked with gold met his bold gaze bravely, and she remained motionless where he had placed her as he quickly inspected the damage inflicted by the night's disaster.

Damien muttered thickly at the chafed wrists and torn hands, holding them gently in his great palms as he determined the extent of her injuries. Then, at Christina's motion, he poured water from the pitcher and watched as she drank it eagerly.

Christina bore his scrutiny proudly, her heart still pounding wildly with the passion his kisses had aroused earlier. He had held her and possessed her for many nights, but this night would be different. She sensed it, and so did he. Her surroundings all but proved it. Never before had he allowed her the intimacy of his private chambers. He came and went as he chose in hers, but she had never shared this part of his personal life. He had held himself aloof all these months. What did he mean to do now? Christina's heart thundered in her ears as she returned the glass to the table and sought his gaze.

Dark eyes held hers with a yearning need she had never before encountered there, or perhaps, only once, that day in the library when he had spoken so oddly of denying himself much for the sake of a principle. Damien's hand stroked the curve of her jaw lightly as he searched her face with care and apprehension.

"Christina . . ." The name was torn from his lips. Dark chiseled features twisted with an agony that Damien could not put to words.

Christina wanted to reach out and caress the pain away, to heal the hurt she read in his eyes. He needed her, and she ached to supply what she knew, instinctively, only she could give, but too many bitter words and moments separated them. She did not know how to chase them away.

"I am sorry, my love." Damien finally forced this much between his teeth, and the rest came easier. "Tonight could have been much worse, and I have only myself to blame. I do not dare ask your forgiveness for all the wrongs done you. I have only one gift left to give you. I hope, I pray, you will take it with more understanding than I have offered to you in the past."

Fear clutched her trembling heart and Christina covered his hands with her own where they rested against her face. She stared up at her arrogant Yankee, noticing how the russet hair escaping from its knot curled softly against a rock-hard cheek and wishing desperately to stroke it. Yet he had never allowed her any gentleness, and she did not dare it now.

"Damien, please, I do not read minds, and you are frightening me. What do you ask?"

He smiled wryly, and capturing her hands, held them between his own. "I ask nothing this time, Christina. I give you your freedom. You have more than adequately accomplished what I requested of you. You may walk out of here tonight if that is your wish, and I would not blame you."

Christina's hands went icy cold and the beat of her heart became a dull thud in her chest. Panic and fear warred behind her eyes and she attempted to jerk her hands from his grip. Damien continued to hold them firmly. Was this it, then? After all these weeks and months, had he tired of her? And why did he choose tonight of all nights to tell her? She wanted to scream her rage, but could not. The pain was too great.

Tears welled up in her eyes when he refused to release her, and she jerked her head away from his steady gaze. Damien allowed himself a small shred of hope as he released one fragile hand to wipe away the trickle of moisture.

"Christina, my love, you are not listening. I do not mean to send you away, though if I were a less selfish man, I should." Light touched the angular jut of his cheekbone as he spoke, and Christina watched the play of light and shadow with fascination, mesmerized by the low, deep tone of his voice. Damien took her silence as permission to continue. He sat beside her and gazed into her eyes as he spoke slowly.

"Tonight may be my last night in England, my love. Until now, I have taken care only to possess your body, Christina, and you have never surrendered more. Though I have injured your pride, I have not dampened your courage, and you have rightly refused me all but what we bargained for. Tonight, I would ask more of you. I am a man without a future. I can make no promises, but with your freedom you take my heart. Can I ask for some small piece of yours in return?"

Christina choked on a cry of mixed dismay and joy as she read the truth of his words in the nakedness of Damien's dark eyes. The flame he kept well disguised behind heavy curtains blazed brighter as it came in contact with the wild flare of joy in her eyes. He made no move to take her in his arms, but waited impatiently for her reply.

"Damien!" Christina cried in confusion, not at all

prepared for this. "You ask too much. I cannot . . ." But she could. So easily she could. She wanted to fling herself into those strong arms and declare her love and eternal devotion and live happily ever after, but there was no ever after, and she had spent too many months denying her emotions to loose them now.

She shook her head in confusion, tousled curls falling in disarray about bare shoulders. The pain in his eyes was reflected in hers, making it no easier.

"Damien, if it helps to know . . . There will never be another man in my life. I could not . . . You are my husband. Do not send me away tonight. I could not bear it. Please." She pleaded for understanding.

In reply, Damien gathered her in his arms and covered her hair with kisses. She had given him the answer he sought, whether she realized it or not. The war might be a long one, but it had to end sometime. Tonight he believed in his own invincibility. If he knew she waited . . .

"Then, my wife, whatever happens after tomorrow, I will return for you. Tonight I will teach you to love."

Tears flooded her cheeks as Damien laid her gently back against the pillows. With excessive gentleness he began to undress her, lingering to caress the rising curve of her breast, to admire the taut flatness between the delicate angles of her hips, to slide his hand lovingly along her flanks.

With all the energy he had previously devoted to his urgent mission here, Damien pursued this new undertaking. Christina discovered the awakening of a long-suffocated joy, a desire to live and love and to return the life he gave to her. To be loved by this man would be a greater miracle than she had thought humanly possible. It did not matter if she could not be wife, it only mattered that she held his heart. An incredible release of love and laughter spilled from the pent-up dam of her heart, and through the magic of her fingertips it spread its contagion to the man above her.

With a laugh of sheer delight, Damien threw off his clothes and came eagerly to her arms. Giddy excitement held them in thrall and they frolicked with the insanity of this new understanding.

Christina pummeled his furred chest as Damien tickled her spine with taunting fingers, then nibbled daringly at his ear as he drew her closer against his nakedness. Purposely burying the specter of fear that haunted them, they laughed and explored each other as if for the first time, daring new sensations, tasting new delights, until at last they loved.

As Damien drew her under him, covering her thoroughly with his male solidity, Christina wondered if he had guessed what was yet only an infinitesimal hope in her center. Still too uncertain of this new plateau of joy they had found, she did not dare speak her hopes, but only offered them with her body.

Wrapping her arms tightly about the muscular strength of Damien's back, she arched welcomingly to his thrust, the piercing ecstasy of this joining sufficient for now.

Limp and exhausted, they lay in each other's arms in love's aftermath. This night he did not leave her, and Christina slept soundly in the security of Damien's embrace.

They woke to face another day. Love had not flown with the night, but as the thunderclouds hid the sun outside, so did reality raise its ugly head to blot out joy. They made love in silence, with heartrending tenderness, clinging long after passion was spent.

As Damien rose reluctantly from the cocoon of warmth they had woven, his hand lingered longingly on the flatness of Christina's belly.

"I trust I have planted a son there, madam," he said almost gruffly, "for then I know I have bound you more thoroughly than words could ever do."

Christina shivered at the depth of passion his words revealed, and she reached out to hold him, but he had already broken the cocoon and escaped. She pulled the blankets over her and watched as he padded about the room gathering his clothes and shaving utensils.

"Is that why you put that clause in our contract,

about the child?" she asked warily, uncertain in the morning's light of the evening's reality.

Damien bent a dark look of mockery upon her before returning to his razor. "Would you have me reveal all my secrets?" he asked tauntingly.

She did not take his words amiss but kept her own silence. She wanted to trust him, but he had erected too large a barrier between them to scale with one night's loving. That she loved him she understood now, though she could not give the reasons why. But she knew that if he returned for her as promised, she would follow this wicked adventurer to the ends of the earth without question.

Christina watched closely as he shaved and washed, sensing this might be the only time she would ever do so. She memorized the way he held his neck up for the razor's scrape, refusing to contemplate the noose that awaited it should his mission fail. Her gaze lingered over the play of powerful muscles along the lean lines of his back and broad shoulders, imagining how they must look in the clean light of the sea air as he sailed his ship toward home. Home. A million miles and a lifetime away. Christina sensed his eagerness to be off, and tears stung her eyes.

Damien turned and caught the surreptitious rub of her hand across her eyes. Beneath the sheets he could see the sensuous outline of the lovely figure he had made love to just moments before. His loins ached to return to that comforting haven, but time had reached a premium.

Wearing only the tight buckskin breeches he had drawn on, Damien crossed the room and sat down at the bed's edge, trapping her beneath the sheets.

Christina drew herself up on one elbow, tawny curls falling about satin shoulders as she searched his dark face. She knew he wanted her, she had learned the signs well, but this time she knew he would not take her. Sadly she waited for his words.

With strong, capable hands Damien drew her to a sitting position. Wordlessly he took her hands in his, examining the delicate ring he had placed on her right hand. With instant decision he drew it off and replaced it on the left.

Their gazes met, ebony eyes impenetrable as always, amber ones open and vulnerable. A small smile lightened and softened Damien's rough-cut visage.

"You said last night that I am your husband. This ring makes you my wife. If all goes well, I will be leaving tonight. My ship is in the harbor and my work is almost done. I cannot take you with me this time, but when I return, you had best be prepared to take our vows before a preacher. For better or worse, we are wedded now."

Love, hope, joy, anxiety, and dismay chased their way across Christina's mobile features. She still feared this arrogant man who held her heart, but she did not doubt his word. She was whore no longer, but wife. An ecstatic glow lit golden lights in her eyes.

"Shall I learn to be highwayman or countess while you are gone?" she asked teasingly, not daring to voice her hopes or fears.

"Neither," Damien growled a mock irritation. "If my lioness cannot wait patiently in idleness for my return, she may occupy herself in whatever pastime suits her fancy, so long as she comports herself in such a manner as not to aggravate an exceedingly jealous husband. Now, give me a kiss and let me be off. I have work to do this day. If you are good, we will attend a masquerade this evening before I go."

He bent to kiss her, but Christina grew frantic at this prospect of seeing him but once more before he left, and that in a public place. She placed her hand upon his furred chest and held him off.

"It is all done, then? Nicholas is gone and will trouble us no more? You will sail safely tonight with all your papers signed?"

Damien caught her hands together impatiently. "The papers will be on their way to Paris tonight. Whether I will be with them or not depends entirely on the outcome of my meeting with Nicholas. I have too much to gain by winning. I will not lose, Christina."

She understood now and her eyes grew wide with terror. He had challenged that foul creature to a duel and would not be satisfied until one or the other of them lay dead. The threat of death had not dissipated with the night's discoveries.

Damien saw the protests forming and rose quickly before she could reply. He wanted no emotional outpourings. He could not afford them now.

As Christina watched him hastily draw on linen shirt and silk stockings, she understood, and kept silent. He had his own private war to fight and she could not do it for him. Hers was here, in this empty house without him. She had her mother to protect, and possibly a new life within her to cherish. She must learn to do both with or without Damien.

He glanced up and caught her sad gaze and flashed a warm smile of approbation and relief.

As he pulled on his last garment, he reached to pull her from the bed. Wrapping her slender naked figure in his embrace, he kissed her soundly, and left without another word.

Eleanor MacTavish watched her daughter's nervous pacing in the downstairs salon. Afternoon sunlight filtered through heavy draperies, casting a dusky haze about Christina's lithe figure, and Eleanor sighed quietly. She knew what it meant to be young and healthy and anxious over love's afflictions. She wished she had some means of easing her daughter's worries, but Christina had not told her of them. Gazing at the new position of the ring on Christina's left hand, Eleanor assumed the marriage would soon be out in the open. If all went well.

After tea Eleanor returned to her room and Christina sat at the desk, desperately attempting to escape her fears by putting them to paper. It didn't work. When Lorna came to tell her it was time to dress, Christina went mindlessly, not knowing what else to do.

The gown laid out on the bed gleamed in a rich emerald velvet suitable for a queen, and as Christina inspected it closer, she understood that to be Damien's intention. The full stiff skirts, squared neckline, and enormous puffed sleeves spoke of an earlier age, and with the wig and tiara provided, she surmised Elizabeth to be queen. Good Queen Bess to Damien's what? Lord Raleigh? That would be to his taste. A more dashing rogue never lived.

Christina donned the sumptuous gown with considerable misgivings. What if Damien already lay dead in the filth of some dark alley? Would the same Bow Street runner come to her door to tell her of Damien's body being found? Or would he kill Nicholas and be caught for murder and the treasonous papers be found on him? Treason meant drawing and quartering. Christina grew nauseated and her own insides felt as if they had just been ripped asunder under the sword.

When Damien finally arrived, he seemed both triumphant and anxious and in too much of a hurry for words. He hugged Christina briefly, then hastened to his own room, shedding clothes as he went. Christina did not dare the welcome pleasure of relief. He was alive, but the night was not yet over.

In the carriage Damien gave a hasty sketch of his encounter with Nicholas. His cousin had not waited to meet Damien's deadly sword, but had flown for Calais, leaving assassins to commit his evil deeds. Knowing his cousin's habits, Damien had suspected such a ruse, and with bribes and threats had been adequately forewarned of both the plot and the escape route. Nicholas had not been particularly pleased to be forced to a halt by a small army of horsemen.

The rest of the story Christina had to piece together for herself. That Damien still lived spoke the outcome. His dangerous cousin had breathed his last, and her Yankee was now free to return to the colonies and his place in the war there. The electric excitement flowing through his veins colored Damien's every move and word. He would leave her tonight with scarcely a second thought.

Damien caught her downcast look and the tense whitening of her knuckles as she sat beside him in the dimly lighted carriage, and his fingers went out to capture her chin and turn it upward.

"Don't, Christina. I will be back, I promise. I must deliver these damnable papers to Mr. Franklin in France. While I am gone, Ben Thomas will be making inquiries as to your uncle's whereabouts. Your mother is not well enough to come with us and we cannot leave her alone. These things take time. But I will come back, if I must rise from the dead to do so."

His grim words terrified Christina more, but she nodded understanding. She searched the dark chiseled face above her longingly, wanting soft words to cling to for the cold days to come, but Damien was not a man of soft words and his thoughts had already flown on to deeds yet to be done. His eyes burned warmly as he tasted her lips for kisses, but his excitement was of another sort.

Christina covered her face with her mask as she realized their destination was not Covent Garden but a private residence on St. James. Damien apparently sought to go out in style, and if he had any pursuers on his heels, they would have difficulty finding him in these rarefied circles. Christina allowed herself a first small quiver of relief. He had strong protectors, to be allowed these halls.

In the throngs of people filling the halls and salons and ballroom, none would notice the masked feminine figure at the side of the dashing young Sir Walter Raleigh. That the rapier at this privateer's side was real and the papers in his cloak more treasonous than any that poor noble had ever possessed would not occur to these garish, boisterous peacocks, either. They were safe here, and Christina acknowledged Damien's wisdom.

She felt the tension in the arm at her back as they entered the ballroom and Damien searched the crowd carefully. With a mocking half-smile he bowed gallantly before her and indicated the dancing caricatures sweeping the floor.

"Shall we join them, my love?"

"Do I have any choice?" she murmured as he pulled her fingers through the curve of his arm and led her into the procession.

A crooked grin flitted across his bronzed features as he met the obstinacy in her eyes. "It is the social event of the season, my dear. After this, all London dissipates to the country. Do you not appreciate the finer side of life I show you?"

If he intended this as a jab at her English-bred views, Christina did not acknowledge it as such. She was as tired of this life as he, and her frazzled nerves were not up to exchanging witticisms. He stood on the brink of another world and dared laugh. For that alone he should be hanged.

Smiling grimly, she followed his lead into the flow of dancers. "I would see the country again, if I could. How will you find me if I should leave here?"

Damien gave her a look of mixed laughter and affection at such naiveté and squeezed her hand tightly. "Unless you marry some wealthy lord, my love, I shall easily trace the path of your earnings. I will find you, Christina, whether you will it or not."

And he seemed to mean it. Christina's heart lightened with the anticipation of the day he would return to her. It could not be long. Paris was not so ver far. And then she would be his wife. It should be a terrifying thought, but her smile glowed in her face like a million jewels.

The brilliance of that smile was reflected in Damien's dark visage, and enrapt, they finished the dance with little awareness of others. Not until the music ended and a blue-doubleted Romeo tapped Damien on the shoulder did they return to reality.

"Jeremy!" Christina cried with delight, causing Damien to flash her a suspicious glance. But since she remained readily within the circle of his arm, he greeted his old friend with a degree of amiability.

Bowing gallantly over her fingers, Jeremy straightened with a joyous grin. "Perfect! Royalty and a knave. I would recognize the pair of you anywhere."

Damien met his friend's mockery with a vague scowl. "I trust we are not that obvious to others?"

"Not yet, but it is only a matter of time. Even disguised, the two of you make a striking couple. Even if that damned craggy map of yours did not send all the ladies into the vapors, Drayton, those amber eyes of Christina's would be eclipsed only by that abominable wig you've hidden her under."

Christina's eyes clouded as they retreated to Damien's unsmiling face. A small smile quirked the corner of his lips as he met her gaze sadly.

"There is one more man I would see before I leave, love. I had best do it now. Stay with Jeremy. He will see you safely home. And remember what I have said."

The look he gave her pierced Christina to the soul, a yearning look of hunger that she could not assuage, could not even touch as they stood alone in the center of the crowded room. Tears welled in her eyes as she realized this would be farewell, and she choked back a sob as his tall cloaked figure became lost in the swirl of dancers.

A hand on her shoulder brought her back to Jeremy, and Christina gave him a brief, watery smile. He did not understand, and his guileless frown lightened her burden.

"If you have brought someone else, I would appreciate it if you would find my carriage. I do not want to hinder your enjoyment of the masquerade," she whispered softly, praying he would not listen. She did not want to leave until she was certain Damien would not return to her this night.

"What in hell is happening, Christina? Where's Damien off to?"

Christina shook her head bemusedly as Jeremy led her toward the banquet table. "He killed a man today, Jeremy. How long will it be before they come after him?"

Jeremy stared at her in horror, the glass of punch he had held out to her frozen in midair. "My God, Christina!" he whispered finally, his gaze instantly sweeping the room for the figure of Sir Walter Raleigh.

Damien was not difficult to find in any crowd. Both their eyes turned to the dashing russet-haired privateer at the far end of the room engaged in serious conversation with a cabinet minister of high rank. The crowd shifted slightly, giving a brief glimpse of the lethal rapier on his narrow hips, then closed around him again.

Troubled blue eyes returned to Christina's shining amber ones. "I heard Bothwell got caught up in some kind of fracas last night that has left him mortally wounded, but no mention of Damien's name was made."

Christina wondered how her cousin had fared in that riot, but cared not for his fate. She shook her head slowly. "He may well have done that too, but today he stopped a coach on the Calais highway. I doubt seriously if its occupant escaped alive."

"Nicholas." Jeremy's lips set grimly at Christina's nod.

Before he could make further comment, Christina's attention wandered to a small commotion at the room's entrance. At the top of the broad sweep of stairs she caught a flash of red and a sparkle of gold braid. Voices rose in disagreement from that direction. Intuition told her instantly, and her fingers dug deeply into Jeremy's arm.

"Soldiers?" she asked breathlessly, nodding toward the entrance.

And then they were stampeding down the stairs in a wide phalanx, hands at swords, boots clattering across marble, blood-red uniforms filling Christina's field of vision. A scream rang out somewhere in the room, her own perhaps, but followed by others as the extraordinary invasion pushed their way through the crowd.

Christina turned frantically to the place she had last seen Damien. Across the room his eyes met and held hers for one last moment's caress, a brave salute, and then he ran for the curtained windows of the ballroom.

With a cry of rage and despair Christina watched as the redcoats spied their prey and drew their swords. They would kill him!

Without another thought she jerked the snow-white linen of the long buffet table. Delicate china and crystal tottered and toppled, spilling punch and jellies and lovely pastries underfoot. As the crush of people spilled backward before the soldiers' onslaught, they slipped and slid and more china went crashing.

Catching Jeremy's eye, Christina fell heavily against the elegant table, her hands coming up beneath it with a vicious shove. In an apparent attempt to save her from falling headfirst into the platter of cut meats, Jeremy completed the maneuver, and the long table crashed sideways, directly in the path of the oncoming soldiers.

Pandemonium ensued. Women in towering headdresses and trailing silks slid helter-skelter through marzipan and cream cakes. Gentlemen in tailcoats and heels toppled beneath rolling melons and plums, crushing the Camembert beneath their posteriors as they fell. Swords clattered to the floor as ladies landed in heaps beneath glittering black boots, and more than one red coat slid through the pool of gravy at the stair's end.

But more than one was not enough. Even as Jeremy grappled in a drunken dance with an unbalanced corporal and Christina trampled delicately on the fingers of another who dared recover his sword, a trio of soldiers safely gained the far side of the room.

Damien had been halted at the window's ledge by the sight of a troop of soldiers in the courtyard below. As he turned to find a safer exit, the first of the redcoats reached him.

Their swords clashed with a metallic clangor that echoed throughout the cavernous interior of the marble room, bringing all else to a standstill. Christina's piercing cry was halted by Jeremy's hand shaking her into silence. The clangor died as swiftly as it began. With swords drawn, the red-coated soldiers surrounded the towering cloaked figure on the window ledge.

Damien surveyed his attackers, and finding himself outnumbered to an overwhelming degree, gave a nonchalant shrug and surrendered his weapon.

Cries of bewilderment rang through the room as the dashing Earl of Westshipham was manacled and surrounded by gravy-splattered soldiers and marched toward the entrance. Damien looked neither to left nor right, his aristocratic profile held arrogantly high as he sauntered casually through their midst. While all else betrayed signs of anger and confusion upon their faces, Lord Westshipham walked calmly.

Only a few yards of marble floor separated them, but he never glanced once in Christina's direction. Jeremy caught her arm and held her as the small party passed by and up the stairs, Damien's russet head held proudly higher than all others.

"Don't, Christina. It will do him no good if you are behind bars too."

He held her tightly, feeling the stiffness in the slender arm beneath his fingers. Tension held her rigid and he feared she would crack beneath the pressure. No tears marred her porcelain cheeks, but her eyes burned with a pain and anguish that could not be extinguished with simple words.

Christina could not remember anything else of that night. Once Damien disappered from her sight, all else disappeared too.

Jeremy led her through the debris and on to the waiting carriage.

19

Ben Thomas shook his head in disapproval at the obstinate glaze of Christina's eyes, but knew better than to express his opinion out loud. He had already used every argument within his capacity to persuade this foolish miss against this escapade, but she heard none of it.

It would not be so bad had they housed the earl in the Tower as his rank demanded, but terrified and furious powers of authority had ordered the treacherous Yankee incarcerated in the notorious Newgate gaol like a common thief. Ben Thomas had feared for his own life that first time he had attempted a visit with his client.

The traitorous papers bearing the terms for which a number of parliamentary figures would be willing to end the war with the colonies had not yet surfaced, but whispers of their existence forced the guilty parties to be even more outraged than the innocent. Those who had most vocally supported an end to the disastrous war now did a drastic about-face in disowning the traitorous earl. No punishment would be too demeaning for the Yankee murderer.

Christina seemed oblivious to the political outcry around her. She had only one thought in mind, to see Damien. Beyond that she refused to exist.

Ben smacked his walking stick against the slimy stone floor of the Newgate corridor, scaring away the wicked yellow eyes of the large rat staring back at them. He cursed as a litter of young raced practically between their feet, swiping at Christina's thin skirts, but she looked stoically ahead, waiting for the gaoler to lead her to their goal.

The slovenly guard watched for some reaction as the stench of open sewage and unemptied slop buckets built in the airless heat of the ancient walls. Christina waited patiently for him to continue, affording him no amusement.

With a shrug and an icy glance at the elderly man who had crossed his palm with gold, the guard threw open a cell door at the end of the corridor.

"This 'un be too dang'rous for the niceties. Me orders is to leave 'im as 'e is, as becomes 'is crime. So don't be comin' to me if you doesn't like what you see."

With that gruff reminder he stepped aside to allow Christina to pass.

Damien's long, lean figure lay sprawled along a narrow cot against the stone wall of the tiny cell. His heavy cloak and rich silks had been stripped away, leaving him but the filthy breeches he ate and slept in. Bronzed muscles rippled with an animallike grace across his bare torso as he turned at the sound of the cell door opening, and dark eyes fastened on Christina's fragile figure with bewilderment.

"Christina?"

He sat up and Christina concealed a gasp of horror as a length of chain clanked with his movement. As her eyes adjusted to the dimness, she realized he was manacled hand and foot and locked to the wall. She cringed at the raw red marks about his ankles and wrists, but she simply gestured to the guard to close the door. Ben would stand outside to guard their privacy.

"Christina? Are you mad, or am I? What are you doing here?" Damien asked in astonishment, not rising from the cot for fear of terrifying her with his chains.

"I brought you some food and clean clothing," she stated clearly, for the benefit of listening ears. She heard a brief exchange outside the door and listened with satisfaction as the guard's footsteps stomped angrily away. Ben's walking stick knocked reassuringly against the door.

In an instant she flew across the room and into his arms.

"Christina, my God, you are insane." Damien lowered his chained wrists carefully about her waist, holding this mad apparition tightly against him, the sweet, clean scent of her bath oil a welcome relief from his own stench. Soft blond hair tickled his chin and neck as she buried her face against his shoulder, and he felt his heart rip from his chest as a hot tear fell against his skin.

Recovering her senses, Christina looked up quickly, eagerly drinking in the hard profile of the man she loved, the rough stubble of his beard scarcely hiding the strong lineaments of his jaw. Ebony eyes caressed her with a warmth they seldom evoked, and she gained courage from the love she found there.

"Tell me quickly! Whom should I go to for help? Give me names, Damien. Tell me where to go, what to do. We must get you out of here, if I have to hold a pistol on the guards myself!"

Her golden youthful face turned up to him, filled with hope and love and anxiety. Damien gazed upon it sadly. He had not wanted to hurt her. She had suffered enough already. He had steeled himself valiantly against those innocent eyes and reluctant, winning smiles, her shy caresses and eager kisses, had sought to teach her how to despise him when he was gone. All to no avail. That night he had found her gone from his side, he had learned the folly of his arrogance. Now he learned the folly of his overconfidence. He might better have left her with Nicholas than to submit her to what would follow now.

Damien shook his head sadly, pleading with his eyes for understanding. "There are no names, Christina," he whispered softly.

"Don't say that, Damien!" Christina nearly screeched at him, dread clamping an icy hand about her heart as she read the message in his eyes and refused to believe it. "You are an earl, a lord of the realm! You know the men with the power that put you here. Those same men can get you out! If nothing else, tell me how to reach your sailors and we will break you out of here!"

Damien had to smile at this naiveté. He could imagine his tawny lioness standing in those stone corridors, sword in hand, silken petticoats trailing the floor. She had her father's spirit, but even that gallant Scotsman would not dare to storm the gaol, let alone in silken petticoats.

"No, my love, you will do as we planned. The court will likely impound Westshipham Hall and all that belongs to me, so you must move out quickly. I wish you had elsewhere to go but Cornwall, but I'd rather you not stay in the city now."

The trial would be a nasty one and its outcome a foregone conclusion. His only hope was that they charged him only with murder and hanged him cleanly. The penalty for treason would be much crueler, but Damien did not speak these thoughts out loud. He had no intention of leaving her to suffer the taunts and cruelties that would grow with each passing day of his incarceration.

"Ask Ben to find you a place in the country, somewhere your mother will be happy and not hear the gossip. If for no other reason, Christina, you must leave to protect her."

He had used this line on her successfully before, but she was a much older and wiser person than that girl had been. Her eyes flashed furiously.

"I am no helpless female who must be cosseted like my mother. I can send her away and stay here. What would *you* do had I been the one thrown in here?" she demanded angrily, throwing off his embrace and striding nervously back and forth. Fear filled every pore, suffocating sensibility, but she would not let him know that.

Damien stood and caught her roughly by the arms, forcing her to face him. "I would get your mother the hell out of here! I don't *want* you here, Christina. Leave me my pride. I want you to remember me as I was, not as they will make me. *Leave*, Christina, and don't ever turn back!"

His tone was strident, his fingers cruel, as they shook her forcefully. Tears poured down Christina's cheeks, and great gulping sobs choked her throat. She had not cried since they had taken him away, but all those unshed tears escaped now. She shook with the ferocity of them, so that only Damien's hands kept her from crumpling to the floor.

He could not bear the sight of her pain. With all the pent-up desperation of his plight, he crushed her to him, unaware of the pain of steel in his flesh as his lips burned fiercely across hers one last time.

Christina clung to him, her fingers digging into his bare arms fiercely, as if to hold him forever. Their tongues clashed and fought and surrendered as their bodies longed to do, and Christina whimpered softly as his kiss became a gentle caress of love and longing.

The clang of Ben's walking stick against the door warned of the guard's approach.

Damien caught her arms and set her firmly from him. "There is one thing you can do for me, Christina."

She searched his face hopefully, but found no promises. Biting her tongue with sorrow, she waited for his request.

"I am not a man accustomed to putting words to paper, but you have that talent and more. My family must be told of my end. Do I ask too much in asking this of you?"

Tears glittered brilliantly in gold-flecked velvet, but did not fall as Christina traced every line of Damien's angular face with her gaze. She committed to memory the tight cord of muscle over his cheekbone, the depth of ebony eyes, the russet curl of hair against his forehead, as he stared down at her. She could feel the pressure of his hands on her arms, knowing his strength would leave bruises there and rejoicing in these reminders he left to her.

"I will write, I promise," she murmured, and as the

sobs tore at her throat again, she jerked away and dashed through the opening door, eyes burning with tears as the image of the proud man behind her, hands falling to his sides, etched itself deep within her soul.

Ben made no attempt to comfort her as the carriage rolled slowly through crowded streets. She had to cry it out before she could go on. And go on she must. The solicitor knew Damien's wishes on the subject and fully meant to carry out his last requests. It was all he could do for him.

Christina's tears had begun to dry by the time they reached Soho, but the burning pain of those yet unshed kept her from noticing all around her. Blindly she took Ben's hand and climbed from the carriage, entering the open door of the town house without awareness of where she was or why.

Raised voices in the salon intruded upon her consciousness, but Lorna's anxious expression as she raced to greet them struck a note of terror in Christina's heart.

"My mother! Has something happened to my mother?"

It was as if some premonition had forewarned Christina of events to come, or her misery had grown so great as to expect the worst of the future. Lorna's grim expression did not relent, but she shook her head negatively.

"Not yet. Your uncle is here. You had best hurry." The questions of Damien must wait, but Christina's pale, tear-stained face had already answered the worst of them. The stern Scotswoman gave the girl's frail shoulders a gentle hug as she led her toward the salon. Over her shoulder Lorna beckoned the solicitor to join them.

News of her uncle's arrival did not produce any feelings of joy. He had come much, much too late to be of any use now. Except to her mother, of course. Perhaps he would help her mother. Christina increased her pace.

Eleanor MacTavish's delicately boned face lit with joy and pride as her daughter hurried into the room. She scarcely noticed tearstained cheeks as she turned to the stiffly upright man beside her.

"Here she is, Thomas. Isn't she as beautiful as I have said?"

Christina came to a halt in the center of the room, her gaze suddenly traveling from the slowly warming smile of her uncle to a slouching figure leaning against the wall. Fury shook her with the wild gust of a hurricane wind.

"You!" she hissed, glaring at her cousin's disheveled appearance. "How dare you set foot in this house again after what you have done! How did you get in? Damien left orders that you were not to be allowed near here ever again!"

Before Thaddeus could reply, the older gentleman at her mother's side stepped forward, his hand going out in a gesture of apology. "It is my fault, Christina. I ordered the servants to let him in. There is much he needs to explain."

Christina clenched her fists and attempted to control her rage. She seldom lost control of herself in this way, but she did not care that her first meeting with her uncle should be so marred. He had raised that despicable excuse of a son and owed much more than explanations for his behavior.

Her eyes coolly inspected the man she must call uncle. Her rage calmed somewhat at what appeared to be sincere apology in the bright blue-gray eyes so much like her mother's. He still retained a military bearing and his unobtrusive choice of garments spoke of wealth and good taste. His mouth was stern, but she thought she detected lines of humor about his eyes. With the natural grace she had inherited from her mother, Christina held out her hand and curtsied slightly.

"I apologize for my outburst, sir, but your son has committed offenses that can never be forgiven. Lord Westshipham had good reason for forbidding him his portals."

Thomas Adderly frowned and Eleanor gasped at the

implication of Christina's words, but Thaddeus only shrugged and stepped forward.

"Drayton's in no position to condemn anyone, and neither are you, lovely cousin of mine."

Pale blue eyes swept assessingly over Christina's trim figure, as if he knew all that lay beneath the modest gown of striped muslin. Christina stiffened, but her uncle squeezed her hand tightly.

"He is no cousin of yours, Christina, but a spoiled young pup I picked up off the streets and tried to make a man of. I failed miserably, as you can see. If he has harmed you in any way, I will make him pay the price of hell for it."

The baron's commanding presence filled the room as he glared at the wayward youth he had raised as a son. Thaddeus had the grace to flinch before those accusing eyes which had once looked upon him with love. Before Christina could accuse him of his faults, Thaddeus took the offensive.

"Do not look at me as if I am the only disgrace to blot your name. At least my blood is not your own, but what will you say of your precious niece when it becomes known she is the whore of that traitorous Yankee they intend to hang from the gallows tree?"

Eleanor's piercing scream froze Christina into immobility. Hatred fired her eyes as she met Thaddeus' venomous glare, but she did not dare face her mother. The hand holding hers continued to squeeze reassuringly.

"That's enough out of you, you young cur. I think it best if you leave now. You know where my rooms are. Meet me there if you wish to carry on this discussion."

Thaddeus turned his glare on the man he had once called father. "You can't order me around any longer, old man. I have listened to your speeches of pride and family for as long as I can stand them. There is your family now!" He gestured crudely at Christina's frozen form. "Ask her where she sleeps at night! And where her lover is right now! Look at her! The guilt is written in her face! And ask that old bastard hovering behind her if I speak the truth. He plays the part of pimp well."

Christina had barely been aware of Ben's presence behind her, but she felt it now as the solicitor strode furiously to the room's center.

He caught Thaddeus by the ear and whacked him soundly cross the rump with his walking stick, then with the strength of a much younger man he flung the culprit toward the door.

"Get out of my sight, you whining, blackmailing little thief. I'll see you hanged if you ever set foot near this girl again!"

Another sound whack of the stick sent Thaddeus flying, but the slamming of the door behind him did not clear the tension in the room.

Christina forced herself to face her mother. Eleanor had grown pale, but she sat calmly upright on the settee, waiting for her brother to break the silence. When it became apparent the stricken man did not know where to begin, Eleanor spoke politely, soothing troubled waters as she had been trained to do.

"The boy made a rash assumption, Thomas. Christina and Damien were secretly married some time ago. I think it would be safe to admit it to your uncle, Christina."

Christina could not reply. Her whole world had crumpled into chaos and she could not think, could not stutter the words, could not face any of them. Shock eliminated all her functioning parts. She continued to stand where she was, all eyes focused on her.

"Christina? What is wrong?" Eleanor's voice rose nervously, and then, with horror, she read the truth on Christina's mobile features.

"Oh, my God, no!" she whispered faintly, before her slight figure crumpled and pitched forward in a swoon.

That galvanized Christina into action. She flew to her mother's side, catching her up before she could fall, screaming to the men behind her to fetch a doctor. With tears streaming down her face, she rocked her mother's tiny, unconscious figure in her arms as chaos again erupted around her.

The doctor shook his head as he left the darkened bedroom, but Christina was already numb and did not respond. As the door closed behind him, she fell to her knees at her mother's bedside, clasping frail fingers in her hands as she prayed silently to the gods who had forsaken her.

Eleanor's lashes flickered briefly, and a small spasm clutched Christina's hand.

"Mama, please, you must listen to me. I am Damien's wife, Mama. I will always be his wife. Do you hear me? Please, Mama, listen to me . . ."

Christina's voice broke with tears, but the fingers clasped between hers moved more strongly now, and a moment later, light lashes flickered open. Blue-gray eyes rested steadily on the bent blond head beside her.

"Christina . . ."

Christina gave a cry of relief and bent to kiss her mother's cheek. "You will be strong again soon, just wait and see. I will explain everything and we will be a happy family again. Uncle Thomas will be with us . . ."

Eleanor shook her head slowly, a sad smile turning her lips as she gazed upon her beautiful daughter.

"You are so like your father," she whispered, so faintly Christina had to bend close to hear.

When Christina opened her mouth to speak, Eleanor shook her head again.

"Let me speak, Christina. I love you, daughter, and I forgive you anything, but you must forgive me also. I have been a poor mother to you. I have tried so very hard . . ."

A tear trickled down skin thin as paper, leaving a silver trail. Eleanor closed her eyes and tried to gain the strength to continue. With a small breath the words poured forth again. "You must forgive me now, Christina. I do not have the strength to carry on any longer. Your uncle will look after you. It has been so hard . . ."

Both women were weeping, knowing the valiant fight

she had maintained these last years. Her life had been Argus MacTavish. For his daughter she had fought to live, but the time had come for Christina to live her own life. Eleanor opened her eyes to gaze fondly upon her daughter one more time, then sank blissfully into oblivion.

Christina cried until she could cry no more, cried until her eyes swelled closed and her sobs brought Lorna running. Someone carried her off and tucked her into bed, but she never knew who it was. Exhaustion took its toll and sleep claimed her and carried her away.

20

Christina would not have left the bed at all had Lorna's questioning not returned her senses and her mind slipped into gear again. While Damien still lived, she could hope. He must live. Life without love could not exist otherwise.

"Shall I tell the gentlemen you cannot come down, then?" Lorna questioned insistently, demanding some response from those frozen features of the girl in the bed. Christina had eaten nothing in days. If she continued like this, she would soon join her mother in the graveyard. Lorna's stern lips compressed tightly. Not if she had anything to say about it.

Christina's eyes lit suddenly, like an unexpected dawn, and she turned eagerly to the housekeeper. "Is my uncle still here?"

"And what do you think I've been telling you these last minutes? He and that Mr. Thomas are downstairs now, wanting to speak with you."

Christina scrambled from the bed, hastily sliding into a clean chemise and splashing water on her face. She had lost all pride and shame. She would beg and plead if necessary. Surely, surely, something could be done.

The men rose politely as she entered the salon. Her uncle's face had gained a grayish cast she had not noticed earlier, and Christina felt a small twinge of guilt. He had lost sister and son and had no one but a niece whom all London knew to be a whore. She no longer blushed innocently at the thought. She had done the only thing possible under the circumstances.

She curtsied and sat primly at the edge of a chair, waiting respectfully for her uncle to speak.

"Christina, I . . . I do not know where to begin. We do not know each other, and that is my fault, as it is my fault that you and your mother were neglected so unmercifully during a time of tragedy. If I had attempted to maintain any kind of communication with Eleanor, this would never have happened. But I was proud, and though I wished your mother well, I knew your father would prefer I did not interfere. So I stayed aloof, and when Thaddeus . . ."

He stood and began pacing the room, a man unaccustomed to explaining his actions, now pouring his heart out to a slip of a girl with huge wounded eyes.

"When I discovered the kind of creature I had raised beneath my roof, it made me violently ill. Perhaps I went a bit mad. I do not know. I left the country without giving second thought to you or your mother, knowing Argus would take good care of you. I received none of your letters until recently, after one of my servants found them opened on my desk. Thaddeus had taken it upon himself to divert my mail."

Christina quivered inwardly at the poor hand fate had dealt her. But for that creature Thaddeus, her mother might as well be reunited happily with her brother today. That in no way eased her present plight.

"Please, sir, you need not make explanations to me. My mother was ill for a long time. She is happy now, I am certain of it. I cannot apologize for what I have done, though I could wish things had worked out differently."

The baron turned slowly and studied her pale features, seeing the heartbreaking emotions lining a face so young. She would be beautiful if she smiled, but all trace of carefree youth had been wiped from her lovely features.

Gravely he asked of her, "Mr. Thomas has told me your story. May I rely on his word?"

Christina flashed the omniscient solicitor a grateful look. "If anything, he will have been too kind to me.

Then you know Damien's . . . Lord Westshipham's plight?"

His blue eyes became almost icy with gray. "A fitting fate for the bastard, I should say. If they do not hang him, I will gladly flog him myself."

Christina's hopes plummeted and her eyes betrayed her misery. "He had no other choice, sir. As his wife I would have been condemned to death by his mad cousin or hounded by the courts and all London now. He had nothing to give me but a name tainted by perversion and treachery. I love him and I intend to do all within my limited power to see him set free. If you cannot help me in this, I am sorry, but I must go my own way. Ben, I must think of moving to St. James. Could you aid me in drawing up a list of names I might petition in Damien's favor?"

Ignoring the warring emotions in her uncle's face, she faced the solicitor with pleading eyes.

Ben did not reply but turned to the rapidly aging man with military bearing who seemed on the verge of some collapse. The baron drew himself together with dignity and met Christina's amber gaze with stern gravity.

"There are courts of law to deal with these matters, Christina. You will not aid your protector by interfering before justice has had its turn. I am certain Mr. Thomas can be prevailed upon to provide the names of barristers willing to defend his lordship."

With a great sigh of relief, Christina realized she had gained a mighty weapon in her small arsenal. The baron's name and wealth would open doors she could never hope to attain. Not daring to hug the stern man she had come to know as family, she held out her hand in gratitude.

The baron clasped it firmly, then with sudden decision drew her into his embrace. His shuddering sob matched her own as the magnitude of their mutual loss crumbled all barriers.

In the days and nights before Damien's trial, Christina worked valiantly at petitions and letters requested by Ben and her uncle. She kept busy in between by copying reams of legal documents for the barristers they had hired. She did anything to keep herself occupied, for she certainly never slept.

Jeremy came and offered his support and that of his family. The marquis was inclined to be apolitical and was affected little by the uproar over Damien's supposed treason. In his stalwart manner he stood up for his son's friend, but his voice counted for little in the courts of law. Still, Christina was grateful for the knowledge of his friendship.

If these friends had not come and gone with words of kindness and reassurance, Christina knew she would have gone quietly mad. The dark paneled halls of this once grand town house held ghosts of too recent presence to accept comfortably. Just to walk down the silent corridors to her room at night awakened images too painful to bear. She must pass the suite she had shared with her mother and remember not to stop and exchange quiet words of the day's happenings. Never again would her mother's gentle smile tell her all would be well with time. Stifling sobs, Christina forced herself to continue to the next chamber of torture.

The room she had shared with Damien held living ghosts. His tobacco pouch still lay upon the mantel, awaiting his return. The scent of his pipe lingered on the shirt Christina had hidden away in her drawer, unable to bear having it washed and erasing all traces of his reality. Though she clung to the hope he might yet be saved, she knew he would never set foot in these chambers again. His tobacco and his shirt and his memory would be all she had to sustain her until the day came when he could return for her.

Writing these thoughts in her journal, Christina came to the vague realization she ventured on the same precipice that had finally claimed her mother. Her whole life had become centered on one man, a man not even her husband, and whose promises she had no right to believe. She had condemned her mother for giving up [illegible] for the love of one man, but at least Argus MacTavish had been the trusted husband of a lifetime. What madness was this that kept her tied to Damien Drayton, the traitorous Earl of Westshipham?

Not so blind that he could not see her torment, her uncle contemplated his niece's plight from the plateau of experience and came to some very grim conclusions. Christina was young and beautiful and had a lifetime ahead of her, but she must recover from this disastrous encounter with the smooth-talking Yankee before she could realize her life had not come to an end. The baron would gladly see the blackhearted cad hanged and this purgatory of waiting ended, but he prided himself on being a man of his word, and he had promised Christina to do everything in his power to see Damien free.

It did not take long for the baron to conclude that he had only one reasonable chance to salve his conscience and free his niece from this destructive relationship. Tapping his hat on his head and taking up his walking stick, the baron stalked determinedly out to his waiting carriage.

Damien glanced up with surprise at the portly gentleman being ushered into his cage. Ben Thomas had brought clean linen, but in the prison's heat Damien had not deigned to fasten it. He made no attempt to do so now, but rose respectfully at the baron's entrance. Ben had informed him of Christina's uncle's attempts to aid him, but he still regarded the older man with suspicion. And rightly so, he decided, reading anger in the man's blue-gray eyes with surprising ease.

"You may sit, my lord. Those shackles hovering above me make me decidedly uncomfortable and it is hardly protocol for an earl to rise for a baron."

Damien slumped back onto his cot, his broad shoulders resting casually against the wall but the knotted muscle of tension over his cheekbones revealing his wariness. With his chained leg across his knee, he carefully watched his visitor's nervous pacing.

"In my country, a man rises out of respect for his

elders and betters. If I am to be hanged for a Yankee, I shall behave as one." The murmured intonations of those cultured tones gave no evidence of the prisoner's emotions.

The baron sent the forbidding earl a sharp glance but found no mockery in that dark gaze. Damien's rough-carved visage and muscular frame had taken him by surprise. He had expected a fast-talking peer of the realm, somewhat akin to the man the late earl had been, but none of that noble's degeneracy gazed back at him from curtained black eyes. The baron took a moment to rearrange his thoughts. More subtle tactics would have to be used than he had anticipated.

"I have come to offer you a choice of fates." Thomas Adderly spoke ponderously, studying his companion with care. At Damien's upraised, questioning eyebrow, he continued. "You and I are both aware that you are as guilty as hell and destined to be hanged, at the least."

Damien did not stir from his casual stance as he continued to probe the old man's expression. He did not like what he saw, but recognized the baron's determination for what it was. He had met an adversary worth the challenge.

When the condemned man made no reply, the baron began pacing the cell in time to his thoughts. "I despise what you have done to my niece, but I despise what she is doing even more. No matter what a man's crime, no one deserves the fate of drawing and quartering."

The baron noted the look of wariness replacing Damien's expression of cool control. Christina was obviously the key to the Yankee's behavior. Adderly used this observation to guide his next words carefully.

"Though I despise what Christina has done to you, she is my niece and I will not see her harmed. When you hear what I have to say, I am certain you will agree I am being most reasonable in my demands."

Damien gestured impatiently. "Explain yourself, sir, but be careful how you speak of your niece. I have murdered at least one man for daring to insult her—with luck, maybe two. Choose your words wisely."

At the harsh tone of the Yankee's voice, the baron drew himself up grandly and stared back in defiant anger.

"You are the cause of those insults and your incarceration here is fitting punishment for the harm you have done that once innocent child! Do not tempt me to walk out of here and leave you to your fate!"

Damien stared back at him and waited.

The other man's unnerving calm was not what Thomas Adderly had expected, and he found himself losing his own temper in recompense. Controlling his ire, he proceeded.

"Christina has informed the authorities of your treasonous behavior. You will be sentenced to drawing and quartering, beyond any doubt—the witnesses named are too numerous. You have only one chance to escape your fate."

The Yankee's handsome visage turned livid with rage. "You lie! You conniving, blasphemous, sanctimonious whoreson of a thousand traitorous bitches . . ."

As the larger man's fists knotted into steel mallets, the baron carefully stepped out of reach of his chains, but otherwise remained undisturbed. "You do not have to believe me. Your trial will prove me true. The female of the species is a more poisonous variety than most men ever know, and Christina had every right to seek revenge. She just went a shade further than I approve." To his own sorrow, the baron knew he spoke of his false son Thaddeus and not his betrayed niece, but his purpose would not be accomplished by this admission.

Damien strained at his shackles, visions of bashing the other man to a bloody pulp relieving the frustration of helplessness, but he retained some semblance of sanity. Christina did have every right to seek revenge, but he would never believe . . .

Sensing Damien still listened, the baron continued. "I can get you out of here. I have a friend in the right position who will see another deserving felon hanged in your place. There are miscreants enough in these walls who deserve your fate and worse. I have only one request to make in return."

Damien nearly snarled at the baron's smug rectitude, but understanding the man offered Christina her only protection, he controlled his rage and made no other reply.

Thomas nodded his approval. "I have been assured you are a man of your word. In return for your freedom, I wish your word that you will immediately set sail from these shores and never attempt to contact my niece again."

Damien reeled under the impact of this blow. Not for a minute did he believe Christina had sealed his fate. He could not have imagined the love in her eyes, the innocent trust she placed in him each time she gave him her body. Just the memory of those moments worked at his insides with an agony he had never imagined possible. Never to see her face again, to feel the cool caress of her hand upon his brow, or the warm press of her lips against his was a crueler fate than any punishment designed by courts. Only death could keep him away.

As if reading his mind, the baron smiled grimly. "I will ask for your answer after the trial. You will see then what I have tried to tell you now. Good day." Bowing politely, he strode quickly from the cell, leaving the younger man in a torment for which there was no relief.

Christina pleaded with her uncle and Ben and Lord Jeremy to be allowed to see Damien again, but all agreed it would be best if she did not. Besides, Damien had demanded that she be kept from him, and they thought it for the best. Damien's irascible temper had taken a violent turn for the worse in these past few days.

Christina had only the word of these three friends that Damien did not suffer. What could they know of [illegible]ffering, they who had never known the stifling suffo-[illegible]on of a single cell and no future? For a man like

Damien, it would be hell. She had felt enough of deprivation to know that firsthand.

She carried his torments with hers as she walked through the days like some creature just emerged from a shell and too shocked to react to its surroundings. Every sight, every sound bombarded her already fragile and nearly shattered nerves with confusion. An unfinished letter in Damien's hand lying beneath a blotter dissolved her into tears for hours. A thoughtless inquiry on the placement of a pair of his boots drove her into a hysterical rage.

She feared for her sanity. Never before had she been privy to these meaningless ups and downs. She had been taught a ladylike passivity that covered the deep emotion only her journal knew. But now these passions came welling out from some deep emptiness inside, and it took all her strength to control them.

Her uncle accepted the tears as normal, but Lorna gave her sideways glances when Christina erupted into fits of rage over nothing at all. It was the stalwart housekeeper who pacified the disturbed servants and led Christina's weeping figure away, tucking her into bed and forcing her to stay there though both women knew she never slept. And it was Lorna Douglass who forced nourishing broths and bits of toast into her when nothing else went down her throat or stayed in her stomach.

She had been ill and confined to bed throughout her mother's funeral, but Christina refused to hide in that haven when the day of Damien's trial finally arrived. By that time, even Ben could tell from the circles beneath her amber eyes and the wraithlike state of her figure that Christina was in no condition to be out of bed. But she refused to remain incarcerated in that prison of torment. Dressed in concealing bonnet and mantle, she descended to the downstairs hall with every intention of accompanying her uncle to the courtroom.

The three men in the salon rose in confusion, not having anticipated this unladylike demand. Christina had not once left the shelter of the house since visiting

Damien. They had protected her from the crowds of sightseers and taunts of passersby, had kept the newspapers rife with ugly rumors and innuendos from her eyes, and she had not objected, had not even been aware of their precautions. The sturdy baron, the wise Ben Thomas, and the gallant Lord Jeremy all fell before the silence of that slender figure now confronting them. Speechless, they knew no words to keep her from the disaster ahead.

Only Lorna Douglass had anticipated this event. Without waiting for permission, the massive housekeeper stormed into the room, and gathering Christina into her arms before the concerned gazes of the staring gentlemen, she admonished, "You are going nowhere this day, miss! That poor boy will have enough on his mind without worrying about you up there in them chairs with people whispering and pointing and carrying on. I promised him to look after you, and I will, if it means tying you to your bed for your own good. Now, come away and let these gentlemen do what they must do. They'll look out for Damien for you."

To the astonishment of all, Christina went without protest. The three men stared at each other in silence as Lorna's clucking reassurances faded away in the halls overhead. They had just seen a living ghost, and they stirred uncomfortably. In a cell not far away waited her counterpart. Death had been planted on Damien's features from the moment the cell bars had clanged closed behind him. It was simply a matter of when and how that they fought for now. It seemed that two lives swung on that verdict today.

They had chosen a courtroom that would hold a crowd, but the spectators still spilled out the doorways and into the hall, chattering like magpies and gesturing excitedly at noted personages as they arrived. The prisoner's entrance met with a moment's awed silence and then a sudden roar of outrage and triumph.

Damien sat through it all with the air of one already parted from this world. He knew there was no de-
...e for his guilt, had known all along that one slip

would condemn him to death. He had spent long hours trying to imagine how he had been caught just at the moment he had every right to believe himself safe, but he no longer cared.

His stony gaze located Christina's uncle at the front of the room. There sat his only hope of life, but what life would that be without Christina by his side? The nights and days of torment behind the miserable walls of the stinking prison had gnawed at his rationality until his only coherent thought remained to protect Christina. He had deliberately ordered her to be kept from him to protect her from his own misery and the filthy curiosity of degenerate minds, but perversely, her absence had wakened ghoulish suspicions.

What did he know of Christina, actually? She was English born and bred, loyal to family and country, and he had overthrown all her beliefs and trampled on all her sensibilities. What arrogance had made him think she would allow a spy and traitor to go free, particularly one who had dragged her down into a life of shame? Had he been in her place, he would have done the same. It had been lovesick folly to imagine she would allow him to escape.

Damien wished for the privacy to hold his head and shut out these poisonous thoughts. If he could not believe in Christina, he had no reason to go on living. She was the only light in the long dark tunnel of his life, the song that sang in his veins and made this fight worth the pain. To believe she had abandoned him would be to abandon all hope.

Accustomed only to the practicality of his logical mind, Damien could not deal with the upheaval of emotions engendered by just the thought of her amber eyes. Logic told him she had every right to seek revenge. Logic told him her uncle had no reason to lie about her treachery. Only madness lit the candle of hope in his heart.

And as the trial began and witnesses were presented one by one, the lone prisoner sat proudly upright, and no one noticed as that small candle flame flickered and died. Only Christina had known of his whereabouts on those nights. Only Christina had known whom he had seen and why. Only Christina could have known when his mission was almost accomplished and warned the authorities to watch his movements those last days.

As the searing stake of her treachery was driven through his heart, Damien glanced up to meet the compassion in the Baron of Adderly's eyes, and his soul withered and died within him. They could have drawn and quartered him then, and Damien would never have felt it. But life would go on, and revenge would be sweet.

Christina did not consciously live through that day. Her mind disconnected itself from her body and followed Damien to the courtroom. Without eyes, she could not see, but she was there, at his side, all the same.

And when the men returned late that evening, she was waiting, standing in the dusky stillness of the center hall like a prisoner awaiting the verdict. Her reed-slim figure was little more than a shadow against the gloom; only the flicker of candlelight against gold spoke of earthly reality.

She did not speak with words, but her eyes were eloquent. Jeremy stepped forward, unable to resist their plea.

"I am sorry, Christina," he whispered softly, holding out his hand. She did not take it, forcing him to continue. "He never had a chance."

That would not do. It was not harsh enough. She wanted the full brunt of it as Damien had heard it. Her eyes lifted to the lawyer. He would tell her honestly.

Ben Thomas understood her need, appreciated the effect of an emotional catharsis, but hesitated over whether it could be healthy for so frail a creature facing him now. But no one else spoke and Christina's silence demanded answers.

"They found him guilty of treason, Miss MacTavish. He has been disenfranchised. The estate reverts to the court, and he is to be regarded as a common spy and murderer. He has been sentenced to drawing and quartering the day after tomorrow."

She heard it as he must have, with the ripping, tearing pain deep in her guts that the words must have engendered. A bleak mental image flashed before her eyes of Damien's tall brave figure hauled upon a scaffold and mutilated before his own eyes and those of a cheering mob.

And then the image went blank and she saw no more.

Jeremy was the first to reach her, catching her crumpling figure before it reached the floor, startled at her incredible lightness as he swung her up in his arms. Then the silence erupted into the baron's shouts for servants and a physician, and the feet of running maids and footmen clattered around them and he had no time to register any more than the direction of the room to which the housekeeper steered him.

Christina woke to the heavily curtained gloom of her own chambers and the familiar features of her mother's physician leaning over her. As her lashes flickered open, the doctor sat back with satisfaction and reached for her wrist, taking her pulse with methodical quiet as she recovered her senses.

"You have let yourself fall into a deplorable condition," he admonished mildly as Christina's gaze focused upon him.

The words seemed to come from another world. They said nothing of death and blackness or the world she inhabited. She had no answer for them.

He did not seem disturbed by her silence. "You could have lost the child this time. The next time you will. If that is your wish, continue as you have been. I cannot promise you will recover, but the child certainly will not under these conditions."

Child. The word connected as no other could, hitting her with a blow as powerful as a steel hammer. A child. How could she have forgotten? She had dreamed of it, hid her burgeoning hopes, not wanting the pain of disappointment. And it had all vanished in a nightmare. But now he was telling her it was no dream but reality. Her fingers slowly crept to the still-flat surface of her abdomen.

The physician studied amber eyes wide with shock and nodded solemly. "Mrs. Douglass mentioned your symptoms, and my examination confirms it. If you can rely on Mrs. Douglass' dates, I'd say you can expect to be a mother by January."

A mother. Damien's child. Damien! Anguish ground Christina's insides to trembling jelly, leaving her weak with pain. She did not even need to think of the reason. She still felt it, deep inside, and had no need to think.

"Miss MacTavish." The voice boomed like thunder and Christina turned blankly toward its sound. "You have a duty toward that child. If you die, it will too. Is that what you want?"

Damien's child! No, never! It had to live, a piece of Damien, his heir, the child he had wanted! She could not desert it as her parents had deserted her. Damien had said she was strong. And she would be. The child needed her now.

She flattened her palms against the bed and forced herself into a sitting position, meeting the doctor's eyes with determination.

"Tell me what I must do."

Lorna shook her head in disapproval when Christina insisted on rising the next morning, but when Christina agreed to eat the meal ordered by the physician, Lorna said no more. She even assisted her down the stairs when Lord Jeremy's arrival was announced, although the practical Scotswoman would have been horrified had she known what her charge had in mind.

But Christina closed the door behind her, leaving her alone with the young lord.

"Christina!"

He flew to her side, grasping her hand and searching

her face with care. The dark shadows had not departed, and a private pain haunted the hidden recesses of her eyes, but she no longer seemed the ethereal figure of yesterday. Life inhabited the flashing gold specks of those dark irises.

"I only meant to inquire about your health. I did not expect you to come down . . ." he protested.

She held his hand as if it were her only support, staring at him intently. "Jeremy, I must ask a large favor of you. Please do not deny me."

"Anything, Christina, you know that. I know how hard—"

She shook her head. Sympathy would destroy her strength and she must be strong, stronger than her mother had ever been. "Take me to see him, Jeremy."

Blue eyes stared at her, shocked, then suddenly clouded with misery as he shook his head. "No, Christina, I cannot do that."

"You just promised me anything, Jeremy," she reminded him practically. "I know it is unfair of me, but I must hold you to it. There is something of utmost importance that Damien must know, and I will go there alone if you will not take me."

Jeremy's amiable expression became one of confusion and distress. "I cannot let you, Christina. He is not himself. He does not want you there."

"I know. He told me that, but for this I must disobey him. It is something I must do, and nothing will stop me."

Her determination worried Jeremy as much as her health. Had the shock affected her senses? Would his refusal make her worse? He wished desperately for the advice of an older, wiser head, but the baron and Ben had buried themselves in some business of their own. Perhaps Christina was right. Perhaps Damien should see her this one last time.

With reluctance Jeremy nodded.

The stench of Newgate had not improved with age, but Christina did her best to ignore it and all else. The shock that had carried her through the first time had worn off. She had not grown accustomed to the thought of Damien's death, but refused to think of it at all. To think of it brought visions too horrifying for her mind to accept. She saw the rats and the slime and the emaciated creatures in their stinking cells and knew Damien had been forced to live like this these past weeks, but she looked no further than that. She clutched her tiny reticule convulsively between her fingers as they strode briskly down the corridors.

Jeremy gripped her elbow tightly as the gaoler unlocked the last iron cell. Christina held her breath, prepared for anything. She had prayed Damien would escape, that her uncle would find influence to have him transported, anything but what must come tomorrow morn, but her prayers had not been answered. They never were anymore, or not until too late. Perhaps God ignored whores. If so, she must take fate in her own hands.

She stepped bravely through the open door into the windowless cell's damp gloom. It took a moment to adjust to the dusky light, but the tattered figure on the pallet saw her easily.

Damien's bellow of demented fury rocked the walls before Christina could even see him. The chains at his wrists and ankles jangled warningly as he jumped to his feet and lunged toward her, but their short length jerked him back. Christina stared at him in confusion, unable to relate the stern handsome gentleman she knew with this wild-eyed savage who seemed bent on murdering her with his bare hands.

"D-Damien, I . . . I wanted—" She attempted to speak bravely, but his curses rang incoherently against the four walls.

Jeremy appeared and tried to drag her away, and the curses turned on him, developing a pattern that Christina could not bear to acknowledge.

"Let me at her! I'll kill her! Jeremy, damn your double-blasted . . ." The curses continued while Christina cringed in horror. He must be mad. Why had they not told her? Yet she could not believe it. Black eyes snapped and flashed with a cold fury that would have killed had they but the means. Powerful muscles bunched and formed fists of frustrated fury that strained against the chains binding him. Only his howl of rage kept her wondering.

"Christina, come on. You must get out of here." Jeremy tugged desperately at her frozen figure, damning himself for a fool.

Christina nodded, her eyes still fixed with horror on the furious figure now pounding at the lock holding his chains. Gently she laid the small reticule she carried on the stone floor, tucking it beneath bits of straw and refuse, knowing the prisoner watched her every move.

"I tried, Damien . . ." she began, but tears flooded her eyes as hatred flared again and his curses carried her name in another violent storm of abuse. Whirling, she fled the room, blindly flying down stifling corridors, his jeers and howls following her every step, tears running hot and wet down her cheeks as she tried to escape the tormented cries of the damned ringing out behind her.

Jeremy caught up with her, grabbing her firmly and half-carrying her from the building. Christina collapsed in his arms, the tears flowing uncontrollably, though she had thought them all dry by now.

Why did he hate her? What had she done to deserve his curses? She had wanted to help, had done everything within her limited power to save him. Why had he turned on her like this? The questions screamed for answers, but she could not push a sensible sound from her tongue. She cried until Jeremy gave her into the care of the practical Mrs. Douglass.

She wept through the remainder of the night, until the sun rose over the horizon with the dawn. The day Damien must die.

21

Since her mother's death the servants had been busy dyeing all Christina's fine new gowns dismal shades of black. The daring silks and satins were packed away, but the sprigged cambrics and striped muslins made modest gowns when topped with crisp white handkerchiefs.

Christina wore one now as she sat in the gloomy parlor, her hands neatly crossed in her lap, waiting. Since the dawn she had waited for some word that would indicate Damien had found the small stiletto she had smuggled in with her reticule. None came. All hope gone, she waited now for the return of her uncle and Jeremy. They had promised to make all the necessary arrangements when it was over. She refused to define "it" any more clearly than that.

She had never seen a public hanging, had never even seen the remains of a body hanging from the tree or gallows afterward, though it was a commonplace punishment for thieves. The technicalities of drawing and quartering she vaguely understood from explicit descriptions she had heard as a schoolgirl, but they did not seem credible. How could anyone live to watch his own entrails drawn out? It was not human. Only savages would contemplate such justice. She could not.

The image of Damien's tall, proud figure climbing steps to the scaffold, however, came easily to mind, as it had from that first time he had mentioned his fate. Christina could see russet hair neatly queued and gleaming in the sun, black eyes flickering defiantly over jeering mobs as the noose lowered over his head. His broad shoulders would be encased only in white linen, and without his cravat, the shirt would fall open to expose the dark mat of hair over his bronzed chest. She had seen him like this too many times to deny the image now. Instead, she closed out the picture entirely.

With deliberately blank mind, Christina awaited the clip-clop of horses and the rattle of carriage wheels that would indicate her uncle's arrival and the end to her death watch. She had prayed long and hard that Damien could turn the knife on himself before they dragged him away, but she would not even inquire. He was dead, but his child still lived.

When the men finally entered the dimly lit room, they showed no surprise at finding her there. All three had returned, still wearing their dark suits of mourning, respectfully doffing their tricornes as they entered. When Damien was here, they would have entered laughing and chattering, exchanging ribald jokes and insults or news of the war and politics. Today they stood silent.

"He is gone, then?" Christina whispered, staring at her hands.

Her uncle stepped forward, taking her hands in his strong ones, forcing her to look up. "You must come with me back to Cornwall. We will open the place up and make it livable again. Your mother said you loved the sea. You can rest there and get well again."

Christina smiled faintly, absently, and withdrew her hand. She turned her gaze to Damien's faithful solicitor. "Ben, can I sell the house in St. James? I have never seen it and do not know its worth . . ."

Short and stout, Ben Thomas hitched up his sagging breeches and came forward with a thoughtful tread. "It is yours to do with as you wish, Miss MacTavish. It is a very valuable piece of property. If you are not intending to remain in London. . . . That is probably a very wise idea."

Behind his glasses, gray eyes studied her carefully and Christina met their gaze with a genuine rush of affection. He had loved Damien too, and he worried that she took his fate lightly. Christina wished to reassure him, but she must take this one step at a time.

"Could you take care of it for me? I have saved the income from the trust, but it will not be enough, I fear."

Before she could explain, the baron interrupted. "Do not hurry into anything rash, Christina. As far as I am concerned, that tainted money can be spent to feed the poor. You need not worry about funds any longer."

Christina squeezed his hand gratefully but ignored his words. She noticed Jeremy hovering uneasily in the background, but he had no right to speak, and held his tongue. She was grateful for his understanding and hoped it went deep enough to understand what she must say next.

"I thank you, uncle, but what I must do now, I must do alone. Ben, you will sell the house for me?" She brushed away all else as she fastened her gaze intently on the solicitor.

"Of course, Miss MacTavish, if you wish. But you should listen to your uncle. He will look after your interests as wisely as I." He watched her cautiously, sensing an underlying determination beneath soft words and wounded eyes.

"I am certain of that, and I appreciate all your help, but there are things that must be done. Damien's family must be notified at once."

An uneasy current swept the room, but Christina would not let their distress stand in her way. Let them think her mad if they must. She would have her way.

"Of course. I have already informed them through correspondence of the events before the trial," Ben replied. "With this war, it is difficult to get letters through, but one of this nature should not be so difficult."

Without asking, the solicitor drew up a chair beside her and settled his weary bones in it. He was not a courtroom lawyer as such, but he had seen enough of human nature to know when an emotional bombshell was about to explode. He had half a notion in which direction this one was aimed and preferred to be prepared when it blew.

"How difficult is it to get a person through?" Christina's question was aimed at Ben, and the others floundered in its wake, not quite understanding.

Crystal glasses gleamed as they met the determined gaze of amber eyes, and a wrinkle appeared at one corner of the older man's lips. "Difficult, but not impossible. Did you have anyone in particular in mind?"

"Myself, if the sale of the house will be sufficient to cover the fare and whatever expenses I may encounter upon arrival."

Jeremy opened his mouth to protest, but the baron beat him to it, his face growing red with hurt and bewilderment and dismay. "Christina! This is madness. You do not know what you are saying. Let me call Mrs. Douglass. She will put you to bed, and in the morning you will see things more clearly. Mr. Thomas, I beg you—"

Ben waved him aside, studying Christina's drawn face with better objectivity than her distraught uncle. "You wish to travel to the colonies to inform the Drayton family personally?" he inquired calmly.

Christina stared back at him. "I wish to travel to the colonies to start a new life there. I will, of course, take that opportunity to inform Damien's family personally, if you will be so kind as to give me a letter of introduction."

"Christina, no! You do not know what you are saying." Jeremy finally pushed his way to the forefront, throwing himself down beside her on the sofa. One hand clenched the delicate scrolled woodwork of the seat, the other curled about Christina's fingers as he pleaded desperately. "You are distraught. It is not a time for clear thinking. Go with your uncle to Cornwall. Tour the continent perhaps. In time, all will be forgotten. You have friends here, Christina, family, people who love you . . ." It was as close as he dared come without declaring himself openly, but he had to chance it. Gentle blue eyes searched hers for understanding. "Christina, please, give it time. There is nothing for you in that wilderness. You cannot make such a journey alone. Say you are jesting."

Eyes moist with sorrow, Christina looked up into his gallant face, seeing for the first time the man behind the amiable facade. Jeremy was much stronger than she had believed, much deeper than the smiling gallantry he showed the world. It would have been so much easier to have loved a man like that. . . .

She touched his face gently and shook her head. "I can and I will, Jeremy. I can do anything I put my mind to, and my mind is made up. I will never forget you, but you must forget me. This is your home, but I have yet to make mine."

The baron and Ben both spoke at once, but she heard only Jeremy's hoarse cry of "Why?"

Speaking only to him, she replied, "Because Damien wished his child to grow up in the Americas."

A sudden silence fell before the explosion of the storm. Christina's soft words produced a most satisfactory bombshell, one right on top of the other. Ben leaned back in his chair with a grunt of satisfaction as both the baron and Jeremy found their tongues and a chaos of voices broke out all around.

Christina waited patiently through it. For the first time in her life she was in full command of her own life, and she had no intention of surrendering it. Perhaps she was a fool or had taken leave of her senses, as the voices around her said. It mattered little. She had had more than enough hours to stare at empty walls and make her decision. She had never been so certain of anything in her whole life. Damien had told her of the colonies and of his family and of his hopes for his children. In one way or another, he would be with her every step of the way. The smile behind her tears brightened imperceptibly.

As it became obvious that she paid no attention to their protests, the three men grew quiet. Until Jeremy broke the spell.

Standing, he caught their eyes. Clubbed hair neatly tucked in a sober bagwig, his dark coat and breeches giving him an unusually somber air, he appeared more than ever the gentleman of substantial means and station, and he commanded their attention readily.

"Please, if you gentlemen will excuse me, may I speak with Miss MacTavish alone?"

With astonishment the baron looked over the young acquaintance who had so amiably held steadfast to Damien's cause these past weeks. He had given the young lord little consideration, but he suddenly saw him in a new light, and his old eyes lit with gratitude and respect.

"Young man, if you can find some means of persuading this foolish child from her folly, I will be eternally grateful. She is my only family."

The words were an unspoken promise but Ben doubted if the young couple heard them. He shrugged as the baron looked his way, and followed him from the room. He would like to hear the conversation they left behind, but he would put high stakes on the outcome.

Christina stared curiously at Jeremy's unusually serious mien. "Yes, my lord?" she prompted him when he seemed to have lost his train of thought. It suddenly occurred to her he had also lost his shy stutter. She stared at him in wonderment.

Jeremy seemed oblivious to her thoughts. His own must be well put or the cause was lost. He finally decided on the seat Ben had vacated, moving it directly in front of Christina so he might watch her lovely features as he spoke.

"Christina, I don't know how to say this, not at a time like this. I thought there would be a time for you to recover from your grief, but with a child in question . . ."

He hesitated, and Christina smiled uncertainly, taking his hand to reassure him. She had no fear of the future. Why should he? Before she could put her question into words, Jeremy waved it aside and continued hastily.

"I love you, Christina. I have loved you from the first

moment I laid eyes on you. But you and Damien . . ."—he waved away her protests—"I wanted to kill Damien. I told you that once, but though you wouldn't admit it then, I could tell it would be like killing you too. You loved him as I love you. The damned eternal triangle—if Drayton ever loved anybody but himself."

Christina's indignant glare was met by an immediate apology. "I am sorry; I spoke in bitterness, but I want you to hear me. I love you and I want you to marry me. It does not matter if you do not love me. You will make me happy and I can keep you secure. You know I can, Christina. It will solve everything. The child will have a name and I will have you, and in time, perhaps you might even learn to love me a little."

Christina wanted to weep but she had cried all the tears she intended to shed. Instead, she shook her head slowly and steadily, clutching desperately at Jeremy's hand. He tempted her much more than he would ever realize. She was all alone now and she wanted to be loved. No woman alive could resist a man such as this one, but she must, for his own sake as well as hers.

"No, Jeremy, you are cruel to tempt me in such a way. I would destroy your life, not make it better. Your family would disown you, society would reject you, you would have to give up everything you know and love for a woman who bears another man's child and who could never love you as you are meant to be loved. Do not make me suffer more by asking again. I cherish your friendship, and above all else, I will miss you when I am gone."

Jeremy looked as if he would weep too, but the habit had been bred out of him too long ago. He set his jaw firmly and met Christina's sad gaze with decision.

"My family would recover soon enough, and I am quite capable of living without society and working to support you. I have thought about it a thousand times, and the only difference the child makes is that it must be done soon. I am sorry if I am being cruel, but the alternative is much crueler. You cannot travel halfway around the world to a strange land where you know no one and have no home. They are at war over there, Christina. It is no place to raise a child."

Christina smiled faintly at his unnaturally stern demeanor. He almost sounded like Damien. Almost, but not enough.

"I thank you, my lord, but I must and I will. If Damien's family in any way resembles him, we will be friends. The child needs to know his true family. I intend to go, Jeremy, and nothing anyone can say will sway me."

Jeremy stared at the firm determination in her pale features and developed some rippling of understanding of the wall he beat his head against. He stood and began to pace the room.

"The child will need a name," he threw out as he paced, one thought madly outracing the next as he sought solutions.

"I will call myself Mrs. MacTavish. Or Mrs. Smith if it makes anyone happier. Names are meaningless."

He turned on her with sudden resolution. "No. They are a means of protection. Names are important. Believe me in this much, Christina. If you will not take my name legally, use it when you leave here. Your own may be known, and mine carries the weight of my family."

Christina stared at him with increasing curiosity. "Why would you do this? I can as easily take my uncle's."

He came to a halt in front of her, impressing her with his intensity. "Take mine. Someday I mean for you to have it legally. In the meantime, take my word that it will provide your best protection."

Christina understood that there was something of importance he was not telling her, something that made it imperative she change her name, but why to his, she could not quite grasp. The thought of calling herself Lady Jeremy Standifer bent her lips in small amusement.

"I hardly think your title will impress the colonists. And what would I say became of my husband? You look very much alive to me."

Jeremy relaxed a trifle and sat down to join the

game. "You will be traveling by British ship to British-occupied territory. The title will be convenient for now and can be dropped later. In the meantime, just tell everyone your husband died honorably. I have always wanted to die an honorable death. Can't imagine what one is, but there you have it. Easy, safe." He shrugged laconically.

Christina stared at this change of attitude, but nodded slowly. What could be the harm? And maybe someday . . . But she would not think these thoughts now.

"If you insist, Jeremy," she answered quietly.

"I insist." Jeremy sent up a silent prayer that this would be all the protection she needed, but in his heart he knew it was not, and he despaired.

Part Two

22

Lorna tugged the billowing cape more firmly around Christina's frail shoulders, but in the June heat it was scarcely needed, and Christina shrugged it back again.

Clutching the ship's railing, she leaned out to find the familiar figures on the dock beyond, spying Jeremy's golden locks with ease, and from there, the more sedately bewigged heads of her uncle and Ben Thomas. A pain tugged at her heart at the sight of these affectionate friends who had stood by her through the worst of times, but she spared no more than a wave of greeting and farewell. She had not strength for any more.

All her strength centered on the child and fighting back the blackness that threatened to claim her every time some small sight or sound reminded her of Damien. If she could think only of the future and not the past, she found some small relief from the pain and the exertion of fighting off his memory.

And the three beloved figures on the dock were part of the past. She waved once again as the wind caught the sails and the width of the river separated them more.

She did not scan the crowds for any other, or she might have noticed a fourth pair of familiar eyes. With malevolence they followed the fleeting ship carrying the tawny-haired lioness who had been the instrument of destruction to all hopes. In harsh tones their owner addressed an equally familiar companion. "She will lead us to him, see if she does not." His companion gave him a dubious glance, as one would to a madman, but shrugging his shoulders, did not disagree.

Unaware of the closeness of evil, Christina meekly acquiesced to Lorna's admonitions and returned to her cabin when the dock drifted from sight. Lorna was part of the past, but part of the future too. She had come from Damien's family and now wished to return, and Christina was more than grateful for her companionship. She did not know what she would have done without her.

And in the weeks to come, it was obvious she could not have done without the Scotswoman, had Christina been conscious enough to admit it.

But Christina's dreams of sailing upon a ship over the ocean's blue waters were lost in the nightmares of illness and fever. The little strength Christina possessed sank beneath the burden of pregnancy and the deprivation of the journey and her own haunting nightmares. Her screams of terror as the scaffold's shadow blotted out all light kept the other passengers complaining, and her confinement to the narrow cabin brought little sympathy from anyone but the faithful Lorna.

For summer, the crossing was a rough one, and when a mighty gale blew them off course from the British-protected waters off New York to the privateer-laden shore of Virginia, rumors became rife. The crew whispered of the notorious *Sea Lion* that had once haunted these waters, and the fact that it had last been seen off Cornwall heading toward France relieved few fears.

The captain of that same privateer stared through his scope at the billowing sails of the British schooner. He no longer held the marque of a privateer and he had no business contemplating this unprovoked attack on His Majesty's navy, but weeks of pent-up rage had need of some release. And his crew would welcome the diversion.

The tall figure at the prow swung around and shouted rapid commands. Sailors went scurrying up the rigging; others jumped to the attendance of the deadly cannon lining the decks of the small clipper. The captain had been in a rare fury this trip, and none were eager for the lash of his tongue should they trip in carrying out of their duties.

The sun glanced off russet hair as the captain relieved the mate at the tiller and steered a course toward danger. Wind whipped through his hair and billowed out the loose sleeves of his shirt as the sails caught and held and sped them on. He seemed scarcely to heed the physical sensations of life about him, so set was the devil's determination to destroy.

Why return home now that nothing awaited him? Somehow he must cauterize the open wounds and numb the pain, and if he were killed in the process, what loss would there be? He would not live half a man, but die a victorious one.

The odds were in his favor of accomplishing that much.

Unaware of the impending combat on open seas, Lorna made a presumptuous request of the weary captain of the storm-driven schooner. He listened with ill-concealed impatience as she suggested she and her ill companion be put off on these enemy shores rather than traveling on to New York, but the thought took hold. The dour Scotswoman and her nightmare-hagged companion had been a constant source of irritation from the outset of this journey. The lady's screams had aroused superstitions in the fertile imaginations of his sailors, and they would be glad to see the end of her.

With the wind blowing in the wrong direction for their northward journey, the captain had no trouble finding volunteers to row the pair ashore.

Black eyes watched the schooner sail inland toward Virginia shores instead of open sea, and they grew bleak with frustration. Denied this fight, they would find another. The captain raised his hand and signaled for departure.

For weeks Christina had been conscious of little more than occasional faces and voices. Lorna's reassuring croons and familiar features were all she had to cling to, and unconsciously she held the woman's hand in a painful grip for much of their ill-fated journey.

Of a sudden, strangers intruded upon Christina's fevered dreams, voices with odd accents, soft hands feeding her warm concoctions, faces that had no place in her memory. The ship's rocking, lurching motion had come to a halt, and sunlight and fresh air streamed through open windows. She drank gratefully of cool juices and warm broths and sank into healing slumbers strangely unhaunted by nightmares.

Christina had no notion of the amount of time that had passed when she woke to a sunlit room and the perfumed scent of a summer breeze wafting through the open window. Her gaze slowly traveled over unfamiliar plaster walls and wide-planked flooring to the delicate lace of mosquito netting swathing the tall posts of the bed she lay in. Only then did her gaze focus on the small figure seated in a nearby chair.

The woman looked to be much her mother's age, but dark eyes gleamed with liveliness from a face scarcely touched by age, and the soft dark hair pulled back in a cap had little hint of gray about it. Christina's gaze came back to fasten on those flashing black eyes, and her stomach lurched painfully.

Her hand instantly went to the small swelling that had grown within her abdomen these past months. She relaxed slightly as she felt its firm roundness, surprised that it could have grown so much in so short a time. A pleased smile flickered about her lips at the thought of the child resting there, and Christina scarcely noticed when the slight woman rose to join her.

"The child is still well, although you had us worried for a while, Lady Jeremy. Would you like some tea?"

The strange address startled her, but Christina recovered quickly and nodded silently. As the woman bent over the tea set, she struggled to sit up and puzzle out her surroundings.

Lady Jeremy. They had taken her passage in that name, she knew. Lorna had called her that in the presence of others on board the ship. But they were not there now. Where was Lorna?

A dozen other questions came to mind, but Christina crushed them down as she accepted the tea from her friendly hostess. It was obvious the other woman barely concealed a number of questions of her own as she watched Christina sip of the bitter brew.

"It is not what you are accustomed to, I am sorry. Since the tea tax we have bought no real tea, but make do with our own or coffee. Would you prefer coffee?"

At Christina's negative shake of her head, the slight woman settled back in her chair and watched her patient with curiosity.

"I have so many things to ask you, my dear, but I fear you are not up to answering them yet. You look much better than you did when Lorna brought you here, though."

The woman had no means of comparison, but she sensed the ethereal translucence of that pale face and those enormous golden eyes were not the natural healthy rose of this young woman's complexion. Still, the young face had gained a measure of dignity and insight that most girls of that age would never gain in their lifetimes, and the older woman studied those lines of pain with interest.

Christina could not wave away her fascination with those piercing black eyes. Abruptly she spoke out loud. "I am most awfully sorry, but I cannot seem to remember your name. Should I know you?"

The slight lady's hands flew to her face and her black eyes danced with amusement at her own expense. "Of course not! How foolish of me! Lorna and Damien and Ben Thomas' introduction have told us all about you, but we've never met. I'm Sophia Drayton, Damien's mother."

At the sound of Damien's name, the teacup bounced off the bedcovers and onto the floor, splattering tea over the colorful quilt and shattering the fragile china. In an instant Sophia Drayton had whipped off the dampened covers and called for maids to sweep up the china shards.

Christina was tucked back among the sheets, and an

anxious Lorna hovered beside her, touching her forehead.

In confusion Christina closed her eyes, but she could not shut out the name she had heard uttered. Damien! How could he have spoken to his mother of her? Butterflies flurried through her stomach and she could not contain her excitement. Restlessly she brushed away Lorna's hand and faced Mrs. Drayton's anxious frown once again.

"Damien?" she inquired weakly, searching the dark eyes eagerly.

The woman sought for the unspoken question, remembering her words and smiling anxiously. "Of course. He wrote all about how he had found dear Eleanor's daughter and brought you both to town. He is an atrocious letter writer, though, and he made no mention of your marriage to Lord Jeremy. I was hoping when you are feeling better . . ."

Lorna snorted warningly as Christina's eyes closed in pain. Mrs. Drayton quieted, but stared down her friend's gaze. The recalcitrant Scotswoman had told her only the bare bones of the girl's story and nothing of Damien. She would not be warned away.

Christina dozed off, and when she woke again, the sun had followed behind the house and the room had filled with dusk. A single candle flame marked the chair where Sophia Drayton sat, crocheting some impossibly frilly lace in the darkness. At Christina's movement she glanced up.

"Good. The doctor says you must eat. I will send for something warm."

Christina made no objection but watched warily as Damien's mother returned to the bedside. The questions between them created an insurmountable barrier.

Sophia Drayton settled herself firmly in her chair and stared at Christina's wan features with decision. "I am going to be extremely ungracious. As you are about to be a mother yourself, perhaps you will forgive me, but my son's well-being comes before all else. Lorna will only mutter dire imprecations when I ask of Damien. That means he has done something awful of which she disapproves, but it is not the first time. As boy or man, I have never seen anyone so hell-bent for trouble as Damien, but he always emerges unscathed. Now, before Lorna drives me away again, can you tell me how my son fared when you saw him last?"

Tears welled in Christina's eyes and rolled down her cheeks unchecked. Why had Lorna not told the poor woman the truth? Why must she, of all people, be the one to break the news? What had happened to Ben's letter?

Sophia presented a handkerchief but waited adamantly for some reply.

Realizing Damien had assigned her this task as his last wish, Christina drew a deep breath and fought for words she had never said, even to herself.

"You received no letter from his solicitor?" she whispered weakly, postponing the inevitable.

The dark head of hair shook negatively, dislodging its crisp white cap. "Besides your letter of introduction, I have heard nothing. Very few ships are coming through anymore. Damien's last letter arrived by a captain we both knew. The man died at sea later, in a battle with a British frigate. This foolish war goes on too long." Sophia Drayton twisted nervously the lace in her lap, not daring to look up again at the open wounds of the girl's huge eyes. She had sat here all afternoon, tearing apart and remaking this same piece of lace a dozen times, knowing she did not want to hear what Christina had to say.

Butterflies again fluttered in her stomach, and Christina's fingers automatically went to cover them.

The older woman caught the movement and smiled sympathetically. "The child moves?"

It came as a revelation. Christina's eyes widened with wonder and astonishment and her fingers sought the movement again with excitement. Damien's child lived! The wonder of it never ceased to amaze her. She had this comfort, but what could she give his mother?

Sadly Christina sought for gentle words. "I wish I could tell you what you long to hear," she whispered.

Sophia continued to stare at her fingers ripping lace. "I knew when he returned to England that he had set his mind to some foolishness. Was it Nicholas?"

The name startled Christina. She had forgotten that evil creature in the greater evils that followed. "He sought Nicholas, yes, but he had another mission, too, a more honorable one, I believe, but the British courts did not quite see it that way," she answered bitterly.

The other woman nodded silently a moment, then asked, "You are telling me he is in gaol or worse, are you not?"

Christina gave the same answer she had once been given. "I am sorry."

The food arrived, and with it Lorna, and Sophia Drayton ran hurriedly from the room, leaving Christina to the housekeeper's care. They exchanged sorrowful looks, but no words.

Christina regained her strength quickly under the constant supervision of Mrs. Drayton and Lorna. After that first outburst Damien's mother had said nothing else of her son and asked no further questions, but as the color returned to Christina's cheeks and the fever dissipated, Mrs. Drayton's quizzical glances became more numerous.

At last, when Christina had the strength to sit in a proper chair, Sophia could contain herself no more. Drawing up another seat and pouring a second cup of "tea," she went directly to the subject.

"Damien wrote me a long letter all about you. He has . . . had . . . never done anything like that before. He even insisted that if anything happened to him, I was to inquire after you and your mother and make certain you were well. I never heard anything more from him. Lorna has told me of your mother's death. Coming on top of your husband's, it must have been a terrible shock, but if you can, I would hear of my son. You two must have been close for him to write to me as he did."

Christina bowed her head. She had never been a successful liar. What could she tell this woman that would not break her heart? But to speak of Damien . . . She had a growing need to speak of him again, to hear of him, to learn more of him, if only to pass on the knowledge to his child.

"He was . . . very kind. He found a physician to help my mother and brought us to London when my uncle could not be found. I do not know what you wish me to say. He had a purpose in going to London, and so far as I know, he carried out that purpose. I hope and pray it was worth the price he paid." The last came out with a bitter twist as she looked away from Mrs. Drayton's hopeful eyes.

"You could tell me why you are wearing that ring and no other. It is an old ring and one I recognize well. Anson bought it for me. He showed it to me many times, but I refused it. When I finally accepted his offer of marriage, we were in a great hurry to leave and left the ring behind. Damien must have found it at Westshipham."

Christina stared down at the circlet of gold and diamonds she wore on her left hand where Damien had placed it. Her mother had commented on it, but she had never thought it could have significance to her unsentimental highwayman. His mother's betrothal ring. She stared at it with new knowledge, then back up into the black eyes so like Damien's own. She did not know what to say, but the burning glow of love in her eyes spoke for her.

Astonishingly, Mrs. Drayton simply patted her hand and nodded sagely. "There now, you need not tell me all. It will come with time, I'm certain. Lord Jeremy was a good man, he and my son were the best of friends, though never were two men more unalike, I believe. Someday perhaps, when you know us better, you will tell me why you came here."

"You have been more than kind and patient. I wish I could tell you what you would like to hear, but I cannot. Perhaps it is time I begin looking for a home of my own. I cannot impose on you any longer."

Dark curls shook vigorously. "I will not hear of it. It

would be like sending my own daughter out on her own. She has been out on the plantation tending to some servants with smallpox, but she should be home soon. You and Mara should get along fine. Yorktown is small and boasts little in the way of society, so she will be delighted to hear of the latest fashions in London. The house is so empty with all of them away . . ."

What had begun as a cheerful speech died out in a sad memory and Christina reached to grasp the older woman's hand.

"Damien spoke of a brother. I trust he is well?"

Mrs. Drayton smiled gently. "The last I heard, he is. Robert is hopeless with a rifle, but the militia finds a use for him. He is with Governor Nelson now, I believe, but he turns up at odd moments. He has an old printing press hidden away somewhere he uses for fiery pamphlets and other, more nefarious purposes, I fear. Like Damien, he is a troublemaker, but his comes from words and not weapons. I do not know why I am not gray by now."

In this manner Christina came to know more of Damien's family and the precarious state of war in which they existed. The Continental Army was perched on some high bluff over British-held New York, Charleston had surrendered to the British, and Virginia had become a battleground of little more than guerrilla warfare. The Virginia militia and Lafayette's small handful of men could do no more than badger Cornwallis' highly trained and well supplied army. The war everyone spoke about seemed no more than the taunts and jeers of small boys to Christina's unskilled ears. The names and places meant nothing to her.

But living without luxuries she did understand. The war had cut off most major supply lines and years of neglect had reduced once fine plantations to mere skeletons of themselves. The housewives of Yorktown made do with what they had as the roaming bands of militia and marauding armies emptied what remained of the countryside. Christina not only learned to live without tea, but once again found herself on a diet lacking many of the essentials.

At least, that is, until the day Robert and Mara returned from the plantation pulling a battered cartload of vegetables and game behind an old mule. Christina hovered in the background as the pair spilled from the wagon into the waiting arms of mother and servants, but she soon found herself caught up in the introductions and stares of the handsome new arrivals.

With unaccustomed shyness she accepted the firm brown hand of the tall stranger who resembled Damien in so many striking ways, and in so many other ways did not. Robert Drayton's hair was the dark brown of his mother's and his eyes a lively green all his own. They flickered over her in a manner reminiscent of his brother's, but his broad grin in no way resembled Damien's stern demeanor. Christina met it with instant delight.

On the other hand, Mara Drayton bore a startling resemblance to her older brother, though she was much his junior. The eighteen-year-old beauty studied Christina with cool composure, dark eyes watching her with suspicion, firm lips unsmiling as the introductions were made. Christina could almost see Damien's cynical nature behind those wide cheekbones, and bit back a smile of mischief at the thought.

"Your brother spoke fondly of you, Miss Drayton. I feel I should know you well," Christina murmured in her best ladylike manner. She listened closley to the reply.

"Indeed, Lady Jeremy, my brother has written so fondly of you, we feared you would be bearing his name and not another's. This is a surprise.'"

Christina's lips quivered slightly as she caught Sophia Drayton's eye. Damien's forthright nature rang true and clear in this miniature replica, and she had a hard time suppressing a smile. "Feared, Miss Drayton? Did you think your brother had turned traitor to the cause?"

Robert's snickers were quickly muffled. Their mother had written of this new arrival and her sad news. It was the excuse he had used to get away from his post to pick up his sister and come back to Yorktown. He had not believed a word of it, but now, standing beside the dignified bearing of this chit no older than his sister, Robert had second thoughts. Christina was as tall as Mara, but her fine-drawn grace brought out protective instincts he had never known he possessed. She met Mara's coolness with a wit and intelligence that commanded respect.

"For your beauty any man would turn traitor, Lady Jeremy. Shall we go in?"

Gallantly offering his arm, Robert smoothly robbed the exchange of any rancor, and the lttle group proceeded inside the modest two-story brick house they called home.

Over dinner the two new arrivals attempted to draw Christina out on the subject of their brother's capture and trial, but Christina quietly deflected the topic, unable to speak more than short phrases in reply. For details, she requested they wait for the solicitor's letter. After a while, even Mara sensed the pain the subject inflicted on their guest, and she withdrew her questions.

That night, Christina lay in the room she now knew had belonged to Damien and tried desperately to commune with his spirit. What was she to tell these people he had loved? Surely he would want them to know of his child, but how would she explain it? She could not. To tell it would wound as much as aid. What could she say?

She cried out her fears to the night breeze off the water, but it gave no reply.

23

Christina had still not fully regained her strength when Robert Drayton offered to show her his hidden printing press, but she accepted the offer gladly. She had sat idly about for weeks and could no longer suppress her restlessness. The printing press held as much interest as her charming escort.

She quickly learned Robert's "visit" entailed a good deal of work, but she instantly succumbed to the intricacies of typesetting, and her own knowledge of the printed word created a speedy partnership. The notices Robert had been commissioned to run off soon developed a style and flair of their own, and his lopsided grin grew broader as he admired Christina's handiwork.

"Damn, but if I had you around all the time, I'd start my own paper. Beat anything Philadelphia or Boston can boast of. Since when did ladies learn to scribble like that?" He bent a quizzical glance to Christina's ink-stained but perfectly charming features.

She sent him a gamine grin. "Did not Damien tell me your Declaration of Independence had something in it about all men being created free and equal? Does that not count for women too?"

The broad smile suddenly slid from his face. "Dammit, Christina—and I don't apologize for my familiarity. 'Lady Jeremy' don't sit well with my tongue and 'Mrs. Standifer' ain't much better; it'd be like calling Mara 'Miss Drayton."

Christina brushed away this meandering and waited

for the reason her new friend had suddenly grown so solemn.

Robert accepted her gesture as permission to continue. "I wish you'd give us the whole truth about Damien. You keep pushing us off until you got Mara thinking you're a British spy who has Damien locked up in a tower somewhere. It's obvious to everyone you're still suffering from whatever happened back there, but you gotta think about *us*. Damn, but even I can't believe the bloody devil is dead!"

Christina's hands fell in her lap and she stared at the ink stains beneath her nails. She liked this brother of Damien's, from the curious bent spectacles he wore when he read to his abrupt honesty. She wanted to offer this same honesty in return, but she had no intention of her child being known as a bastard. She evaded the truth with another truth.

"I am sorry, Robert. Sometimes even I find it difficult to believe he is dead. The emptiness is there; I cannot hear his voice or touch his hand. But when my mother died, she was gone. I felt she was gone. I did not go around expecting to hear her laugh behind a door or see her figure coming down the stairs, as I do Damien. I simply cannot believe he is not there any longer."

She choked back a sob and Robert averted his face in embarrassment at what he had heard in her voice. He noticed she made no reference to her husband's death, and his sorrow deepened.

"I'll not mention it again, Christina. My mother swears Damien has nine lives like a cat, and until she sees his dead body she will never believe he's gone. Maybe there's something in that."

Considering the wretched manner in which Damien had died, Christina doubted very much if his mother would wish to see his dead body, but she had told no one of that particular grisly detail. Let them think he died honorably, as an earl, with his head through a silken noose. She would not deny them this small comfort.

She accepted Robert's hand and slid from her high stool. They walked back over the hill to the main street of town, hand-in-hand. Dusk had fallen, and the peculiar cries of the gulls had silenced. Yet the air held an element of tension, of expectation, as if any moment now this dreamy landscape would erupt into life.

Christina smiled to herself at this flight of fancy and gently rubbed her free hand over the small protrusion of her stomach. In the heat she had abandoned the stylish abundance of petticoats, and her thin black muslin did little to disguise the small bulge beneath her still-tiny waistline. Soon she would need to let out the seams of her bodice.

A blaze of candles lit the downstairs parlor window. An oddity, for the fat for their making was a scarcity at the moment. The shutters were closed, however, and Christina and Robert could not see inside. Still, their step quickened as they approached the stately brick structure.

Entering, they could hear the distinct sound of a male voice behind the closed parlor door, and Christina hesitated in the hallway, rubbing nervously at the smudged spot on her nose. Gallantly Robert produced his handkerchief and attempted to rub the spot away, wickedly muttering "Vanity" under his breath.

The door swung open on this tender scene, the sudden light mixing with a furious intake of breath before the vibrating thunderclap of a deep voice shattered the silence.

"*Christina*! What the hell!"

Flashing black eyes swept from Robert's lanky frame to the slim golden-haired creature practically in the lad's arms. As Christina turned in dazed shock, the eyes instantly swept downward to the new rotundity of her figure, and their owner's bronzed face developed a sudden pallor.

Christina scarcely noticed the direction his gaze had taken. Dumbfounded, she stared at the dark apparition in the doorway, his lean figure garbed in the navy broadcloth and gold braid of a ship's captain, whispered only the one word, "Damien!" and fainted.

With a violent curse, Damien reacted more quickly than his brother, catching Christina's falling figure before she tumbled to the floor. The cries of female voices behind him prevented any more than a glare being sent to Robert as Damien casually swept the slight burden into his arms.

"I knew it was too soon for her to go out! She is much too frail to exert herself in such a way. And then, seeing you . . ." Sophia Drayton came flying out of the parlor after her son, taking in the situation instantly, and immediately heading for the stairway. "Bring Lady Jeremy up here. She has been occupying your old room, Damien. She does not carry the child well, poor thing. Hurry!"

Damien followed the trail of words upward, each statement hitting him with the force of a hammer blow until his face had twisted into a grim mask of itself by the time he reached the bedroom door.

Depositing his fragile burden among the bedcovers, Damien watched implacably as Christina's eyes began to flicker. She turned her head in agitation against the pillows, uttered a pleading moan, and then dark lashes suddenly flew open to encounter the stony mask of hatred hovering above her. The shock as their gazes met sent a trembling quake through every fiber of her being.

Mrs. Drayton hurried in with smelling salts and cold compresses.

"Damien, get out of here. The child has been ill and you have just given her the shock of her life. Shoo! Scat!" The tiny woman peremptorily motioned away Damien's tall, lithe frame.

Damien moved only enough for his mother to slip by him, his black gaze still fastened on Christina. "What are you doing here?" he intoned furiously, ignoring his mother's chattering protests.

"They told me you were dead!" Recovering some of

her senses at this sign of the apparition's reality, Christina responded with vehemence.

"I trust that made you happy, but that does not answer my question. What in hell are you doing here?" Damien roared, his fury rattling the windows.

"Damien!" Mrs. Drayton straightened to her full height and turned from her ministrations to face her tall son. "I will not have you speaking to a guest in this house in that manner. Now, leave at once or I will be forced to call the servants to drag you out!"

With furious control, Damien met his mother's irate glare. "That won't be necessary, madam. Any house she remains in will not hold me."

Turning on his heel, he strode out, slamming the door behind him. An altercation arose in the hallway below, but Damien's curt tones decided the matter, and again a door slammed. Amber eyes filled with tears as they met the sorrowful dark ones above her. Strong strides died away in the distance and silence fell.

"Perhaps now you would care to tell me what is between you and my son," a soft voice murmured pleadingly.

Christina's heart felt like it had been yanked from her chest and trampled on by a cavalcade of horses, and the pain of it filled every corner of her soul. Her uncle had lied to her. Jeremy and Ben had lied to her. Why? Why had they all conspired to put her through this misery? Why would they say he died so horribly when they knew he lived? How could he be alive afer what she had seen and heard? And worst of all, why had Damien perpetrated this outrage upon her? What had she done to deserve his hatred?

She tried to escape the anguish of uncertainty by focusing on the kind woman beside her. Sophia Drayton deserved better than that demented monster she called son. What point was there in denying her wishes now?

Slowly the words formed on Christina's tongue, a steady catalog of facts of these past fantastical months since Damien had come into her life. She made no excuses, placed no blame, simply emptied her soul of the dead waste left behind. It had no place in her life now. Damien had left her more certainly than if he had died. Before, at least she had had pleasant memories.

Sophia Drayton shook her head sadly at this outpouring of facts, understanding more than was said and mentally castigating the foolishness of men. She said nothing, however, until the tale was fully told.

"The child is Damien's, then?" she asked thoughtfully when Christina fell silent.

"You will not tell?" Christina asked with sudden alarm. She had wanted to unload this tangled tale, but had not thought of the repercussions.

"I think he should know. He is angry for your following him here, it seems, but he must accept responsibility for the child."

He had been angry before she had followed him here, but that signified nothing. Perhaps the gaol had sent him over that fine line from sanity to lunacy. She had called him mad before. Now he seemed to have proved his madness.

Christina shook her head. "Jeremy must have known Damien's feeling on the matter. That is why he insisted I use his name. The child has a name and sufficient funds for support. We do not need Damien's assistance."

Mrs. Drayton shook her head in dismay at the girl's wrongheaded obstinance, but held her tongue. Time had a way of straightening these things out. She would wait.

Christina did not return downstairs again but undressed and retired to the lonely emptiness of her bed. Damien's bed. She must leave this haven and find another soon. She could not come between him and his family, for his family's sake. Damien could go to hell for all she cared. She had suffered the torments of the damned these months, and he had blithely sailed off without a care, without even leaving word, actually blackmailing her friends and family into silence. She had hated him before, but it in no way measured against the depth of her hatred now after this betrayal.

Christina tossed restlessly in the warm night air. No

breeze seemed to stir through the open widow. Her mind was a jumble of racing thoughts, but her insides had a hollow where her heart used to be. She must learn to think without a heart.

The effort sent her into a fitful doze. Damien's bronzed angular features twisted into a grimace of hate and madness behind her eyes, and she woke in a cold sweat to the knocking of the shutters against the wall.

She turned over, her nightdress a pale blur against the pillow. A shadow detached itself from the wall, and Christina stifled a gasp as a ghostly apparition formed beyond the bedposts.

He had shed coat and waistcoat and now stood before her in only open linen shirt and tight white breeches, without benefit of stockings. The dark coloring of his arms and legs blended into the shadows, leaving only the outline of his powerful torso in the moon's light.

"What are you doing here?" Christina whispered in horror, not certain that he was not a ghost, after all.

"I believe I have already asked that of you. This time I expect an answer." Damien stepped menacingly closer, his broad shoulders blocking out the outline of the window behind him.

Anger surged to replace fear, and Christina sat up against the pillows, pulling the covers to her throat and pointing at the window through which he must have entered. "You have given up any rights you had to question me! Leave, before I scream for help!"

Damien ignored this, his fists knotting into balls at his hips. "Scream, and let Lady Jeremy be found in bed with her lover. They do not look so lightly on whores here as they do in London."

Christina quickly slid to the edge of the bed, but Damien trapped her neatly beneath the covers, not touching her, but holding the linen tightly in place while he glared down at her. "Don't tempt me, Christina. I have never killed a woman before, but I could throttle you easily now. Where is Jeremy? Why do you bear his name?"

She sensed the tension of rage in those knotted muscles on either side of her and did not dare test his threats. She had never been able to lie to him, but she refused to give him the truth. "Even a widow generally bears her husband's name," she answered disdainfully, skirting the truth neatly as he had taught her to do.

Damien's fists knotted tighter and his face contorted with rage. "Fool! You could not even wait for a decent period of mourning, I suppose! Why was that? Because of the child? Is it his or mine? Dammit, Christina, start giving me answers! What happened to Jeremy?" He grabbed her shoulders and with each word shook her head against the pillow.

He was mad. He was demented. He had to be. How could he believe such lies when he knew how much she had loved him? He accepted everything she said, and more, of his own. His own depravity tore at his insides. It served the cad right to feed on his own traitorous behavior. Christina fed his fury gladly.

"Jeremy wished it to be known that he died an honorable death. If you wish details, simply write to your dear friends who claimed they had seen you drawn and quartered and buried!" she spat out with the rage of weeks of anguish.

She thought for a moment he would strangle her. His arms bulged with the effort of restraining himself before he stepped back out of temptation's way.

"They simply told you what you wished to hear, my dear," Damien replied with deceptively calm tones. "How did you rid yourself of Jeremy so quickly? Let me guess—a duel, defending your dubious honor. I trust the title is worth it, though it is scarcely anything to the child. Mine would have been much more illustrious, but I denied you that, didn't I? Whose child is it, Christina, his or mine?"

The sudden change from calm to ominous warned her she had best think quickly. If he must ask, he did not deserve to know, but how could she state so bald a lie? Even a madman would detect it. With relief, she heard a hurried knock on the door.

"Christina? Are you well? I heard voices. May I come in, dear?"

Mrs. Drayton! Christina dashed for the door, knowing Damien dared not follow her, praying he found a hiding place. She would not be thought a whore again. She cracked the door a fraction and peered out.

"I am sorry if I woke you. It was a bad dream."

Sophia Drayton took one look at Christina's pale, frightened face, the amber eyes wide and glowing feverishly, and pushed the door open. She threw a quick look over Christina's shoulder and noticed the girl did the same, sighing visibly when nothing out of the ordinary met their gaze.

"Let me get you back in bed. I will sit with you this time. You've had too many shocks and you're not quite recovered yet."

The older woman bustled about the room, tucking Christina into bed, then drawing the sash and locking the window shutters decisively. "There. The night air is not always so healthy." She threw another quick look around the room and then seated herself comfortably at Christina's bedside. "You have nothing to worry about now, my dear. Go to sleep. You need your rest."

Christina made no protest. With his mother in the room, Damien, or his ghost, dared not interfere again. Throwing a final nervous glance at the shuttered window, Christina slipped into exhausted slumber.

Not daring to show himself in a public tavern, Damien sought the refuge of the remaining rum in his ship's cabin. He had thought all feeling dead with the discovery of Christina's betrayal, but anguish carved at the remains of his heart now. Pain ripped at his insides, and his only solace was the liquid inferno of drink.

But even rum could not blot out the memory of Christina's frail pallor and her silhouetted figure beneath the thin nightrail. The child had to be his, unless she had deceived him in her faithfulness too. The thought of her in another's arms did nothing to assuage his fury or pain, and Damien heaved the empty bottle across the cabin, watching blindly as it shattered into tiny shards.

At the sound of shattering glass, one of his men stuck his head in the door and raised a questioning eyebrow.

Damien sat slumped at his desk, hands in pockets, stocking feet stuck out in front of him, staring morosely at the broken glass. "Women are hell, Jake."

Jake grinned at this piece of news. "Hell is living without 'em, cap'n."

Leaving Damien sagely contemplating this drunken philosophy, he closed the door behind him. So that was what had been bothering the man! The terror of seven seas, and felled by a woman! Wait until the crew heard that.

24

"Will you help me find shipping out of here, Robert? Your mother insists I must stay, but you must see that I cannot."

Christina perched on the high stool in the press-room, watching Robert stare dutifully at his work, his wire glasses sliding down his nose in the sweaty heat of the tiny hut. She had seen him out chopping the vines beneath her window earlier this morning, but he had disappeared down here before she had time to dress and find him.

Robert stared down at his work, then up at the tawny-gold goddess inhabiting his filthy abode like a ray of sunshine through nonexistent windows. He frowned. "I can see that you and Damien are at odds over something, but I'll be damned if I know what. And until some explanations are forthcoming, I'm not taking anybody's side in this thing."

Robert had quickly gathered the import of his mother's orders to cut those vines outside Christina's window. He and Damien had used them often enough as kids for midnight forays into the countryside. It had not occurred to him how easily accessible Christina's room would be until his brother had returned. Leave it to Damien. His frown deepened and he returned to his work.

"Are you beginning to think like Mara, too, Robert?" Christina inquired softly, sensing the pain behind those open green eyes. "Do you think I am a British spy who would have your brother hanged?" Christina slipped from the stool and turned sadly toward the door. "It would only be sensible, I suppose. Damien is your brother and I am a stranger. I'll not worry you again."

Robert threw down his tools with exasperation. "Get back here, Christina. Don't be a fool. Maybe you are a bloody British spy, but I sure as hell don't claim Damien is any angel. I just feel like I'm entitled to a few explanations before the two of you go for each other's throats with me in the middle!"

Christina picked up the crudely lettered notice he had been given to work on and began idly making corrections in wording and spelling. "Damien is obviously under the impression that I was responsible for his imprisonment. I cannot ask you to take my word against his, but he has refused to enter the house while I am in it. For that reason alone, I must leave. If I had known he lived, I never would have come here without his permission. Now I must return to my family. If you cannot help me, I will begin looking for myself. I will not stay here."

Robert sighed and shoved his glasses back up his nose again as he turned to stare at her. "Even if I should be fool enough to find you a ship out of here, you cannot travel alone and in your condition. Lorna might go with you if you ask, but this is her home. It is scarcely fair to ask it of her. If you cannot live under the same roof with Damien, then go to Williamsburg. We have friends there. It will be easy enough to find you a respectable place to stay. The British are holding the town and most of the rest of the area, from the last reports I heard, but I reckon they'll not play games with a Lady Jeremy. *You'll* be safe enough, like as not."

Christina noted the trace of bitterness in his last words, but did not try to puzzle it out. She could not quite grasp the differences between herself and Damien's family and the British soldiery. They all came from the same place, and political differences were part of their upbringing. But she did understand Robert's references to Williamsburg, and she contemplated this alternative carefully.

Her last ocean voyage remained clearly imprinted on her mind. She would not have survived without Lorna. Perhaps it would not be wisest to travel too far until the babe was born. That would give her time to write to her uncle and solicit his aid and advice and to locate a companion for the return journey. She very much wanted to know what had sent Damien off on this wild tangent, and why they had lied to her. Perhaps Ben Thomas would tell her if her uncle would not. Yes, the idea had definite possibilities.

"How soon could I go?"

Robert had watched Christina's black study from the corner of his eye as he worked. Now he met her reply with relief. "I've got to be getting out of here by tomorrow night. If you can be packed by then, I'll take you as far as I can. It shouldn't be difficult to find someone to accompany you and Lorna the rest of the way."

"Over my dead body, little brother."

A shadow covered the room's only light as a lithe figure lounged insolently in the doorway, little more than a silhouette against the sun's light outside. "She'll have you in those stinking British galleys before you know what hit you, and I'd have a devil of a time getting you out, provided, of course, I manage to escape her little trap."

"Damien!" Christina slid off her stool again and seriously contemplated bringing it down over his arrogant head. Well-bred ladies did not behave like that, however, so her fury sought refuge in words. "I cannot believe I was so foolish as to mourn your death! Drawing and quartering would have been too good for you! A devil like you should have a stake driven through that black lump that passes for your heart."

At the mention of drawing and quartering, Robert blanched and stared aghast at his older brother, but Christina's bitter tirade contained too much pain to ignore.

"Christina!" he interrupted sharply, catching her arm and placing himself between the slender, irate figure in black and his brother's potentially dangerous and much more powerful one.

Having added only stockings and shoes to the scanty garb of the prior night, Damien tensed visibly beneath this tirade, but not until his brother intervened did he step forward.

"Let go of her, Robert. She is my responsibility and I will not have you interfere."

Christina shook off Robert's hand, and hands on hips, glared at Damien's rigid features. "I am my *own* responsibility! Every man I have ever known has failed me. Now *I* will look after *me*! I do not even wish to be in the same part of the world with you, Damien Drayton!"

"You were going to send a British bombshell like *that* back to your comrades?" Damien asked sarcastically, looking over Christina's head to meet his brother's gaze. "Why not just make a map of our camps and send it on to Cornwallis personally? I have a better place for our little spy."

He caught Christina's arm in a biting grip and jerked her forward, sending her stumbling into his arms.

"Where are you taking her?" Robert demanded, gauging the situation carefully as Christina disdainfully shoved his brother's arm aside and stood up of her own accord. Even in the thin muslin gown and the filth of this hovel, she held herself like a duchess. He had a hard time thinking of this tawny lioness as a spy.

"To the *Sea Lion*. She may have some measure of difficulty sending messages from there." Damien continued his hold on his prisoner's arm, twisting it slightly when she attempted to jerk away.

"The *Sea Lion*?" Christina caught these words with astonishment, staring up into Damien's piratical face with horror, remembering well the tales of that dastardly ship and its notorious captain.

Robert grimaced. "Did he not tell you? He holds the marque of a privateer. The *Sea Lion* is his ship."

"Oh, my God. The mad Yankee," Christina whispered, remembering that day when she had dreamed of sailing the seas with the gallant privateer. Of course. What had made her think there could be two mad Yankees? A highwayman and a spy, why not a privateer? Her heart sank further as she realized just how dangerous an opponent Damien could be.

Damien bent a wicked leer toward her. "Is that what they call me? 'The mad Yankee?' Most fitting, I suppose." Then, twisting her arm to a better position, he inquired abruptly, "Now, how do you wish to go? Kicking and screaming through the streets? Or will you go peacefully?"

"Damien! You cannot haul her off like one of your sailors! She is a lady, a girl scarcely older than Mara, and in a delicate condition, if you did not care to notice. You have no right to treat her like this!" Robert protested vigorously, not certain of any of this affair, but horrified at his brother's ungentlemanly tactics.

Damien slowly transferred his gaze from Christina's furious features to his younger brother's anguished eyes. With calm directness and an icy stare, he silenced them both.

"On the contrary, I have every right. That is my ring she wears, and in all probability, that is my child she carries. Now do you understand me when I say she is my responsibility?"

The cold words broke like an icy torrent of rain from a thundercloud, leaving Robert speechless. He stared helpless at Christina's stunned expression, and acknowledged Damien's next words with a nod.

"I am carrying messages out tonight. You had best get back to your post immediately. If I do not miss my guess, you will be seeing action soon." Damien turned from his brother's frozen nod to stare at Christina. "Will you go peacefully?" he repeated.

"You will take away my name, here too, so I cannot hold my head up and raise my child in pride in any home I make?" Christina asked, staring back at him through bitter tears, no longer caring about anything else but this. She wanted a home and a life of her own, and the right to hold her head up and meet anyone's eyes, and once again he was tearing it away from her.

"Kicking and screaming will certainly draw attention to that fact, as you have already learned. Go peaceably, and we will settle the matter later."

Shadowed by the sunlight behind him, Damien's face remained hard and unyielding, but his voice lost its cold, grating quality when she spoke of the child. Christina stiffened when he moved a hand to hold her elbow in a more respectable manner, but she did not protest as he turned her toward the door. She did not look back as they emerged upon the sandy street looking no more than a sailor and his lady.

Christina lifted her dark skirts from the sandy debris of the narrow path along the water's edge. She felt as if all eyes in the village were upon her, but in truth, here below the hill, few but fishermen noted their odd progress. Kicking and screaming would have availed her nothing among them, she surmised.

Damien's hard hand burned patterns along her skin, and his tall masculine presence beside her stirred memories best laid to rest. She had buried those feelings in the grave she had thought held his body. What dismal mockery was this that raised to take their place?

Damien led her to an unpainted, splintered fishing craft, its laconic owner staring out to sea and scarcely noticing the couple as they climbed aboard. Christina found herself shoved into a cramped cabin possessing only a filthy straw pallet. This she settled on resignedly. At least Damien did not join her, and she would not be seen from above. Her humiliation would be a private one.

She had no idea how long they traveled or how they avoided the vigilant eyes of the British ships upriver. A decrepit vessel such as this probably attracted little notice. It scarcely served for fishing, and as a seagoing craft it would be beneath anyone's notice. Christina hung onto her precariously churning stomach and waited.

They made poor time, and it was almost dark before

the sail flopped limply against the mast and they came to a halt in the midst of a protected cove. The skeletal bones of a low-lying clipper floated silently on the lapping waters, deceptively passive in the placid breeze off the cove. But Christina guessed this to be the notorious *Sea Lion,* and from the number of guns it sported, not a ship of peace.

The *Sea Lion*, the nemesis of every British ship from Virginia to France—Christina stared around at it as Damien brought her aboard, remembering that day so long ago when she had longed to be standing on its heaving deck, feeling the wind lift her hair. She instinctively glanced upward, but no flag waved overhead, and no breeze lifted the sails.

As she watched, the fishing boat slipped away, and Damien made some gesture to the idle crew that set them all in motion. Immediately the deck came to life, and in the fading rays of sun men scurried to the rigging, and the process of setting the ship in sail began.

Damien gave Christina no chance to observe more, but led her belowdeck, through the narrow passageway, to the captain's cabin. He followed her in, his six-foot frame seemingly filling the limited space of the interior, his head narrowly missing low-lying beams.

He rummaged among the maps and charts on his deck, producing a flint and lighting the lantern overhead. The flame threw burnished highlights over neatly queued russet hair and illuminated angular cheekbones as Damien bent over the desk. Satisfying himself on their position, he straightened and turned to observe Christina's quiet figure.

She stood where he had left her. The modest cap she had taken to wearing over loosely looped flaxen hair had been dislodged in their voyage, and she held it in her hand now, tidily tucking its pins into the folds. She had knotted her large linen handkerchief at a respectable height above the square-cut neckline of her bodice, and appeared every inch the prim, respectable lady of quality she wished to emulate. Only the gleaming golden highlights of tawny hair, the generous curves beneath thin muslin, and the amber spark of wide eyes betrayed anything of the passionate nature concealed beneath modest attire.

"I'll have a meal sent in. Don't wait for me. I'll eat when I can, with the men," Damien spat out in curt phrases, unable to conceal in any other way the emotions she stirred in him. "The bunk is over there when you grow tired."

He indicated the neatly made bed against the far wall, buried now beneath cast-off garments of various sorts.

Christina flicked a disdainful glance over the accommodations. "Will you sleep with the men, too?" she inquired cynically.

Her words and tone cut deeper than she had any notion of doing. She stood there, the bereaved widow of his best friend, a woman Damien had thought above all others, whom he had wished to love and protect for the remainder of his days, and who had stabbed him in the back in the most callous manner he had ever encountered in any man, woman, or child. The conflict tore at Damien's insides, but her biting words resolved the issue.

"I sleep in my own bed," he replied emphatically, then strode briskly out the door, slamming it behind him.

Christina stared at that solid oak panel and mused upon the wisdom of keeping tight hinges when Damien was around. The mad Yankee would demolish any normal door.

Sighing, she glanced around her prison and attempted to sort out the oddly tranquil state of her emotions. Since Damien had come to claim her, resignation had become her only response. Did she possess some means of fighting his will?

She had more than enough time to contemplate possibilities. She straightened his cabin, ate her meal, glanced through his odd assortment of books, undressed, and wrapped herself in an old quilt, and he still did not return. She glanced at the inviting bed and grimaced.

Her eyes hung heavy, the babe stirred uneasily, and she wished only to curl up and sleep. How did one fight a madman in such a state?

Pride would not allow any lessening of her principles. She was not a whore but the prisoner of a mad Yankee. That she had once loved the madman and now bore his child had no place in the matter. He thought her capable of a treachery and duplicity beyond the bounds of human decency, treated her as if she were a piece of trash found in the street, and she could not allow it to continue.

Wrapping the quilt around her, Christina sat stiffly upright in the captain's chair, her eyes slowly closing with weariness as time passed and Damien did not return.

25

Christina jerked fron an uneasy doze with the first sound of footsteps in the cabin. Damien sat at the bed's edge, removing his shoes and watching her steadily.

"You chose a poor berth for sleeping," he commented dryly.

"It suits me well." Christina pulled the gaping quilt more snugly about her. She had contemplated remaining dressed, but she had only the one gown and did not trust it to his temper. However, at the moment he did not appear particularly violent.

"Whose child is it, Christina?" Damien asked, deceptively softly.

"I don't intend to tell you," she replied steadily, returning his stare. "How did you escape?" she countered.

"With difficulty." Damien threw his shoes to the floor with a thud. "This argument goes nowhere. Why did you come here? Answer me that one question, Christina."

"You would not believe me if I told you." Uneasily she felt those black eyes stare into her very soul, stripping her of all defenses.

"You are right, but give me an answer anyway. If I had thought you easily parted from your mother, I would have installed you upon my ship long ago and saved myself much grief. Give me some explanation of how it came about."

At mention of her mother, her eyes flared with fury and anguish and Christina's weary passivity faded. "That is an easy one, my lord. She is dead. We killed her, you and I. What reason had I to stay after that?"

Damien crossed the small space in a single stride, jerking Christina to her feet and searching her face for truth. "No one told me. When did she die, Christina? If you lie to me, I'll shake you until your teeth rattle."

"What difference does it make?" Christina cried, the anguish of this loss still too painful to consider calmly. "What need was there to burden you with my sorrows when I thought you had more than your share of your own? Let me go, Damien! You have killed everything that has ever been between us. Unless you plan to kill me too, let me alone."

Her cries went unheaded. The quilt had slipped when he grabbed her, and Damien's gaze followed the easier path from the painful truth in Christina's eyes to the silken flesh of her shoulders and the rising curves of her breasts. His breath constricted in his lungs at this sight he had been denied for so many months. She was even more beautiful in the flesh than in the tormenting dreams of these many nights past.

"Everything, Christina?" he whispered huskily. "Do you really believe that what went between us was so easily killed? Unless you played me false from the very start, you bear the burden of our lovemaking even now. Do you think it so difficult to kindle those fires again? Behind that mask of coldness, you are dry tinder, Christina. Shall we test it with a spark?"

Devil's eyes gleamed as they challenged hidden depths of amber. Christina knew of what he spoke. The same magnetic current that had brought them together that first time pulsated demandingly between them now. Hard fingers were like burning brands against her skin and the heat of his gaze aroused a need for a more physical contact against her flesh. Why could not hatred erase these hungers he had taught her so well?

"Don't, Damien," she whispered faintly, knowing the argument was already moot. "I am your whore no longer. If only for the child's sake, leave me alone."

"You are my woman for so long as I have need of you, and since you saw fit to follow me here, I see no reason why our relationship should end. A damp prison cell brings new meaning to a man's hunger for a woman's warmth."

Christina frantically clutched the quilt over her breasts as Damien's hands began to roam over the skin exposed above it. The pressure of his fingers against her shoulder blades demanded response, but Christina continued to resist.

"I will give you your money back. You may have it all," she answered frantically. "The house was sold and Ben invested it in goods to be sold in New York so I might have funds here. It will show a tidy profit, Damien. You may have it all. Just give me fare to return to my uncle. I ask nothing more. Please, Damien, don't . . ."

She wept as his kisses fell against her hair and continued downward, raining against her cheeks and forehead as his hands continued to stroke her gently. Her chemise came untied and fell loosely about her arms, awaiting only Damien's touch to divest it further.

"Do you honestly think I would let you carry my son back to England, Christina? Don't be a fool. If I must, I will hold you prisoner until the child is born. You may do what you will then, but the child remains with me."

Damien gave the quilt a tug and it tumbled from Christina's trembling hands, falling about their feet as his palms cupped young breasts already filling with milk for the child she carried. Christina tried to pull her chemise back to cover her, but he shoved it aside, consigning it too to the floor. Now he held her as he wanted her, and he drank of the loveliness of the vision. His desire for her had only multiplied with distance, and he knew he could not play this game much longer.

Christina sank beneath the passionate depths of his response. He would do as he promised. She would be damned to a living hell. His revenge would be a mighty one.

"Kill me, it would be easier," she answered miserably.

For a moment Damien hesitated. The tawny sheen of her bent head reminded him of an earlier time when he had taken an innocent girl against her will. She had been innocent then, full of life and love, and he had taught her fear and hatred. Now she stood like a wax doll between his hands, and he still could not prevent himself from taking her.

"Look at me, Christina," he demanded.

With pain she stared up into the chiseled hardness of his face. His eyes no longer struck at her like flint, but opened before her like a bottomless well into whose depths she would fall and never return. She longed to find the warmth of love in them, but saw only emptiness. Her heart cried out for the man who had once looked out at her from those depths, but he had retreated from her sight.

Instead of speaking, Damien lowered his mouth to her trembling lips.

Christina tasted the salt of the sea breeze in his kiss, smelled the wind in his hair, and succumbed to the hungry grasp of his fingers. He was alive! No matter what else they said or did, nothing could halt the incredible surge of joy she felt at finally grasping this fact. He lived! God had brought him back to her! And her hands wrapped ecstatically about his linen-clad shoulders, clutching him for dear life as he swept her from the floor.

"My God, Christina!" Damien muttered hoarsely against her hair as they paused for breath.

He did not enlarge upon the point, but buried his lips against the slender column of her throat, drawing Christina's breath and setting her heart racing. It had been so long since he had held her like this. She had thought never to feel his lips upon her again, thought the rough grip of his hands to be gone forever, lost as all else had been. How could she deny him now?

She couldn't. What they did now had no place in a world of practicality and common sense. It belonged to another world where senses were all, where she could touch his mind by holding his body, explore his soul while surrendering her own. Christina wanted to lose herself in the tumultuous ecstasy that his lips—and not his words—promised.

Damien laid her gently against the freshly made bed, his kisses covering her while his fingers nimbly loosened his own clothing. Christina clung joyously to the heavy body of this man she had been given to love this second time, writhing impatiently beneath his caresses until they could wait no longer. They merged swiftly, breathtakingly, and Christina cried out with the joy and pain of it.

Afterward Christina lay in his arms, her face against the open linen shirt he had not had time to doff. She could feel Damien's heart beating strongly beneath her palm and prayed he would say nothing to break the spell. If they said nothing, she could pretend all was as it had been before, that they shared this adventure together, anticipated their child with pleasure, and would live happily together forever after, just like in books. Damien was not the gentle white knight of her dreams, but a man more exciting than dreams could portray. Why, then, must they ever be at odds?

As if sensing her thoughts, Damien moved restlessly, and turned, laying her back against the pillows as he propped himself on one elbow and stared down at her, his black gaze a shadow in the flickering lamplight.

"Damn you to hell, Christina," he muttered thickly, gazing with longing at lovely, innocent features blurred with the satisfaction of their lovemaking. Her full, ripe body lay open and inviting beneath him, but she denied him what he sought most. Even now, amber eyes flared malevolently at his curse.

Damien grabbed her before she could wrench away.

"Go to sleep, Christina. I will not bother you again."

He spoke wearily as he lay back against the bed, keeping her firmly within his grasp. He did not believe in dreams; his practical mind told him their differences were irreconcilable and that this way lay madness, but he did not release his hold on this woman he had thought never to see again. Christina remained stiff and unyielding at his side, but eventually exhaustion took its toll, and they slept.

When she woke in the morning, he was gone. With a mixture of sorrow and confusion she ran her hand over the dented pillow where Damien had slept. She had not dreamed the night past, then.

The lurch of the ship warned that all the rest was no dream either. Her stomach heaved threateningly as it had not done these past weeks, but she had not forgotten its meaning. With incredible agility Christina scrambled from the bed and to the chamber pot.

It was there that Damien found her, her shoulders heaving with the burning nausea racking her slight frame as she crouched over the lowly pot. Instantly comprehending her plight, he grabbed for towel and water pitcher and knelt beside her, holding her gently and applying cloths as needed.

Stomach emptied, Christina curled up wearily within the strength of Damien's embrace and allowed him to carry her back to bed.

"You are still ill," Damien muttered with concern as he sat beside her, smoothing back golden curls to touch her forhead.

A wan smile curved Christina's lips as her hand traveled to the small bulge of her stomach. "Your son is a poor sailor," she murmured lovingly as she felt the babe's restless movements within her.

The words hung on the taut thread of tension between them, frazzling it further. The muscle over Damien's angular jaw twitched, and dark eyebrows drew down over eyes black as midnight, but the look in them wavered and softened as his large brown hand covered her small one. Beneath the light covering of sheets he had thrown over her, a slight movement undulated their joined hands.

"You are willing to admit the child is mine, then?" he asked cautiously, searching the warm glow of her amber eyes.

"It is pointless for me to lie to you, but it changes nothing. The child is mine. You cannot take that away from me," Christina stated firmly. She would have him understand now that she had no intention of parting with the babe.

"Nor will I give it up," he replied, crushing her fingers in his powerful grip as he stared down at her.

"Nonsense!" Christina jerked her hand away, and holding the covers firmly to her breasts, wriggled to a sitting position so she might stare back at him on more even ground. "You sailed away without any intention of ever coming back. You threw away any claims of fatherhood!"

"You forget the clause in our agreement, Christina," Damien reminded her calmly. He watched steadily as she absorbed the full impact of his statement. "I never had any intention of leaving the child homeless, whatever you chose to do with him. Ben Thomas would have seen the child brought to me."

Christina gulped and searched Damien's hard, dark face closely. She had not considered this possibility. What man ever claimed his bastards? But if he meant what he said, she should never have told him of the child's parentage. He would make life a living hell for her now, of a certainty.

"And what would you have done if I had chosen to keep the child?" she asked suspiciously.

Damien shrugged. "At one point, I only thought to see the child cared for. I had no doubt you would be a proper mother, and Ben would have notified me of the child's well-being."

"Good. Then he can do the same when I return to England, for I certainly will not."

"You are not returning to England," he pointed out. "You are in no state to travel, and until Cornwallis and the British Navy hold the port, you will find no shipping out. You chose to come here for whatever reasons, and now you will have to stay."

Damien rose and stared down at her, his impenetrable mask once more firmly in place. "Until you are honest with me, I cannot decide what to do with you, but I can tell you of a certainty—my child stays here."

With that statement he turned around and strode out.

Christina had the remainder of the day to contemplate this ultimatum. What good would being honest do? He would only believe what he chose to believe, in any case. If he thought her capable of betrayal, he would never believe she came here solely because she wished their child to grow up as he had wanted. Even if he did believe it, it would give him a hold on her she had no intention of allowing. Without trust there could be no love between them. And she would kill him before she allowed him to make a public whore of her again.

With that thought firmly in mind, Christina awaited Damien's return to the cabin. If he thought to keep her a prisoner aboard this ship for his own perverse pleasures, he would soon discover she could make life a hell for him as easily as he could for her. He might think her mild-mannered and meek, but the blood of Argus MacTavish did not flow in her veins for nothing. For the second time in her life, Christina was prepared to fight for her beliefs.

Little suspecting the rebellion waiting for him, Damien flung open the cabin door late that evening, sweeping into the room like a hurricane wind. Ignoring Christina's irate figure in the room's center, he threw open the lid of his trunk and began rummaging through its contents.

At his haste, Christina grew uneasy, and when he armed himself with a brace of pistols and drew out the long black cape she had reason to remember well, she shivered with fear.

"Where are you going? What is happening?" she asked anxiously as he checked his powder and ammunition.

"We are just off the Delaware Bay and I am taking precautions. The British Navy finds New York a cozy harbor, but they have been known to wander. Go to bed. You will know soon enough if we meet with trouble."

All rebellion fled in sudden fear. "You cannot fight

the navy with pistols! Where in the name of heaven are you going?"

"To Philadelphia, if luck be with me. Do not worry yourself, little Tory. If the *Sea Lion* is captured while I am gone, my men will swear you are a prisoner and you will be treated quite royally, I daresay. If I do not make it back, they have orders to return you to Yorktown. You are quite safe, my dear."

Damien flung the lid closed, shoving a package of papers in his coat pocket as he fastened his cape and drew on his tricorne. Appearing even taller than usual in his gold-braided uniform and black boots, he cut a dashing figure that brought horror to Christina's heart. With pain she realized he had found some new desperate mission to plunge into, and she could not bear to imagine its outcome.

"For the love of God, Damien! Have you not had enough of death for one lifetime? I will not bear those tidings to your family ever again!"

A wry smile twisted his lips as he halted long enough to look at her. "Do not get your hopes up, Christina. Philadelphia is no longer in British hands. I have every intention of returning to decide your fate. Good evening, Lady Jeremy." Tipping his hat gallantly, Damien strode out without a further look back.

A shoe sailed over his head before the door closed and another struck viciously at the oak panels where his shoulders would have been had he not slammed the door faster. A shattering of glass echoed down the passageway as he walked off, and Damien chuckled to himself. If nothing else, he had succeeded in disturbing that ladylike composure that rebuffed his every effort to conquer her.

Not fully realizing Damien had finally succeeded in breaching her most formidable defense, Christina threw herself upon the bed and cried herself to sleep. It seemed the least she could do under the circumstances.

26

The ship rolled idly somewhere offshore of some land Christina did not know and could not see. At least her bouts of sickness remained confined to the mornings, but that held no consolation for her heart. Each day she walked the decks, straining for some sight of a returning sail, and each night she sank into a misery of her own making in the captain's cabin.

Damien's sailors kept careful watch over her, but none spoke more than a few words at a time and she had no heart for making friends with his rough-garbed crew. For aught she knew, they thought her a Tory spy too, and she could not bear the hatred of any others. Had she made some mistake in assuming this country large enough to welcome someone like her?

That question and others nagged at her thoughts as Christina slipped into Damien's large empty bed each night. She had come here with every intention of starting a new life, a life she chose for herself. The sale of the house and the goods purchased with the proceeds ensured the capital to start her own business. She wished to support herself and save Damien's funds as the child's inheritance. She had wanted the child to know his father's family. She had come this far on her own. Must she give up all her plans because of Damien?

The thought of returning to Cornwall as her uncle's dependent and a figure of shame repelled her. She did not want that, but what else could she do if she returned to England? She wanted a family for the child, and her uncle would provide that, but he would never allow her to live independently. She had played with the idea of supporting Robert's printing press and the newspaper he wished to create from it. Would she have such an opportunity in England?

She would not. Christina knew it instinctively. Her uncle would see her married. His fortune would attract many suitors, even with her tarnished reputation and possibly because of it. In desperation she would be forced to accept Jeremy's devotion as the only alternative, and she would be consigned to the lot of country wife, unacceped by society, raising a brood of "honorables" under Jeremy's protective concern—a life she might have envied once, but no longer.

With a sigh, Christina was forced to admit Damien had shown her horizons she had never dared dream existed. He had shown her she could accomplish anything she wanted, if she but put her mind to it. And she would, just as soon as she decided exactly what it was she wanted.

She slept soundly upon that decision, until the squeak and shifting of the bed woke her. Sleepily she sensed Damien's heavy masculine presence beside her, bringing with him the scent of salt and sea and a wild tanginess that aroused hidden longings.

When he curled up beside her and drew her into his strong embrace, Christina came willingly. He had returned, and his kisses were like gifts from heaven. She responded to them joyously and felt Damien's shudder of pleasure with thanksgiving. Whatever came between them, she knew he needed her as much as she did him. Her proud Yankee would never have come to her bed otherwise.

With that discovery, everything else fell in place, and Christina gave herself freely to the sudden passionate flow of their lovemaking. As if they had been parted years and not days, they merged with a wild abandon they had never before allowed themselves, and Christina's cries of joy only echoed Damien's own.

They slept then, but woke again before dawn to distribute the caresses they had not had the time for the night before. This time their joining was a bittersweet foreshadowing of the harsh reality dawn would bring. Christina clung tightly to his shoulders even as Damien cursed her with the first eruption of their bodies in the throes of ecstasy their joining brought.

Afterward she lay curled against his arm, running her fingers through the dark mat of hairs on his chest as she felt him retreating into the black humor separating them.

Rather than waiting for Damien's doubting questions, Christina took the reins in her own hands. "Why do you accuse me of betraying you when you must know how hard I tried to save you?"

"Save me?" Damien asked incredulously, midnight eyes turning with derision to the fair face that had haunted his dreams these last weeks and months. "Your uncle told me how you 'saved' me. Do not make me hate you or myself any more than I do."

Hurt and anger warred within her breast, but Christina had regained her shaken confidence these last days. She would fight for what she wanted, whatever paths this war took.

"My uncle? I cannot imagine what he said or why he should lie, but would you take his word over mine? Fie on you, milord! You are more a milksop than I knew."

She pushed away from him, but Damien stopped her, holding her pinned against the bed while he glowered down upon her.

"Milksop, am I? I cursed your uncle for every foul fiend in hell and would have throttled him had the chains not interfered. Not until I heard the testimony at my trial did I believe. Only you could have known those things, Christina. You knew I had murdered Nicholas—could you not have been satisfied with that charge? Was the shame I brought upon you so great it justified the punishment you would have inflicted upon me?"

Anguish scarred every note of his cry, jarring Christina in a manner that twisted her insides. Yet there was that in his words that gave cause for hope, and she nourished it carefully. He must feel guilt for what he had done or he would never have framed the question in such a manner.

"I repeat, I do not know what my uncle said or why, but I had no part in it. I begged him to use his influence to see you freed, and he agreed, though reluctantly. I see no reason to tell you more, since I can offer no proof, and you are too warped with hate and distrust to see things rationally."

Stubbornly Christina refused to say more. With fury, Damien noted her set jaw and implacable glare, and cursing, he threw himself from the bed. He wished heartily Argus MacTavish had had a son so he could rip the devil's heart out with his sword, but Christina's feminine contours effectively ended such conjectures.

Even as he set aside such thoughts, his eyes continued to wander over Christina's nicely rounding figure as she rose from the bed. Tawny curls rippled in tousled disarray across breasts filling rapidly to ripeness. His gaze roamed over the slight curve that carried his child, scarcely disfiguring her slender grace yet, though he guessed her at least four months gone by now. The illness had taken its toll and left her too fragile. The greenish hue of her face now as she fought back the nausea of the ship's motion jabbed him with a pang of remorse.

Quickly donning his breeches, Damien caught her before Christina could begin the task of garbing herself. With decisiveness he lifted her back to the bed and covered her. Producing the empty washbasin, he placed it on the stand beside her.

"Stay there until your stomach settles. You have no reason to be up and about, and the sea is likely to be rough today. I will have the cook concoct one of his herbal brews. It is not tea, but it will warm you."

Christina stared at him with astonishment but could not find the strength to argue. She only wished he would leave before she embarrassed herself before him again.

As if sensing her thoughts, Damien gave her an anxious glance, and grabbing up his shirt, quickly departed. Christina promptly brought up the prior night's meal.

By the time he returned with the hot brew and some toast, Christina had restored herself to some order. Wearing only her cotton chemise and tying her hair back neatly with one of Damien's ribbons, she managed to reconstruct her ladylike exterior as she sat primly against the pillows.

Damien took in this remarkable change with some amazement and dryly set his meager offering before his regal patient.

"You look damned good for a green lady," he admitted gruffly.

Christina shot him a scathing glare. "Keeping me prisoner here is your brilliant idea. What enchantment do I have to look forward to next?"

Damien shrugged and arranged the tray over her lap. "You did not seem to mind my company so much last night. When is the child due?"

Christina watched him suspiciously as she sipped the herbal brew. "In January. Will you hold me prisoner here till then?"

Damien shook his head and helped himself to a piece of bread. "I'm fitting the ship for battle. You will only be in my way. January," he mused, counting backward. "At that rate, we will never be childless. I must have caught you in the very first week. Surely you did not expect Jeremy to believe the child his?"

Christina sent him a look of disgust. "Jeremy is no fool and I am no liar. Those appellations belong to you alone."

He ignored her sarcasm, following his own thoughts. "Why did you not tell me of the child? You must have known."

Exasperation clanked the cup against the saucer. "I only suspected and forgot that in my overwrought concern for your foolish neck. When I came to see you to tell you of it, you nearly murdered me. The child is mine now. Do not concern yourself further about it."

"On the contrary, I have a sincere interest in the

child's fate, and plan to see it well cared for." Damien watched her curiously, his dark gaze contemplating her golden innocence with bemusement. "Why did you leave the knife for me? At the last moment, did you regret what you had done?"

Christina gave up and shoved the tray aside. Her stomach trembled distressingly, but anger more than nausea caused it.

"I am regretting everything at this moment. If you do not intend keeping me here, where are you taking me?" Christina refused to linger on his reference to a battle. She had lived in fear of his life for too long. He could risk it all he wished now. She must get on with her own.

"That is a question I am pondering." Damien pushed the tray back into her lap again. "Eat. The child needs nourishment."

Christina clenched her fists and struggled to control a scream of frustrated rage. The child! All he thought of was the child! He did not care how brutally he had treated her, that he had ruined her reputation in London and now worked at destroying her here. He cared nothing about how she felt or what she wished to do. His only concern centered on himself and the child.

This time her control reached its tether and fury won. The tray went flying through the air, landing upside down on the spotless deck.

"Do not *ever* tell me what to do again, Damien Drayton! I am a grown woman, as I have pointed out to you before. I will do what I want with myself, and you and your demands can be hanged!"

Christina dragged the covers around her and fled the bed, seeking her clothing.

Damien stared at her in astonishment and mounting anger. He knew he had stripped away her most effective defenses, but the furious creature he had uncovered left him confused and uncertain. He had relied on her innate sense of propriety more than he had realized, and she had thrown him off balance by shucking it entirely.

"Where in hell do you think you are going?" he inquired gruffly as she began wriggling into chemise and petticoats beneath the protection of draping bedcovers.

"Anywhere you are not," Christina retorted from the confines of the muffling blankets.

Damien grabbed the bundle containing his obstreperous mistress and threw her bodily back to the bed, then towered over her, hands on hips, daring her to flee again.

"You are going nowhere until I have had my say. As displeasing as you may find my person, you are bearing my child and I have every intention of seeing that child born and raised in a healthy manner. It seems to me the best manner of ensuring that is to legalize the vows we exchanged."

Christina shoved away the hindering blankets and gaped at this awesome stranger in amazed wonder. "Legalize?" she cried incredulously. "Will that make you abide by them for a change? Can I have you hanged the next time you leave me? Put the punishment for breaking our vows in writing, and then I might consider your suggestion. Legalize!" she snorted inelegantly.

Damien grasped the back of his desk chair to keep his hands from straying about her tempting neck. He had just asked this traitorous bitch to be his wife, and she had flung the words back at him with taunts. He ought to kill her, but his urge was of another sort. The splendid tangle of her tawny mane fell across rising curves of ivory perfection where the blanket had slipped away. Damien checked his anger with his lust, though he would not admit it out loud.

"The child is mine. I want him to bear my name. Since you say you will not give him up, the simplest solution seems marriage. I cannot compromise your reputation if we say we are wed."

Christina could not believe he had the temerity to utter such words. After what he had made her suffer, how dared he even contemplate such a ludicrous fate? She stared at his imposing frame with disbelief.

"You are insane! I have no need of your name or your money. You have no hold over me any longer, Damien Drayton. I am free to come and go as I please, unless you intend to keep me under lock and key. Make claims to my child, and I will go back to my uncle and you will never see the child again. Now, leave, and let me dress!"

She held all the cards this time, and she knew it. Damien's knuckles whitened around the chair back as he contemplated for the first time the possibility of losing a battle. He had always won whatever game he played, no matter how high the stakes, but this time, with the prize more precious than his own life, he seemed on the point of losing.

He gave a ragged sigh and straightened to his full height, narrowly missing an overhanging beam. "You are my wife, Christina, regardless of what you may wish. I do not make vows lightly. Dress if you must, but I will be back by evening and it is my bed you will grace tonight and every other."

Visibly regaining control of his seething temper, Damien nodded a curt farewell and strode quickly from the room.

Christina stared at the door for a long time after, not daring to think, but wallowing in a state of shock.

27

He spoke the truth. By evening the ship rolled alarmingly, and Christina literally fell into Damien's arms when he entered. The comfort of his reassuring strength wrapped about her prevented all protests as he carried her to the bed. At moments of fear and confusion like this, Christina needed him desperately, and she willingly surrendered her newfound independence to his soothing caress.

But as Damien succeeded in carrying her from frightening reality to the pleasure of their union, salt tears coursed unchecked down Christina's cheeks. She wanted his love, but he offered only lust. How could she continually fool herself into thinking differently?

She curled miserably against the sunburnt hardness of his chest, seeking comfort in the regular rhythm of Damien's heartbeat. Silently Damien held her there, feeling the wetness of her cheek against his skin. Their thoughts were better left unspoken, the gulf between them too wide to bridge easily.

When dawn came, the ship rolled idly in some protective cove. Damien rose and donned his breeches, then stood staring down reflectively at the golden dawn upon his pillow.

"Yorktown is near. I must stock supplies."

Her golden curls sprawling in tangled knots across the pillow, Christina stared back up at him, memorizing the dark line of his jaw, the ebony gleam of jet eyes as he gazed upon her. If he would let her ashore, she must find some means of leaving him far behind. She could not fool herself into believing they could ever live peaceably in the same town, or even country. She must go before he destroyed her, but she would hold him in her heart for just a while longer.

"And what will you do with me?" she asked quietly.

"I will wait until I hear news from town. I would prefer to keep you at the plantation, but the British have the river blockaded. A storm is gathering, Christina, a violent one that may change the course of our lives. I cannot stand aside and watch, I must join it, but I fear to let you go."

Christina understood. He feared that while he battled for his country, she would escape with the life he had bred in her. It did not seem possible that so cold and arrogant a man could evince such concern for a child not yet born. A man she had not been given time to know lay behind the callused facade of the domineering privateer. She might never have time to know him.

Shaking her head slowly, she replied softly, "The only promise I make is that I will do what is best for the child."

"And I am to believe that?" Damien whispered hoarsely, with barely disguised anguish, before turning quickly and striding from the room.

He stayed aboard ship. Christina could hear his restless pacing overhead as he awaited the return of his men and supplies, but he did not stroll below again.

She rose and dressed, grateful for the ceasing of the violent pitching. She would be prepared for whatever he decided to do next.

It grew dusk again, and Christina ate her evening meal, delivered by a shy cabin boy. The restless pacing had halted and the sounds of a boat being hauled aboard and laughing curses overhead told her the crew had returned. What news did they carry? Christina took up the restless pacing the man above had left off.

When Damien finally appeared in the cabin doorway, he had a strange expression on his face and a loosely wrapped bundle in his hands. His gaze seemed to look upon her with a new light, and he remained oddly silent as he studied her apprehensive stance.

Christina said nothing, but waited stoically to hear her fate. Amber eyes glimmered in the lanternlight as Damien finally moved forward and closed the door behind him.

"I believe this belongs to you." He indicated the package in his hand, but made no move to give it to her. He shifted it uneasily between his hands, as if reluctant to let it go. "I have not read it. I glanced through it and read one page until I realized what I held."

Christina gasped in shock as she recognized the sheaf of papers he held. "My journal!"

She reached for it, and Damien yielded it slowly, watching her with curiosity. As she riffled through the pages, checking to see how much of her personal life had been placed between his hands, Damien stepped a little closer.

With some small amount of wonder in his voice, he added, "There were tearstains on the page I read."

Christina's head jerked up to meet his steady gaze, her heart setting up an erratic rhythm as she caught the look in his eye. He had read her innermost thoughts, words she had spoken to no one. What must he think? She could say nothing, though a mist of tears shimmered in her eyes.

"Christina, I . . ." Damien gestured helplessly, torment warring behind the black messages of his eyes. "I did not need to read the rest to know I was a fool."

His hands fell to his sides as Christina warily backed from his reach. Sadness swept briefly across his features, the same sadness she had detected that day in the library when he had looked on her with such despair. She did not relent.

Damien guessed as much and crossed the room to pour himself a swift drink. "Your cousin Thaddeus is the most likely culprit, I suppose. I should have guessed, had I not been so crazed with grief and guilt." He swung around and contemplated Christina's pain-filled eyes. "Guilt, Christina. I used you and left you to bear the brunt of my trespasses. Death was the easy way out compared to what I left you. I had wanted it to be otherwise."

Christina could not quite believe she heard him aright. For too long now he had used and manipulated her, made her think white was black and up was down. Now he offered apologies, and she could not quite accept them. Not now. Not yet.

"I am sorry too, Damien. I trusted in you, believed in you wholeheartedly—until that day you walked into your mother's parlor. It is not the same any longer, Damien."

"Will you give me time to make it right? I admit my guilt, but could you not listen to the circumstances? Your uncle is as much to blame as I."

He seemed almost to be pleading with her. The dashing black-eyed privateer, the terror of London, held out his hand in supplication to *her*, a merchant's daughter. Christina could not quite comprehend the change.

"What do circumstances matter? My mother died because of what we did. Circumstances will not bring her back. I nearly killed myself and the child for your sake, and you left me all alone and bereft of all I loved. I crossed half the world to raise your child as you would want, and you accuse me of treachery. What circumstances would relieve my pain?"

The glass crumbled beneath Damien's tense grip, but he did not seem to notice. The chiseled features that could look so stony now contorted with a pain from which there was no escaping, a pain of his own making.

"You never married Jeremy, did you? He helped me escape, he and your uncle and Ben Thomas. Your uncle made me promise I would never return for you or try to contact you. That was a condition of my escape. I thought of a dozen ways around that vow, but your uncle must have sensed my determination. He did what he thought best for you by keeping me from your door, warning me of your betrayal. Jeremy knew that too. He must have felt most confident of himself that he loaned you his name until you returned to him."

Trembling with a tumult of emotions she could not readily assess, Christina clutched the sheaf of papers to her chest as she regarded him with tears in her eyes. "Will you let me go now, Damien?" she whispered, not daring to risk more.

"Where will you go? Back to Jeremy? I would follow you, you know."

He discovered the broken glass in his hand and threw it aside, binding a gash on his palm with a handkerchief. Christina did not dare move forward to help him. Just to touch him would be death to all her firm resolves.

"I cannot make that journey now. I must think of the child. If Williamsburg is safe, I think I would go there, for now," she answered cautiously.

Not allowing any sign of hope to flare, Damien approached her slowly. "Until the British leave, I would feel safer if you remained with my family. They know this country and you do not."

"Damien, I cannot—"

He interrupted her protests with an impatient wave of his bandaged hand. "For the child's sake, if not for mine, promise me you will stay here."

The intensity of his gaze burned through all Christina's defenses and scorched her soul. She had loved this man with a passion bordering on madness, perhaps loved him still, but she did not really know him. How could she know him, when he wore so many disguises? To linger in his presence long was akin to playing with fire, but she had felt the flames before and survived; she would do so again. He had become a passion she did not want to do without.

"I will stay, so long as you do not compromise my reputation," she answered evasively.

"I want you for my wife, Christina. I have told you so before. Against my better judgment I have wanted you from the very first, and then even when I thought you had betrayed me. I am not likely to change my mind anytime soon."

Damien did not touch her, dared not. She stood poised on the precipice of flight. Any abrupt movement of his own would send her fleeing from him. He must pull her to the safety of his arms with care and patience, if only he had the time. Damien cursed the war that would keep him from wooing her as he ought. He wished the child to bear his name, but even more, he wanted the woman carrying the child. For that, he would have to wait.

Christina sensed the brutal control he held on himself. It was unlike her Yankee privateer not to reach out and grab what he wanted. Clutching the sheaf of papers, she did not argue with his statements for fear he would lose that control once again.

"Where did you get my journal?" she inquired instead, diverting the subject.

"From the description my men gave, I gather Lorna brought it to them. Do not chastise her too severely when we return. She knows my temper and probably fears what I may have done to you. But I have not sunk so low yet that I would read a person's private thoughts, though I would most dearly like to know yours."

She stood bewildered and uncertain, not inches from him, her hair gleaming softly golden in the lanternlight. Knowing her vulnerability as he did, how could he have mistaken her innocence? Damien cursed his own stupidity, knowing that his guilt alone had caused him to think the worst of her. She had admitted nothing, given him nothing to cling to; she might still be a spy or worse, but he must learn to trust. Their futures depended upon it.

Christina shied away from the warm light of his eyes. "Which page did you read?" she inquired softly, needing to know, wanting to know what had brought this drastic change in him.

"It must have been the day I was sentenced. Your words are very evocative, as I have told you before. I read no more than that; I still know nothing. One day perhaps, you will tell me all."

Sympathy burned brightly in coal-black eyes and Christina could not bear the burden. She turned toward the cabin door.

"May I go now?"

For answer, Damien drew out a long cloak and wrapped it firmly around her shoulders. "It is a long row and the night is chilly."

They stood beneath the darkened windows of Drayton House, Damien gently grasping the folds of the old mantle concealing Christina's slender figure in its darkness. Though she held herself stiffly upright, his silhouette still towered a head above hers, and he bent closer to hear her words.

"Will you not come in?" It seemed strange to be parting at the door. They had spent so many nights together. How would she get through one now, knowing he lived but could not come to her?

"It will be dawn soon. I must return before I am seen. Christina . . ." Damien's voice broke over her name, and he halted, searching for better words. They came briskly, as of old. "Cornwallis is expecting fresh troops by ship. He has discovered Williamsburg is not a suitable encampment and will be marching here to meet his ships. I am relying on you to do whatever is necessary to protect our child. I cannot tell you how I know, but there will be a battle soon—most likely by sea, at first. Yorktown has not escaped unscathed before. You must follow the advice of others, and if you need me, send word to Nick at the tavern below the hill."

Christina nodded understanding, her hands involuntarily knotting below the folds of the cloak. "I will be fine. Robert says they will not harm a Lady Jeremy." She kept her words short, to prevent his hearing their trembling.

Damien's fingers dug deep into her shoulders, forcing her to look up into his shadowed face. "You will wait for me?"

Amber eyes gleamed like warm summer suns. "I will be here."

It was all that he could ask, for now.

Within minutes his tall shadow disappeared over the rim of the hill, and Christina prepared to return to his home, alone.

Never would she know how difficult it was for him to turn his back on her and walk away, knowing the tide of war would soon engulf them and perhaps separate them forever. He had to trust in fate, and in Christina's courage. Damien forced one foot in front of another and kept his eyes on the future.

28

Sophia Drayton wept tears of relief at Christina's return. Lorna remained stoic but hugged her warmly. Mara watched her with open hostility. Robert had reluctantly repeated Damien's words in explanation of the kidnapping, but neither brother appeared to give explanation of Christina's return—both had returned to war. Mara's hostility was not unreasonable, and Christina bore it with understanding. Damien demanded loyalty of everyone.

Little time was spent on the topic of Christina's disappearance and mysterious return. As Damien had warned, Cornwallis had evacuated the upper regions of Portsmouth and Williamsburg, and already the first of his troops had begun to dig in on the bluffs overlooking the sea and Yorktown. Tents and troops began to fill the horizon, and the first loose earth appeared as hasty fortifications began. Yorktown waited below in tense expectation of the next act.

Mara urged her mother to pack her things and move to the plantation in the wagon, their only surviving means of transportation, but Mrs. Drayton remained adamant about remaining in her home. The chances of the plantation being overrun with troops were as great as in town. At least here they had neighbors.

Those were the excuses she gave, but Christina read the fear behind the older woman's eyes too well, knowing it herself. If there were any battle, her sons would be there. Word of them might not reach her at the plantation for weeks. The suspense would be unbearable.

Christina took no side in the argument, but breathed a sigh of relief when Sophia Drayton prevailed. Damien had said the first battle would be at sea. He would be in it, she knew, and she could be no closer than here. Here she wished to stay.

So when the first British troops rode into town, the three women waited alone and unprotected, with the exception of the few remaining servants. Many of their neighbors had already fled. Others waited behind locked doors as the proud officers pranced their strong horses through the center of town. Their uniforms gleamed with polished brass and gold braid, a far cry from the disreputable, barefoot state of the meager volunteer militia hiding in the woods and barns of the countryside.

Lorna came up the stairs to warn them of the soldier's approach. The larger houses and taverns were being appropriated for the officers' use. The servants had already carried word that Cornwallis had taken Governor Nelson's house for himself. Drayton House would not be left unmolested.

The occupation was orderly, without any violence, for there was no one left to fight the swarms of British troops. Every man able to stand on his own two feet had joined the governor's militia or Lafayette's Continental troops in the countryside. Those remaining in town were loyal Tories and offered no resistance.

So the sudden furious pounding at their own front door came with great surprise to the women in Drayton House. They had fired no shots, offered no resistance other than a cautious bolting of the door, yet the redcoats below had taken a violent dislike to their portals. Shouted orders brought a vicious crash and splintering as the double doors swung open. Within minutes, booted feet rang in the uncarpeted hall below.

Lorna grabbed the old shotgun one of the men had left behind. Mara hefted a pewter candlestick from the mantel. Sophia appeared gray and drained as she glanced at Christina and gripped a knitting needle tightly.

A maid's screams echoed up the stairwell. Coarse laughter and curses followed as someone muffled the screams, and the thumping sound of boots continued through the downstairs rooms.

They could hear the maid's strangled cries of distress and Christina grew pale as she recognized the source of their anguish and terror. She had heard those cries in another place, in another time. The cries of rape victims did not differ widely whether in a brothel or at the hands of British soldiers. The horror stories she had heard of this vicious war took on new meaning.

Amber eyes swept the room for some means of escape. The vines were gone and she doubted if they could have climbed them encumbered as they were in petticoats and stays. Mara's pitiful candlestick and Lorna's rusted old gun would not stand up against angry men. And those men below sounded exceedingly angry. Christina's gaze fell thoughtfully upon Mara's slender beauty. Damien's sister's worldly cynicism was of the mind, not the body. She knew nothing of what those men could do to her. And Sophia Drayton would die as Christina's own mother had done at any cruel violation of her daughter.

Christina's amber eyes grew cold as gemstones. She would not allow people she loved to suffer the torments of hell she had known. She had learned the wisdom of protective coloration from Damien. She would employ his techniques now and be condemned for it later, if she must.

Rising determinedly, Christina gave swift, curt orders to the other women. "Mara, put down that candlestick and get beneath the covers. Look sickly, use powder, hot compresses, anything. Lorna, guard the door. Allow no one in until you hear my voice."

At Mara's furious protests, Christina turned to Sophia Drayton. "Make her do as I say. She has smallpox and is hysterical, if anyone asks."

Before anyone could stop her, Christina swept from the room, slamming the door behind her in Damien's best style. Instinctively she straightened her mourning gown, tucked the fichu a little lower, and patted her curls into place. Lady Jeremy must not look in the least perturbed.

She descended the stairs in quick, staccato steps, instantly drawing the attention of the officers in the hall who were about to ascend.

Her sudden appearance left them openmouthed; her haughty tirade brought them up short.

"I have never heard such a commotion in all my life! Colonel, tell your men to stop that caterwauling at once! I never thought to see the day British officers would turn a house of illness into a brawling tavern. What are they doing to that poor maid? Colonel, I demand an explanation of this at once!"

The ringing, well-rounded tones of British aristocracy in this den of Yankees startled them momentarily, but the man on the steps below was no fool. In his mid-forties, he wore his years of experience well, the sprinkle of gray at his temples giving him a distinguished look that blended well with his aura of authority. Cold gray eyes studied Christina's slender figure warily.

"We've had warning that Damien Drayton has been hiding in this house. We've come to search it and appropriate it in the name of His Royal Majesty's army. Stand aside and let us pass."

His hand rested on the hilt of his sword, but Christina sensed this man would not draw a weapon against a woman. She stood adamantly in the center of the stairs, her long skirts blocking their path.

"You have been listening to fools, then. Damien Drayton, Earl of Westshipham, was executed in London not two months since. Broke his mother's heart, but what man cares about that? Now Lady Mara is taken ill and may die, and you dare to come to a house of such sorrow in such a manner! I shall notify the marquis at once of your behavior!"

Taken aback by this harping string of diatribes and

noble titles, the colonel hesitated, then turned to one of his aides and snapped curt orders to cease looting at once. Then he faced his golden-haired persecutor and proceeded up the steps.

"My orders are to search the house, madam, and search it I will. We will attempt not to disturb the ladies."

Christina instantly softened her approach, nodding approval and sweeping her skirts aside so only the colonel might pass.

"We are a house full of unprotected women, Colonel, and you have terrified us into a state of shock. I do not understand all this nonsense about poor Lord Westshipham. He was a rakehell, I admit, but the family history is a sad one. As an officer and a gentleman, I appeal to you to treat the family kindly. Lady Drayton has been desperate to return to England, but this dreadful war . . ."

She allowed her words to trail off meaningfully as she appropriated the colonel's arm and began to climb the stairs with him, necessitating his forceful tread to slow to the pace allowed by a multitude of petticoats.

"I did not catch your name, Colonel . . . ?" Amber eyes swept questioningly upward from the youthful innocence of a face framed in golden ringlets.

Slate-gray eyes softened slightly as they looked down upon ivory curves pushing modestly above the lace fichu, and traveled lower to the thickening waistline of motherhood straining at a still provocatively small bodice.

"Colonel Jamison, madam, at your service. And may I have the pleasure?" he inquired politely.

A tiny dimple appeared as Christina acknowledged his gallant bow. "Lady Jeremy Standifer, Colonel. I knew you were a gentleman the instant I laid eyes on you."

What the soldiers behind them thought of this gallant play did not concern Christina. Colonel Jamison was obviously the officer in charge of this particular troop. She was grateful he was not some belching, potbellied, doddering old man. Yet he had a distrustful wariness she must overcome.

In the upper hall he ordered a man to each of the rooms, reserving for himself the room Christina indicated as the sickroom.

She knocked lightly at the panel, praying Mara had obeyed and all had gone well. At Christina's quiet call, the massive housekeeper threw open the bedroom door.

"Lorna, this is Colonel Jamison. He and his men have some astonishing idea they will find ghosts in here. Is Lady Mara sleeping? He must search the room."

The dour Scotswoman frowned at the red-coated officer, then moved aside to allow a view of the room's interior. Mara lay still and pale upon the bed, feverish pink spots flushing her high cheekbones, ebony hair strewn in chaos about her shoulders. Sophia Drayton glanced up distractedly at their entrance and returned to applying compresses to the "invalid's" forehead.

"I am sorry, my lady, but some troublemaker has been carrying foolish tales and the colonel must follow his orders. May he come in a moment?" Christina inquired politely.

Lady Drayton looked up again, nodded absently at the strange officer, and returned to her work.

The officer stepped respectfully into the obviously feminine bedroom, glanced cursorily at the stricken girl in the bed, noted the emptiness beneath the quilted, tall-posted canopy bed, and fastened his gaze on the large wardrobe. Gathering the path of his thoughts, Lorna grimly threw open the doors for his inspection, revealing a froth of feminine frippery. He nodded gratefully and left the room at a call from one of his men.

Christina followed, determined to stay in command of the situation.

"Ain't nothing much up here, but there's men's clothes in the room across the hall." The young soldier held his hat respectfully before the lady, but looked only at his commanding officer.

The colonel raised an inquiring eyebrow to his female bodyguard.

"The late Lord Westshipham's room, I fear," she replied obediently. "His mother will not let us dispose of his effects. She is most distraught, you understand. I have taken the room for myself, hoping to take some of the loneliness from it. I understand much of her feelings, Colonel, having only just lost a husband myself. It cannot be much different from losing a son."

Christina's wide-eyed gaze did not flicker from the officer's attractive face. Her lies poured like molten honey from her tongue. Damien had taught her well, too well. She felt repugnance for this charade, fawning over a man who would allow rape and pillaging, but if Damien could do it, so could she. She even felt some pride at her newfound ability to lie without giving herself away. If only she had learned it sooner.

Interest flared instantly in the colonel's eyes at this mention of her widowhood. A beautiful woman with no husband presented all manner of interesting possibilities, particularly a lady with breeding and obviously high-placed connections. The colonel smiled reassuringly.

"I am a widower myself, Lady Jeremy. I understand. I must apologize for our unseemly intrusion, but Damien Drayton is a known privateer, a captain in the Continental Army, and a wanted criminal. His ship has been seen in these parts and I have had reports of his comings and goings from this house. I had to do my duty."

Christina's brow puckered into the slightest frown. "Who can be saying such ghastly things? Please do not repeat it to the countess—she would be most dreadfully disturbed. Damien Drayton was executed in London; you may write to your superiors to confirm it. It is the reason I am here. I knew the news would destroy my dear friend, and I desperately wished her to return with me. But it was not to be, I suppose." Christina sighed and gestured dispiritedly. "Damien's ship was sold long ago. I suppose that is what your informants have seen."

"Of course. That is possible. I am sorry we must impose on you in such a way, but my men need a place to stay and General Cornwallis has ordered us to take command of this house. We will endeavor not to disturb the ladies, but we will be quartered here for the duration."

Colonel Jamison held a protective hand to the small of her back and spoke apologetically and politely, a far cry from his earlier gruff wariness. Christina hovered within the circle of his strong arm and let her lashes drop demurely.

"We will feel most secure under your protection, sir."

The red-coated soldiers moved in as if they meant to stay. Runners raced in and out with messages, and the front parlor filled with aides-de-camp scribbling lengthy tomes or idly pitching cards. The upstairs hall rang with their booted feet and male voices, and the women hovered in silence behind closed doors.

Lorna Douglass took it upon herself to oversee the protection of polished floors and delicate china, and in so doing, placed herself directly between the soldiers and the kitchen servants. No man dared trespass on the formidable housekeeper's territory, and no further crimes were committed against the terrified maids.

Christina was grateful for the release from this one burden, for the burden of her dual role weighed oppressively upon her shoulders. Not fully understanding the protection Christina's lies afforded her, Mara complained bitterly of her imprisonment and glared resentfully each time her brother's mistress entered the room. Christina's laughter and coquettish flirting floated up the open stairwell clearly, and Mara never noticed Christina's sighs of relief when she escaped to the safety of the bedroom, or her reluctant steps when forced to return below.

Christina frowned in vexation at Mara's churlish gripes, but made no attempt to explain herself. She had learned the pointlessness of contradicting Damien's stubborn opinions. His sister would be no different. At least his mother offered some sympathy, vaguely understanding that Christina stood between them and the enemy. But Christina's continuing flirtation with the handsome colonel caused even Sophia Drayton to occasionally glance askance at her performance. Christina shrugged away their doubts as Damien had done. Her madness had as much purpose as his.

For she had finally come to understand the precipice on which Damien had hung in London. He was a British lord as she was a British citizen. But war respected neither title. These soldiers understood only that the Yankees were enemies. It did not matter who they were or what they were; to be named Yankee meant a sentence of death. The Drayton women teetered continually on that brink. If it became known that Damien lived and that they had harbored him, the colonel would not hesitate to order them all hanged.

Christina could not sit idly by and wait for that day to come. She unashamedly eavesdropped on the gossip and conversations of the men around her, read what papers fell into her hands, curried every bit of information available. She would be prepared for every circumstance.

And so it was that Christina was among the first to hear the news of the fleet of ships seen upon the open sea. She flew up the stairs to her bedroom, grabbed Damien's old spyglass from a shelf, and securing it beneath her shawl, slipped into Mara's "prison cell."

As she excitedly adjusted the glass to look out over the water, Sophia came to join her, and even Mara jumped from the bed to watch suspiciously.

"They say it is the French, not the British!" Christina announced excitedly. "Damien must have known of their coming. He said there would be a battle by sea. Do you think he is with them? He went to Paris after he left London. Does that mean the French will protect us?"

She was rapidly learning the details of this war of Damien's, and Sophia Drayton gave her a shrewd look.

"Robert says they have joined our side, but have been more hindrance than help, except for the young marquis, of course, and he joined much before this new agreement." She watched patiently as Christina located the ships and studied each one. "Well? Are they French? Do you see the *Sea Lion*?"

"They are French, but I cannot find the *Sea Lion*. My hands are shaking. Here, you look." Christina passed the glass to Mara, who stood beside her. Not only were her hands shaking, but her eyes had grown misty. Damien could be out there now, his tiny clipper dwarfed by the towering frigates of the French. What if Clinton's ships sailed down from New York now? That would be the battle Damien expected, and he would be in the thick of it! Christina clasped her hands tightly together, fighting back fear and hope. If only Cornwallis would retreat at the sight of that brave French fleet!

But of course, he did not. He cursed and he railed and he dug in deeper. The tension within the walls of Drayton House intensified as messengers ran back and forth, day and night, their heavy boots ringing clarion warnings in the dead of night, jarring nervous sleepers awake.

The notorious Virginia heat began to take its toll on the troops frantically digging the huge redoubts on the bluff, and left tempers simmering throughout the town. Part of the French fleet sailed up the York River, cutting off supplies from that direction, and tempers grew in extravagant proportions.

In the privacy of their quarters, the officers could throw off their heavy coats and paraphernalia and find an occasional cooling breeze in some open window to dry their sweat-soaked linens. But up on the hill, in the unforgiving August sun, the troops worked in full regalia, and dropped like flies from the heat sickness.

September brought no relief. Dysentery swept the camps, and the British and Hessian officers were at each other's throats over the slightest details. By now, Christina had learned that the Marquis de Lafayette and his motley army were cutting off supplies by land, and the officers argued over the various attacks they might make to eliminate the obstreperous young Frenchman once and for all. But no one did anything. Christina heaved a sigh of relief, for young Robert would be out there with that army somewhere in those cotton fields among the bursting bolls.

While Damien waited somewhere out there on the sea. The women took turns watching through the spyglass for some sign of the *Sea Lion* or the British Navy or any action at all. The tension had become so unbearable, even Christina dared not venture below too often, and her obvious anxiety relieved some of the distrust between them.

The fifth of September brought the wind for which they had all been waiting. Fresh sails billowed on the horizon, and a rousing cheer from below made no secret which side they belonged to. The British navy sailed gloriously into the bay.

Men and women poured from the houses to watch the great white beasts glide gracefully in some strange dance upon the glittering waters. Sophia and Christina exchanged glances and rushed to join them, leaving Mara bewailing her fate in Lorna's protective custody.

The majority of the French fleet had been caught in the bay, with a number of their troops on shore gathering the abundant sand crabs for meals, but Christina's small spyglass told her little of the story. The sails seemed to bounce just over the horizon, maneuvering like graceful butterflies in the fresh sea breeze.

They heard no clash of cannon, no explosions of gunpowder, saw nothing but the dancing sails in the distance. The British officers in the crowd cursed mightily as their navy came no closer, indeed, even seemed to be waiting for the French to gather their troops and escape from the trap of the bay.

Many drifted away as the day grew longer and hotter and nothing of interest seemed to occur. Christina and Sophia Drayton remained, waiting for that one small glimpse that would tell them whether the *Sea Lion* sailed the seas in that mighty company.

It was midafternoon before the first roar of cannon fire warned of the approaching battle. The cliffs began to fill with people again, and Christina was jostled from side to side as she strained to see what the earth's curvature hid.

Smoke poured over the horizon and the wind carried the noise and the stench closer. Great shuddering waves of sound boomed and echoed in the distance and Christina trembled before the fury of it. How could any man survive those powerful explosions?

And as the battle warred on, it became apparent many had not. Bits of debris bobbed upon the waves, then larger shards, and finally heavy bodies, thrown up and down by the dance of the waters, sucked under by the current and flung up again to float tauntingly just out of grasp. Christina shivered and prayed and clutched desperately to her piece of glass, searching for that one familiar sail.

The sun began to lower behind them, but none of the crowd relinquished their vigilant stance. Bodies drifted ashore and some went to claim them before the sea did; the rest stood above and watched as part of the battle drifted gradually closer until the crowd could spy the sails and determine the size of the ships involved.

It was just then, as the sun disappeared behind the town and dusk turned the horizon to crimson and indigo, that the two ships appeared. Blown by wind and tide toward shore, they separated from the rest—one badly crippled and the other bearing down in hard pursuit. The smaller, French ship was clearly outgunned by the copper-bottomed British frigate, but it continued to fire bravely at the fragile rigging of its pursuer.

Damien Drayton propped himself on the bulkhead of his clipper, gazing through his glass at the unequal battle. He had felt helpless in this fight between giants, able only to aid a disabled French ship that had hobbled from the battle beyond the Capes. This small skirmish sailing toward him now offered the opportunity to engage in this great fight, but the cost would be high.

He did not hesitate. Barking a few curt commands and signaling to the men in the rigging, Damien set his swift ship in motion. Well-trained, his men leapt to their stations without questioning, though the course indicated would set them in direct line with the towering three-tiered British frigate.

As the intrepid *Sea Lion* swept on a collision course with the larger ship, Damien gave one last glance toward shore. With a tug of sadness, he wondered if Christina had waited, if she stood there now, watching him tempt a watery fate. He had not meant to drag her into this cruel war. He had wanted her far away, safe within the circle of her friends and family, but he could not contain the small leaping flame of hope and joy at her presence. She had sailed halfway around the world for his sake. Surely she would wait to hear his explanations.

If she had not, he was destroying all chance of following her by his actions now. As the explosion of cannonballs tore through the rigging, Damien's jaw set with determination. He would survive, and she would be waiting. He could not allow himself to believe otherwise.

His shouted orders rang out above the shattering fire of artillery and his tall figure for one moment was silhouetted against the outline of the setting sun.

The crowd watched breathlessly as the British frigate moved to deal the death blow to its crippled victim. The small clipper slipping from a concealed inlet caught them by surprise. Darting boldly at the towering British vessel with all cannons blazing furiously, it aimed to maneuver the attacker from its course. Christina gave a gasp of horror as she recognized the *Sea Lion*'s bold insignia waving from the upper mast.

Sophia Drayton clenched her arm as she gathered the import of Christina's hasty words, and both pairs of eyes strained desperately to see what happened next.

No one in the crowd dared cheer as the daring Yankee clipper cut across the bow of the frigate, giving the French ship time to slip to safety. But the British soldiers did not hold back their jubilation as a wayward wind sent the heavier frigate on a collision course with its lighter adversary.

Cannons blazing, both ships struggled to come about, but the tide had finally turned for the courageous *Sea Lion*. As Christina watched with anguished prayers and waves of horror, the huge frigate crashed against the fragile bow of the light clipper, splintering it with a mighty blow. A cannon roared, and an explosion shuddered through the stricken *Sea Lion*, sending a burst of flame flaring amidship.

Christina screamed in horror and nearly dropped the spyglass. As she swayed weakly, Sophia grabbed the glass, and from behind, Christina felt unseen arms grab and hold her firmly on her feet. With desperate intensity a voice whispered in her ear.

"Hold yourself together, lass. There be eyes watchin'. The Drayton boys say ye're one of us and their word's good enough for ol' Nick, but there be others who ain't too certain and will give you away. Watch out for yourself, lass. Too many questions are abroad, and I don't like the looks of the ones askin'."

Christina scarcely heard the words or understood. Even without the glass she could see the sheets of flame from the *Sea Lion* illuminating the dusky sky.

Sophia shoved the glass back in Christina's hands. "Your eyes are better than mine. Can you see him? Is there anyone in the water? Did they escape?"

Frantically Christina surveyed the debris for signs of life. The flames cast an eerie glare over the darkened waters and shadows bobbed crazily among the waves. The British frigate hobbled slowly away, leaving its sinking prey behind. As they watched, the flames died down and guttered among a few shards of mast and bow. And then there was darkness.

Even the distant sounds of battle had died away.

Nothing remained but the muted roar of waves and the bobbing bits of debris in their grasp.

Christina lowered the glass and stared bleakly at the white-faced woman beside her. Without another word, Sophia Drayton took her into her arms, and together they slowly dragged themselves back up the hill toward home. No one dared offer sympathy or acknowledge their plight.

29

Christina sat dry-eyed in the rocking chair, eyes fastened on the netting of Mara's bed as she rocked slowly and steadily to a rhythm of her own making. Mara gave her a look of disgust and stalked to a far window, but Sophia sat close at hand, watching anxiously.

"He may have survived. Damien is a strong swimmer. We thought him dead before, and he was not."

Christina made no reply.

Sophia tried again. "We cannot give up now. The French have returned to the bay and they say the British have retreated to New York. Surely that means good news?"

Christina rocked silently, locked in her own thoughts.

In desperation, Sophia pleaded, "Christina, you must think of the babe now."

"I am thinking of the babe," came the gruff reply.

Mara swung around at this break in Christina's silence. "The bastard, you mean," she said crudely.

Christina disregarded Sophia's cry of dismay. "Damien's child," she stated flatly. "We may not have been wed in the eyes of the church, but in the eyes of God, he was my husband." She had thought of this long and hard and worked now on the edge of resolution.

"If he had wanted you for wife, he would have married you," Mara replied disdainfully.

"I refused him."

The flat statement hung on the air between the three women, two pairs of dark eyes focusing with astonishment on Christina's golden fairness.

"You refused him?" Sophia's incredulity could not be harnessed.

Christina gave her a brief, sorrowful smile. "He wanted to marry me because of the child and I would not let him. Pride is a terrible thing and he left me so little of it . . ."

Sophia clasped her hand with understanding. "I have done the same myself, under different circumstances. It took a long while before I realized the Drayton men are not given to changing their minds. I sincerely believe, given the opportunity, they would cross the portals of hell to finish what they set out to do. Had not the war intervened, you would be his wife now. He would not take no for an answer."

It was Mara's turn to remain silent. There might never be a chance to learn the wrong or right of this argument. Damien held the key, and the fish might even now be feeding on him.

Rumors ran rampant throughout the garrisoned town. The British Navy had deserted Cornwallis. General Washington marched to join the Marquis de Lafayette to push the British into the sea. Cornwallis had a secret plan to lure the colonials into a trap and destroy them once and for all. No one had the whole truth, and Christina's interest in the matter lagged. Only one piece of news mattered to her, and she would not likely gather it from the British.

She had scarcely comprehended the warning given her that day at the cliffs and made little attempt to deal with it now. The town was rife with rumors. If she were the subject of some, it mattered little. If there were those watching her, they had little opportunity. She seldom left the house any longer.

Until the night Lorna knocked at her door and gestured for Christina to follow quietly. Men stirred in the rooms below, but the upper hall was quiet and fully dark. Christina wrapped herself in a robe and trailed questioningly in Lorna's path to the back stairs.

They slipped unobserved from the back door into

the walled garden. A shadow detached itself from a seat among the shrubbery and Christina caught her breath, but its youthful slightness and noticeable limp in no way resembled anyone she knew. In disappointment she waited for some explanation.

The youth looked questioningly from Lorna to the silent lady garbed in only a robe, and at Lorna's nod, rushed to deliver his garbled message.

"Hit's Robert, ma'am. He be bad wounded by a scoutin' party. He wouldn' go back to the camp. Said they'd take his leg. But he can't walk no more and I can't get him by the guards. He wants me to bring him some grub and says he'll stay hid out there, but I don't know, ma'am . . ."

Christina easily read the look of concern on the youth's mobile features. Without care, the wound would be festering, and his leg wouldn't be all the obstinate Robert would lose. Christina set her lips in a grim line. These Drayton men had more courage than sense and more obstinacy than was good for anybody.

"You can lead me to him?" she asked curtly.

The boy nodded uncertainly. "But we got to get through the British line, and them woods ain't no place for a lady—"

Christina cut him off by turning to Lorna. "Can you and this boy and old Ned carry Robert if we rig up some kind of stretcher?"

Lorna nodded unquestioningly, but their young visitor protested. "We can't get no stretcher through them—"

"Yes, we can, if you are able to hold up your end without my aid. Go on down to the kitchen and get a bite to eat. I'll need to dress."

Christina left Lorna to show the boy the kitchens, and hurried back the way she had come. Dawn wasn't far off. They would have to hurry. Her mind spun rapidly as she reached her room and quickly changed into one of her black gowns. Plausible lies began to form, and she had her story nearly packaged as she slipped down to the kitchens and her traveling companions.

Deemed too old to fight, the black servant Ned had stayed with the family, but with neither fields to work nor horses to drive, his function in the household had become jack-of-all-trades. Roused from sleep, he waited patiently for whatever was asked of him. Beside his gnarled figure lay a makeshift stretcher.

"Do we have a flask of brandy?" Christina inquired immediately as she joined the trio in the kitchen.

Lorna disappeared into the back cellar and returned moments later with a silver flask and a bottle. Cleaning and filling the flask, she handed it to Christina.

Christina slid it into the pouch beneath her mantle and glanced inquiringly at the obviously ravenous youth as he polished off the remaining crumbs of his meal.

"Are you ready?"

"Yes, ma'am, but I don't see how . . ." He stared up into stern amber eyes and grew silent. Though the lady had the appearance of some golden angel in the candlelight, a closer look at set lips and determined jaw told him he'd best follow the lead of Lorna and Ned. He shut up.

Christina nodded approvingly and they strode silently through the kitchen garden to the back gate. The officers in the house slept, and the only sentry kept a silent vigil in the front hall, unconcerned with the comings and goings of servants in the kitchen.

The boy led them through dark back lanes, past tents in distant fields, corrals of restless horses, and to within sight of a flickering campfire at a guard post. Beyond that point the countryside stretched blackly into a no-man's-land of deserted roads and woods.

Their guide gestured toward a thicket of trees well beyond the earthen redoubts that marked the British barricades.

"He be out there, but them sentries walk up and down that wall and there ain't no way we can drag him—"

"Can we slip out when the guard turns his back on that center section?"

Christina pointed to the spot where she had seen the

guard walk and turn around and head back toward his campfire.

"But . . ." The boy gulped at Christina's scathing look and nodded hesitantly. "We can get out."

"Good. Then let's go."

They stole as close to the narrow gap as they dared, and waited until the sentry had stopped and turned about before, one at a time, dashing silently into the field beyond.

Christina waited until the others had safely disappeared into the outlying darkness, then checked the guard's position along the wall. He chatted with his companion at the campfire. Taking a deep breath and pulling the dark mantle securely around her face, she doubled over and scurried across the recently thrown-up earthen mound. The gap they had chosen was easier traversed than the larger hill on either side, but her heeled shoes sank in the loose earth and she nearly stumbled and fell before she made it into the open field.

She heard a guard shout but ignored it, racing frantically for the broken bush she had seen the others run toward. Behind it, she took a deep breath to steady her rapidly racing heartbeat, listened for sounds of pursuit, and hearing none, scurried quickly for the thicket of trees.

She was grateful for the cloud cover overhead, closing out the night sky and enveloping the landscape in a thick blanket of humid darkness. Even the mosquitoes had given up and gone home to bed. The enervating heat made it easy to relax into a lethargy too heavy to worry over night animals scrambling in the underbrush. The guards didn't even look up as Christina covered the remaining yards of open field and delved into the protection of the trees.

She found the others easily from the faint murmur of their voices. As she strode silently into the small clearing, the lengthy male figure on the ground raised himself painfully on one arm and held the other out in greeting.

"Christina! My God, but you're a sight for sore eyes, though what in heaven's name you're doing here is beyond me."

Green eyes eagerly drank in the sight of Christina's slender figure as she threw back her mantle and knelt beside him. The strong cut of his jaw and the crooked tilt of his lips beneath matted hair and stubbly beard reminded her so much of Damien that she could not resist an impulsive kiss on his cheek. Robert grinned, and covered the spot with his hand.

"I'll never wash that cheek again, my lady."

Christina grimaced in mockery. "Fie on you, sir. From the smell, I daresay it has not been washed for some time. Here, have a sip of this before I waste it on those fools back there."

She handed him the flask, which he took eagerly. While he drank, Christina glanced at Lorna, who had already cut through filthy matted bandages to the wounded leg. At Christina's glance, Lorna shook her head.

"The lead's gone through and the bone's whole, but it's festering," she murmured in low tones.

Robert lowered the flask, wiped his mouth on his sleeve, and handed the container back to Christina. "I'll live, if you've brought enough victuals for me to gnaw on." He glanced uncertainly at Ned and the crude stretcher. "You planning on taking me somewhere?"

"Home," Christina answered crisply, straightening to her feet before he had time to protest. "Load him up, boys. I'll help carry until we get to the bushes, but then I'll need to go on ahead. Can you do it?"

Robert's protests were drowned out by Lorna's straightforward negative.

"Ye'll not carry nothing, lass. Do you wish to lose that babe?" she asked indignantly. "I've put up with your nonsense, knowing it's for the best, but ye're not Damien, as much as you try to be. Go on ahead. I'll carry this great fool."

The gazes of the two women met and clashed as they had upon first meeting, Christina's stubborn amber meeting its match in crystalline Scots blue. But the affection between them had grown deep, and Christina knew this was one battle she would not win. Lorna had fought for Damien's child as hard as she. Neither could bear to lose it now, not with Damien's fate unknown. Christina bowed her head in acceptance and turned to leave.

Robert's voice halted her.

"Christina! Are you mad? They'll shoot us all if we try to cross that line."

She turned slowly and gave him a sad smile. "I'm a Tory spy, remember? I can do anything."

Her look, as much as her words, silence him. She left them behind without a further word.

Christina heard them following haltingly behind her and hurried on ahead. This next part would take careful timing, but she had little to lose. Vaguely she wondered if they hanged pregnant spies, but she did not have time to worry over it. She had become a mechanical device, acting without thought.

Waiting until the sentry had turned his back, she slid back within the lines again and cut through a yard until she came upon the path to town. Throwing back her hood, loosening her mantle to expose creamy skin uncovered by fichu or kerchief, Christina strode boldly along the lane toward the guards' campfire.

A dark figure stood and hurriedly fumbled at the straps of his musket, but as Christina's figure emerged from the darkness, the sentry lowered his gun and stared unashamedly.

"Ma'am?" he inquired, his voice splitting the before-dawn silence with a loudness that made them both start nervously.

Bringing her hand to her throat in a gesture of surprise, Christina stepped forward with curiosity, amber eyes studying the young foot soldier with amusement. Under her scrutiny he shifted uneasily from one foot to the other.

Hearing his companion's voice, the second sentry hurried his pace and ambled into the feeble light of the fire to join them. He too stared at Christina's blond beauty with bewilderment.

"Ma'am, it ain't safe to be out here like this. A person could get shot, or worse," he amended badly, embarrassed, as Christina's amused gaze fell on him.

"Thank you, soldier. I will remember that the next time the colonel asks me to meet him. I fear he will be a trifle disappointed when I refuse, but I will explain his own men have assured me it is too dangerous to be about."

The young men glanced at each other uneasily, neither wishing to take the blame for her presence or her absence. Christina's light laughter returned their attention to her.

"Never mind. It seems as if he has found more important matters to attend to this night. I am returning home and will bother you no more." Drawing out the flask, Christina offered it smilingly. "Since he will not be needing this, perhaps you would care to share a drink or two in return for your vigilance? I believe it is almost dawn. Your watch must be nearly over."

The man closest to her reached out hesitantly, glancing to his comrade for reassurance. Receiving a shrug in reply, he closed his fingers eagerly about the flask.

"Mighty kind of you, ma'am. It's been a long evening, that's certain. Would you join us?" he asked politely.

Christina smiled absently, scarcely aware of his existence as she tried to guess how close her friends had drawn and whether or not they had crossed the line. She had no intention of drinking until dawn with this duo. A faint scraping noise caught her ear and she hurriedly turned her undivided attention to her companions of the moment.

"Thank you, sir, but that's not my particular vice." She continued to chat amiably as the young soldiers greedily polished off the liquor, but when their hot gazes began to fasten on her, she drew up her hood and closed her mantle. Accepting the flask's return, she spoke gracious farewells, and left the two happy soldiers to stare after her rapidly retreating back.

The sun had begun to rise over the horizon as Christina's thinly shod feet flew down the dusty back roads the others must have taken. She saw no sign of them, and prayed they had met with no mishap. Damien would never forgive her . . . She would never forgive herself if anything happened to Robert.

She met Ned coming out the gate and he grunted with relief and followed her back in. The officers garrisoned inside had already begun to stir and Christina threw the old man a questioning glance. He nodded toward the cellar and she followed in his path.

Beneath the house, in the nearly barren vegetable bin behind the wine racks, Christina found Lorna working over her fevered patient. The filthy wound had been cleansed and fresh bandages were being applied, but the housekeeper shook her head in dismay as Robert uttered a groan and tossed restlessly.

"We'll have to get him out of here if he keeps that up. They'll hear him above."

Christina knelt beside the rough pallet and placed her hand over Robert's forehead. The last part of his journey had taken its toll. He had lost consciousness and his skin burned with a fire that did not bode well. She wrung out a rag in the cold bucket of water beside him and applied it to his brow, but his restless tossing did not cease.

"I still have some of my mother's laudanum. If we give him a few drops, would that quiet him?"

Lorna nodded, but the skeptical look in her eyes did nothing to reassure Christina. If the leg had already become gangrenous . . . Christina glanced down at Robert's youthfully handsome face, seeing Damien's square jaw and chiseled nose, and her heart cracked a little wider. She might never see Damien's face again, might never watch his black eyes snap with anger, or his thin lips part in a wicked grin. She could not let this small part of him be lost, too.

She kissed the fevered cheek and rose quietly, slipping through the kitchen and up the back stairs to the room Mara and Sophia now shared.

They stared as if she were a ghost when she entered. The previous level of hostility had suddenly intensified, but Christina made no attempt to examine the source.

"Is there a physician to be found in this town?" she asked hurriedly, ignoring Mara's contemptuously turned back.

"Why? Is there something amiss with the babe?" Sophia rose worriedly, stepping forward hesitantly as she examined Christina's pale face.

"Anyone with any decency would be ill after a night with that villainous colonel, but I suppose we cannot hope that is the case." Mara swung a venomous look to Christina's hastily donned costume.

Somewhat confused by this vicious attack after the truce of the last few days, Christina glanced from Mara's proud features to Sophia's. The dark eyes of the older woman watched her sorrowfully.

"I heard noises in the hall last night and worried about you. When I went to your room, you were not there, nor anywhere else, though I searched everywhere but the colonel's room." Sophia spoke sadly but bluntly. She had admired Christina's honesty and had hoped for the best for Damien's sake, but the evidence of her own eyes had convinced her. Without Damien, Christina had found another protector.

Christina grimaced at this unspoken accusation, but did not answer it directly. Instead she stated quietly, "Robert is below, in the cellars. He has been seriously wounded and I fear he is fevered. He needs a physician. I have told Lorna I will bring her some laudanum to quiet his cries, but perhaps one of you should take it to him. I would not wish to arouse any further suspicions."

Holding back her tears, carrying her head high, Christina turned and left the room, leaving the two stunned women to stare at each other in dismay.

To be the object of suspicion and disgust wherever she went seemed a cruel fate for the mistake of loving too much. Digging through her trunk of precious mementos for the bottle of laudanum, Christina felt the sobs choking at her throat. All she had known and loved was gone, swept away in the debacle of her love for a man she would never be allowed to know.

Furiously swiping the hot tears from her eyes, Christina set the laudanum bottle outside the door, and unable to control the pain and sorrow any longer, threw herself across the bed and buried her face in the pillows to prevent the sobs from being heard.

She wished for her mother's loving words, her father's kind sensibility, even Jeremy's amiable chatter, anything but this barrier of tension and distrust Damien had thrown up about her. She had told him she would wait, but for what purpose now that he was gone? She could not bear to live like this any longer. Lorna was right. She did not have Damien's strength.

Christina ignored the quiet knock on her door. Robert's fate no longer concerned her. They would accuse her of poisoning him next. She would go tonight, pack a bag and slip out through the lines and sleep in the woods. To be free would be a great relief after the burdens she had carried these past months. When love caused such pain, what good was it? She had no need to suffer for it any longer.

The door opened and Christina sensed someone standing just within it, but she feigned sleep. Sophia Drayton would have returned to apologize, but Christina had no heart for apologies. She was tired, too tired to be understanding and patient any longer.

The intruder moved further into the room with uncertain step, closing the door quietly. Christina clenched her eyes closed and gritted her teeth. Could they not leave her alone just once?

"Christina?" The quiet voice cut through the early-morning stillness.

"Mara!" Curiosity overcame irritation, and Christina turned over, staring at Mara's abject figure with amazement. The haughty Mara had come to her! What world-shaking event had brought this about?

"Christina—I am sorry." Mara's voice broke with tears, but she fought valiantly to maintain her composure. "Lorna told us what you did . . . how you saved Robert.

She said more . . . she said terrible things about Damien. Oh, Christina, I don't know what to believe anymore!"

Mara's anguished cry and crumbling composure reminded Christina of how young Damien's sister actually was—younger than herself, and much less experienced, despite her arrogant reserve. Lorna must have scolded her fiercely, and Lorna's scoldings could be most vehement. Christina grimaced in remembrance.

Sighing, Christina ran her hand through her unruly curls and gestured for Mara to take a seat. "Lorna tends to the melodramatic upon occasion, I fear. She is angry right now, but will regret what she has said later. She loves Damien as dearly as you do."

Mara looked up with some wary semblance of hope. "How can you not hate us all for what we have thought of you? And for what Damien has done? How can you sit there so calmly and not scream and yell at me for my stupidity?"

To tell her she was too tired to scream at anyone would not serve the point. Christina smiled wearily. "I learned the foolishness of screaming from your brother. It is a waste of breath. When I wished to tell him something, I waited until he was ready to hear it. Sometimes it was too late." She gestured apologetically for the weakness of her reply.

But Mara seemed to accept it with all seriousness, nodding her head thoughtfully in agreement. "Screaming at Damien would be most useless. But I am willing to listen, and perhaps a little screaming would not harm me."

Christina felt some lessening of the heavy weight about her heart. It would be so nice to be accepted again, to have a family, a friend . . . But she was much too tired to pursue this path now.

"Mara, you should not be out of your room. I doubt if the soldiers will bother you now, but they will not be pleased to think we have been making fools of them. Give me time to rest, and I will come to your room later. I do not expect you to understand what I have done, but I would not have you think ill of Damien, either. I am only just beginning to realize what he suffered myself."

Mara stood up hastily. "I am being selfish again. You have not had any sleep, and in your condition. . . . I will go, but tell me one thing." She hesitated, waiting for Christina's attention. "Do you still love him?"

Christina's lips turned up ruefully. "Life would be a good deal easier if I could hate him. But life is seldom easy, is it?"

Mara nodded solemnly, digesting this new information, and hastily retreated, leaving Christina to herself.

She slept then, the sleep of the exhausted, for the first time since the *Sea Lion* went up in flames. Her imagination could not handle the image of the man she loved surrounded by a sheet of flame, but it took strength to quell the vision of the burning ship. Exhaustion had the same effect, and Christina slept without dreams.

When she woke, she washed and dressed hastily and hurried to find out how Robert fared.

Sophia's drawn, tired face gave the answer. She glanced up as Christina entered her daughter's room, and wordlessly she rose and took Christina into her arms. The two women clung to each other for strength, the only strength available in times of trouble, the strength of love.

Separating, Christina eased the older woman back into her chair and glanced at Mara's worried face.

"Is Lorna with him now? Shall I go down for a while?"

Mara glanced at her mother and waited for her to speak.

"The colonel has been asking for you. We have told him you are not well, but now he wishes to see you to ask if there is anything he might do. You had best go down and keep him occupied so he does not wonder where the rest of us are spending our time."

Mara waited patiently for her mother to stop speaking before intruding with her own plea. "I feel utterly useless confined in here, Christina. Can you not tell them I am well again so I can move about more freely? Then I could be with Robert for a while."

Christina sank thoughtfully into a rocker, her brow puckered up in a frown. The child drained too much energy from her and she wished desperately for Damien's strong shoulders to lean on. Hateful, despicable bastard that he was, he always knew what to do, and his arms about her now would ease this agony of indecision.

"The fever is much worse, then?" she asked, stalling for time as her thoughts raced rapidly. "Is there no physician we can call on?"

"The fever is worse and the leg festers. Colonel Jamison has offered to fetch the company physician for you, Christina"— Sophia Drayton made a moue of distaste—"but he can hardly be called on for Robert. There is no other. They are all with the militia."

The militia. From all she had gathered, Christina knew the Yankee militia were close at hand and General Washington had actually made the tremendous journey down from New York to join them. The British had trapped themselves on this narrow strip of land and must either wait for ships to carry them off or launch a full-scale attack against the body of the Continental Army. Somewhere out there in the countryside must be a physician who could heal Robert's wounds. If not there, then among the French ships guarding the coast, waiting eagerly for the return of their British counterparts. If only she could reach them.

A small plan took shape in her mind, and Christina worked at the edges of it, making certain it had no weak point. It would be a long shot, but a relatively safe one.

"Damien told me I must contact a man named Nick in the tavern below the hill if I should need anything. Do you think there is any possibility this person might be able to find a physician?" Christina asked, nibbling on her lower lip as she continued to contemplate all aspects of the case.

"Nick knows everything that goes on. You met him, Christina. I saw him talking to you that day on the cliff

. . ." Sophia hesitated, not wishing to clarify that horrible day further.

The old man who had told her to beware. Christina had forgotten him. She wondered if he were quite sane, but if Damien trusted him, so must she.

"We must tell Colonel Jamison that Mara has taken a turn for the worse. Under the circumstances, we could not think of calling upon the camp physician, but we will ask if we might send for our own. He will be too busy to deny us. Ned will have to be sent to the tavern with our message. Surely, if it is possible, they can find someone to help with Robert, or at least move him to where he can be helped. We have no other choice. They will discover us for certain if he grows worse."

Silence shrouded the room as they contemplated this audacious plan. To harbor a Yankee soldier beneath the noses of the British was foolhardy enough, but to contact the other side while behind enemy lines, and perhaps even smuggle one in, ventured on insane. But Christina was right. The only other alternative was to watch Robert die.

Mara made a face and curled up on her "sickbed" and Sophia Drayton nodded reluctantly.

"I will leave you the task of manipulating the colonel, Christina. I will find Ned and have him carry the message. I cannot imagine what Nick can do, but we must try everything."

"That means I can still do nothing but groan convincingly," Mara wailed. "Why cannot Christina be the patient for a while? She should be the one lying down, in any case."

Christina smiled tiredly and thought the idea of spending a few days in bed would be a welcome one, but her reply in no way reflected her feelings. "Are you prepared to keep the colonel and his men entertained while your mother and Lorna smuggle food and water up and down those cellar steps?" she asked quietly.

Sophia looked horrified as her daughter obviously contemplated the idea, but Mara finally saw the sense in what Christina left unsaid and reluctantly acquiesced to her part in the plan. Christina not only had more experience in dealing with the unwanted attentions of less-than-respectable gentlemen, but she had the protection of her pregnancy and her "widowhood" to keep their attentions to a minimum. An attractive, unmarried maiden had none of these advantages.

With growing distaste for this part she played, Christina returned to the parlor below with her plea. She had come a long way since that fateful day when she had hidden from a dirty-minded butler and screamed in outrage at Damien's overardent attentions. She had learned to use her looks to obtain what she wanted, to use words and feminine wiles to hold off eager advances, to lie almost as convincingly as Damien. And she did not enjoy it. She almost wished Damien would burst through that front door in a fury to put an end to this pretense. She would welcome his fury and accept gratefully any punishment he chose.

But Damien's suspicious rages would never trouble her again. She must oversee her own fate, and a dreary task it was. Christina had wanted to live her own life, unhampered by any man's demands, but the loneliness of it blotted out any satisfaction she might gain at knowing she could do it. She had known she could do it. Why did she have to prove it? But it was too late now to go back and accept any of the offers she had been made. Her path had been chosen.

So, smiling brightly, Christina declined the offer of the camp physician, murmured about an "old friend of the family" being sent for, and listened intelligently while the colonel carried the subject off to his own complaints. Mara's "illness" meant little to this man, who saw the future of his career and the lives of his men balanced on the decisions of a general who wanted nothing more than to go home and leave this weary war behind.

Christina's sympathies lay elsewhere, and she escaped as soon as it was reasonably safe to do so. The man lying fevered in the damp cellars had a more immediate hold on her thoughts than the young bored soldiers in outlying trenches or a cynical old general in his comfortably usurped headquarters. The colonel could take care of his own problems.

She joined Sophia in the dimly lit vegetable bin and knelt beside Robert's prostrate form. Under the influence of laudanum he lay deathly still, and even in the poor candlelight the waxen state of his skin held an unhealthy pallor. Christina glanced worriedly at his mother.

"Lorna is resting?"

Sophia nodded and wrung out another cold compress. The icehouse had yielded the last of its precious contents weeks ago. Their only weapon against the debilitating heat of fever was the icy spring water from the well out back, and it appeared to have no effect on Robert's fevered flesh.

"Did Ned deliver his message?" Christina laid her cool palm against Robert's scorching cheek and nearly cried out with the heat of it. No one could survive such a fever for long.

"Nick heard him out, but sent no reply. They may be watching him. Perhaps there is nothing he can do." Sophia shrugged with a cynical acceptance of the ways of the world.

Watching the life drain from Robert's gentle soul, Christina could not be so resigned to fate. She raged at the cruelty of it, clenched her fists at her helplessness, and prayed for deliverance. Surely, *surely*, this one man could be spared.

And outside the house, in the form of a fate Christina would have recognized had she seen them, a pair of mad eyes carefully contemplated the well-guarded walls of Drayton House and the secrets within.

30

Christina had spent half the night at Robert's side, helplessly applying cold compresses and soothing his murmured wanderings, when Sophia finally ordered her to return to her room. The large circles under her eyes had given away her weariness, and Damien's mother revealed a remarkable obstinacy that Christina could not refuse.

But instead of returning to her room, she joined Mara, and they spent long hours speaking of things that could not be said in the presence of their elders. Though their differences were many, by the time both girls fell asleep they had formed what promised to be a lasting friendship.

But the contentment of knowing she had adopted not only a mother but also a sister was not sufficient to ease Christina's dreams. She slept poorly and woke with the strange sensation of Damien's closeness as if he had just been gazing upon her or stroking her hair as he was wont to do. It sent a tingling sensation up her spine and her stomach lurched painfully as she came fully awake and realized she had fallen asleep in Mara's room and that Damien would never do these things again.

Her hand covered the gentle kicking of Damien's child within her, and Christina sought the pleasure of imagining the babe she would soon hold in her arms. She had little time to feather her nest with cradles and tiny gowns and blankets, but when she could, she tried to envision a peaceful nursery somewhere beyond the reaches of war. It brought a smile to her face when nothing else could.

Returning to her own room, she washed and changed into her black silk gown, pinning a white lace kerchief about her shoulders to conceal the low neckline and knotting it in front. The starched apron she tied about her waist did little to conceal the definitely noticeable bulge of her growing waistline, but Christina admired it. If the British soldiers below should ever learn she carried the child of the notorious Damien Drayton, they would probably have her head, but she carried the burden proudly.

A noise in the front hall attracted her attention. She had heard messengers clanking through the halls much earlier and knew the officers were already on duty, but this noise did not fit the usual pattern of sound from below. With astonishment she realized someone knocked at the front door, a nicety totally ignored by the garrisoned soldiers.

As she cautiously descended the front stairs, a redcoated private threw open the door and listened patiently to some explanation from their early-morning visitor. Christina lingered in the upper hall, listening for some indication of what this might portend.

The soldier called for the colonel, and overcome by curiosity, Christina descended the stairs at the same time the colonel spoke with their unseen visitor. He turned and saw her, and smiling benevolently, gestured for her to join them.

"It seems your physician has arrived. Perhaps you should be the one to lead him to Lady Mara."

With a warm smile he reserved for Christina, Colonel Jamison took her hand and gallantly assisted her from the stairs before gesturing to allow the visitors in. With a great show of concern, he continued speaking as the physician entered.

"Perhaps you would consent to his examining you as well, my lady. You have seemed unwell these past days, and I would have you come to no harm while you are under my care." Slate-gray eyes caressed her with concern, and his hand squeezed hers with gentle care.

Christina scarcely heard the handsome colonel's words after his announcement of the arrival of a physician she knew had never existed. Eyes riveted on the doorway, she paid little heed to the soldier's eager attentions.

The short dapper man who entered first Christina had never seen in her life, but the tall, lean, bearded figure who sauntered in behind him held her frozen—unaware of the man holding her hand or whispering in her ear, unaware of the drafty hall or any of her surroundings. Over the colonel's shoulder, her eyes rose to meet the piercing glare of a furious midnight gaze.

Voices murmured around her, but not until the bearded figure spoke did the shock lessen enough to let her mind work.

The cultured voice of Lord Westshipham spoke from behind that dark beard, reassuring the officers with his Oxford accent, smiting Christina's ears with disbelief. The devil had returned from the dead to punish her for her sins! And with that astonishing thought her heart took wing and soared wildly into the heavens. A dancing smile curved rose lips and lit amber lanterns and the words she had heard long moments ago began to make sense again.

"Dr. Samson, it is good to see you again. If your assistant will take your bags and follow me . . ."

As Christina calmly took command of the situation, brushing off her ardent suitor, directing the dapper stranger up the stairs, watchful black eyes grew wary. When they met mischievous amber lights over the heads of the interfering redcoats, fury died to a suspicious smolder. Christina's grin widened as she threw her hair back and proceeded grandly up the stairway. Let the devil steam in his own juices. He was back! He was alive! She almost sang a song of rejoicing and danced up the stairs, knowing Damien's strong presence followed close behind.

She knocked briefly at Mara's door and threw it open without further warning. The physician must be smuggled down to Robert immediately, but for the benefit of anyone watching, she led them into the "sickroom."

Having heard the commotion below, Mara and her mother waited eagerly within, and when the two men entered, Christina had to slam the door hastily before their ecstatic cries gave them all away.

Mara flung herself into her brother's arms and Damien lifted her easily, squeezing her tightly before setting her aside and turning to his mother with a more sedate hug.

Christina and the stranger stood quietly by the door, watching this family reunion with heartbreaking emotion. Christina longed to feel Damien's powerful arms about her again, but she did not know whether it would be in joy or rage, and she withheld her own feelings, content to enjoy the others' happiness.

The stranger muttered his pleasure at the scene in French and Christina replied in the same language, explaining how they had thought Damien dead. He beamed appreciatively and introduced himself as Dr. Girondeau and asked after the patient.

Whether it was their exchange of French or the young physician's admiring gaze as it rested upon Christina that caught Damien's attention, Christina did not know, but before she could reply, strong fingers bit possessively into her shoulder.

"Dr. Girondeau, this is my wife, Christina. My mother will show us to Robert." Damien swung her around until Christina could feel his breath upon her forehead. He stared sternly down into her face, daring her to deny him. "If you will excuse us a moment, my love, we have risked our necks to see brother Robert, so we had best do so first. But I will be back. Do not go away."

Black eyes held a hundred messages that sent Christina's heart into a frenzy of activity, but she nodded understandingly, satisfying herself with only a touch of her hand to the bristly beard covering his hard jaw. He looked more than ever the pirate now, and her radiant smile melted the hearts of the two men watching.

Damien caught her hand and kissed the palm slowly, not taking his eyes from hers. Then he abruptly followed his mother's path out the door.

The door closed behind them and Christina continued to stare at it blindly until Mara spoke.

"He looks awful. You'll have to make him shave it off, at once."

Christina could not suppress a wildly irrepressible giggle, and within seconds the two of them were in each other's arms, stifling gales of mirth from dangerous ears below. They harbored a known spy within the midst of an enemy encampment, but their joy could not be contained.

Minutes later, Mara wiped the tears from her eyes and giggled delightedly. "Did you see his face when you smiled at that strange little man? I thought he would strangle you. What have you been doing to make poor Damien so upset before he's barely even entered the house?"

Christina bit back a grin. It was so much easier to see the humor in things when someone else shared the burden. Another age ago, Damien's fury would have terrified her, but she knew a security now that she had not before, and she dared meet his anger with impudence. If he truly wanted this child, he would have to take her with it, and she had no intention of quailing before his anger ever again.

"He saw Colonel Jamison holding my hand," Christina whispered surreptitiously, as if it were a terrible secret.

Mara went into another fit of laughter and buried her face in the pillow to hide it.

So when Sophia Drayton slipped worriedly back into the room, followed by Damien with a threatening frown, they found themselves met with beaming faces and barely controlled laughter, scarcely the terrified air of suspense the occasion demanded.

A state of tension cannot be maintained forever, and any small occasion gives reason for relief. The joy of Damien's return had snapped fragile threads, and Sophia Drayton's lips began to curve upward at the sight of the two girls' good humor. Dark and light, they contrasted beautifully, but in these past months Christina's delicate fairness had gained a radiant beauty surpassing all others'.

"Dr. Girondeau is working on Robert's leg now. He says it is not gangrenous, and with good care can be saved."

Sophia sailed to her daughter's side and they hugged each other with relief, while Damien and Christina continued to watch each other warily across the room.

"Lorna claims you saved Robert's life by bringing him through enemy lines. What did you have to give your good friend Colonel Jamison to turn a blind eye to that episode?" Damien's cold accusation silenced all chatter.

Christina did not answer immediately, though her eyes still danced with amusement and the blood pumped crazily through her veins. The madman was actually jealous! Of her! She could not believe it, but could not interpret his words in any other way. If he felt nothing for her, he would not care what she had done to save his brother's life. Gratitude from this impossible man would have been a death knell to her hopes.

Before Christina could loosen her tongue, Mara let fly with hers.

"Damien Drayton, you are a horrible, selfish beast and somebody ought to see you horsewhipped through the streets! You don't deserve somebody like Christina and it would serve you right if she decided to love somebody else, but if you drive her away with your beastliness, I'll never forgive you. Never!"

Mara drew herself up in indignation, black eyes flashing like mirrored pools of her brother's, and Christina had to hold herself back to keep from throwing her arms around both of them. Stubborn, arrogant, independent, containing depths of character that gave and demanded a loyalty and love no other could surpass—these Draytons were a breed unto themselves. And she carried one within her now.

Holding her chin proudly high, Christina met Damien's gaze with love and a shared understanding. Mara's tirade had shocked and amused, but it had become rapidly apparent they could not speak without her defensive interruptions or her mother's anxious interest.

"I see if I am to beat you as you deserve, it will have to be in another room. Would you excuse us, ladies?" Damien peremptorily appropriated Christina's arm and steered her firmly toward the door.

They could hear Sophia hushing Mara's outraged cries as they closed the door behind them and slipped down the hall. Christina made no attempt to free herself from Damien's rough grip, but swept along at his side, quickly turning the latch to her room so he could guide her inside.

The door shut and they stared at each other over a space measured in inches. Christina's proud golden head came just to Damien's roughly bearded chin, but their eyes clashed on an equal basis.

In somber tones of wondering resonance, Damien broke the silence. "You waited."

"I waited." Christina's heart beat a frantic beat. Had he begun to understand, then? Had he finally learned to accept that she was her own person, free to come and go as she pleased, to lead her own life just as he lived his? Could she expect that of him? If he would just give her this recognition, everything else would fall in place. She did not even ask that he love her. She just wanted him to see her as a person, not a possession.

"I vowed to trust you, so I will not question what you have done, but I still want to break every bone in that Jamison's head."

She read the pain in his eyes and hid a wild surge of hope. "He is a source of information and nothing more. We saw the *Sea Lion* go down."

Damien accepted the change in topic without blinking an eyelash. His hand still clenched the doorlatch, to prevent it straying elsewhere. Even his gaze remained stationary, not leaving hers, avoiding the temptation of following the curve of full breasts to the very real evidence of their nights together.

"I am sorry you had to suffer through that again. I had no way of communicating with you. The French had boats out looking for us. I have been with them. Christina . . ."

Her heart leapt to her throat as the dark curtains fell from his eyes and she read the bewildering conflict of emotions in their depths. Without thinking she raised her hand to the open linen shirt covering his broad chest.

The contact sent electric shock waves jolting through both of them, and before Christina could jerk away, Damien had caught her up in both arms and smothered her against his chest. Their lips met with ferocious hunger, and days and nights of uncertainty vanished in this renewed pleasure.

Christina's arms crept about Damien's neck and clung wildly as his kisses covered her face, then fastened demandingly to her mouth as his tongue plundered and possessed honeyed interiors. If he had loosed his grip, she would have fallen to the floor in a swoon, but he held her firmly, and Christina melted eagerly into his embrace.

Not until they gradually realized time was running short did they separate, and then reluctantly. Damien ran his hand longingly through cascading golden curls, unwilling to let her move from his touch.

"Christina, will you reconsider your decision now? It may be months before I can get back here again. Let me give you my name legally."

He seemed almost to be pleading, and Christina's heart lurched with a desperate longing to answer his plea, but he had not yet given her what she wanted.

"Me? Or the child?" she asked cautiously.

Damien's black eyebrows drew down in a thunderous

frown beneath a thick wave of russet hair. "If my only concern were the child, I would have dragged you by the hair of the head to a preacher long ago. I know one who frowns on bastards and obstinate females and would marry us whether you were willing or no. I want your consent, Christina. I want you to admit that you want to spend the rest of your life with me."

His stern frown did not terrify her as it once might have. She knew now that he hid his feelings behind it, and hope surged wildly in Christina's heart.

"And if I should say I would prefer to spend my life with Jeremy? My uncle wishes it and would give the dowry Jeremy needs to make his family happy."

Damien's shoulders slumped wearily as he studied Christina's coolly controlled features. He knew how much she treasured family, and Jeremy would be a much safer, saner husband who could keep her comfortably on familiar shores. Damien could offer only the possibility of years of war without the certainty of home or civilization. If things went badly, he could expect to be hanged as spy or traitor. What choice was that to a woman five months gone with child and desiring safety? Particularly with what he knew now and had not yet told her.

Sighing, Damien shoved the hair back from his forehead and eyed her sadly. "I would say if Jeremy makes you happy when I cannot, then you must go to him. I love you too much to ruin your life all over again."

Wild joy fired her blood and tears sprang to her eyes as Christina heard these words she had never dared hope to hear. With a trembling smile she raised her eyes to meet his, and slid her fingers against the rough grain of his beard as she fought to find the words that would bind them for eternity.

"You had best mean that, my love, because I have no intention of giving up my pursuit of happiness for yours once we are wed. I am not your frightened country miss to be bullied about any longer."

A small grin began to tug at the hard lines of his

mouth as her message became clear. Damien's hold on her curls became tighter.

"I never bullied you any further than you would let me, and I meant every word of what I said. You may pursue your happiness anywhere you like, just so long as its path winds its way to my bed every night. I will not share you with another."

"Nor I you, my mad Yankee." Christina resisted his pull, joy written upon every feature but firmness ringing in her words. "If I am to give up the rest of my life for you and endure your impossible humors, then I must be allowed the satisfaction of knowing I am the only woman in your life."

Damien's grin grew wider. "You drive a hard bargain, wench, but I am desperate to get you to the altar. Do you have any other ugly surprises you would visit upon me before I make the arrangements?"

He jested now, and Christina relaxed beneath the warm gleam of coal-black eyes. With a soft sigh of surrender, she allowed him to enfold her once again in his embrace. His chin rested upon her hair as she spoke softly.

"I only wish I could make you promise to come back safely, but I fear that promise is beyond your power."

Above her, where Christina could not see, dark eyes grew grave and troubled.

"I have not been fair with you, Christina. I know how much you long for home and family, but until this war ends, I can offer you only tokens of each. Knowing this, I have tried to bind you without telling you of another opportunity that might suit you better."

Puzzled, Christina attempted to pull back to examine his face, but Damien held her too tightly, forcing her to continue resting against his chest.

"Damien, I—" she began, but he interrupted without heeding, bringing his words out in a rush as if to get them over with quickly.

"Jeremy is here, at the inn. Nick and the others wouldn't tell him where you are or even that you are here until I arrived to vouch for him. I've talked to him. He wants to marry you and take you back to England. He thought perhaps your infatuation with my ill humor might have worn off by now. He can offer everything I cannot, Christina."

Shock had kept her silent throughout this speech, but fierce joy and new pride brought a speedy recovery.

"Jeremy is here? He must be madder than you. What in heaven's name would he want with a woman known to all London as the mistress of a notorious pirate and traitor? And who bears another man's child? To come across an ocean for such a person is an act of madness."

"Or an act of love," Damien replied softly. "He has persuaded his family they must either accept you or he will remain here. He is most anxious to see you again. He loves you, Christina. If he would make you happier, I cannot stand in his way."

Amber eyes flashed furiously as Christina shoved from his grasp. "But I do not love him! Would you give me away already? Men are such fools!"

She tried to escape his menacing presence, but Damien snatched her quickly, catching her arm behind her back and forcing her to face him.

"What does it matter if you do not love him? You have said no words of love to me either. As a matter of fact, the last words I heard on the subject had more to do with hate than love. What do you want, Christina?"

"You have to ask?" she answered incredulously. "I have given up my name, my family, my country—to follow a madman! I bear your child willingly, wish to raise him as you ask, have agreed to spend my life with you. And you doubt that I love you as much as you profess to love me? Fie on you, sir, for you know no more of me than yon wall. Let go, and I will go find Jeremy. He cannot be so thickheaded."

Damien's long arms locked behind her back and flashing black eyes met amber easily. "Damn you for a caterwauling shrew, woman. You purr like a kitten and preen yourself beneath my caress when you should be clawing and scratching, and then when I come to expect your softness, you bury your teeth in my flesh. I will enjoy beating some sense into you once you are mine."

"Oh, Damien, this is madness." Christina melted back into his arms again, hiding the stinging tears in her eyes. "I have ever been yours, though I fought you in ways you will never know. But I fear you will never be mine. You will always be off on some new venture, sailing the seas and leaving me behind."

Damien's hand moved up to caress her curls, long fingers entangling themselves in golden strands. "Then you had best learn to be a sailor, my love, because I have no intention of leaving you to your own devices for very long. You have a most singular aptitude for getting yourself into trouble. Now come, we must break the news to the family and make some plans, though I sense I would be stoned had I brought you back without the announcement of our impending nuptials," he finished wryly.

Christina bent a wicked grin upward. "I believe Mara mentioned horsewhipping."

"I cannot imagine how you wrapped that stubborn tyke about your finger."

"It comes with experience, my lord." Shaking herself free from his embrace, Christina straightened her crumpled gown and picked up a brush from the dresser to rearrange her mussed curls.

Damien eyed her proximity to the bed hungrily. "And Robert? Have you used your 'experience' to bewitch him too?" He strove for a tone of irritation, but was too conscious of the fact that she had seen past his gruff exterior and knew him better than he did himself. She tilted a saucy smile at him, and it took all Damien's strength to keep from throwing her across that tempting bed that by all rights they should have been sharing from the first.

"Robert is much to easygoing for his own good. I prefer a challenge. He wishes to run a newspaper and I wish to write for one, and since you have so generously allowed me to keep my money . . ."

Damien groaned and caught her by the waist, shoving her toward the door. "I don't want to hear it. The only words I want out of your mouth right now are 'I do.' "

Christina stuck her tongue out at him, then checking the safety of the hall, dashed out into the corridor and out of his grasp.

Mara and Sophia looked up eagerly as Christina came flying through the door, their uncertain smiles slowly fading as she entered without Damien. When Damien finally followed, dismay wrote itself across their faces while they watched him stalk the room after his obstreperous prey.

Backed into a corner, Christina could not escape as powerful arms lifted her bodily from the floor, but her giggles relieved all concerned as Damien proceeded to tickle her into submission.

"Damien! Stop that! Whatever in the world has come over you? Let that poor girl down and tell us what you have decided," Sophia demanded, but her eyes twinkled happily as they rested on the obviously happy couple.

"I am going to tie a noose around this saucy twit as soon as I can find someone to do the job. Have you any suggestions?"

Damien returned Christina to her feet but kept his arm about her waist. Christina accepted that position gladly, and leaned against his strength as she faced his family. A pink flush of excitement had colored her cheeks, and she met their gazes with some embarrassment at this discussion of a wedding at such a late date, but nothing could destroy her present happiness.

Mara nearly jumped with joy, then, remembering herself, sedately stepped forward to plant a kiss on Christina's cheek before regarding her bearded brother coldly.

"I suggest you shave that ghastly appendage before you set foot inside a church. I cannot imagine what Christina sees in such a foul-tempered creature as you, but you could at least have the decency to appear as a human instead of the beast you are."

Christina giggled at Damien's irascible growl behind her, but clutched his arm to prevent his doing bodily harm to his sister. "He can come in rags if it pleases him, but I fear no church will accept me as I am, and I do not know what will happen if word of our wedding spreads. Perhaps now is not the time to make such plans." She dared not consider the consequences if their British gaolers learned she had wed the notorious privateer.

Anxiety swept across Sophia's dark eyes as she looked to her elder son, but Damien had already taken the matter firmly in hand.

"We will be wed before I leave, if it must be from a prison cell. Is Reverend Hathaway still around?" he addressed his mother last.

Sophia looked relieved. "Yes, of course, but there are soldiers quartered in the church. The ceremony cannot be conducted there."

"Where does not matter, so long as it is legal." Damien released Christina and turned her around to face him. "We will have to move Robert out of here tonight. His presence is too much of a danger to the rest of you. Tomorrow I will send Jeremy for you. That should delight your officers and give you good excuse to get away. Can you keep out of trouble until then?"

Mara interrupted before Christina could reply. "I want to go too! I am sick and tired of sitting in this room while everyone else has adventures. I want to go to the wedding."

Before the annoyed look in Damien's eyes could become sharp words on his tongue, Christina intervened, touching her hand to his chest to draw his attention. "Take care of Robert and the arrangements, my love. I will take care of our guests. Have some confidence in me, if you will."

Dark eyes softened as they rested on fragile upturned features, and a look of regret briefly crossed Damien's face. "I have every confidence in you, my pet.

I only wish I could take you with me. But there is always tomorrow."

He smiled lightly, kissed her warmly, and after hugging mother and sister, disappeared down the hallway. The house felt suddenly empty as his boots tramped out the door.

31

On hearing of the impending ceremony, Lorna insisted on spiriting one of Christina's extravagant satin gowns from the house, refusing to allow her charge to marry in the false widow's weeds she had donned. With Robert safely in the doctor's care and gone from the cellars, the housekeeper felt safe in coming and going as she pleased.

Not so Mara, and it took some masterful planning before a maid could be persuaded to play the part of her mistress while Mara donned the maid's drab homespun. Elated at the prospect of escaping the house for the first time in weeks, Mara cared little what costume she wore. Attended by the properly attired Sophia Drayton on an ostensible errand of mercy, she slipped from the house without notice.

That left only Christina to wait impatiently within the house of soldiers. Demurely serving tea and quietly discussing whatever caught their fancies, she felt she would scream if someone did not come to rescue her soon. Surely Damien's plans had not fallen through? They could not have discovered him yet! Please, Lord, let all go well just this once, she prayed.

A brisk knock at the door sent her cup clattering on the saucer, but she gently set it aside and assumed an air of indifference as one of the young aides-de-camp sauntered off to answer it. She picked up a piece of needlework and pretended to be engrossed in its intricacies as the door in the entrance hall opened behind her.

But the stir of excited voices prevented any further pretense, as even her companions began to look interested, and she rose unsteadily and turned to meet the approaching party of men.

Jeremy's amiable grin spread across his face as he held his arms out to her, and the party of British soldiers watched with interest at this reuniting of a happy couple. Christina gladly completed their illusion by flying into Jeremy's arms and kissing his cheek, ecstatic at seeing his friendly features once again, knowing he would take her to Damien.

"Jeremy, I cannot believe it! What happened? Tell me . . . Oh, darling, you cannot believe what I have been through . . ." she chattered mindlessly, saying anything to keep them believing her long-lost husband had returned from the dead while thinking only of the man who waited for her somewhere beyond.

Jeremy's grin grew wider as he fitted Christina's slender frame snugly against him and listened to her outrageous endearments. With lordly benevolence he gestured toward their audience.

"It is a long story, my dear, and I will tell it in due time. Meanwhile, I must thank these gallant gentlemen for protecting you on these traitorous shores. I really should beat you soundly for being so foolish as to run here instead of staying safely where I could find you without crossing an ocean." He tried to pull a stern face, but the mischievous twinkle of his eyes forced Christina to bury her face in his lapels to keep from laughing out loud. His imitation of Damien was hopeless.

"It has been a delight associating with a lady such as your wife in these savage lands, my lord," Colonel Jamison spoke up. Disappointed in his plans of matrimony, he quickly hoped to turn the advantage in another way. It could not harm to have the acquaintance of the son of a marquis.

Well acquainted with this type of self-serving modesty, even if Damien's outraged description of the man's fawning attendance on Christina had not still burned his ears, Jeremy became the very picture of arrogant British aristocracy.

Sweeping a nonexistent hair from the lapels of his stylish blue superfine tailed coat, adjusting the gold buttons of its tightly fitted waist so it rode smoothly over white breeches daringly molded to his trim figure, Jeremy inspected the colonel with a bored air of disdain.

"It is much more than any soldier could expect in these savage wild lands, Colonel. I cannot imagine how it came about that your men were quartered in the same household as three ladies of quality, but I will inquire into that later. Is Lady Westshipham or Lady Mara at home? I must give them my regards."

"Mara is very ill, darling, and cannot be disturbed. And Sophia has gone on some foolish errand and won't return for hours. Could we not go somewhere and . . . talk for a while?"

Christina's suggestive tone as she ran her fingers lightly down the fine material of his coat brought a knowing leer to Jeremy's face. "Of course, my dear, though it looks as if talk might be all we can do." He gave her growing waistline a wicked glance from beneath an upraised brow.

Before she could berate him as he deserved, Jeremy continued smoothly, addressing the colonel, "Give my regards to the ladies and explain I have stolen away their companion for a while. It has been some time since we were . . . ahem . . . together, and I think the privacy of my room at the inn might suit my needs of the moment. We have much to discuss and will not be returning today, if you take my meaning."

With a repulsively smug look on his face, Jeremy made their excuses and escorted Christina out into the broad light of an early September morning. She felt as if she were seeing sunshine for the first time, and nearly hugged Jeremy's neck, despite his insufferable performance.

"Oh, Jeremy! It is so good to see you again! How is Seraphina? There is so much I want to say! But first I ought to beat you for saying such things! I am not so fat as that, am I?" She glanced anxiously at her thickened waistline.

Jeremy swept her up in his arms, and there in the center of the street for all to see, he hugged her thoroughly and swung her around in a joyous circle.

"You are the most beautiful creature on God's earth and I swear I ought to kidnap you before letting that cad lay claim to you." He set her down gently and studied her eyes with growing anxiety. "I worried about you, Christina. I knew Damien left England thinking you the one who had betrayed him. I could not bear to think of the misery he could cause you. It took a while to accumulate the funds to follow you, but I am here now. Are you certain you know what you do? Damien is not forcing this marriage for some reason, is he? He is such a hard person—"

Christina placed a finger over his lips and tugged his hand to urge him down the road. "You are creating a scene, silly. If I did not love Damien so much, I would have to love you for being so utterly foolish. Damien can force me to nothing. I go willingly to the altar. Be happy for me, Jeremy."

Her feet skipped quickly down the cobbled street, practically dragging Jeremy in her path in her eagerness to see Damien again.

"I came to rescue a lady in distress, only to find her enamored of the dragon. How will I ever explain my failure?" Jeremy wailed good-humoredly as he caught up with her and secured her hand.

"If it is a lady in distress you seek, I have the perfect specimen. You will recover from your sorrow quickly if I do not miss my guess." Christina flirted him a mischievous grin, then followed more sedately as Jeremy took the lead. She had no idea where Damien might have arranged for the ceremony to take place. For all she knew, the caves under the hill would be their chapel.

With a sigh of relief, she realized she was being led to Nick's inn. She had never been inside, but the two story clapboard structure seemed neat and well-kept and better than the caves or ramshackle huts below the hill.

She did not expect a church or a fancy ceremony, but a respectable minister and her closest friends would be more than she had ever dared dream. Once she had thought herself doomed to a single life and had accepted it as her only choice. Had it not been for Damien, she might still think that the best of fates, but she had learned the folly of trying to live without Damien. She had no desire to try it again.

Christina's feet fairly flew across the threshold, but came to an abrupt halt when she found no one waiting in the spacious hall. Surely they could not all be in the tavern, though she cast a dubious glance in that direction.

At that momnent Mara, ebony hair streaming down her back, came clattering down the back stairs. Christina heard Jeremy's muttered "My God!" behind her and hid a smile as she imagined Jeremy's expression of stunned disbelief at meeting this feminine replica of Damien. Christina rushed forward to meet the suddenly hesitant dark-haired beauty.

Though she was dressed in the maid's old homespun, Mara's regal stature betrayed her true upbringing. No man in his right mind would mistake those haughty cheekbones or flashing eyes for those of less noble heritage. A princess dressed as a pauper decorated the suddenly bare boards of the inn.

"Mara, I would have you meet Lord Jeremy Standifer, a very noble but equally silly friend of mine and Damien's." Christina threw Jeremy a crinkled glance of amusement. "Or at least, once a friend of Damien's. I trust you two are still speaking."

She choked back a gurgle of laughter at Jeremy's bemused nod. He had not yet removed his eyes from Mara, and she doubted he had heard a word she said. "Jeremy, this is Lady Mara Drayton, if you have not already surmised that. It is high time the two of you met, and it couldn't be a better opportunity. Damien would have your head for looking at his sister like that on any other day, Jeremy, but he will scarcely be in any state to notice it today."

Christina giggled out loud as neither of the two took

notice of anything she said. They made polite murmurs of introduction, but neither noticed as the bride-to-be shrugged and walked off, leaving them alone in the wide hall of the inn.

Christina found the room occupied by Lorna and Mrs. Drayton without much difficulty. Lorna's fussing and fretting as she hurriedly stitched the let-out seams of Christina's ivory satin carried easily in the empty upstairs hall. Where Damien was she could not imagine, but she entered the spacious bedroom eagerly.

"Where is Mara?" Sophia asked absently as she removed the last of the pins and smoothed the satin lovingly.

"Discovering the course of true love never runs smooth." Her spirits floated so high, Christina could not find it in her to be serious, and Sophia's startled glance only brought a brighter smile.

"I never saw a less nervous bride in all my life. We have sat here frantically piecing together this bodice for you and I swear you would not have cared if you'd been married in black. Hurry, let's try this on and pray it fits. Damien is champing at the bit and will not tarry much longer." Sophia lifted the gown as Lorna hastened to undress Christina. With a look of curiosity, Sophia asked, "Where exactly did you say Mara is?"

Christina stepped out of the black silk and kicked it aside. She would not have to wear the wretched thing again, though besides the satin, it and the others like it might be all she had that fit. She did not care. She would soon be Damien's wife and not a "widow" any longer. She would flaunt her new respectability readily.

"I just introduced Mara to Lord Jeremy. They seemed to have much in common." Christina giggled at Lorna's muttered imprecation behind her as the bodice was lowered over her head. Damien had run the good woman a ragged chase. Mara might be the death of her.

As the bodice lowered in place, Sophia gave Christina's innocent expression a shrewd glance. "Mara and Lord Jeremy? I thought he came here to marry you."

Christina squirmed the slippery satin into place, modestly adjusting the neckline so that it at least covered the lower half of her newly full bosom. She had always been slender; her new fullness pleased her. Christina looked up and caught Sophia's eyes and shrugged.

"He came to slay dragons and rescue fair maidens. Once Damien discovers he courts Mara, Jeremy will have fire-breathing dragons aplenty. He does not need me."

The dark-haired woman looked bewildered, not certain whether to be happy or shocked. At last she settled on the obvious. "But Lord Jeremy lives in England!"

Christina held her breath as Lorna struggled to close the gap of hidden buttons over her no-longer-flat waistline. "And Mara has never been to England. Somehow I think the adventure of going will suit her nicely. And if she decides she does not like it there, Jeremy is amiable enough to return and live here. He has no estates to tend. The only objection might be that he has no funds of his own, but it never stopped the poor boy before." Christina let out a gasp of air and relaxed as the straining seams held.

"Mara's father left her a healthy dowry. They will not starve," Sophia answered dryly. The couple had just met, and already they had them wed and across the ocean. One wedding at a time was all she wished to handle.

Christina accepted the closing of the subject serenely. Soon she would see Damien again. He would look at her with love and take her hand and they would be married legally and then . . . She sent up a little prayer over the next step. Surely, *surely* he would not leave before they had their wedding night. Just the thought of it sent a shiver of excitement coursing to her fingertips.

A heated argument outside the door sent Christina's blood racing faster and her hand automatically went to her hair. She had not yet had time to arrange it; they could not let Damien in yet!

Mara slipped through the door, her cheeks flushed

with an unusual excitement and her dark eyes sparkling merrily as she shut the door on the commotion. Heavy boots stomped angrily over bare floorboards and the argument carried safely down the hall.

At the expectant faces turned toward her, Mara blushed even brighter, but she spoke with cool control. "Damien has quite lost what few brains he possessed. He swears you have been kidnapped, Christina, or that you have run away, and he is bound and determined to go looking for you if we do not produce you at once." She paused thoughtfully and added as if in afterthought, "Since he has shaved his beard and is most likely to be recognized if he goes out in the streets, you had best hurry and put the poor man out of his misery."

Knowing Damien's mercurial nature, Christina flew to the mirror and hastily began rearranging pins and smoothing naturally untidy curls. She had no desire to meet with his black humor on her wedding day.

But when the time came and all was ready, Christina began to tremble nervously. What had she committed herself to? Marriage with a madman? A privateer? She would never know another moment's peace. But remembering the monotony of her days of drudgery and poverty in Cornwall, with no expectation of ever experiencing life, Christina straightened her shoulders and stepped forward bravely. Peace could be had in the grave.

As she crossed the threshold into the common room of the inn, Christina halted in surprise, almost sending Sophia into a collision with Lorna to avoid knocking her down. Christina scarcely noticed. Her gaze had found Damien's tall, lean figure easily. From somewhere he had obtained a forest-green coat embellished in gold braid and accented by snowy white folds of lace at neck and sleeve. The dramatic contrast with his dark coloring made a handsome portrait, but Damien's good looks had not brought her to a standstill. Beside him, for all the world looking like some Turkish sultan propped upon his throne, sat Robert.

As his gaze fastened upon her, Christina grinned

joyously, but remembering the occasion and all too aware of Damien's suspicious eyes upon her, she maintained her best composure. The French doctor must have been a miracle worker to reduce Robert's fever so quickly, but though she was grateful for his return to health, her thoughts had another focus now. The dawn of a brilliant smile began to play upon her lips as amber eyes locked with black.

Christina was aware that she was being introduced to the Reverend Hathaway, that the French physician offered effusive congratulations, that Robert had begun a mixed outpouring of gratitude and best wishes, but her whole being had attached itself to Damien's vibrant presence. He held her hand possessively, his dark gaze seldom straying from her face as events rushed on without them. She had come home at last.

The ceremony was brief but appropriately solemn. The summer heat had broken for this day, and a cool sea breeze poured in the open casements on beams of sunlight. The beams cast brilliant sparkles of gold through tawny curls and highlighted shimmering folds of creamy satin over sensuous curves. Beside the delicate filigree of Christina's feminine finery, the groom stood straight and tall, proudly pledging the vows that bound them forever. Russet hair pulled back in a simple queue accented the harsh planes of Damien's dark face, but the velvet softness of dark eyes as they rested on his new bride betrayed a more sensitive emotion beneath.

As long fingers wrapped about her slender ones in the final words of the ceremony, Christina dared look up into the deep wells of Damien's eyes. What she found there brought a smile of such radiance it bedazzled the sun, and few who watched could hold back their tears. The Sea Lion had found his proper mate.

Thoroughly bewitched by the promise in her eyes, Damien lowered his head to capture that smile for his own. Their lips met, and the shock waves of excitement sent tremors through both of them, but with friends and family looking on, they could do no more than that. Damien's hard hand rested protectively at the small of her back, keeping her well within the circle of his arm, and Christina had to be content with that as their lips reluctantly separated.

Damien's ring had been on her finger all along, but it glittered with new meaning on this day. Christina kept casting wondering glances upon it as she accepted the greetings of all around. But her husband's gold band that Mrs. Drayton had produced for this occasion glittered even more brightly now against Damien's dark finger, and Christina considered it with awe. He had accepted this symbol of their shared vows with an alacrity she could scarcely believe. In fact, she could scarcely believe any of this had happened.

They stood in the eye of a hurricane, surrounded by the mighty forces of war, and soon the winds of violence would whip across the land, but for this magic moment, this wide-flung collection of friends and family had been drawn together to be blessed by the sun.

Christina was grateful for the beauty of the day and the support of this gathering of people, but she wished also for its swift end and the moment she could be in Damien's arms, alone. She intercepted his glance conveying the same thought, and felt the tightening of his arm about her. No longer would she fear the physical act that had brought them together.

Contemplating the merriment of their assorted guests, Damien maneuvered around the room until they reached the door. With a conspiratorial wink he slipped into the hall and drew Christina after him, cautiously closing the door after them. With a finger to his lips, he silenced any protest, and Christina followed eagerly in his footsteps.

The room she had used for dressing had magically become a bridal chamber, complete with a bottle of liquid suspiciously resembling champagne. A small bowl of fruit sat upon the table, and a gossamer silk chemise lay across invitingly turned-back covers.

Christina turned an amazed look to her new husband, but he shrugged carelessly and began unknotting his cravat with a look in his eyes she knew well.

"Shall I turn my back and allow you to prepare for bed modestly?" Damien asked politely as she continued to stare at him.

"The sun is still up!" Christina protested weakly, knowing he laughed, but suddenly uncertain of everything.

"I noticed," he replied solemnly, throwing aside the cravat and starting on his coat buttons, dark eyes never leaving her slender figure.

"But our guests are still back there." Christina gestured desperately toward the other room.

"So they are," Damien agreed amiably, and threw off his coat. The billowing sleeves of his loose shirt clung to the outline of powerfully muscled arms and shoulders as his hand fell suggestively to the buttons of his breeches.

Christina gasped and turned away. She had wanted this moment most urgently, but had imagined the friendly concealment of darkness to cover her burgeoning figure. How could she face his calm inspection in the vivid light of day?

Strong brown fingers came to rest on her shoulders, caressing a polished curl before moving to the fastening of her ivory bodice. Christina tensed as the material began to part and her shoulders emerged from the froth of lace, but Damien's careful administrations removed all fear.

He slid the satin from her shoulders and lightly kissed the curve of her throat as Christina freed her arms from the entangling cloth. The filmy chemise she wore barely concealed the voluptuous thrust of her breasts, and she felt her nipples hardening against the silk as Damien's dark gaze burned her flesh. He remained behind her, but brought a hand up to gently cup the heavy weight of one breast.

"Your beauty takes my breath, Christina. Let me enjoy it as it is meant to be."

The words murmured against her ear had as electrifying an effect as his hand cupping her flesh, and Christina melted weakly against the hard strength of his masculine frame.

"I fear you will find me ugly now that the child has grown," she whispered faintly, forcing him to bend closer to catch the words.

"My God, still a fool," was his only reply as strong fingers impatiently snapped fragile ties. Her breasts spilled from their confinement, and Damien filled his hands joyously, stroking hardened crests with growing excitement. "You are as ready as I, my love. Introduce me to our son."

With sudden impatience, Christina's fingers fumbled at the fastenings of skirts and petticoats. Damien eagerly assisted, and within moments, only the partial covering of the silken chemise separated her from the broad light of day. Where Damien pressed against her from behind, she could feel the hard line of his maleness against her buttocks.

With a groan of delight Damien bent his lips to a tender earlobe, one hand supporting the tempting weight of ivory curves while the other explored the small roundness of Christina's distended belly.

"You are more beautiful than I dared imagine, my love. I think I shall arrange to keep you this way."

Christina shivered as the chemise joined the petticoats in a puddle on the floor, but she straightened and stood proudly before him. His child weighted her belly, and she was glad of it. Turning, she met his gaze boldly.

"I think I shall enjoy that arrangement, sir. Would you care to keep in practice?"

Joy danced in the dark fires of his eyes and with one sweep of his hand Damien sent her stack of intricate curls tumbling over her shoulders. A golden cascade fell over ripe curves and his grin widened.

"I would, indeed, wife. To bed with you, then."

With a gasp of surprise, Christina found herself seized in a powerful grip and dropped unceremoniously upon the linen-covered feather mattress. Before she could locate a more respectable position, Damien fell beside her, the weight of his heavy frame burying them in the soft ticking.

Christina giggled as she fought to return to the surface, but her giggles quickly became something else as Damien's hungry kiss found her mouth and she was swallowed whole by a desire as old as mankind. She surrendered quickly to his plundering tongue and cried out with the heat of his fiery touch as he drew his hand across her nakedness, pulling her closer to his embrace. He devoured honeyed interiors with starving kisses, then moved on, fastening demandingly on the sensitive crest of her full breast.

Floods of aching emotion swept through Christina and her cry of joy joined the call of a mockingbird outside the window as Damien suckled hungrily at tender flesh. There would be no slowness in their love-making this time. The gnawing emptiness of many weeks' duration craved immediate fulfillment and a celebration of life. Eagerly she helped Damien jerk free the remainder of his clothing.

The touch of his hard flesh along the length of hers sent shuddering earthquakes of excitement up Christina's spine. His lean body covered hers, pressing her down into the feather ticking, and she welcomed the strength of his maleness. This was the counterpart she needed, the balance that made life stable, the give-and-take that created life. As he gently took her as wife, his maleness piercing her aching emptiness, tears of joy rolled down Christina's cheeks.

They blended quickly and easily, the weeks of separation culminating in a joyous reunion that left their bodies spent and satisfied.

Neither having slept much these past days, they slept now. The warmth of the afternoon sun covered them, and they curled together contentedly.

Damien woke first, and with newly discovered joy gently explored the smooth contours of the woman he held in his arms. Christina sighed in her sleep and snuggled closer, giving him the opportunity to communicate more fully with the faint stirrings in her womb that was his child.

A particularly hard kick brought a gasp of surprise and Christina's lashes flew wide, then relaxed as she realized Damien held her. A small smile tinted her features. "Your son is as adventurous as his father. You will have your hands full with him."

Damien placed his hand over the undulating movement of her belly. "A daughter would suit me nicely. I have a partiality for golden curls."

Christina grinned. "I can see it now: golden curls, dark eyes, and her father's silver tongue. You will have to marry her off at the age of twelve."

"I will teach her to sail and hire eunuchs for crew. My daughter will know how to defend herself from rascals."

Christina grew serious and turned so that she faced him. She had memorized every line of that hawklike visage hovering above her, but sometimes she felt she would never know the man beneath.

"Will she ever know a home or normal life? When this war ends, where will we go? What will we do? Must I expect to spend my life in your mother's house, ever awaiting your return?"

Amber eyes lost their gleam and melted to brown as she studied Damien's somber features.

Damien brushed his knuckles against her cheek and dark velvet eyes grew warmer. "The war has made me what I must be, Christina, not what I wish to be. I told you once I am a farmer. When this war ends, I intend to rebuild my plantation. It may be a while before the fields are productive enough to allow you to decorate the house as you wish, but it will be a roof over our heads and a home of our own. You will see it soon enough. As soon as I get Robert out of here, I am coming back for you and the others. The plantation will be safer than a town under siege."

Christina smothered a leap of hope and studied his face cautiously. "Now that you have no ship, you will stay with us?"

Damien smiled and shook his head at this ingenuousness. His hand began to play temptingly with a rosebud crest. "I have been given permission to act as privateer and spy because it suited the purpose of those above me, but I am a captain in the Continental Army. I will be expected to return to my regiment as soon as I can possibly do so. Save your questions until later, Christina. The sun has set and I must be leaving soon."

Before she could cry out a storm of protests at this injustice, Damien covered her lips with his kiss, and their awareness of time and place became nil.

32

Damien carried out his claim, leaving Christina to an empty bed while he used the dark of the moon to smuggle Robert and the French physician past British noses to the French ships beyond. Christina understood the necessity, but punched her pillow with exasperation. Perhaps they had celebrated their wedding night early, but when would she ever have a husband?

Jeremy escorted her back to Drayton House the next morning, but he barely acknowledged the knowing leers and jests that greeted their arrival. As a long-lost husband he was a dismal failure, and Christina quickly steered him past the soldiers before they could question his decided lack of interest in his "wife." He brightened perceptibly as they approached Mara's "sickroom," the only room left to the family as parlor.

They were greeted with joy and anxious inquiries and the small family circle easily enveloped the newcomer from across the ocean. Sophia Drayton watched him with the wariness given to a prospective suitor, but greeted him cordially, then quickly softened to Jeremy's warm nature. Christina watched with amusement as Lorna kept her wary eye on the more tempestuous Mara, but she too obviously approved of the young lord.

In whispered tones Mara and Mrs. Drayton excitedly spoke of the news that had roused the colonel the night before. Overnight, French and rebel troops had surrounded the town, and they could be seen digging trenches and parading up and down in the far fields. General Washington had finally arrived!

Christina flew to the window to see for herself. These were the troops Damien meant to join when free of his other obligations. How odd that she should be looking upon them from the wrong side of enemy lines! Odder still that the enemy were her fellow countrymen.

She could see little more than smoking campfires and flags and dark figures scurrying across the landscape in the distance. What harm could those distant figures do to this enormous British garrison with guns bristling from behind earthen redoubts up and down the hill? Red-coated soldiers paraded in military splendor in the fields above the town, while others dug furiously at bigger and better trenches. Dark-coated Hessians marched and swore and fought in the streets, eager for battle. What could that tiny band of men out in the fields accomplish against such an army?

It did not take long for Christina to discover the effectiveness of Washington's troops. Cornwallis' supply lines were completely severed. They had no food but what was stored in town and camp, and that would scarcely feed the combined population of troops and townspeople. Rationing began immediately.

The dysentery that had begun in the summer's heat did not improve with the overcrowded strain on limited sanitary facilities. War did not need the use of artillery to strike its victims. Men died before the first shot was fired. The ground floor of Drayton House slowly became a calamity ward.

Christina paced her room nervously each night, staring at the window Damien had once used to make his entrance. The vines were gone now, the house filled to overflowing with British soldiers. How would he come for them? It seemed impossible. They were neatly trapped until they starved or British ships returned to drive out the French. With each passing day the former seemed more likely to occur.

Jeremy found himself caught in an awkward position between rebel friends and fellow countrymen. He and

Mara came to a violent disagreement over the matter of using his position to spy on British communiqués, and as a result he spent much of his time elsewhere. Christina could not imagine what he had found to occupy his time, but she could not blame him for his desertion. He must return to England sometime, but this would be her home now. She had no problem with the decision of loyalty.

But a decision did little good when no action could be taken. Once the ground floor became a hospital, she had been forbidden access by both the Draytons and Colonel Jamison, her "delicate condition" prohibiting nursing the sick. She sat uselessly at the upper-story windows, watching the mass of rebel troops slowly creep closer, wondering if Damien were among them.

Occasionally Christina had the uneasy impression of someone watching her while she watched the troops. She could find no reason for the feeling, unless some nameless soldier in the woods had a strong field glass, and it was absurd to think she could feel his eyes upon her. But it was equally absurd to think someone watched from the street below unless it were Damien. Her heart leapt with hope each time she considered the possibility, but she scanned the street without avail. Men came and went on the cobbled streets, a quickly turned back or bent head occasionally struck a familiar chord, but none had the stature or presence of her Yankee husband. Christina blamed her overactive imagination and sought other outlets.

The shelling began the first week of October.

At first, the sound seemed little more than thunder, and Christina paid it little note until the sudden trampling of boots below betrayed the furor in other quarters. Sophia Drayton clattered up the broad staircase to join them, dark eyes sparkling with a mixture of excitement and worry.

"General Washington is attacking the redoubts on the bluff! Look, you can see the smoke from here!" She pointed through the window, past the yellowing leaves of trees to the hill beyond.

Christina and Mara gathered around her, staring at the battlefield, unable to determine what the action represented. Thunder continued to roll and various figures raced back and forth behind both lines while smoke curled from rifles and cannon, but it seemed a futile cause. Neither side moved from their emplacements and little ground could be gained from stationary positions. Was this what war was all about?

In the next few days the meaning of war became a little clearer. Artillery fire rattled the windows. The dysentery patients on the floor below were replaced by groaning apparitions sporting sickening bandages of filth and gore. Their moans laced the air through night and day, and Christina's nightmares took on a new realistic quality. Somewhere out there, Damien risked these same dangers.

That thought preyed constantly on her mind. She had played the part of widow for so long, surely fate could not be so cruel as to make her one in reality, not before they had even a taste of married life. But in the dark shadows of night the horrors of possibilities haunted her thoughts.

Until the night that the Yankees began shelling their own governor's house just down the road.

The explosion sent them scurrying from their beds, wrapping dressing gowns hastily about shifts as they gathered in Mara's room to watch the destruction. This was a rebel town, Governor Nelson led Virginia militia in the fields beyond, and so they had thought themselves safe from attack. But as the stately mansion slowly crumbled beneath the cannon fire and stray shots fell dangerously close to their own backyard, they began to realize the deadly seriousness of the situation.

General Washington meant to drive the British into the sea, and the small town in his way would not stop him. The purpose of this war had a mightier weight on the scales of history than a few individuals. Yorktown and its inhabitants were dispensable.

Others quickly came to that same conclusion. Hastily garbed townspeople carrying rough bundles and baggage scurried through the streets toward the relative safety of the shoreline beneath the hill. If nothing else, they could cower in the cave until the shelling ended.

Even before Jeremy came bounding up the stairs, the Drayton women had donned their gowns and gathered their valuables. If British headquarters in Nelson House was the first target, the garrison in Drayton House would be next. They had no intention of waiting for the shell to hit.

As Jeremy burst unceremoniously through their door, the silent tension with which they had set about their tasks suddenly broke with a wave of relief. To prepare for departure was one thing; to actually make that first step from home to the unknown was quite another. Jeremy would provide the impetus to set them on their way.

"Jeremy, thank God!" Christina exclaimed for all of them as his gentlemanly figure burst in with most ungentlemanly abruptness, but he interrupted hurriedly before she could say more.

"Damien has a ship down in the harbor. He can't come ashore for fear of causing suspicion, but his men have a boat down by Nick's ready to take us out. I told the officer below I'm taking you out of here, but it's so hectic down there, I doubt they care. Let's go!"

His sudden outburst of speech without a trace of hesitation or stutter did not seem shocking under the circumstances. That he allowed Lorna to aid Christina, while he escorted Mara and her mother down the stairs, brought only a wry smile of acknowledgment.

They were out in the streets before Christina could inquire after Damien. She saved her eager questions. Shortly, she could ask them of Damien himself. It wasn't just the excitement of danger that surged through her veins as they raced down the darkened streets under the shelter of buildings still standing.

And then she realized that in her haste, she had left

behind her journal and the small package she kept with it, the necklace Damien had given her that first night of their affair. What if other hands fell upon them? Other eyes read those pages? Her journal alone would be sufficient to send them all to the gallows! She must retrieve it at once.

Jerking hurriedly from Lorna's grasp, Christina whispered a quick explanation and sent the Scotswoman on ahead to inform the others. The shelling seemed to have eased. Perhaps they were safe for a while. The danger would be greater if she did not turn back.

As Jeremy and the others hurried unsuspectingly down the hill, Christina turned her footsteps in the other direction.

No one questioned her as she dashed back in the house and up the stairs. The grim young soldiers on duty scarcely noticed as the black-gowned lady hurried out again, desperately clutching a small package to her breast. These were perilous times. Civilians must look after themselves.

Christina breathed with relief as she reached the darkened street. She had hoped Jeremy would hurry back to accompany her after he left Mara and her mother with the boat, but a quick glance down the street discovered only running soldiers and a few stray refugees moving to join the others beneath the hill. It seemed strange to see so much activity at this time of night, but the cannon fire on the ridge explained much. A second bombardment would soon begin.

She had not had time to be afraid before, but as she stepped quickly down the cobbled street strange shadows silhouetted by eerie fires cast their darkness across the night, and she shivered. The warm, dusty streets she had grown to love became frightening apparitions at night. The few people rushing by were strangers, not the helpful neighbors she had known. A few drunken soldiers lurched up the hill from one of the taverns, and Christina hastily sought a protective alley. The streets at night held more dangers than she wished to encounter.

As she quickly learned to her detriment.

As the soldiers tramped by, singing boisterously at the top of their lungs, a gloved hand reached over Christina's shoulder and caught her by the throat.

Her brief scream died a gurgle in her throat as the rough hand tightened about her slender neck.

"I've never broken a neck before, but I'd be more than happy to practice on yours."

That voice! Why did it sound so familiar? Christina quickly ceased her struggles as the hand tightened menacingly. Whoever it was meant what he said. Her breath came in short gasps.

"That's better. Come with me quietly and we might live to see another day, although another day in this godforsaken place seems scarcely worth the effort."

The taunting sarcasm rang bells of warning. Christina searched her memory, finding the answer in a sudden jarring realization. Thaddeus! Only Thaddeus spoke in that sarcastic whine. What in heaven's name was he doing here?

She commenced her struggles again, but his effetely slender frame had more strength than hers, and he lifted her bodily from her feet, jerking her chin back until she thought her neck would snap.

"You're the reason I'm in this hellhole and you're my ticket out. Stop the nonsense and we'll get this over quickly."

He carried her deeper into the shadows of the alley, giving her no opportunity to speak. The shells bursting over their heads held less terror than the peril of her cousin's deadly embrace. Christina wanted to scream, but could not. The sound would go unnoticed on such a night, in any case. Thaddeus had chosen his moment well.

At last they arrived at a stone hovel on the brink of the hill. Thaddeus kicked open the warped wooden door and shoved Christina into the dark hole of the interior.

Christina kept herself from falling by grabbing at the

rough wall as Thaddeus entered behind her, slamming the door and kicking it in place again. He struck a flint to a candle, illuminating the hollows of his empty face before holding it out to examine his victim.

Murky blue eyes surveyed her dishevelment with satisfaction. Tawny curls hastily tied back in a simple knot had come loose and hung now in limp tendrils about Christina's pale face. The bodice of the black silk had developed a tear in her struggle, revealing a tempting glimpse of lacy chemise beneath. But amber eyes glared mutinously above a jaw of defiant set, contradicting any notion he might entertain of her imminent defeat.

"Well, cousin, you have led me a merry chase, but this meeting should be a little more satisfactory than the last. With that damned lover of yours feeding the fishes or reclining at the end of a rope, you should be a little more cooperative this time."

Christina's stomach churned painfully at this mention of Damien. Surely they had not come through this hell to be separated by a fool like Thaddeus? But he knew Damien's identity, and if he had turned him over to the British . . .

It would not do to dwell on the impossible. She must get out of here and find out for herself. Her hand closed about some object on the table beside her and she moved it quietly into the folds of her skirts.

"Nothing to say to me after all these months? Shame on you, Christina. But we will have plenty of time to converse later. First I had better secure you in a safer place. To the right, Christina, and down the stairs. We have a place reserved just for you."

Thaddeus gestured toward the gaping blackness of a doorway. Christina gripped the object—a bottle, she had discovered—tightly, as she moved slowly in the direction indicated. She must let Thaddeus get within reach.

As he shoved her shoulder impatiently in the direction of her prison, Christina swung swiftly, raising the bottle above her head and hurtling it downward at her captor's skull.

The satisfying thud became a splintering crash of glass against stone instead. As Thaddeus deflected her arm with one hand, his other came up with a powerful crack to Christina's chin. The room swirled and went black and Christina crumpled to the floor.

33

She woke with a throbbing jaw and a dry thickness in her mouth. She tried to swallow and gagged on the motion. Her head pounded and her jaw ached. She tried to brush the filthiness hampering her lips, but her hands wouldn't move.

Frantically Christina twisted her wrists, and discovered them bound together and tied above her head. A gag deadened the screams she sought to loose. As awareness gradually seeped into her brain, her eyes flew open and searched desperately for explanation.

She found herself in a dim stone cellar with no window in sight. A candle guttered low on a rough wooden table in the corner, casting terrifying shadows against thick stone walls. Even could she scream, no one would hear through that barrier of dirt and mortar.

She lay on a rough cot, her hands tied to some unmoving object out of her sight. The crude hemp cut harshly at tender skin, and Christina quickly learned to lie still to prevent further pain.

A door hidden in the shadows opened and Thaddeus entered, a grin drifting across his slovenly features as he noted her wakefulness.

"Thought maybe I'd killed you, but as much fun as that would be, the future we have planned for you is much more entertaining. Besides, Nicholas has a nasty temper when his whims are thwarted."

Christina could say nothing, but her eyes widened in terror at the mention of that hated name. How could Nicholas be here? Damien had killed him, hadn't he?

Producing the bottle he had carried in, Thaddeus set it down with a thud on the table and collapsed his lanky frame in a rickety chair beside it. He noted Christina's reaction with satisfaction as he began to work at the cork on the bottle.

"A cat has nine lives, so they say. No telling how many that bastard has. 'Tis a pity your gallant lover cannot kill a man when he's down, or Nicholas would be pushing up daisies now. As it was, if I hadn't been hiding in the bushes, he would have bled to death before anyone found him. Your lordship wields a cruel rapier. I have made it a point to stay out of its way."

The cork popped and Thaddeus took a thirsty swig. Christina's parched throat ached for refreshment, but she would die of thirst before drinking after that pig. She understood little of what he said, but it was obvious the coward had fled and hidden while his companion attempted to fight off a furious Damien. Damn Damien for being such a gentleman! He should have cut the cad's throat when he had the chance.

That left her to wonder what the devious Nicholas had in store for her. Thaddeus apparently believed Damien safely out of the way. Was that what Nicholas was up to now? If she could get free, would there be time to warn Damien of his danger?

She did not have long to contemplate the possibility. A halting step sounded upon the stairs, and Thaddeus glanced up eagerly.

The door swung open, revealing a distorted caricature of the man she had known as Nicholas. Thick dark locks hung in dishevelment about a pale face twisted to one side in a hideously disfiguring scar. Once-powerful shoulders had shrunk and bent at an awkward angle, leaving one arm dangling uselessly in a filthy sleeve. The dandy of the gambling hall and the terror of half the whores in London had deteriorated to a shell almost beyond recognition.

Christina's expression of horror brought a grimace resembling mirth to that scarred face.

"Enjoy what his lordship has done to me? His revenge was more thorough than he imagined, but I shall have the best of him yet." The mirth died to a black glare.

Christina's skin crawled beneath the creature's malevolent inspection, but he soon turned it toward Thaddeus. Taking away the bottle, he shrugged in Christina's direction. "Have you told your charming cousin of the exalted position we have held open for her?" He lifted the bottle to his lips and swallowed, a small trickle dribbling out the stiff corner of his mouth.

Thaddeus grinned wickedly and shoved his hands deep in his coat pockets. "I was saving that for you."

Nicholas wiped his mouth with his filthy coat sleeve and turned a dull stare toward Christina's helpless figure. A bruise had begun to blacken along her jaw and the small swelling of her pregnancy left her particularly vulnerable, but she returned his look with a defiant glare. He shrugged again and turned back to Thaddeus.

"Tell the bitch carefully. I have no intention of explaining a second time."

At his harsh tone, Thaddeus sent him a sidelong look, but the anger seemed directionless and he complied with his boss's wishes eagerly.

"Nicholas thinks the colonies are ripe for a string of brothels and gambling houses like he had in London. The fire and his, uh, incapacitation lost him a lot back there, but we can gain it all back here in half the time, and this time I'll be his partner."

Nicholas set the bottle down and spat into a far corner. "Stop the blather, fool. You're easily replaceable, but convenient."

Thaddeus jerked nervously and continued without the smile. "You're going to be the main attraction, cousin. We're aiming for a high-class operation this time, and you'll give the place the air of distinction we're looking for. You're already well trained for the trade; with that lover of yours gone, you'll have to find some other means of support. Nicholas is more than willing to make you the same offer he made before."

Christina shivered uncontrollably as that mad stare returned to her. She could feel the heat of his dagger against her skin, just as if it had been yesterday when he threatened to brand her as his. Nicholas had not forgotten either, and the heat of his gaze told her his thoughts followed the same path.

He stepped closer, blocking the candlelight with his massive figure, throwing his warped shape into silhouette as he stared down at her.

"It's too late to rid you of the bastard, but we'll find a use for it later. Mayhap it will be a girl as beautiful as its mother and can carry on the family trade. I will be happy to train her in the same manner as my cousin has trained you."

Nicholas' leer was all the more evil in that it never reached his lips. Christina trembled with the horror he promised with look and voice as much as words. He hovered like a malevolent devil over her trembling figure, and it took all her strength to look him in the eye. Bound and gagged, she could not convey her message any more strongly.

Nicholas laughed shortly. "I like you even better with your tongue silenced. Thaddeus, take your bottle to bed with you this night. I have it in mind to slide between a woman's legs this time."

Christina glanced wildly at her cousin and back up to the menacing darkness above her. She struggled frantically at her ties, screaming against the gag in violent protest.

Thaddeus seemed prepared to offer a protest of his own, but Nicholas had his back turned toward him and any sound died in his throat. Crippled as he was, Nicholas was still the stronger man, and the one who held the purse strings. Thaddeus well knew the source of his partner's dementia and had no desire to stand in his way. His sexual cravings had grown as misshapen as his figure in these past months. Let Christina satisfy him this time.

Christina watched in horror as Thaddeus rose and strode out the door, leaving her with this demented monster. As the room filled with the silence of her ragged breathing, amber eyes fled to the nightmare at her side.

Nicholas watched her without expression as the fingers of his good hand worked their way down the buttons of his breeches. They jerked spasmodically over each fastening, slowing his progress, and horror-bound, Christina followed their path with sick dread. She doubted if Damien's wounds had caused this loss of nervous control. The disease that had destroyed his father must already be eating at Nicholas' brain.

At this realization her stomach heaved and her gaze once again flew to the devil's face. As if reading her thoughts, Nicholas attempted a caricature of a grin.

" 'Tis a pity I did not take you that first time and pass this pox on to all your lovers. But it will not mar your pretty face until after half the colonies have enjoyed your body. By then it will not matter. Your daughter can take your place. Or perhaps that haughty sister of Drayton's. I like the idea of spreading Drayton women as the whores they are."

Christina screamed into the gag as his hand grasped the torn fragment of her bodice and tugged. The fragile muslin gave easily as he ripped away the bodice and began on the skirts below. She had worn little in the way of petticoats in her haste to dress, and these fell quickly in his violent assault.

She scarcely noticed the resumption of shelling above her as she twisted and turned and attempted to evade the grasp of this madman. The noise of cannon fire had become part of the nightmare and had little meaning. Her world consisted only of this maniac whose burning hands crawled and scorched across her skin, branding her with horror beyond the imagination as he bent to kneel over her on the cot.

A violent thud interrupted by a piercing scream directly overhead intruded more forcefully than bombshells. Nicholas halted his obscene attentions and listened carefully. A shell exploded somewhere nearby, but in the interlude a step could be heard upon the stairs.

More quickly than Christina thought possible, Nicholas scrambled from the bed and reached for a stout bar lying in a far corner. Christina forgot her nakedness in her attempt to tear free and scream a warning to whoever approached. The moment anyone stepped through that door, Nicholas would bash his head!

The door swung open and in a flashing instant Christina caught Damien's horrified expression, the swing of Nicholas' club, and the bright silver arc of a swift rapier.

And then Nicholas' cry of pain exploded in a roar of cannon fire and crumbling stones and dust and the room plunged into darkness.

Christina fought off the smothering cloud of debris choking her nostrils, struggling at her ties in an effort to be free to find Damien. Walls had collapsed all about them, he could be buried beneath them even now while she lay tied helplessly to this beam now lying crazily over her!

His hand reached out of the darkness, locating her ankle and clutching it desperately. "Christina! My God, Christina! Are you there?" The cry developed a heartbreaking note of despair as he discovered the cot laden with debris.

With frantic swiftness Damien swept aside the bricks and stone until his hands encountered the welcome warmth of bare flesh. Sliding his hands over his wife's uncovered bosom and along her throat, he finally located the gag and roughly tore it away.

Christina gasped with relief as the smothering rag fell away, but choked with dust and dryness, she could only cough raggedly as Damien hastily found her wrists and sawed her ties. But when she was finally free, she threw herself into his arms and buried hysterical sobs against his chest.

Gentle arms held her close, rocking her patiently as small stones slithered down broken walls and the cool night air rushed in through gaping holes. The whole world had fallen down about their heads, but nothing else mattered at this moment but that they were alive and in each other's arms.

After a while the sobs slowed to a racking cough, and Damien drew his cloak about her slender nudity, tucking it warmly to cover her as he drew away.

"The stairs are blocked. I must find a way out of here. Sit still." He brushed a kiss across her forehead and rose to inspect the cellar walls.

Christina held the heavy cloak and breathed deeply of its masculine odors of salt air and tobacco and whiskey and felt as if she had returned from the dead. Through whatever means, Damien was alive and by her side. She could ask for no more.

Damien retained a little more sense than that, knowing if he were discovered, they would both hang. The thought gave him speed, and he soon had an opening wide enough to crawl up and out into the night beyond. He had only to push his wife out first.

As he lifted her into his arms, Christina clung to him, unwilling to be parted from him again, content within this shelter for the moment. She resisted his attempts to push her out into the night until his curses woke her ire, if not her senses.

"Climb out, damn you, Christina! I don't have all night to dawdle with you. Any half-witted idiot who goes running through the streets after pieces of paper . . ." His curses continued as Christina kicked viciously and struggled to free herself from his grasp.

"Idiot, am I? No time to dawdle? You tire of me so soon, then? Fie on you, you miserable cur! And to think I worried whether you'd hang or not." Christina gave a mighty heave and scrambled out the opening, nearly losing the protection of the cloak in the process.

As she grabbed at the folds, Damien popped from the hole, grabbed her by the middle, and swung her up in his arms.

"I'll hang when I'm damn good and ready. Until then, madam, it is my bed you will dawdle in and my babe you will bear and my name you will answer to."

Each word carried them another step farther from town, another step farther from danger, another step closer to the future.

As Damien's tirade continued, Christina wrapped her arms around his neck, no longer caring how the cloak fell as her lips sought the sensitive hollow beneath his ear and began their sensuous journey toward shutting his mouth once and for all.

Epilogue

The October sun gleamed golden through the window pane Christina polished lovingly. The plantation house had been seriously neglected in Damien's absence, but she had already begun the process of making the house her home. She loved the airy spaciousness of the wide halls, the verdant view of rolling pastureland from every window.

From which she now saw billowing clouds of dust along the road beyond. Her fingers tightened on the rag as she strained to see the horse and rider furiously pounding up the path. Surely no other . . .

"Damien!" she screamed with joy, alerting the entire household as she flew down the elegant stairway to the wide front doors. "Damien!" she cried with the delight of just hearing his name.

Damien's heart thumped a little faster as his eager gaze scanned the facade of the modest brick plantation house. Home! His heart waited here, and soon, he had every reason to believe, he would be able to stay. For now, he contented himself with absorbing the vision.

Except for a small vegetable patch in the kitchen garden, the fields lay bare, but an old black servant and a limping Robert worked with their cantankerous mule to till a nearby field. Damien absorbed the fact that the stable appeared newly scrubbed and a major cleaning was apparently under way in the basement kitchens. Empty bottles and rotted vegetables lay in discard piles, and sparkling clean black kettles covered the walkway. Even as he watched, he caught Lorna's industrious figure carrying out further trash with the aid of a servant. His bachelor household was definitely in the process of being turned inside out.

He sought eagerly for the source of this mayhem, knowing instinctively she would be watching for him, but his gaze faltered as it encountered another sight. He hauled back on the reins and his eyes narrowed suspiciously.

Beneath the rose trellis at the side of the house, safely out of the view of the other inhabitants, a couple had found the haven of each other's arms. Even as Damien watched, their lips met in a kiss that he could easily ascertain was not their first. Uncapped, Mara's dark hair fell intimately over Jeremy's embracing arm.

With a spur to his horse's side, Damien covered the remaining distance in moments.

The black stallion reared to a halt in the courtyard, but a whirlwind of activity preceded by his wife prevented Damien from reaching the source of his ire.

As Christina flew down the porch steps, Damien swung effortlessly from the saddle, his buff-and-blue uniform sparkling with freshly laundered glory. Just the sight of that golden hair floating about a face of pristine joy brought Damien's mood back to the ecstatic.

Christina dashed into his waiting arms and squealed with happiness as he swung her clear of the ground and covered her face with kisses.

"You're here! Can you stay? Did they give you leave? Is the war over yet?" Questions tumbled eagerly from rosy lips each time Damien's mouth slid from hers to explore other territories. Christina gasped as his teeth tugged gently at her earlobe, but she hugged his neck tighter.

"One thing at a time. Wait until the others catch up with you so I need do my explaining only once. Which reminds me, where did that bastard Standifer go?"

Damien gently deposited his wife on the ground and gazed belligerently in the direction from which Mara came running. His mother and Lorna were emerging from the house and Robert was hobbling in from the field, but Jeremy had not yet appeared.

Christina tugged impishly at his hand, sensing the path of his thoughts, and a corner of her mouth twisted upward in a wry grin. "He'll not be far behind Mara, I wager. He's just being discreet about intruding on a family reunion."

"The hell he is!"

Mara came to a grinding halt some distance from her brother as she read the fury in black eyes so similar to her own. An equal temper began to rise in hers as Damien aimed his next words in her direction.

"Where is that scoundrel? While I'm out risking my life to protect my family, the bloody bastard seduces my sister! I'll have his head . . ." Spying the offender sauntering from the direction of the kitchen garden, Damien turned his attention that way. He would have followed his gaze with his feet, but Christina dug in her heels and held him back while his mother quickly intercepted his path. "Dammit, Christina, let me settle this so we can get on." He shook off her grasp impatiently, his hand straying toward his buckled scabbard.

"Get on with what?" Jeremy reached speaking distance and eyed his friend warily.

Ignoring the question, Damien asked pointedly, "What are your intentions toward my sister?"

Mara squealed with fury at this rudeness, but Lorna caught her by the shoulders and prevented any more physical show of anger. Only no hold could be put on Mara's tongue. "That's unfair, Damien! You have no right—"

"Hush, Mara, and let me handle this. He does have a right." Jeremy faced his interrogator calmly.

To everyone's surprise, Mara obediently grew quiet and waited as the two men she loved most in the world met as if to do mortal combat.

"I have waited for your return to ask your permission to ask Mara to marry me. I meant to present the proposal at a more propitious moment, but if you prefer to press the issue . . ."

This amazing speech came out without a trace of hesitancy, causing several muffled gasps behind him and leaving Damien momentarily nonplussed. Taking the advantage, Christina plunged recklessly where angels had better sense than to tread.

"No one is pressing any issues until Damien has come in and sat down and had a bite to eat and told us the news he rode in here with." Christina met the gazes of both men with defiance, determined not to mar this homecoming with anger.

Damien's grin widened as he stared down at the belligerent figure of his very pretty, very pregnant wife. Her words had reminded him of his reason for being here, and with Jeremy's proposal safely solving the question of Mara's reputation for the moment, he had time to regroup and strike again.

"You win this round, madam," he agreed easily. "I have better things to do with this day than argue with prospective brothers-in-law. Tell Ned to harness up the wagon—I wish to show you the end of a war!"

Instantly, from all round him, excited voices questioned eagerly. Robert's booming voice drowned out all others, but still remained incoherent in the general babble as he attempted to gain his brother's attention. Christina watched with amusement as Mara sought Jeremy's company in the confusion, but her own thoughts had turned to other matters now, and she directed her gaze upward to search Damien's face.

"An end, Damien? Can there truly be an end?" she asked softly.

As if attuned only to the woman at his side, Damien met her eyes immediately. "Cornwallis has surrendered. If you will hurry, we can see the British army lay down its swords before us. Hurry, my love. It is the beginning of the end."

With a wild whoop of joy, Robert dashed toward the stable to hitch the wagon. The mules were all that remained of Damien's once fine stables, but they needed much persuasion before they could be harnessed. Christina could not bear the wait.

Throwing her arms about Damien's neck, she pleaded, "Take me up with you. I cannot bear to ride behind those animals on a day like this! Please, Damien?"

The dark visage she had once found stern and forbidding now turned upon her with tenderness and concern and love. "I do not wish to harm the child, Christina. You have been through so much . . ."

"Don't treat me like an old lady! I am healthy. I will not break. I want to ride, Damien. I want to see the end of this wretched war. I want to tell our son of this day. Please, Damien. We will miss everything if we linger."

A grin twisted the thin line of his mouth upward as Christina molded herself closely against him, her breasts flattening against the parade of golden buttons across his chest, her skirts successfully concealing the telltale bulge rising beneath his tight breeches. Even five months gone with child, his lioness had the power to seduce him. Damien crushed her closer, nibbling her ear before catching her up in his arms and swinging her into the saddle.

"You've learned how to twist me into putty already, you little minx, but if our son protests this treatment, you are the one to take the blame."

He threw himself up behind her, gentling the nervous stallion as it strained at the bit. Jeremy and Mara had joined Robert in battling the mules beneath Sophia's and Lorna's admonitions, and none noticed as the couple began to move down the road.

Christina squirmed into a more comfortable position and smiled sunnily. "Not I, sir. 'Twill all be your fault for not being properly stern with me. Can we not go faster? All will be over before we get there."

Damien growled something irascible but soon they were flying down country lanes, through woods colored in autumn and long grasses wet with dew. Freedom was within their grasp at last.

Christina could hear the ceremony before she could see it. A monotonous roll of drums beat like thunder across the horizon, followed by the high piping of flutes.

Her heart quaked at the sound, trying to grasp its full meaning.

General Cornwallis and the mighty British army had surrendered to a ragtag, mutinous disarray of farmers and Frenchmen. The notion was most difficult to grasp, but Christina clung to it with hope. With the main part of the British Army incapacitated, surely Damien's talk of peace would come to pass!

They topped a wooded rise and looked down upon the fascinating spectacle below. Line after line of immaculately red-coated figures paraded in perfect formation through the grassy fields surrounding Yorktown. On either side of their path stood the proudly triumphant armies of Washington and Rochambeau, Washington's garbed in buff-and-blue and buckskin and whatever else could be found, Rochambeau's in the gaily colored finery of the French monarchy. A splendidly colorful sight for a sunny October morn.

Around this tableau scattered the wagons and steeds and women and children of the towns and fields surrounding, all drawn by the hope and excitement and triumph this moment promised. The war had lasted an eternity, torn loyalties deeper than birth, devastated lives and land, but a glittering promise hovered on the horizon.

Freedom. The air breathed the word, though no lips formed it. It whispered with the sound of the Liberty Bell in Philadelphia, murmured through the words of that brave Declaration of Independence written years before, but none yet knew its meaning. Only hope and prayer and persistence had brought them to this new day, and no one dared yet breathe the word too loudly. The end had not yet come. But it was closer.

Guns and swords began to mount in a disorderly pile at the end of that long scarlet line. For a while the defeated British soldiers marched with their faces averted from the rough-clad army of Yankees, preferring to accept their surrender to the respectable old foe of France. But as they watched, Lafayette's troops began to pipe a strange refrain, and an oddly unmilitary song began to float mockingly above the roll of drums.

As Christina realized what was happening, her shoulders began to shake with mirth until she could no longer resist looking up to dancing black eyes. In unison, they joined the refrains of "Yankee Doodle" and laughed until the tears rolled down their cheeks and they clung together to keep from falling.

And so the others found them, their faces wet with tears of joy and hope, their lips sealed together in a kiss of love, while three armies marched and paraded to the roll of drums and the piping strains of "Yankee Doodle" below them.

About the Author

Patricia Rice was born in Newburgh, New York, and attended the University of Kentucky. She now lives in Mayfield, Kentucky, with her husband and her two children, Corinna and Derek, in a rambling Tudor house. Ms. Rice has a degree in accounting and her hobbies include history, travel and antique collecting.